SEVEN TEN THIRD

SARA MACK

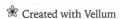

Dedicated to MLR
Without you, this story would remain unfinished
Thank you

~ Please read ~

Seven Ten Third is a work of fiction that deals with subjects that may be sensitive for some readers. This story discusses events around bullying, suicide, drinking, and drug use. Please be aware of the potential emotional response this could cause.
If you are having suicidal thoughts or problems with addiction, free and confidential support is available. Please reach out and call the National Suicide Prevention Lifeline at 1 800 273 8255 or SAMHSA (Substance Abuse and Mental Health Services Administration) at 1 800 662 4357.
Thank you for reading.

CHAPTER ONE

Lucy

J uvenile delinquents aren't a very social bunch. Then again, I'm not here to make friends.

"Miss Anderson."

My head snaps to the left at the stern sound of my name. I know who is calling me, but I still have to blink to focus and find him. Between the blazing sun reflecting off his yellow safety vest and the waves of heat rising from the pavement, the police officer is a blur.

"A word," he says.

I stop what I'm doing and walk toward him. Sweat that previously peppered the ground from my forehead now drips down my face, running between my nose and one eye. I use the back of my dirty work glove to wipe it away, while my other hand drags a trash bag behind me. The weather is already humid this morning, and my clothes stick to every inch of my body. Apparently, for this particular day, August has decided to mimic hell.

How fitting.

When I reach Officer Hodge, I squint up at him. He towers over me with crossed arms; arms which, when I was little, used to wrap me in bear hugs and toss me giggling into the air. Not anymore. For one, I'm seventeen. For two, he's on duty. And for three, I don't remember the last time I giggled.

"Luce." His voice is gruff yet hushed. He shouldn't be singling me out; we discussed this. "Slow down," he warns.

I don't see the point. "Why? We have miles to go."

"You're not the only one here."

True. However, the others are taking their sweet time. They're collecting trash off the side of the road like they have a choice. They don't. There's a reason for this community service, and it's not to earn volunteer hours for college applications.

"Leave some work for the others," he continues. "I don't want you to get dehydrated and pass out. Your mother will kill me."

I meet my uncle's eyes and lower my voice. "Fake bomb threats and selling your parent's oxy doesn't compare to what I did. If the court said–"

"What these kids did was intentional," my Uncle Tony says. "You're different, and you know it."

My mouth twists. I'm different all right.

Leaning toward me, he enunciates his next words. "Take. It. Easy."

There's no point in arguing with him. It will only draw attention to the fact we know each other. "Yes, sir," I mutter and look away, even though slowing down is the last thing I want to do.

"Five minutes until water break," he says before dismissing me.

I close my eyes and fill my lungs, then let the air out in a whoosh. I know he cares about me, but my rapid pace was keeping me focused and my negative thoughts at bay. What he's asking will do the exact opposite, and I don't want to move any slower right now.

Turning around, I look past the other fluorescent yellow vests dotting the roadside. For a local two-lane highway, there's an awful lot of garbage to pick up. I wonder if it was placed here on purpose, just for us, because I don't remember seeing all this junk when I've driven this way before. Then again, I was going the speed limit ... or slightly over.

My eyes land on a chain link fence that sits off the highway, up a small embankment at the top of the grassy area we're obligated to clean. Papers and who knows what else are pinned at the base, so I decide to head there and remain separated from the group. A few of the kids seem to know one another because they're working side by side, but I don't know if that means they're partners in crime or just repeat offenders. My uncle didn't give me a rundown of everyone's rap sheet, only a brief overview of their various offenses. His lack of detail will disappoint my best friend Izzy when I talk to her, I'm sure.

Reaching the fence, I bend over to grab a plastic grocery bag while looking through to the other side. In the distance, two soccer fields and a baseball diamond are set amongst other small buildings and an outdoor basketball court. The sports park is full with players and parents; a ref's whistle blows and I watch the running soccer kids stop in their tracks. They must be dying in this heat.

"Fascinating, isn't it?"

Startled, I look to my right. One of my comrades has broken rank to join me. She's about my age and height, which means she's too young to vote but tall enough to lay a decent spike on a volleyball. Features-wise she could be any regular girl from any small town if it weren't for the plugs stretching her earlobes and the tattoos trailing down her arms like sleeves.

"What is?" I ask.

"How we're stuck playing games our entire lives."

I'm not sure what she means. My expression must give away my thoughts because she elaborates. "When you're young, it's for fun." Her eyes follow the kids on the other side of the fence. "When you're older, it's out of necessity." She throws a glance over her shoulder at my uncle and his partner.

I concede her point with a nod. She has an interesting take on our situation.

As we start to work the fence line, she introduces herself. "I'm Delaney."

"Lucy."

"After Lawless or Ball?"

I stop walking to throw away a crushed water bottle. "After Maud Montgomery."

Delaney pauses and tries to blow her bangs off her forehead, but they're stuck to her skin with sweat. "As in the author of *Anne of Green Gables?*"

I'm impressed she knows the series. "Yeah. My parents are into literature."

"Nice." She bends over to pick up some nasty crumpled napkins. "Mine are into Jack, Jim, and Johnnie."

Ouch. I'm familiar with whiskey, since my grandfather likes his neat, but I doubt Delaney is referring to the liquor in a refined sense. "I'm sorry," slips out of my mouth before I can catch it.

She shrugs and continues to work. "So, what are you in for Lucy Anderson?"

She must have paid attention when my uncle called me over. I decide to ignore her question and swipe some newspaper off the ground.

"Let me guess," she continues. "You're into art like me."

I squint at her. "You got in trouble for art?"

"I draw on more than just my skin." She stops in her tracks and holds out her left arm. The sun reflects off her ink, off a black raven perched on a thorny branch permanently etched into her bicep. Except ...

I step closer. "Is your tattoo blurry on purpose?"

"No. It's what happens to Sharpie when it's a million degrees outside."

"You mean they're not real?" I'm impressed. They look real.

She shakes her head. "There's only one artist I trust, and he won't touch me until I'm legal." She sighs and then adds, "And by touch, I mean in more ways than one."

Sarcasm escapes me. "You shouldn't break the law."

Her eyebrow quirks up. "And yet, here we are."

She has me there. Our attire and uniformed chaperones don't exactly scream National Honor Society.

"Anyway," she continues, "my last masterpiece landed me here." She winks. "I needed a bigger canvas."

I'm confused.

She rolls her eyes and says, "I used the side of an old train station."

Ah. I get it. "You're a graffiti artist."

"Aspiring." She looks proud.

Silently, I mull over her offense. Even though what she did is frowned upon, judging from her arms, I bet whatever she created was amazing.

We continue along the fence, picking up grease-stained fast food bags and straw wrappers.

"I take it you're not into urban graphic design like me," Delaney presses.

I shake my head. Why is my crime so important? I wish she'd drop it.

"That's too bad," she continues. "I thought maybe I'd found a kindred spirit."

My eyes land on hers and she smiles, asking, "You see what I did there?"

A small laugh slips out. "Yes." She quoted Anne, from *Anne of Green Gables*. Under different circumstances, I think I could be fast friends with Delaney.

"So, spill," she says. "What'd you do? It can't be too bad if you're on garbage detail."

Apparently, she doesn't understand how the legal system works. Honestly, neither do I. I'm only doing what I'm told to avoid screwing up the rest of my life. Relenting a bit, I say, "Let's just say the punishment doesn't fit the crime."

Now she's confused. "As in it's too much or too little?"

Way too little, I think, although I'm not going to complain. "It's not enough," I say and move along, dragging my trash bag behind me. The plastic crinkles in my hand making me wonder if, when I'm done for the day, tossing away what I've collected will allow me to throw away some of my guilt, too.

"Hey, we're all bad apples here," Delaney says. "Don't tell me you're trying to be a martyr and suffering for the greater good."

I snort and glance behind me. "I'm not. I'm just rooted in reality."

She accepts my response with a nod and finally drops her line of questioning.

We continue to work as the sun beats down on us. Man, I'm hot. This vest doesn't breathe; I swear it's absorbing the sun's rays instead of reflecting them. Didn't Uncle Tony say we had a water break in five minutes? It feels like it's been twenty.

As we move farther away from him, we get closer to a parking lot, one that backs up to the fence line. I'm focused on the ground to pick up more crap when a car pulls in a couple spaces ahead of me. Diligent delinquent that I am, I don't look up. I just keep moving.

"Hey, Lucy," Delaney says as the car door slams. "It looks like it's time for a break. Schmidt and Jenko are waving at us."

I crack half a smile at her *21 Jump Street* reference and stand up straight.

"Lucy?"

My eyes lock on the person who said my name. My shoulders instantly tense, and I skip a breath. Standing on the other side of the fence is Aaron Matthews. Uber popular, super athletic, God of my high school, Aaron Matthews. I haven't seen him since …

Since the night I killed his best friend.

CHAPTER TWO

Aaron

L*ucy.*
  I shouldn't have said her name, but it just slipped out. I haven't seen her in months, not that her big, dark eyes don't haunt my dreams. Or my nightmares. I'm not sure which are which anymore.

She stands there, immobile, staring at me. I stare back because I can't help it; I'm hung over, and I'm pissed I had to come out here today. My mind registers what she's wearing: work gloves, cut-off jeans, and a neon yellow vest which is way too big for her. She looks tired and sweaty. My eyes fall on the trash bag in her hands, and it takes a minute before everything clicks.

Shit.

"C'mon." A goth-looking girl taps Lucy on the shoulder. "Let's go. I'm dying here."

Lucy pulls her eyes from mine and follows her friend. After a few steps, they disappear down a hill on the other side of the fence. When they're completely out of sight, I lace my fingers behind my neck, let my head fall back, and look at the sky.

Damn you, Cody. The words swim through my pounding head. *Damn you.*

When I finish cursing someone who will never hear me, I turn around and let my arms flop against my sides. Out of the corner of my eye, Cody materializes, clearly a figment of my imagination. He sets his hand against his chest and leans back with over-the-top fake shock, like he's offended I would think badly of him.

Dick.

My eyes scan the soccer fields from beneath the brim of my baseball hat, searching for my sister so Cody will disappear. I've been sent to pick her up because my mother's hair appointment is running late. Her demand that I get out of bed ruined my plans to sleep off my latest attempt to forget.

Spotting a cluster of lime green jerseys, I walk in that direction. My sister's game should be over soon, and she's not expecting me; she's expecting Mom. Arriving at the sidelines, I stand with the other spectators and spot Ayden right away. Her blonde ponytail bounces above the number five, her jersey number, as she handles the ball. My sister heads right, then fakes left, maneuvering around the other team's defense.

Just as she passes the ball off to her teammate, I overhear a sickly sweet "Thank you so much! All the proceeds will go to support the senior class. It's what Cody would have wanted."

My scowl is immediate. Why is *she* here? June's voice grates on my nerves, and I pull my hat lower, hoping she'll walk past me.

"Aaron?"

Well, that plan didn't work.

I pretend to be invested in the game and barely glance at her. "Hey."

"Ohmygod." All three words come out of her mouth at once. She steps beside me and throws her arms around my chest, hugging me from the side. "How are you?" Her question is muffled against my arm.

Confused as to why she's touching me, I lean out of her weird hug. "I'm fine. What are you doing?"

Her eyes meet mine, and she bites her bottom lip. "Selling these." She holds up a bunch of plastic wristbands.

That's not what I meant, but now I'm curious. "What are they?"

"Bracelets. The class reps got together and decided it would be a good fundraiser for homecoming. You should have one."

She offers me a wristband, and I take it. Stamped in white letters on blue plastic are the words *Cody Cunningham ~ Forever a Husky.* My blood pressure rises. "Who thought this was a good idea?"

"I did." She shrugs. "I know Cody would've loved it. He was so dedicated to Holton High."

I stare at her in disbelief. Her boyfriend died three months ago, and the school is profiting from it? "Unbelievable," I mutter.

"Right?" June mistakes my reaction as a compliment. "I posted a picture on my story and everyone thought the bracelets were great." She pauses and tips her head. "You didn't comment, though. I thought you would."

Suddenly, the crowd around us bursts into cheers and applause. My attention shifts to the soccer field, and I see Ayden's team celebrating with high fives. They scored.

Remaining focused on my sister, I clap and tell June, "I didn't see your post." If I had, I would have told her to shove the Cody fundraiser up her ass. If she had known him like she thought she did, she would have known he wasn't dedicated to Holton. He had his sights set on college and getting out of this small town. This is the perfect example of why I've avoided people from school all summer. If I read the online tributes or heard the comments about my best friend, I'd be tempted to open my mouth and set the record straight. Everyone has an opinion about him.

And none of them know the truth.

"Well, maybe you should pay more attention." June ignores the fact I'm not here to see her. "Now that Cody is gone, everyone will be relying on you."

My eyes snap to hers. "For what?"

"Direction." Her forehead creases, and her perfectly shaped brows mesh together. "They need to know how to deal with the loss."

That makes no sense, and my expression shows it. "I'm not a counselor."

"Aarrron," she whines like I'm being impossible and sets her hand on my arm. "We both know you and Cody were the most popular guys at Holton. You were leaders. People looked up to you, they followed you; hell, most of them wanted to *be* you. They still do."

"No one wants to be me."

She steps closer. "Yes, they do."

Maybe they did before, I think. *But no one would want to be me now.*

Glancing down, I brush her hand away and get a whiff of her flowery perfume in the process. "It doesn't look like you've needed my help to adjust."

Yeah, unfortunately, I've noticed. June's always been hot, but way too high maintenance. It's obvious she hasn't missed any pool time since her boyfriend died because her little shorts and tank top reveal a rich tan in addition to her defined quads and curves. She takes my words the wrong way again and shoots me a flirty smile. "Thanks. It's been hard to keep things normal."

My thoughts are brutal. *No, it's been hard milking this for everything it's worth.*

"June. I'm out of wristbands."

I look past Cody's girlfriend at the sound of Katherine's voice. Now there's a girl I genuinely like. She's funny and honest, and she can hold her own with the boys. I have no idea why she hangs out with June. If I've told Kat once, I've told her a thousand times: if she would just break her rule about not dating high school guys, I could make her one of the happiest girls on the planet. Well, I said that before I became a moody mess. I probably couldn't pull off one good date now.

When June turns around to hand over more bracelets, Kat notices me. "Hey, Aaron." Her smile morphs into concern, and she walks over to wrap her arms around my waist. Unlike June, Kat hugging me happens all the time. She squeezes me and asks, "Are you okay?"

"Of course I'm okay. Why?"

"Because you look kind of rough." She leans back and squints up at me. "Late night?"

"Just a party. I didn't sleep much."

June is instantly intrigued. "Party? What party?"

She probably wants to know why she wasn't invited. "It was up at CMU. Craig and Ben told me about it." Cody and I played varsity lacrosse with the guys. They graduated last spring, and Cody and I were set to take over the co-captain reins at the end of the season. Now, I'm flying solo.

"A college party?" One of Kat's eyebrows jumps. "Well, haven't we joined the big leagues."

I crack a smile, and it feels foreign after the last few months.

"Figures it wasn't around here," June sniffs.

"Why?" I let go of Kat. "Because you didn't know about it?"

"No. Because everyone is watching us like hawks."

It's true to say the three of us, amongst others, are to blame for the new local curfew. Around these parts, if you're over the age of thirteen, be prepared to justify why you're hanging out with more than two people. Ever since Cody's death enlightened the community to our underage drinking "problem," parents, neighbors, and the local police have been on high alert.

"You have to admit it's for a good reason," Kat says.

June's eyes narrow. "No, it's not for a good reason. We never had a problem until *Lucy* forgot how to drive."

June practically hisses Lucy's name, and her anger surprises me. After we lost Cody, all I saw from her were tears and a blatant need to be the center of attention.

"How many parties did we have where nothing bad happened? Like a million."

I want to tell June she's wrong. Plenty of questionable things happened out at the Field; we just never got caught.

"And then *she* had to go and ruin everything." June looks at the wristbands in her hand and starts to pull on one, forcefully stretching it like she's trying to break it in two. "My senior year is trashed thanks to that loser."

11

Both Kat and I frown. June's words make me wonder if she's more upset about losing Cody or losing the ability to drink on the fifty-yard line of an abandoned football field.

Suddenly, she smiles. "Get it? Loser, *Luce*-er?"

An air horn sounds, signaling the end of my sister's game and distracting me from June's strange behavior. Stepping away from the girls, I look for Ayden and find her making her way to the obligatory handshake line. Glancing at the scoreboard, I see her team won.

"I need to grab my sister," I say and take a few more steps. "I'll catch you guys later, when school starts."

"Hopefully before then. Right, Kat?" June nudges Kat's arm. "I told him he should pay more attention to what's going on. People want to know how he is."

Even though I grimace, I see Kat nod. "It's true." She looks sympathetic. "A bunch of people have been asking about you."

They should worry about themselves, I think and give the girls a dismissive wave as I walk away. Once I flag Ayden down, she grabs her stuff and skips up to me. "Where's Mom?"

"Her appointment ran long. Good game."

"Thanks."

The two of us are silent until we make it to the edge of the parking lot. "Do you think we could stop for ice cream?" My sister pulls her damp jersey away from her skin and tries to fan herself with it. "I'm so hot."

"Sure." There's a place on the way home, and it would probably be wise for both of us to eat. She's been running around all morning, and I skipped breakfast. Plus, if I treat Ayden, maybe our parents will leave me alone for the rest of the day.

When we reach my truck, I unlock the door for my sister before walking around to the other side. Out of the corner of my eye, I catch a spattering of neon in the distance. Lucy's earlier stunned expression slams into my brain, making me wince. I was never close to her; I never talked to her. I knew her name, but we weren't friends. Regardless, it doesn't ease the weight I feel settling on my shoulders. It's been there for months, but it suddenly feels worse.

Heavier. More permanent.

I could blame the hang over, but I know without it I'd feel the same way. Seeing Lucy physically pay for what happened, running into June, Kat's confirmation people are talking about me …

I take a deep breath and curse beneath it. I need to pull my shit together or the guilt will eat me alive. That can't happen. I can't break my promise to Cody.

Opening the truck door, I glance in Lucy's direction one last time. Yes, she may have been the one who killed my best friend.

But I let it happen.

CHAPTER THREE

Lucy

Izzy swings her tiny Chevy Sonic into a parking space and cuts the engine. "Well." She looks at me without taking her hands off the steering wheel. "We're here."

Yeah, we are.

Across from us sits Holton High, and I stare at it through the windshield. Thoughts of the last time I stepped foot on campus make me clutch my backpack a little tighter. This will be my fourth and final year at this school. I'm a senior, and I should be rejoicing.

Instead, internally, I'm freaking out. Izzy knows it, too. I haven't been back here since that horrid day last May.

"It'll be okay," she reassures me. "Your locker is right next to mine, and we have three classes together. Plus, today will seem short with the welcome back assembly."

I nod without speaking.

"Luce. Look at me."

I comply, and her expression softens, revealing a hint of a smile. "What reminders do we need today?"

My eyes roll. "Stop."

"She speaks!" Izzy dramatically throws her hands in the air, making me laugh. Well, more like snort.

"I don't need any reminders," I say. "They won't help." Not even the pills my doctor prescribed for anxiety help. All they do is make me tired.

Izzy frowns. "Yes, they will, and we only have a few minutes. Start walking, missy."

With a heavy sigh, I open the car door. Izzy created a list of reminders, or daily affirmations, which she likes to recite to me. She thinks if I hear the words enough, I'll start to believe them. To be honest, most of what she says I already believe. I am a rational person, despite recent events.

Rounding the front of the car, she hikes her bag onto her shoulder and says, "Reminder number one. You look cute today."

My expression twists. "You're straying from the list."

She stops in front of me to primp my messy curls. "I swear. If I had your hair ..."

"I slept in braids, Izz." It's not like the waves are natural. Izzy's been after my hair since kindergarten, when hers was a straight chin-length bob and mine hung down to my butt.

"Yeah, but it's this awesome reddish mahogany color. I'm stuck with plain 'ole blondish-brown."

"Please. Your hair is anything but plain." Today she's twisted it into two cute knots on the top of her head. My best friend has a very unique fashion sense; right now, she's wearing hot pink Chucks with khaki capris, a gray crop top, and a tattered red and white flannel. I'm nowhere near as adventurous with my wardrobe. My standard black leggings and slouchy white tee practically scream "one of the herd."

Dropping the subject of hair, we start to walk toward the school. Cautiously, I glance from side to side. Other students walk near us, joking, laughing, or squealing hello. No one seems to notice me. I don't know what I expected; I wasn't here to witness the fallout last spring. My parents thought it would be best for me to finish my last month of school from home, since I'd run over one of the most popular kids to walk the halls of Holton since the nineties. I didn't disagree.

But now, time has passed. The police report has been filed, and I've completed my community service. It's time to start moving forward.

"Reminder number two," Izzy continues as we get closer to the school, "you can't change the past."

"I know." We're back to the standard list.

"Reminder number three, it was an accident."

"I know."

"And reminder number four," she stops short of the door and turns to me, "what happened doesn't define you."

I grab her arm to keep her moving. "You shouldn't be allowed on the internet."

As we step over the threshold into the school, we find it buzzing with first day excitement. Come next week the vibe will wane, but right now students roam every which way. In addition to the masses, I notice the spirit committee has been busy; posters supporting everything from the football team to the robotics club grace the walls. The farther we get from the main entrance, the more I can tell the freshmen apart from the upperclassmen by the way they hold their schedules and folders like security blankets.

"Remember that feeling?" Izzy asks. "Poor babies."

I nod. "They'll get over it by tomorrow, though." It's the truth. The school might be big, but it's easy to figure out.

Turning a corner, we pass the cafeteria and the auditorium, then enter the senior wing. I should have known my invisibility was too good to be true because as soon as I appear, every pair of eyes land on me. Thankfully the hallway doesn't go silent, like it would in a movie, but it's still as if my arrival has been announced by megaphone. Heat crawls up my neck to my cheeks, and my gaze immediately hits the floor. I let my hair cover one side of my face, and Izzy's body stiffens next to me.

"Don't you dare," she mutters. "Look up. Don't be intimidated."

Easy for her to say.

Reluctantly, I do as I'm told, even though I'm sure I look anything but confident. I focus on the red exit sign at the end of hall, since our lockers are the last two before the door. We requested them last year, when we had the ability to choose because we're seniors. Back then, we thought it would be cool to be somewhat secluded; now I'm ecstatic we made that choice.

Once we make it there, I let out a breath and pull up my schedule on my phone to find my locker combination. As I focus on the dial, someone taps me on the arm.

"Hey, Lucy."

My head snaps up. A few of my classmates have wandered over. "Hey," I manage, unsure.

"It's good to have you back." Nick gives me half a smile.

"Umm ... thanks."

"We ..." He pauses and glances around the group. "We weren't sure if we would see you today."

He looks sincere, and it confuses me. I mean, I know these people; Izzy and I have hung out with Willow and Brooke from time to time, and Nick has been my alphabetical locker neighbor since middle school. What I don't get is why they care if I'm here.

"We kind of lost contact over the summer," Willow says. "It's good to see you're okay."

"Of course she's okay." Izzy drapes her arm over my shoulders. "What'd you expect?"

"I don't know. I just ..." Willow looks at her shoes, then offers me a smile. "I just wanted to welcome you back."

"Me, too," Brooke adds.

"Thanks," I say again. "I'm ..." I search for words. "I'm glad to be back."

Liar.

Loud voices and a small cheer pull our attention away from one another. Farther down the hall, back the way we came, a bunch of kids applaud the arrival of none other than Aaron Matthews. I know it's him because the small crowd parts as he makes his way to his destination. Despite the scowl on his face, he looks like he always does: like he stepped off the pages of an Abercrombie catalog. He swipes a gray

17

beanie off his head, I'd say in frustration, revealing perfectly tousled brown locks. If I wore a hat and tried that, my hair would be shot to hell.

"Well, nothing's changed there," Izzy muses in my ear before the warning bell rings.

"Gotta go," Nick says, backing up. "We'll see you guys around, okay?"

"'Kay."

Shrugging out from beneath Izzy's arm, I open my locker and toss my backpack inside. Grabbing a notebook and pen, I ask, "What was that about?"

"What? The welcoming committee?" We start to walk. "I'd say they were concerned about you. You did disappear, after all."

"What I did was heinous. Are you sure they weren't dared to speak to the freak or something?"

"Did it look like they were faking?"

"Well, no," I concede. I know Izzy wants everything to be perfect, but I can't help my doubts.

When we arrive at our English class, we find desks side by side and survive the period with only one chapter of reading assigned. Mentally, I smile. With my parent's love of the written word, I've already read *The Scarlet Letter*. The first semester of this class is going to be a breeze.

Second and third periods wind up being the same, with minimal homework if any. Izzy is by my side in U.S. History, but we don't have the same foreign language class. When the bell rings at the end of Spanish, everyone shoots out of their seats like they've been electrocuted. As we file out the door, I'm surprised to see a few smiles directed my way. Now that I think about it, I got a few "hellos" last period, too. It feels weird. I wasn't a social outcast before, but I assumed things would be different now.

"Hiya." Izzy finds me on the way to our only fun elective, yearbook. "Everything going okay?"

"Yeah." My face scrunches. "I wonder why."

She shrugs. "I doubt people have forgotten, but honestly, who would bring it up? No one is that cruel."

"Maybe." If there's one thing I love about Izzy, it's her optimism. I've learned to take it with a grain of salt, however. Recent experience has taught me everything can't be roses and rainbows.

"See. I told you not to worry." She grins and unexpectedly bumps her hip against mine, throwing me off balance and sending me stumbling into a group of people.

"Jesus, Izz!"

Some guy I don't know jumps out of the way, but I still end up falling. In less than a second my brain registers who I'm crashing into, and I curse Izzy, gravity, and karma all at once.

It's Aaron Matthews.

"Whoa," he says, catching my forearms before I completely hit the ground. "You all right?"

I stand up straight and look at him, mortified. He blinks and, once he realizes who I am, drops my arms like they burn his palms. I jerk back. "I'm fine. Sorry."

"Are you sure?"

"Aarrron," June Summers flirts as she rounds the corner. "Do you think–"

Both of us turn and look in her direction. June stops in her tracks. Her eyes lock on mine as an expression of pure hatred consumes her face.

Shit.

"What. The. Fuck?" She enunciates each word.

I don't know what to say. I've never spoken to her before – ever. All I know is she's popular, has the body of a swimsuit model, and ... I killed her boyfriend.

"What do you think you're doing?" She walks up to me and stops inches from my face. "Are you trying to talk to him?" She stabs a finger in Aaron's direction. "You don't get to talk to him. You're not allowed anywhere near us or any of Cody's friends. Got it?"

My heart wants to pound out of my chest.

This. This is what I was expecting.

Speechless, I step back. I want to say I never planned on breathing near them, let alone striking up a conversation, but I can't. My tongue feels swollen in my mouth.

"What are you waiting for? Get out of here!" she screeches. She's so close, I can smell her wintergreen gum. Other students notice us and start to stare.

"June. Stop." Her friend, I think her name is Kat, grabs her arm. "Calm down, okay?"

"I will not calm down." She shakes Kat off. "I can't stand the sight of her." Her steel blue eyes bore into mine. "Murderer," she spits.

I hear gasps and silently pray the floor will open up and swallow me whole.

Before it can, Aaron steps between us. "That's enough." He sounds angry as he turns his back to me. "Knock it off," he warns June.

"Let's go," Izzy whispers, and I don't think twice. We take off in the direction we came from as unshed tears prick my eyes. I think I hear June shout, "You're defending her?!" before I'm out of earshot, but things are muffled from my racing pulse.

Izzy apologizes as we walk. "I'm so so so so sorry. I didn't see him there; I didn't think you'd fall."

I dismiss her with a shake of my head. "It's fine."

"It's *not* fine." She steers me into the nearest restroom. Once we're inside, she checks the stalls before throwing her arms around me. "I'm the worst best friend ever! What can I do?"

"You can stop squeezing the life out of me," I say, trying to take deep breaths. "You didn't mean it."

"Of course I didn't, but ..." She moves away and holds me at arm's length. "Seriously, are you okay?"

I nod, but I'm a little shaky.

"June is insane," Izzy says, squeezing the top of my arms.

"She misses Cody."

"That doesn't give her the right to attack–"

The bell rings. "Great." I sigh. "We're late to fourth period."

Stepping around Izzy, I take a quick glance in the mirror. I look relatively unscathed; a little red in the ears and cheeks, but it will fade.

"C'mon. We need to go." I don't want to call any more attention to myself than I already have.

We stick our heads out into the hallway like spies, looking right and left before leaving the restroom. The coast is clear.

As we speed-walk to yearbook class, Izzy says, "You know what she said isn't true, right? You're not a murderer."

I shrug. Does it matter?

BY THE TIME the welcome back assembly rolls around, I'm more than ready to go home. I've been walking around on eggshells since I fell. Aside from a few whispers and stares, nothing else has happened with June. In fact, I haven't seen her at all, not even during lunch. Maybe she's avoiding me, but I doubt it. She doesn't come across as a coward. I'm sure she'd relish the opportunity to let me have it again, especially in front of a crowd.

That's why, when Izzy and I enter the gym for the assembly, my eyes bounce everywhere. I've been tense all day; I'm not sure I can handle a sneak attack.

"I don't see her," Izzy says as we find seats in the senior section, climbing several rows and sliding to the end of one of the bleachers. "I don't see Aaron, either. Oh, wait." She frowns. "There they are."

I follow her line of sight and sure enough, both of them, along with Kat and a bunch of their friends, are walking into the gym. June doesn't look upset anymore; she's all talkative and bouncy. They stop in front of the first row of bleachers, not bothering to climb higher to find seats.

"Good. Stay down there, you evil, worthless, ugly–"

"Lucy?"

I stop listening to Izzy's color commentary and turn around. Ms. Wright, our class advisor, is standing beside me.

"Yes?"

"I need to speak with you for a moment."

Confused, I stand and follow her down to the gym floor where she leads me around the side of the bleachers. Ms. Wright is a new teacher and one of the more popular staff members at Holton High. She's young, fresh out of college, and can relate to us, which is why she was appointed advisor. I don't know why she needs to speak to me, unless it has to do with the student council. My stomach sinks. What if the council is part of the assembly? No one told me. We haven't even had one meeting.

"Lucy," she starts, "I heard there was an incident today."

I frown. "An incident?"

"Yes. In the hallway before fourth period."

This is about June? "I didn't start anything, I swear." It's the truth. I never uttered a word.

"Regardless ..." She grimaces, twisting her perfectly made-up features. "I think it would be best if you step down as student council treasurer."

Wait a minute. "You want me to resign?"

She nods.

"But I was elected."

"As advisor, I can overrule the election. In light of what's happened, I don't think you're fit for a leadership role."

What is she talking about? "Are you referring to June attacking me or Cody?"

She closes her eyes and takes a deep breath. "Both."

She can't do this. "I'm sorry, Ms. Wright, but it was an accident. It wasn't premeditated. I didn't mean to–"

She interrupts. "My decision stands."

"But I was going to use the experience on my college applica–"

"I think this is what's best for all involved. I will inform the other officers you have resigned effective immediately."

For the second time today, I can't find words.

With that she leaves me, shocked and alone. I stand there frozen until the marching band strikes up the Holton High fight song, making me jump. Willing my legs to move, I climb the bleachers and find my seat next to Izzy.

"What's going on?"

"I just got kicked off the student council."

"What?" Her eyes pop out of her head. "Why?"

"I'll tell you later." It's hard to talk over the band.

Izzy's face falls, and she wraps her arm around my waist. I rest my head on her shoulder, and the two of us sit together, slumped, while the other students stand, clapping and singing the fight song:

"Go, go, go, go

Fight, fight, fight, fight

Win, win, win, win

Yaaaay Holton!!"

Screw Holton, I think. The cheers, the drums, the cymbals, the horns … my mind replaces the cheers for the football team with ones for my most recent demise; as if the entire school saw what Ms. Wright did and *loves* it. My head starts to pound. I don't want to fight or win. But I do want to go.

Go home and hide.

CHAPTER FOUR

Aaron

I t's so loud in here I can't think.

June is glued to my side, which is annoying as hell. She's been clingy all day, and I need some space. When we walked into the gym, I tried to sit next to Kat, but somehow, she slid in between us. On top of that, to my left, my lacrosse team is being obnoxious in their own right. People have been acting crazy all day; it's like I've stepped into some sort of twilight zone. Cheering when I showed up this morning? What was that? An entourage following me to each class? Why? June confronting Lucy in the hallway? It's psycho.

"That's you, man." Harrison claps me on the shoulder.

"What?"

"They just called your name."

I look up and some kids from the spirit committee are motioning for me to join them. Judging by who they're standing with, they've selected a student from each grade to compete in some sort of game. *Ugh.* This is the last thing I want to do. When I hesitate, everyone around me starts to cheer. I get a few nudges from behind and, before

I know it, June grabs my hand, pulling me to my feet. "You can do it! Good luck!"

She's touching me again. I realize this is my chance to get away from her and jog out to the center of the gym floor.

"Okay, Holton High," some kid says into a mic, his voice echoing through the PA system, "based on an informal vote taken by our committee, these four guys are your choices to compete in ..." He cues the band for a drumroll. "The Hottie Hula Hoop!"

The crowd roars, and I try to stop my eyes from rolling.

A pink plastic circle appears in front of me, and I take it from a committee member's hand. The movement causes the hoop to light up from the inside. The first thing I think of is Ayden. She would love one of these. The second, I can't hula hoop. Cody was the one who could; in fact, he was the one who taught my sister when we were younger.

"The rules are simple," committee man continues. "Whoever can hula hoop the longest, wins. If the hoop falls, make sure you catch it. Once it hits the floor, you're out."

I'm tempted to drop it on purpose.

Music starts to blast through the speakers, and the four of us who got suckered into this game back away from each other. I have to try to do this. Sliding the hoop over my head, I spin it around my waist and move my hips in an attempt to keep it in place.

Nope.

Catching it against my leg, I try again. Things don't go any better the second or the third time around. I look over at my lacrosse buddies, and they think this is hysterical. Kat and June are covering their mouths and giggling too, and an image of Cody pops in my head. I can picture him right in the middle of all of them, recording me with his phone to torture me later. The urge to smile creeps up on me, until my eyes sweep the senior section and fall on Lucy.

She's easy to pick out. While everyone else is standing, she's sitting with her friend. Her head rests on Izzy's shoulder, and she looks miserable. They both do. I remember what June called her earlier today, and a realization slams home. How is the attention on us, four dudes epically failing at a child's game, when there is someone who obviously needs it more? Has anyone, staff or a teacher, bothered to ask her if she's all right? They should, because I know exactly how she feels.

"What are you doing? Keep going! Don't just stand there!" My friends yell at me from the bleachers. They care more about this dumb game than anything else. There's only one person in this gym who understands how ridiculous this all is.

In a silent show of solidarity, I go with my earlier thought. I let the hula hoop drop, and it bounces off the ground. I'm the first one eliminated.

And the last one to care.

IT WAS the first spring night warm enough for a party out at the Field. People were everywhere, from the old overgrown parking lot to the forgotten fifty-yard line. A decent bonfire was licking the sky, cars with good sound systems streamed the same radio station, and anyone with a legal connection – or parents who wouldn't notice a few missing bottles – provided the booze. My teammates and I had just finished an animated retelling of our latest victory, mainly to entertain ourselves, when I noticed my cup was empty.

"I can see the bottom," I announced. "Anyone else?"

"Me." Cody downed the last of his beer. "I'll come with you."

Our feet carried us away from our group and shuffled through the grass toward the keg. Cody's cell buzzed in his pocket, and he pulled it out for the umpteenth time that night.

"Who keeps blowing you up?" I asked. "June's here, isn't she?"

"Yeah." He silenced his phone and tucked it away. "She's pissed at me."

"For what?"

"I was supposed to come over last night, but I didn't."

I remembered Cody telling me June's parents were out of town. "You passed up an opportunity to get laid?" Passing on sex was something Cody didn't do. It's something no seventeen-year-old guy did, including me.

"I just didn't feel like it. You know?"

I chuckled. "No. I don't."

Cody stopped walking. It was clear he didn't share my hormonal humor. "What is it?"

His phone sounded from his pocket again. He hung his head, then pulled out his cell and looked at the screen. I could tell his thoughts on the call were confirmed when he grimaced and held the phone out toward me. "It's not June. It's Allie."

He had to be kidding. "You're not serious."

All he did was shake his head.

"Cody. What the hell?" I stepped closer to him so no one could hear me, even though the closest group of people was several feet away. "I thought you called that shit off."

He ran a hand through his hair, exasperated. "I tried. I talked to her last week; I told you she flipped out."

"Yeah, but you haven't said anything since."

Cody glanced around and focused on an object in the distance. My jaw dropped. "Is this a conversation for the bleachers?"

Nothing has been that serious since we were eleven, when we accidentally broke his neighbor's window with a rogue baseball bat. Yes, the bat, not the ball, slipped from Cody's grip and went flying into Mr. Daniel's front window. We'd been warned about playing in his yard and when the glass shattered into a million pieces, we were convinced we were going to jail. We ran to the Field to hide. It was a mile from Cody's house, but we didn't care. We hid under the dilapidated bleachers, plotted our escape to Canada, and started collecting cans and bottles party goers had left behind to fund our trip. That was when Cody's dad found us, roaming the Field with our arms full of empties.

"Let's walk," I suggested. If we stood in one place for too long, our friends were bound to find us. We gravitated toward the bleachers.

"So, what does she want?" I asked.

"Me, apparently. She keeps sending threats."

27

"Like?"

"Like she'll tell my parents. Tell other people."

"Would she?"

"Hell if I know. I wouldn't put it past her."

I let out a heavy breath. As soon as this whole thing started, I told Cody I didn't like it. I told him to stay away from Allie, but he thought it would be a rush. He was seeing June, but he said things between them were getting difficult. He said he needed to live a little, since he was busy trying to keep up appearances as Holton High's star athlete. I had to admit if Allie came on to me, I'd have been tempted, too. But there are lines you just don't cross.

Trying to sort through what he said, I asked, "Okay, so what? If she outs you to everyone, it only implicates her. She's the one with the most to lose." Well, that's not entirely true. He'd probably be grounded for life, lose any monetary support until he's thirty, and his girlfriend would dump him, but he'd survive.

"I'm stressed out enough; the last thing I need is for this to get out." Cody crushed his party cup in his hand. "My parents will kill me. Her latest threat is to tell my recruiter I tried juice. I'll lose my spot at Notre Dame."

My eyes grow wide. That's low, even for Allie. Even a hint of a drug scandal would be scholarship suicide.

"I need another beer." Cody tossed his cup on the grass.

I needed to help him find a solution. "How many times did you hook up? Two? Three?"

He shoved his hands in his pockets and stared at the ground. "Or more."

I tried not to raise my voice. "More? How many more? Christ, Cody. What were you thinking?"

"Listen. I don't need your shit," he said, suddenly angry. "I get I fucked up, okay? Now I have to pay for it. Happy?"

"No, I'm not. I'm trying to help. There's a way out of this, we just have to find it."

He snorted. "The only solution I see is to keep seeing her. She's just going to come up with more threats."

"Why do you sound like you're giving in?" I asked. "Let's fix this."

"How?" Cody crossed his arms.

I stared at my shoes while I searched for answers. Maybe he should be proactive and take a drug test. He only tried steroids on and off one summer; he would pass now with no problem. His family is well-off, maybe – wait. "Offer her money," I said, snapping my fingers. "She must want cash."

"I'm seventeen," he scoffed. "I doubt my allowance will satisfy her. Am I supposed to hack into my dad's bank account?"

I stood there, thinking. Unfortunately, there was only one idea that made sense.

"You have to tell your parents," I said, resigned. "I know it sucks, but they can help. Bite the bullet and come clean. Even though they'll be upset, they will have to respect your honesty."

"Are you insane?" The veins in Cody's neck bulged. "You know I can't do that."

"You can. I'll be there with you. I'll tell them you were coerced or whatever you want me to say. I know you'll feel like pissing your pants; I know you'll get in trouble. But at least they will have heard it from you and not Allie."

Cody's hands clutched the back of his neck, and he started to pace. We remained silent for what seemed like forever until he let out a deep breath and finally looked at me. "Okay."

"Okay? As in you'll do it?"

"You're right. It's the only way."

Relief flooded me. Why I don't know; this wasn't my problem. However, Cody was my best friend. I'd warned him off Allie, but I'd also asked for details, too. I encouraged him while not encouraging him, if that made sense. "So, when do you want to do it?"

"Not tonight." His voice was adamant as we started walking back toward the keg. "Tonight I'm getting wasted because it will probably be my last taste of freedom for God knows how long."

I didn't question him. His logic seemed sound; it's what I would do if I were in his shoes. As we walked, I draped my arm over his shoulders. "I've got your back. Just tell me when you've had enough, and I'll get you home."

He nodded.

When we made it to the keg, it was in use. Despite everything that just went down, my eyes lit up at the sight of the person filling her cup. Since Kat wouldn't give me the time of day, Paige Brewer and I had fallen into an undefined something.

"Hey, guys." She smiled at us. "I see the bromance is still going strong."

"Paige." I moved away from Cody and gave her a lopsided grin. "Where've you been?"

"My car has been making some stupid noise, so I was late."

"What kind of noise?"

"It's a weird hum. I think it's coming from under the hood, but I'm not sure." She took a drink, then pouted behind her red party cup. "I wish I knew a mechanic."

"Do you want me to take a look at it?"

Before she could answer, Cody let out a sarcastic laugh. "You're not a mechanic."

I shot him my "shut up" death stare. "At least I can try."

"Whatever." He reached for a cup and the keg tap at the same time. "I don't know who you're trying to fool. We all know which hood you'll wind up under."

I had to restrain myself from punching him in the arm. I didn't know how Paige would take his comment. Even though we were really into each other, I only hung out with her off and on. What we had wasn't dating or even considered official, although the thought of changing our status was on my mind.

A lot.

"C'mon." I stepped to her side. "Where's your car?"

"This way." She nodded toward the sea of haphazardly parked vehicles. "Thanks for volunteering to help. I'm in serious need of a tune up."

I was about to tell her that was the cause of her noise problem when she winked at me. I caught her meaning and looked at Cody.

"You going to be okay?"

He was chugging his beer and didn't answer me.

As soon as we were out of earshot, I wrapped my arm around Paige's waist and pressed her to my side. "A tune up? Is that what the kids are calling it nowadays?"

She laughed. "I'm glad you got my hint. Although, there really is something wrong with my car. I was late because my dad was trying to figure it out. I need a new wheel bearing."

My lips found her ear. "I love it when you talk auto shop."

She smiled. "I love it when we don't talk at all."

Seizing the opportunity, my mouth found hers. We stopped walking, and I got lost in the bitter taste of beer mixed with something strawberry on her lips. Minutes later, a playful scream from someone being chased startled us apart.

"Race ya." She grinned and took off running, tossing her cup aside. I ran after her, and when her car was in sight, she reached into her pocket and tossed me the keys. Snagging them out of mid-air, I pressed the unlock button and we jumped into the backseat from opposite sides of the car, slamming the doors behind us. Within seconds she was in my lap, I was unzipping her fleece, and we were both panting from our run – amongst other things. Her lips found mine, her fingers found the button on my jeans, and I couldn't get her jacket off her shoulders or her t-shirt over her head fast enough.

Afterward, as she pulled her clothes back on and I made sure my fly was up, I thought about asking her about us. About where she thought we were headed and if she wanted a committed relationship. For the first time since we started hooking up, I felt the urge to ask her to be my legit girlfriend.

"So," I started out slowly, "I have a question for you."

"I hope it's not about prom," she said, gathering her hair into a ponytail.

"Why?"

"Because I'm moving." She was very matter-of-fact. "My dad got reassigned."

All the air left my lungs. I knew her dad was military, but ... just ... damn.

"We leave for Florida in two weeks."

She reached for her jacket, unaffected by the bomb she had just dropped. I, on the other hand, searched for words to hide my disappointment. Shifting my weight on the seat, I kicked at the condom wrapper on the floor. "Well, at least it's warm there."

"Right?" She smiled. "There are worse places to live."

She finished pulling herself together and then slid over next to me. Her eyes roamed my face before she planted an innocent kiss on my cheek. "I'm glad I got to know you, Aaron. Hanging out with you was fun."

"While it lasted," slipped out of my mouth before I could catch it. She frowned and looked confused by my tone. Thankfully my phone went off, distracting us. I reached for it, but it wasn't in my back pocket.

"Here." Paige leaned over and grabbed it from under the front seat. "It must have fallen."

She handed it to me, and I glanced at the screen. It was Cody. *I can't* were the only two words he sent.

You can't what? I sent back.

It took him a few seconds to respond. *You kniw.*

He had to be talking about Allie and his parents. *Why?* I typed.

His started to reply and stopped multiple times; I could tell when the conversation bubble on my cell kept appearing then disappearing. Finally, he sent *I can't lie anymore.*

I sighed. *I know. We need to talk to your mom and dad.*

No. Not what I'm talikng about.

I could feel the confusion on my face. Cody didn't sound like himself. He wasn't the melodramatic type.

"What's going on?" Paige asked.

"Cody isn't making sense."

"He's probably drunk."

That would explain his spelling. He did say he was going to get wasted.

With that thought, I realized I should go find him. I'd been alone with Paige only an hour, but in that time something had changed. "I should go check on him," I said and reached for the door handle. "He doesn't need to embarrass himself."

She followed me out of the car, and we started back toward the party. After a few steps, she bumped her body against mine. "I'll get to see you before I leave, right?"

I smirked. "I would think so. We go to the same school."

"That's not what I meant."

I knew what she meant, but I wasn't sure about seeing her anymore. Not after I let my emotions sneak up on me. Now I understood what Cody had said earlier, about not "feeling it" with June. I wasn't necessarily feeling it with Paige right now.

"Things are busy," I said, trying to be non-committal. "Playoffs are around the corner, and coach has added another hour to each practice. I'll let you know, though."

She nodded. No sadness or disappointment crossed her face, only acceptance. Obviously, she never questioned our relationship like I had.

My phone went off again. The message from Cody read *Im gonna pass out.*

I groaned and stopped walking. "I'll catch up with you later," I told Paige. "Cody's sick."

"Okay." She smiled and kept moving. "Call me."

Not likely, I thought.

Standing amongst the cars, I sent Cody a message. *Where are you?* When he didn't respond, I guessed *The bleachers?*

Still nothing. He was acting really strange. *What did you drink?* I typed as I started to walk. He had to be around here somewhere.

To my surprise, my cell rang. I hardly ever used the actual phone part of my phone. "Hey," I answered. "Where in the hell are you?"

"Shots." Cody's voice sounded muffled. "Too many shots."

No wonder. "I'll take you home. Tell me where you are."

"No."

"No? Do you want to spend the night out here?"

"I found a good place."

There was no good place to sleep out here. We learned that lesson when we were kids. "Have you lost your mind?"

No answer. All I heard was shuffling, like he was moving and bumping against stuff. Was he walking through the trees? There was a wooded area at one end of the Field with a stagnant swamp in the middle of it.

"Cody." A bad feeling took root in my gut. "Tell me where you are."

"You can't tell anyone," he slurred. "Promise."

"I promise." My pulse started to race. I hadn't told anyone about Allie or his two seconds of doping. Was he talking about something else?

"I can't …" He drifted off. "… just a kid. You can't tell her mom … she'll cry. I hate it when she cries."

Huh? "It's not that bad. You can fix the Allie thing."

"I can't."

"You can."

Through the phone I heard a door slam, like he got into his car. My walk turned into a run through the parking lot. "Get out of there! You can't drive."

"Not … driving."

What was his problem? This wasn't my best friend. I raced in the direction of where we had parked, and I heard an engine start on his end of the line. It sounded loud, like he had the windows down or he was in a garage. "Dude. Listen to me. Don't screw things up any more than they already are."

It was hard to hear. "Winners never give up," he mumbled. I recognized the line his dad used all the time. "Don't tell them I gave up."

"What? Cody, you're not making any damn sense."

The engine revved and I heard a crunch, like he dropped his phone. I could see our cars, but his hadn't moved. He wasn't there. I skidded to a stop and turned around in circles, my eyes darting everywhere. "Cody?" I said into the phone. "Cody? Are you there?"

Moments later, I heard the scream. My head snapped to the left, and I started running again. In the distance I could see a girl, but it was dark and I didn't know who she was. I made it to her in seconds and stopped, trying to catch my breath as I stared at her over the hood of her running car. Her eyes were wide with fear, and her entire body was shaking.

"Lucy?" I asked, recalling her name.

Her eyes fixed on mine. She could barely speak. "Call," she choked out. "He's stuck."

She lifted her hands, and they were covered in blood. It was as if I'd been slapped, and I stumbled back. Looking down, I recognized Cody's black Chucks right away; his legs sticking out from beneath her front tires. Without thinking, I dropped my phone and fell to my knees, grabbed his ankles, and tried to pull him free.

"Cody!"

He wouldn't move and my hands slipped, causing me to lose my balance and fall back on my ass. Righting myself, I scrambled forward and made the mistake of looking beneath the car. All I could hear were muffled sobs as something fed a growing puddle of blood. My muscles refused to move as the dark stain morphed and started to run downhill, winding its way through the blades of grass as if seeking me out.

My body jolts awake, my heart hammering in my chest. With clenched fists, my eyes sweep the darkness until I realize I'm in my bedroom and not out at the Field. Bile rises in my throat, and I swallow it back while scrubbing my face with the palms of my hands. It does nothing to erase the memory.

Goddamn it.

I lived this nightmare. I hate that I'm forced to dream about it, too.

CHAPTER FIVE

Lucy

"Hello, Huskies. As the end of this first week draws to a close, we have some late afternoon announcements."

I look up from highlighting my chemistry book as the principal's voice interrupts sixth period over the PA system.

"First, your class representatives would like to remind everyone homecoming is two weeks away. Tickets for the dance will go on sale Monday in the cafeteria. Please consider supporting the event by purchasing a Cody Cunningham memorial bracelet, also available during the lunch hour."

My cheeks turn crimson, and I slump in my seat. Every time someone says his name it's like a punch to the gut.

"Second, staff would like to remind students to park in the student lot only. Parking in lot A is forbidden during school hours. From now until the end of the year, students will serve detention if their vehicle is found in lot A."

Someone groans behind me.

"And finally, the results of the Holton High Alumni Association Scholarship Contest are in."

My ears perk up a bit. I forgot I entered an essay before the shit hit the fan.

"The third-place winner of a $100 scholarship is ..." Mr. Hughes reads the name. I don't know her or the second-place winner.

"In first place, and the winner of $300, is senior June Summers."

I smirk. It figures.

"And, last but not least, the $500 grand prize goes to senior Lucy Anderson."

Did he just say my name?

"Well done, Lucy. Congratulations to all the winners. Awards can be picked up in the main office." The principal pauses, then says, "Don't forget we have a home football game tonight against Kensington. Go Huskies!"

I'm stunned I won.

"Nice job." Nick compliments me from the lab table beside mine.

"Thanks."

My cell vibrates in my pocket, and I pull it out just enough to glance at the screen. It's a text message from Izzy: *Congrats! Victory Freezy Wheezy on me.*

I smile. Freezy Wheezies are what we call frozen drinks from the gas station. In all reality I should buy her one, because she's been driving me to school all week. The police returned my car this summer after their investigation, but I've yet to drive it. Just the thought gives me hives.

"So," our chemistry teacher continues after the interruption, "homework for the weekend."

Irritated groans surround me.

"Read through chapter two. Our first lab will be next week." The bell rings. "And make sure you think about a lab partner!" She raises her voice over the slamming of book covers and shuffling feet.

"Lucy." Nick catches up to my side in the hallway. "Are you going to the game tonight?"

I shake my head.

"Why not?"

37

Telling him I have an appointment with my therapist is out of the question, so I say, "I have other plans."

"Like what?"

I bite my lip while I search for an excuse. "Stuff with family," finally comes out of my mouth. The truth is, even if I didn't have something to do, I wouldn't go to the game. Being social isn't high on my list of priorities lately.

We reach his locker before we get to mine, and he hesitates, like he doesn't know if he should stop or not. "Okay, then. I guess I'll see you Monday."

"Yep. Have a good weekend."

"You, too."

My attention shifts down the hall, where Izzy is jumping up and down and waving her arms around like a lunatic in front of our lockers. What is she doing?

"Con-grat-u-lations!" she sings and hugs me when I reach her. "Let's go claim your prize."

"Why are you so happy?"

"Because." She steps back and throws her bag on her shoulder. "It's Friday, it's sunny outside, and you just beat June."

"I'm glad I could oblige." Ever since I told her the details regarding my student council impeachment, Izzy's been convinced June went to Ms. Wright and requested my resignation. Why a teacher would listen to a student and act on her recommendation is beyond me, so of course I think she's wrong.

"You don't deserve what happened to you," Izzy says as I gather my things. "I still think you should report it."

"To who?" I ask as I shut my locker. "I highly doubt the principal would take my side over staff." I didn't even bother to tell my parents. They don't need any more stress.

"Ms. Wright's only been here a year," Izzy disputes me. "This is a democracy, not a dictatorship."

I shoot her a side-eye as we start to walk. "Look around. We're in high school. This is the definition of a dictatorship."

She sighs. "I was referring to the fact you were voted into office."

I refuse to comment. Losing my position is a sore spot, but in reality, probably for the best. The relief that overcomes me when I get home each day tells me I'm not ready for more Holton High than necessary. I know I've encountered only one nasty person, but I still feel the weight of people's stares. Nick, Brooke, and Willow are the only people who have had a real conversation with me since the first day of school. Losing the student council gig is most likely a blessing in disguise.

As we near the main office, Izzy asks, "Are you seeing the Doc tonight?"

I nod. "Are you going to the game?"

"Not without you."

Her response hurts my heart. "Izz. Don't miss out on things because of me. It's your senior year. Go have fun."

She frowns. "It wouldn't be fun without you. And besides, between your shrink and me, you'll be back to the old Luce in no time. I can wait to watch football players in tight pants."

My brow jumps. "Can you now?" I know how Izzy feels about tight pants. She practically swoons at the sight of a guy in skinny jeans.

"Hey. I'm not *that* addicted."

I smile, ready to prove her wrong. "Really? Did you get a good look at Wes today?"

Her eyes grow wide. "Oh my god, I did." She sets her hand against her chest. "So. Hot."

I laugh. "My friend, you are beyond addicted."

We reach the office, and I pull open the door just as someone is leaving from the opposite side. She stumbles forward and I shuffle back, both of us caught off guard. Our eyes meet, and my laughter fades. Not her. One confrontation is enough this week.

June's features twist as she regains her composure. "Coming to pick up your pity prize?"

I try to walk past her, but she steps in my way. Does she really want an answer?

"You only won because the committee felt sorry for you," she snipes.

Despite my suddenly dry throat, I manage, "They don't even know me."

"Everyone knows you." She looks me over from head to toe, clearly unimpressed. "They shouldn't."

Just then, the office door opens and secretary sticks out her head. "Lucy?"

I blink. Maybe everyone does know who I am. "Yes?"

"I'm getting ready to lock up. Come on in so I can give you your award, and we can go home."

She disappears and I start to follow her, but June grabs my arm. My muscles tense, and I sense Izzy take a breath, ready to tear into her. I shoot my best friend a look and shake my head no.

"Wise choice," June says and releases me. "Stay out of my way."

"Or what?" Izzy asks.

June gives us a condescending smile. "Trust me. You don't want to find out."

MY THERAPIST FURROWS her brow and shifts her weight, resting her elbow on the opposite arm of her wingback chair. "And what did you say?"

I shrug. "What could I say? Thanks for the warning?"

When Dr. Marie asked me how school went this week, I told her about my latest run-in with June. I knew I had to tell her something substantial; she wouldn't let me get away with a simple response like "It was okay."

Dr. Marie purses her lips. "June is projecting."

"She's what?"

"She's projecting. She's focusing all her anger toward you."

Ya think? I want to say. Instead, I mutter, "Who else would she blame?" To be honest, I thought I'd get the cold shoulder from a lot more people than just her.

"Who do you blame?" The Doc, as Izzy likes to call her, crosses her legs. "Who are you angry with?"

Should I be mad at someone? A lot of her questions confuse me. "I'm not angry."

"Don't you think you should be?"

My head is starting to ache. "You know, if you told me what I'm supposed to say instead of asking me vague questions, things would be so much easier."

She smiles. "Okay. I think you should be mad at someone."

"Who?"

"You tell me."

Ugh. I take a deep breath and let it out; obviously this is what we're working on tonight.

"Well," I start with the obvious, "I'm not mad at June. I think she's sad and doesn't know how to handle it. She hasn't done anything but snap at me, so ..."

"So, you think her behavior is acceptable and you deserve it."

"No," I say quickly. "I just understand what she's going through." I pause. "I think."

"Maybe you don't," Dr. Marie encourages me. "Could there be a teeny bit of resentment there?"

Do I resent the fact that I've tried my hardest to avoid June and all her friends this week and she still ended up in my face? Yeah, I do. Despite my best efforts, we're going to cross paths from time to time. It's inevitable. Part of me says she needs to get used to it. The other part says I did something that hurt her, so she has a right to be upset.

"Lucy?"

"What?"

"Your thoughts?"

I sigh. "I don't know. It's complicated."

"All right. Let's go back. Tell me someone else you should confront."

Hang on. "You think I should confront June?"

Dr. Marie leans forward and rests her clasped hands on her knees. "It sounds to me like this girl has issues. Issues she's not dealing with properly. If her behavior escalates, you need to stand up for yourself. Something traumatic happened to you, too. She has the right to her feelings; however, you're not required to suffer the consequences. Remember that."

I nod to appease her. *Stand up to bullies, kids.*

"Now," she glances at her watch, "I have a homework assignment for you."

Dr. Marie stands, walks to her desk, and retrieves a spiral bound notebook and pen. "Speaking of confrontation," she returns and hands the items to me, "who else deserves to hear how you feel?"

"I don't know," I confess. My parents and Izzy are the closest to me, and they already know everything. They know how guilt weighs me down. They know how certain sounds or smells will set off images in my head, making me nauseous. It's weird; I can look at a picture of Cody and feel fine, but I can't smell smoke without remembering the bonfire from that night. Or, like the other day, when my younger brother, Will, accidentally dropped a watermelon as he was bringing it inside the house. It splattered on the tile, and the sound of the pop and the sight of the red, mushy fruit was enough to make me equate it to Cody's smashed skull. I couldn't help clean it up because all I saw was blood on my hands.

As if sensing my thoughts, Dr. Marie says, "You wouldn't be sitting here if it wasn't for Cody. Don't you think he needs to hear how his actions impacted your life?"

My eyebrows shoot up. "You mean how he got so drunk he passed out in front of my car?"

She nods. "And how that choice wasn't fair to you."

"You want me to talk to a dead person?" I frown. "I never spoke to him when he was alive."

"I want you to pretend to speak to him." She taps the notebook. "Write him a letter. Write him several letters. Get everything off your chest and share what you're going through. It might take a few tries, but I think you'll find the exercise helpful."

I stare at the paper in my hands. "Then what? We set the letters on fire in some sort of ritualistic cleansing?"

Dr. Marie laughs. "We could. But I think ..." She opens the note-book cover. "I think you should deliver them instead."

Written on the first piece of paper are the words: Whispering Oaks, Section Seven, Tenth Row, Third Plot.

My eyes grow wide. "You want me to go to the cemetery?"

"When you're ready, yes."

The Doc may have lost her mind.

"I'm going to leave you alone for the rest of today's session," she says. "I want you to work on your first letter."

"But–"

She starts to walk away. "I'll be back in about fifteen minutes."

I start to panic. "Will you check my work?"

"No." She shakes her head. "This is between you and Cody."

The door closes behind her, and my relieved eyes land on the notebook. It's a good thing she doesn't want to see what I write because what the hell? I've never thought about what I would say to him. There's plenty I could ask, but it's not like I'm going to get any answers.

As the time passes, I doodle on the paper. Swirls and shapes and designs. I write my full name a few times, then Izzy's.

Isabel. Isabel Ann.

Lucy. Luce. Lucifer. I cross that one out.

Holton. Dictator. Wright. June. Summers.

I draw a sun, then a tree, and then a flower. It kind of looks like a tulip, which makes me think of spring. The Field appears in my head.

The party.

I shade in the sun; it's night. I draw a fire next to the tulip, then turn the petals into flames.

It's late. I'm tired. I'm stuck. On what?

Hit the gas. Thump. Can't back up. My dad is going to kill me. What did I hit?

Familiar pressure settles in my chest, along with the sick feeling in the back of my throat. Turning the page, I write the only words I can think to say to Cody:

I'm sorry.

43

CHAPTER SIX

Aaron

I stare at Coach in disbelief. "You can't be serious."

"I'm sorry, son. Your counselor should have caught it sooner. But, in order to graduate and remain sports eligible, you can't take four years of PE. You need at least one other elective."

"And yearbook is the only thing available?"

"I'm afraid so."

I groan. When Coach found me in the hallway before fourth period, I knew it was about lacrosse. I thought he might want to talk about selecting another co-captain, even though it will be hard to replace Cody. Instead, I'm faced with sitting out the season or taking a class I have no interest in.

"I don't think you understand," I argue. "I'm not a creative person; I'll fail."

"No, you won't. It's not an art course." Coach slides my revised schedule across his desk. "You'll find a way to make it work. Why? Because I need you. The team needs you." He taps the paper with one finger. "We all need our captain."

My shoulders slump. He should really save the pep talks for the locker room.

"You should get going," he says, grabbing a late excuse slip. "You've already missed twenty minutes."

He starts writing, and I rest my elbows on my knees. "Do I really have to do this?"

"Do you want to graduate?" He looks up at me. "Lacrosse isn't the only thing on the line here."

He's right. I just wish there were another option. Computers, accounting, anything other than yearbook. If Cody were here, he'd tease me, although I suspect he would be in the same boat. If so, at least we'd be able to screw things up together.

"Here you go." Coach stands and hands me my papers. "Go learn something new and useful."

My eyes roll. "PE was useful. This ..." I want to say sucks but settle on "isn't."

"You never know." Coach almost smiles. "The situation's not ideal, but try your best. We won't make the playoffs without you. Plus, I got a call."

"From?"

"Notre Dame." He pauses. He knows that was Cody's school. "They wanted your contact information."

My brow jumps. "They're interested?"

"I think so, but we'll have to wait until they call you."

This is news. D1 recruiters start looking when you're a freshman, and the only school I've heard from is U of M. It would be nice to have another offer on the table, so I can compare it to what Michigan proposes. From what I've been told, it's better to be able to negotiate.

"Thanks," I tell Coach before he makes me leave his office.

Wandering the empty halls, I take my time because I have a late excuse. I need to re-visit my locker and trade my gym bag for a pen. I doubt I'll need an old t-shirt and shorts for whatever it is you do in yearbook. With a resigned sigh, I make it to my destination and turn the dial, entering my combination. At least one good thing came out of my conversation with Coach – the possibility of another college opportunity.

"Shouldn't you be in class?"

My eyes close. I knew it was only a matter of time before she found me.

Slowly, I take a step back so I can see Allie. She's standing on the opposite side of my open locker door, wearing a thin black sweater over a fluorescent pink top. She's also wearing two silver charms, one a heart and one an arrow, on two really long chains. They land right on her chest. Why do girls do that? My eyes are automatically drawn to that part of her body, to the shiny, sparkly things.

I re-focus on her face and get sarcastic. "Shouldn't *you* be in class?" I know I should check my tone, but I'm still angry. She's the reason Cody did what he did; he felt trapped because of her.

"I'm on lunch," she says.

Awesome, I think and turn my attention back to what I was doing. The cafeteria is two hallways away. I suppose she was randomly roaming around and bumped into me? I finish stuffing my bag inside my locker. "Is there something you need? I had a schedule change, and I'm late."

"Schedule change?"

"Yep." Grabbing a pen, I shut my locker door. "You can ask Coach Carlson if you're concerned."

"No, I ..." She looks a little confused. Crossing her arms, she adjusts her posture and stands up straight. "I wanted to see how you're doing, that's all. I've been thinking about you and how hard it must be without ... without your best friend."

My expression twists. Now she wants to pretend to have a heart? After she was the one threatening Cody?

"Thanks, but you don't have to worry about me. I'm good."

"You're sure?"

"Positive."

"Okay, well ... if you need someone to talk to, you know where to find me."

I snort. She's the last person I would talk to about Cody.

"Is something wrong?" She steps closer.

"As if you don't know."

She frowns. "No, actually, I don't."

This is stupid. She has to know Cody confided in me. From the first second he thought she was hitting on him to the last nasty text message. Leaning forward, I say, "Think about it. What did you call Cody just now?"

She doesn't hesitate. "Your best friend."

"And what do best friends do?"

I turn my ear toward her, anticipating an answer. She still looks confused.

Taking a few steps back, I say, "Gotta go. You know, class and all." I don't want to give her a chance to respond. There's nothing she could say to justify her actions, at least not in my mind.

As I turn and walk to the end of the hall, to the room for yearbook, I sense her watching me. Maybe I stunned her into paralysis or something, I'm not sure. All I do know is she'd better be gone by the time the next bell rings.

Stepping into yearbook, I'm surprised to find organized chaos. I thought my arrival might be noticed, but with the desks arranged in scattered groups and everyone talking to each other, I might as well be invisible. As my eyes sweep the room to find the teacher, they catch on a sign hanging over a date-covered white board: *Deadline has dead in it for a reason.* My eyebrows jump before continuing my search. I notice a bank of computers next to some drafting tables before I find Mrs. Ryan buried in the back corner.

"Ah, Mr. Matthews," she says when I hand her my excuse slip. "I was told you'd be joining us. Have you given any thought to your position?"

"My position?"

"On the staff," she says. "What interests you?"

Should I tell her I have no idea what anyone on the staff does? "Uh ..." I glance around her desk. "What are my options? Honestly, I just found out about this less than an hour ago."

Mrs. Ryan nods and then stands. "Lucy?" She calls out over the students' chatter. "I need you."

Lucy? I blink. She doesn't mean–

Mrs. Ryan waves her over, and I turn around in time to watch her stand. She's talking to her friend, Izzy, and doesn't even look in our direction. She finishes their conversation by walking backward toward the teacher's desk and, when she's about a foot away from me, she turns around.

"What's up, Mrs. Ry–" She freezes, her entire body going stiff.

"Aaron has just joined our staff, and he's not sure where he fits in. Could you give him a rundown of the available positions? I need to go make some copies."

"I'll do it." Lucy's words rush out of her. Then, her cheeks turn pink. "I mean, I'll go make the copies, and you can tell him what we do."

Mrs. Ryan shakes her head. "You already assigned the rest of the class, and Aaron is no different. Consult Isabel if you have to. I'll be back in a few minutes."

Gathering her papers, Mrs. Ryan rounds her desk and leaves. Lucy opens her mouth like she wants to say something, but she changes her mind and looks down. I do nothing but play with the pen in my hand. I feel like I need to step up, but I don't know where to start. I've only ever stared at this girl. Over the hood of a running car, through a chain link fence, and when she fell in front of me last week. As she tries to look everywhere but at me, I notice the pink hasn't left her cheeks. Her neck is turning red, too. I've never seen a girl blush so much. But, then again, she probably thinks I hate her.

That's when it hits me.

"Listen," I say, stepping toward her. "I don't want–"

"Me talking to you. I know." She holds up her hands. "Please tell June it wasn't my idea. I won't talk to you ever again if I can help it."

I frown. I was going to tell her I didn't hate her, but my words change to, "I don't care if you talk to me." Not that we've had anything to discuss in the past, but she shouldn't listen to what June says.

Lucy looks unsure. "She made it pretty clear to stay away from all of you."

It's true she acted bat shit crazy in the hallway the other day. "Well, June doesn't speak for me," I say. "So, don't worry. We can talk."

Some of the tension leaves Lucy's shoulders. Not a ton, but enough to make me feel better about what she thinks of me.

"Okay." She takes a breath. "About this class. There's different–"

"What's going on?" Izzy appears protectively by her side. "Why are you here and why does my friend look like she's about to hyperventilate?"

"I'm not going to hyperventilate." Lucy rolls her eyes. "I'm explaining what we do here."

"Why?"

"Because I got transferred," I say. "This was the only elective available to fix my schedule."

Izzy looks suspicious. "What was wrong with your schedule?"

"I can't take four years of PE. If I do, I won't graduate."

"Well, duh." Izzy stares at me like I'm dumb. "Everyone knows that. It's, like, the first thing they tell you in orientation."

I suppress a smile. Obviously, this girl doesn't care who I am or what anyone says.

"Anyway," Lucy interrupts, "there are all kinds of things you can do here. Photography, copy writing, layout design, even marketing. All of our section editors have already been assigned, but you could work under any one you'd like."

I'm confused. "What's a section?"

"Sports, student life, seniors, the underclassmen ..." Lucy drifts off.

"Each section has an editor, and each section has the positions she mentioned under it," Izzy clarifies. "So, for example, if you chose sports, you would work with that group over there," she points, "and you could go to all the games and take pictures, if you wanted."

I'm starting to like the sound of this class. "What do you two do?" I ask.

Izzy drapes her arm over Lucy's shoulders. "We're the senior co-editors." She grins. "We oversee everything and basically run the show."

Now I know why Mrs. Ryan requested Lucy's help.

"So, what do you think?" Izzy presses. "Anything pique your interest?"

I catch Lucy giving her friend a look that tells me she thinks she's acting weird. "I don't know," I say. "Sports stands out to me, but I have no idea what I'd do. All I've ever done with my yearbooks is thrown them in the closet."

Both Lucy and Izzy's eyes double in size, and I know I've said something wrong. "That's blasphemy," Izzy whispers. "Do you know how much work went into those?"

Suddenly, I feel bad and rub the back of my neck. "I guess I do now."

"You should sit with us," Izzy decides and leaves Lucy's side. She grabs ahold of my forearm and leads me to a desk. "To appreciate the process, we must start from the beginning."

For the rest of the class, Lucy sends me small, commiserative smiles as we're subjected to The History of Yearbook according to Izzy. Lucy says nothing, and I can tell she's just as bored as I am. Neither of us stops her friend, though. I assume it's to save us both from the awkwardness of talking to one another, although I hope Lucy will feel less tense around me now. I didn't like her reaction earlier. It was almost like she was afraid of me, and that's not okay.

When the bell rings, the three of us walk out of the room, but it doesn't stop Izzy. She keeps talking until finally, when we're in the hallway, Lucy speaks up, exasperated.

"Enough!" She pulls on her friend's arm so she moves farther away from me. "Class is over, Izz. For the love of God, leave him alone."

I let myself smile a genuine smile. Lucy shakes her head at me and steers Izzy toward their lockers. When I get to mine, my grin fades. June is there, waiting.

"Were you talking to her?" she demands.

"Does it matter?"

I start to open my locker so she's forced to step aside. She's silent until her next question comes from out of left field.

"Are you taking her to homecoming?"

"What?" My face contorts. "No. We were just walking down the hall."

"So?"

"So that means we're dating?" I yank open my locker door. "You're delusional."

She's quiet while I grab my stuff for my next class. When I'm finished, she holds out what looks like a voting ballot. "We were nominated for court," she says. "I thought you'd like to know."

I glance at the paper but don't take it. This isn't any different from past years. "And?"

"Who are you taking?"

"To the dance?"

"Yes, to the dance," she huffs. "Why are you being so difficult?"

Am I? I shut my locker door. "Look, this day has been insane. I haven't even thought about homecoming. I probably won't go."

June's eyes consume her face, reminding me of Lucy and Izzy's reactions in class. It must be a girl thing. "You have to go," she says. "You're on the *court*."

She emphasizes the word court like I was born royal. "No, I don't."

"Yes, you do."

She stares at me, like she can't possibly fathom the idea of my wanting to sit this one out. Then, without warning, tears start to well in her eyes. She blinks, forcing huge drops to roll down her cheeks. What the–? Why is she crying?

"June …" I start.

"Don't," she says and wipes her face. "Just forget it."

"Forget what? I don't understand what you're trying to say." Obviously, this is about more than the dance.

"I just thought …" She sniffs. "I just thought you might take me. For Cody's sake." The tears keep falling. "Because he's not he – re."

Her voice breaks on the word "here," and she steps into me. I have no choice but to catch her in a clumsy, one-armed hug. She sobs against my shoulder, and my first instinct is to let her down easy. That is until I catch several people, including Kat, giving us curious looks. Shit. How can I get out of this? June is a mess. If I reject her now, my friends will think I'm a total ass.

Wait.

Friends.

"Why don't you ask Kat if she wants to go?" I suggest. "I'll ask the team, and maybe we could go in one big group."

"You'd do that for me?" Her voice is more hopeful than I'd like.

"Yeah."

She steps back and wipes her cheeks. "Okay. I didn't mean to break down on you; I just miss Cody so much. And I don't want to miss out on anything else. It's our senior year."

I give her an understanding nod as the warning bell rings. Then, she smiles and walks across the hall to Kat with a skip in her step.

"Man, I think you've been played," Cody says in my head, like he's standing right behind me.

I glance over my shoulder to make sure he's not there, because, you know, going crazy is fun. He's not, of course, but I know his – my – thoughts ring true.

"You're gonna have a *great* time," he snickers in my ear.

CHAPTER SEVEN

Lucy

S tanding in front of Cody's grave is surreal. My mind spins trying to figure out what I did, prior to the obvious, to bring us both here. Clearly, it was something horrible for karma to deliver these consequences.

A few days after my session with Dr. Marie, I worked up the nerve to ask my mom to drive me to the cemetery. I wanted to leave my "I'm sorry" note for Cody. The exercise the Doc had given me was weighing on my mind, and I thought if I delivered the letter, I'd feel one of two ways: better or the same. If I felt better, then I'd consider writing another note. If I felt the same, I would tell the Doc I had completed her assignment and it did nothing for me.

But now that I'm here, it's hard to define how I feel. My world has stopped. Reading his name, seeing the dates ... it's not like I was pretending it didn't happen, but this makes is more real, if that's even possible. Memories wash over me in waves. Why? Why did this have to happen? I didn't want it to; I never thought something like it ever *would*. Guilt creeps up on me, like a ghost slowly wrapping its invisible arms around me from behind. Tears sting my eyes, making me blink and look away from Cody's blurry name. I never knew him in life, but we're inseparable now.

Looking for a spot to leave my note, my eyes fall to the flowers on the ground. They look fresh, like someone has recently been here. Immediately, I think of his parents, which makes me think of my own mom, who is patiently waiting in the car while her daughter places a note on the grave of the boy she killed. It makes me feel awful, putting them both through this. Never once had she imagined this for me, and I know Cody's parents never thought he'd die at the age of seventeen.

Why? Why? Why?

Suddenly, I want to scream, to release the one-word question. Would anyone answer? I didn't plan what happened, and I'm sure he didn't wake up that morning deciding to die. Is this what Dr. Marie wants me to realize? That we're all pawns in some game we have no control over? Because it sucks. Hard. How am I supposed to live life knowing everything is left to chance?

A tear snakes down my cheek, and I wipe it away. Getting back in the car upset is not an option, not if I want my mom to keep chauffeuring me to places like this. She'll refuse if she thinks it hurts me, which is one of the only things that makes sense anymore. Realizing I've taken up enough of her time, I bend down and do what I came here to do.

I leave my apology behind as requested, wedged between the flower stems.

"Hellllllo. Lucy." Izzy waves her hand in front of my face. "Where are you today?"

"Hmm?"

"I've been talking to you forever. Didn't you hear anything I said?"

My eyes snap to hers. "No. Sorry."

I'm beyond distracted this morning. I didn't tell Izzy I went to

Cody's grave, and I keep seeing his name in stone when I close my eyes.

"In that case," Izz wags her eyebrows, "just say yes."

"Oh, no," I say and reach for my English folder. "You've tricked me too many times." Once, I ended up on a carnival ride that made me so dizzy, I puked. I'm sure I won't like whatever diabolical plan she's come up with now.

"Why do you always assume the worst?" She frowns. "We'd have a blast, plus we can stay the night. We're not going to the dance, so I thought we should have some fun."

I have no idea what she's talking about. "Come again?"

She sighs. "I secured us an invitation to Central. This guy B likes, his fraternity is having a party."

B is her older sister, Bianca. "And she wants us to tag along?"

Izzy shrugs. "She's the one who offered. I told her we were skipping homecoming this year, and she said we could come up and party with her."

My stomach sinks. I feel awful Izzy is missing the dance because of me. I've told her as much a million times over the last week, so she'd change her mind and go with Wes. He asked her, and I was genuinely excited for them. But she turned him down, saying she couldn't leave me alone, and she owed me. Owed me for what, I don't know. When I questioned her, she said I'd find out sooner or later. I really hate secrets.

"So? We're heading up to Central, right?"

I force my concentration back on Izz. "I guess so." The idea of a road trip never crossed my mind, but then again, I haven't been driving. The more the idea settles, the more it sounds nice to get away. Plus, Izzy gave up a date with skinny-jean-wearing Wes. She says she owes me, but, in reality, I owe her.

"Yay!" She claps. "We're going to have so much fun. Just like old times."

Eh … I turn back to my locker. *As long as this time doesn't repeat the last 'old time.'*

With my mind half on our plans and half on the place I visited last night, we start to walk to our English class. On the way, the sea of students parts in front of us. The principal, Mr. Hughes, is headed in our direction. It appears he's on a mission to find someone, and when he spots Izzy and me, he waves.

My eyes immediately jump to my best friend. "Did he just wave at you? Because there's no way he waved at me."

Izzy swallows. "I think you're about to find out why I owe you."

I'm confused. "What?"

"Just remember you said yes," she says, anxious. "You can't back out on this weekend."

Judging from her demeanor, she's done something she regrets. My stomach starts to knot. "What did you do?"

"Girls." Mr. Hughes calls out and signals for us to follow him. "I need to speak to you for a moment."

He does?

All eyes swing to Izzy and me, and I feel my cheeks flare. Ugh. I never used to blush this much. It's an annoying habit I didn't know I had until recently.

"This way." He gestures to a nearby classroom, which he reaches before us and unlocks.

"I wonder what she did now," June snarks loud enough for everyone to hear. Her comment draws a few muffled snickers from the crowd, and I take a deep breath. Of course *she* would be around to witness this.

Once Izzy and I walk across the hall to join Mr. Hughes, he wastes no time getting to the point. "Lucy. Your friend Isabel here brought a very perplexing situation to my attention last week." He frowns. "Why didn't you report Ms. Wright removing you from the student council?"

My eyes grow wide. "Because she's the advisor."

"She may be," he says, "but she overstepped her bounds."

I'm going to kill Izzy. Well, not literally, but she should know better than to go behind my back. I thought we'd moved past this.

"I wish you would have come to me," Mr. Hughes continues. "I would have corrected the matter immediately. Now, from what I've been told, your position has already been filled by another student."

Good, I think. I didn't want it anymore anyway.

"Regardless," he crosses his arms, "I've spoken to Ms. Wright personally. She's been made aware of her error in judgment. I told her the treasurer position is rightfully yours, should you want it." He studies me. "The question is: do you?"

I open my mouth then close it again like a fish. I don't like being put on the spot. My mind races; if I refuse, will I look ungrateful? There were reasons I didn't want the extra stress before; now I can add pissing off Ms. Wright to the list. It sounds like she got her hand slapped because of me. It would be awkward if I came strolling in to the next council meeting. And, what about the other person who filled my job? What happens to them?

"With all due respect," I finally say, "I wouldn't want to take the opportunity away from someone else. It would be too much like what happened to me. So, no. Thank you, but I don't want the position."

Mr. Hughes nods. "I admire your response, although I'm not happy it came to this. I'll inform Ms. Wright of your decision." He walks around us and reaches for the door, but stops short of opening it. "Girls, please, remember my office is always open. If there's something you feel I need to know, don't hesitate to share it with me. I can't be everywhere all the time."

Both Izzy and I nod, and he allows us to walk out of the room ahead of him. As we go our separate ways, I turn on Izzy and hiss, "Seriously?"

She hugs her English book to her chest. "What?"

"I told you I was good with the student council thing."

"And I saw a wrong that needed to be made right."

My mouth forms a thin line, and I pick up my pace to our English class.

"See, I told you I would owe you." Izzy catches up to my side. "I knew you'd be mad."

"Then why did you do it? I don't need any more attention. The entire senior hall saw the principal speak to us privately!"

"I didn't know he'd handle the situation in public," Izzy says defensively. "Besides, I did it because you wouldn't stand up for yourself. Ms. Wright needed to be put in her place." She sticks out her chin. "Are you saying you wouldn't do the same for me?"

"No, not at all. But things are a little different. I'm already watched and talked about."

"By who? Just June, and she doesn't count."

I shake my head. She may not notice the stares, but I do. And June *so* counts.

We make it to class and slide into our seats just as the bell rings. What can I say to make Izzy understand? All I want is to fly under the radar.

Is that too much to ask?

BY THE TIME mid-day rolls around, Izzy and I have shared few words. We're not mad at each other, but this is what we do. When one of us annoys the other, we take some down time to deal with it. It's one of the reasons our friendship is so strong. Instead of getting dramatic, we simply give each other space.

That's why, during yearbook, we aren't talking. We're in the middle of silently passing cover designs back and forth until she randomly gets up and leaves. Curious, I watch her ask Mrs. Ryan for the hall pass and walk out of the room. Since I assume she's headed to the bathroom, I take advantage of my alone time to close my eyes and focus on my breathing like Dr. Marie taught me. I haven't had time to really process the events from this morning.

"Hey."

I jump. Aaron has slid over two desks to end up beside me. His presence still makes me a little anxious, even after seeing him in class day after day.

"What's up?" I try to act casual.

"I ... uh ..." He clears his throat. "I need to show you something."

Of course he does. This is what editors do. "Is it the copy for the ad campaign?"

To my surprise, Aaron chose to market the yearbook instead of covering sports like I anticipated. He said his community connections would help sell ad space, and his looks would promote book sales to students. He said the last part with a smile, and I secretly agreed. Having the most popular guy at Holton endorse your product can only be a good thing.

"No, it's not about the copy." He looks around before handing me his cell. "Did you know about this?"

I look at the screen. It's a picture of me. Well, it's a picture of the photo the office secretary took when I won the alumni scholarship. It's been hanging in a glass case along with all the other winners except now, my face bears the word "BITCH" across it in red marker.

My shoulders tense. "Uh, no. I didn't know." I hand his phone back to him. "Do you mind if I ask who sent that to you?"

"June," he says. "Although it didn't come directly to me. It's a group message."

Fantastic. Both anger and embarrassment run through my veins. How many people know about this? I've avoided her like she asked. I can't help it Aaron was transferred into my class.

"She says she didn't do it." He shrinks the picture to show me the text message: *I don't know who did this but it made me LOL!!*

Right, I think. Who else would've done it? She's the only one who's said anything nasty to me about Cody.

"I'm not defending her, if that's what you're thinking," Aaron says quickly. "I just thought you'd want it taken down."

He's right. "Thanks," I say and reach for my phone. Hopefully Izzy will make a pit stop. If not, I know where I'm headed after class. I start typing my plea for help.

"You're not fighting with your friend, are you?" Aaron asks. "I noticed you two weren't talking much today."

He did? "No. We're just ..." How do I put this? "We're just being us."

"Being you?"

"Um hmm." I finish my message to Izzy: *Someone got artistic with my scholarship picture. Can you make it disappear?*

Aaron sounds hesitant. "She wouldn't do this to you, would she?"

"Izzy?" My face contorts. "No. Never."

"Just checking," he says. "I don't know how close you guys are."

I decide to volunteer the information, so her loyalty is without question. "We've been best friends since kindergarten."

Just then, my phone vibrates against my desk: *I'm on it.*

"Izzy's taking care of the situation," I say.

"Good."

With my crisis solved, I expect him to move back to the desk he came from. He doesn't. Instead, he rights his body in the seat, stretches out his legs, and gets comfortable. When he opens a folder and starts to thumb through some papers, I redirect my attention and pretend to go back to critiquing cover designs. It's useless, though. With Aaron's proximity, the questions swirling around in my brain, and my eyes constantly darting to the door for Izzy's return, I can't concentrate on anything. He didn't have to warn me about the picture, and I wonder why he did. I know June wouldn't be happy if she found out.

Less than five minutes later, Izzy walks through the door. Correction: Izzy marches through the door. She sets the hall pass on a distracted Mrs. Ryan's desk and hightails it over to her seat beside me.

"What the hell is this?" she whispers as she holds up the scholarship pic. It's been folded in half.

I shrug. "Red looks good on me, don't you think?"

She smirks. "Very funny."

"Was it hard to get?"

She shakes her head. "The case was unlocked."

Of course it was. How convenient for those who don't like me. "Thank you," I sigh.

"This is crap," she says quietly before crumpling the picture into a ball. "How did you find out?"

I stay silent and try to inconspicuously nod in Aaron's direction. I'm not sure if I'm allowed to share the intel, in case he broke some sort of code with his friends. Izzy looks around me and her eyebrows jump. "He told you?" she mouths.

Nodding, I point to my phone. "Group text," I mouth back.

Izzy looks impressed before her expression softens. "That was really nice of him." Her voice is hushed.

I glance at Aaron who seems oblivious to our conversation.

Yeah. It was.

CHAPTER EIGHT

Aaron

I f the homecoming committee's goal was to make the gym look like a giant Smurf exploded, they've succeeded.

Everything, and I mean everything, is dripping in blue and white. From the walls, to the tables, to the balloons and the metallic streamers, it looks like someone hosed the place down with Holton High's school colors. Even the liquid in the punch bowl is an unnatural shade of blue. I say liquid because I have no idea what it is. As I watch Harrison take a drink of the stuff, my expression twists. The color reminds me of toilet bowl cleaner.

"It's not too bad," Harrison says, smacking his lips. "It tastes like pineapple."

"Mmm." I pat my stomach. "Tropical Tidy Bowl."

My teammate scowls. "When you put it that way ..." He tosses his plastic cup in the trash. "Why can't they serve Coke and Pepsi like normal people?"

Shrugging, I grab a few pretzels off the snack table and toss them in my mouth. The Cody bracelets had to pay for something. Why not a punch that will turn your piss blue? I snicker. Cody would have gotten a kick out of that. Actually, the more I think about it, the color would probably be greener with the yellow mixed in …

I stop myself. Why am I thinking about this?

Because you don't want to be here, Cody's voice answers in my mind.

"So." Harrison shoves his hands in his pockets and rocks back on his heels. "Are you planning to dance with anyone? 'Cause there's a group of ladies about ten feet away who haven't stopped staring at you."

I take a quick look. Yeah, I've felt some attention tonight. It can't be because I made any special effort with my appearance; I skipped the suit jacket completely and opted to wear only dress pants with a black button down. I also left the collar of my shirt open and my tie at home, much to June's disappointment. When we all met up at the restaurant before the dance, I thought she was going to have a heart attack when she saw me. *"You're dressed too casual!"* she screeched. *"Please tell me you have a tie in the car. Are you kidding me? Do you have time to go back and get one?"*

So, no. It's not the clothes. Or maybe it is. Maybe they think I'm "too casual," too. Honestly, they're probably more concerned with the fact I haven't left the refreshment table since I got here. Oh, and I didn't bring a date. I'm sure that's headline news.

"No, I wasn't planning on sweeping anyone off their feet," I tell Harrison. "You should, though. You don't have to keep me company."

"You're sure?" He glances over my shoulder. "Because I think the girl in the red dress is looking at me now. Do you know her?"

I shake my head. I didn't look long enough to focus on faces. "Go for it."

Harrison smiles, then gives me a good-natured slap on the arm as he walks away.

Left alone, I decide to head in the opposite direction to lean against the wall and observe. From here I have a direct line of sight into the dancing mob. My eyes catch our group – Kat, June, a few of their friends and a few of mine – coordinating their arms and singing along to the music. Kat looks really nice tonight, but then again, I'm partial. Out of the blue, Cody appears in the center of the mix, jumping around like a flopping fish – his go-to dance move. He looks over at me and grins. You would think seeing him so much in my mind would weird me out, but I actually like it. It means I'm not forgetting him.

"Can I talk to you?"

My head snaps to the right, and I frown. Allie has appeared out of nowhere. As I take in her appearance, my frown grows deeper. Curled hair, black dress, bare shoulder, tiny waist ... and a Cody memorial bracelet on her wrist.

"Please?" she asks when I remain silent. "It'll only take a minute."

Sighing, I stand up straight and gesture for her to go ahead. I have no idea what she wants to say to me.

"I –" She glances around to see if anyone is watching us. "I need to know what you know. All of it."

I get smug. "I think you know what I know."

She looks a little nervous. Or maybe impatient. "Could you be more specific?"

Does she really want details? I reach for my cell. "I'm sure the pictures Cody sent are still in my phone. Do you want to see?"

She frowns. "What pictures?"

I'm about to say the half-naked selfies you sent him, but we're interrupted for a quick second by some students dancing by and waving hello.

Once they're gone, Allie steps closer to me. "I really don't know what you're talking about, but if you do know certain ... things, are you planning on saying anything?"

Ah. The real reason she wanted to talk comes out. "I wasn't." I slide my phone back into my pocket. What good would it do to spill their secret now?

"You're sure?" She looks skeptical. "I think it might be too personal and shouldn't be spread around."

My brow jumps. "What changed your mind?"

"Excuse me?"

"Last I knew, you were threatening to tell the world."

"Aaron ..." She shakes her head. "I honestly don't understand what you mean."

I don't buy her excuse. I can't. Not after the pressure she put on Cody. She should have been the bigger person all along, but she wasn't.

"Allllll right, Holton High."

Allie looks over her shoulder at the interruption, and I look past her. Like a game show host, the DJ drags his voice over the thumping bass. "It's that time of the night. The time you've all been waiting for. Let's crown your homecoming king and queen." The song fades out into something more subdued. "Can we get the senior court on stage please?"

Thank god. Saved by the DJ. I start to leave.

"Aaron." Allie brushes my arm. "I meant what I said. If you need someone to talk to, I'm here." Her eyes bounce from her hand to my face, and she squeezes my arm through my shirt sleeve.

"Just stay away from me," I say.

As I leave, I barely catch a breath before June rushes out of the crowd.

"There you are!" she gushes and loops her arm through mine. She plasters a huge smile on her face and starts to lead me toward the stage. "Where have you been?" she asks without moving her lips. She's mad.

"I wasn't aware I had to stay by your side."

Her smile falters for a quick second before she regains it and flips her hair. We make it to the top of the stage steps before she leans into me and whispers, "You're supposed to be Cody, remember?"

My entire body tenses. I didn't agree to *be* anyone.

"Are we all here?"

Principal Hughes holds a mic away from his mouth so the entire gym can't hear his question. As our fellow nominees gather on the stage, June finds us a spot front and center next to the DJ. Since I can't address her comment until after this is over, I look out into the sea of waiting faces. I wonder if anyone out there has been in a situation half as messed up as mine. My dead best friend's girlfriends are driving me insane.

"Good evening, everyone," Mr. Hughes says into the mic. "I hope you're having a great time tonight. Are we ready for the big announcement?"

Clapping and hollering ensue, and June clutches my arm tightly in anticipation. When the noise dies down, Mr. Hughes pulls an envelope out of his jacket pocket and ceremoniously rips it open. "Without further ado, please give a round of applause to your Holton High homecoming king ..." The DJ plays an auto-tuned drumroll. "Aaron Matthews!"

He did not say my name.

June squeals and jumps up and down as hands surround me and pat me on the back. A class representative appears beside Mr. Hughes holding a goofy blue crown and white sash. Both she and the principal look at me expectantly as the student body cheers. When I don't move, Mr. Hughes gestures for me to join him, and the same hands that congratulated me push me forward so I don't have a choice. Pasting a fake smile on my face, I walk forward and slouch down, to let the class rep place the "King" sash over my head and the crown on top of it. As I stand up straight and give a half-hearted wave, I know I look like the biggest idiot.

"Congratulations, Aaron," the principal says before moving on. "And now, to announce our queen. This year's Holton High home-coming queen is ..."

As the same drumroll plays, I silently pray: *Don't let it be June. Don't let it be June. Don't let it be June.*

"June Summers!"

Shit.

She appears by my side in the blink of an eye, fanning her face to ward off tears I know she can conjure on command. The same class rep loops a sash over her head, and then takes her time carefully placing a glittery silver tiara in her hair.

"Congratulations, June," Mr. Hughes says. "You two make a lovely couple."

No, I think. *No, we don't.*

"Let's hear it for your royalty!"

Principal Hughes addresses the crowd and gestures like we're prizes on a game show. Everyone claps and June clings possessively to my side, smiling like Miss America. Cameras start to flash and I glance down at the gym floor, at the students taking pictures with their cell phones. Standing among them is one of the yearbook photographers, who uses better equipment. Noticing him makes me think of Lucy, who I haven't seen all night. If she's here, she's good at hiding. If she skipped, she had the right idea.

"If the court would now proceed to the dance floor, I believe this next song is for you."

Mr. Hughes hands the mic back to the DJ, and the beginning notes of a slow song start to play. In a matter of seconds, June pulls me off the stage and on to the gym floor, snaking her arms around my neck before we stop walking. As she tries to press her body flush against mine, I wrap my hands around her waist to stop her.

"What's wrong?" She looks confused. "We're supposed to dance."

"And that's what we're doing." I'm very matter-of-fact. She needs to understand I'm not into her, nor am I trying to "be" Cody.

"Aaron. You're acting like we're in middle school." Her hands leave my neck, circle my wrists, and move them to rest against her lower back. Moving closer, she sets her palms against my chest. "I get it. It's been awhile for me, too." She's quiet before she adds, "But, we can figure it out together."

What is she talking about? "You've lost me."

She sighs. "I'm talking about dating. Liking someone. Hooking up. Whatever you want to call it." She plays with the collar of my shirt. "I haven't seen anyone since Cody. I know you had that thing with Paige …"

My brow furrows.

"… but I think I'm ready to move on." She stops messing with my shirt, and her eyes lock on mine. "With you."

If I had something to choke on, I would.

"I mean, the whole school thinks we should be together." She smiles before sliding her fingers across my chest, over the sash that matches hers.

I have no words. No feelings below the belt, either. Never in a million years did I think June would come on to me. She's never expressed any interest since I've known her, including the time before she was dating Cody.

"I think you're hot," she whispers when I don't respond. She tips her head and bites her lip before winding her arms around my neck and zeroing in on my mouth.

"June," I say and jerk back before she can kiss me. "No."

She frowns. "What do you mean no?"

"You don't like me."

She laughs. "I think I know what I like and what I don't like."

"Well, same here." I know this girl isn't used to rejection, but she's going to have to get accustomed to it real fast. Stepping back, I untangle myself from her arms. "I know you're not into me, so why pretend? I can't date you. You were sleeping with my best friend. It's not right."

Her face immediately falls. At first I think she's going to cry again, but when she realizes her reaction gets nothing out of me, her expression morphs from disappointment to frustration. "It's not right? Are you serious?" Her eyes narrow. "What's wrong with you? There are a million guys who would die to be with me."

"That may be true," I say. "But I'm not one of them."

June's jaw drops in disbelief. I have to admit her short strapless dress leaves little to the imagination. Yes, she's physically attractive, but I know too much about her. Her heart is ugly, and I don't want any part of it.

"I can't believe this. If Cody knew how you were treating me, he'd –"

"He'd what?" I'm getting irritated. "Be happy I don't want his girlfriend? Be pissed at you for flirting with me? What, June? What would he do?"

"He'd hate you," she snaps.

This girl is so out of touch with reality it makes me laugh. Snickering, I say, "Okay. You go ahead and believe that."

June slams her hands on her hips just as my cell vibrates in my pocket. Pulling it out, I see a text message from Ben, my old lacrosse teammate up at Central: *Party tonight at Phi Nu. You in?*

Nothing sounds better right now than getting out of here. I glance at the time. It's a little after nine. If I leave now, I can make it there around eleven. My thumbs fly over the screen: *I'm there.*

"Who are you talking to?" June demands. How dare I ignore her.

"Ben," I say and take a few steps back. "I've got to go."

"You're *leaving*?" She looks incredulous. "We came together!"

"As a group," I remind her. It's a good thing she rode with Kat and a few of the other girls.

"I'm the homecoming queen!" She stomps her foot. "The king can't leave the queen on the dance floor alone!"

I hate to break it to her, but ... "Yes, he can."

And, turning around, I do just that.

AFTER STOPPING at home to change clothes, grab a few things, and get disapproving looks from my parents, I make it to CMU in roughly two hours. As I drive past the frat house, I see the party spilling out onto the lawn and quickly remember parking close by will be impossible. Since I've been here before, I'm familiar with some of the side streets. Lucky for me, I score a parking spot in the road just a few blocks away. The night is finally looking up.

"My man!" Ben gives me a high-five after I find him inside playing pool. "I'm glad we could save you from the torture of homecoming."

"It was hell," I exaggerate, but not really. "Thanks for the invite."

"Any time. Kegs are in the kitchen." He leans over the table to line up his shot. "We've got liquor too, but it's not free. Gotta pay for this crib somehow."

I nod and look around. The house is packed. "Where's Craig?"

Ben sinks his ball into the left corner pocket. "Probably upstairs with his new woman."

"A different one?" The last time I was here he had a "new" woman.

"Yeah." Ben stands. "This is college, man. Too many flavors to try just one, ya know?"

He grins, and I shake my head. Ben has always thought of himself as a ladies' man, yet he rarely has a lady. "I'll be right back," I say and point toward the kitchen.

"Okay. We're almost done here. You're in next game."

"Sounds good."

Weaving my way through two rooms and countless bodies, I eventually make it to the line for the keg. Once I have a full plastic cup in my hand, I start to make my way back to Ben but change my mind. Loud music has been blasting through the house since I walked in the door and, since I have a few minutes before Ben's game ends, I decide to people watch. Valuable lessons can be learned from observing. For example, the last time I was here, I learned it's never a good idea to throw up in your girlfriend's purse.

After sidestepping a kissing couple and a shirtless dude with "Anarchy" written on his chest, I wander into the dining room just off the kitchen. Usually it holds a table big enough to seat twenty and tonight it still does, although it's been pushed aside along with the benches for seating. In a dimly lit corner, I find the source of the music; a girl wearing headphones mixes songs on a laptop hooked to small but mighty speakers. A cluster of people move to the beat in front of her, and I lean against the wall to take in the scene. As soon as I bring my beer to my lips, my eyes land on someone intriguing.

Her back is toward me and, unlike most here, she moves effortlessly with the music. Her hair falls over her shoulders in waves that sway when her body does, and she's wearing a pair of jeans that mold to her ass perfectly. Maybe my observation makes me shallow, or maybe it just makes me a guy, but when she brings her hands up to lift her hair off her neck, the bare strip of skin exposed at her lower back is one of the hottest things I've seen in a while. It does a hundred times more for me than June's barely contained chest at the dance.

Half of my beer disappears as I watch her and try to think of something to say. Part of me wants to talk to her and the other part says it's not worth the effort. I'm a senior in high school, and this is a college party. She'll probably blow me off just as her linebacker boyfriend shows up to punch me in the face.

I'm about to leave and find Ben when I see something that makes me freeze mid-swallow. On the opposite side of the room, through the other entrance, walks Izzy. I know it's her, but I still blink because why is she here? She holds a cup in each hand and approaches the girl I've been watching. She hands her a beer, and when the girl stops dancing and turns, I'm floored.

It's Lucy.

Never, and I mean never, has she shown up to school looking like *that*. Her clothes don't hide her body, they hug it. Her hair doesn't hide her face, it frames it. She's an inch or two taller due to heels rather than sneakers, and she has to be wearing make-up. It doesn't look like she went crazy with it, but even in this light her features look fuller. No, she's never looked this way at school. I would have noticed.

Right?

Swallowing, I watch Lucy take the cup from her best friend, say something, and point in the direction Izzy came from. Izzy nods and starts talking to some other girls, so my eyes follow Lucy. I watch her make it to the edge of the room, set her drink down, and leave.

My eyes grow wide. What the hell? Why would she do that? Doesn't she know what can happen at parties, especially one this big? Immediately, I spring into action. I make it to her beer and grab it before anyone can put anything in it. Catching a glimpse of her leaving through the sliding patio doors, I decide to follow her. Someone needs to tell her she shouldn't leave her drinks lying around. Someone needs to tell her it's not safe.

That someone should be me.

CHAPTER NINE

Lucy

Pulling a deep breath of fresh air into my lungs, I let it out slowly. It feels good. So does the cool outdoor temperature against my skin. Since Bianca, our ticket into this soiree, volunteered to help her crush set up for his party, we've been here for hours. Hot and tired are now my middle names. It's not that I haven't had fun; I have. But, for someone who hasn't been very social lately, there are a lot of people here. It's starting to wear on me.

Glancing around, I hold little hope of finding an empty seat on the patio. Party guests occupy every surface, so I decide to walk to the far side, if for nothing other than to look at the sky and hang out for a few minutes. When I get there, I gaze at the stars and take another deep breath. It will only be a matter of time before Izzy finds me and tries to talk me into dancing with her sister's friend Carson again.

"Please tell me you didn't plan on drinking this."

A firm voice speaks over my shoulder, and I turn around. "Aaron?"

Concern colors his features, and it confuses me. Where did he come from? I glance at his hands. He holds a plastic cup in each, one fuller than the other. "Did you pick up my beer?"

"The one you just abandoned? Yes." He gestures with it. "You can't walk away from your drink at a party. It's a good way to get drugged."

I frown. Apparently, he thinks I'm clueless. "I didn't want it," I explain. "Izzy insisted on getting it for me, and I only took it from her to be nice."

Aaron's shoulders relax, and he looks between me and the cup. "Oh. Sorry. I just ..." He closes his eyes and gives his head a quick shake. "I didn't want you to get taken advantage of."

Really? I find it odd he would care. But, then again, he did warn me about my scholarship picture. "Well, you don't have to worry about me. Thank you, though."

He nods. "No problem."

You can leave now, I think.

But he doesn't. Instead, an awkward silence falls between us, and he raises what used to be my beer to his lips. He glances around the patio, interested in what's going on. It doesn't appear he has plans to move anytime soon.

Suddenly, I'm self-conscious. What is he doing here? Does he expect me to carry on a conversation? I look in the opposite direction and wrack my brain for something to say. It would be rude to just walk away, but it's not like we're buddies. It's then that it dawns on me. Where are his friends?

"Shouldn't you be at the dance?" I ask.

His expression twists before he lowers the cup from his mouth. "Been there, done that."

"You left?" I know it's late and the dance will be over soon, but I would expect Holton's most popular senior to stick it out until the end.

He smirks. "Let's just say I've only been here twenty minutes, and things are way more interesting. I should have followed your lead and avoided the thing all together."

"My lead?" My eyebrows jump. "Nobody follows my lead."

"Sure they do, yearbook editor."

One side of his mouth quirks up, and I'm stunned for a second. I've never been on the receiving end of one of his flirty smiles. It's kind of ... wow. If I didn't know better, I'd say he was paying me a compliment. That can't be the case, so my eyes roll. "I meant socially. I'm a pariah."

"Says who?"

I give him a blank stare. I know he said he's only been here twenty minutes, but ... "How much have you had to drink?"

He laughs. "Social outcasts don't get invited to frat parties. Especially if they're still in high school."

Aaron looks behind him and leans against the back of an occupied patio chair, crossing his feet at the ankles before taking another drink. He looks comfortable and casual, the exact opposite of how I feel. I don't get why he's talking to me. Discussions in class I understand, but this ... there are so many other girls here. Plus, he had to have come with someone. Immediately, my mind jumps to June. I pray it's not her.

"So," he sets the full cup in his hand into the empty one, stacking the two, "who do you know in the house?"

"No one," I admit. "Bianca has a crush on a member, and she invited Izzy and me."

"Who's Bianca?"

"Izzy's older sister. She goes here. To Central."

Aaron nods. "Ben invited me. I got his text about the party at the dance. Do you remember him? He graduated last year. We played lacrosse together."

"No, sorry. I don't follow lacrosse." Not to mention last year's graduating class had over three hundred students.

"What do you follow then?"

"Um ... sports-wise? Nothing really, except when the Red Wings are doing well. I tend to pay attention then."

Aaron looks amused. "You like hockey?"

I shrug. "It's fun to watch." The truth is my last and only serious boyfriend was big into hockey and turned me on to the game. It's the only thing I took away from our brief six-month romance.

"Physically speaking, lacrosse and hockey are pretty similar,"

Aaron says. "They're both fast paced. You should come watch me play sometime."

I blink. Did he just invite me somewhere?

He frowns. "What's with the face?"

I quickly relax my expression. "What do you mean?"

"You look like I'm speaking a foreign language."

"I think you are."

Aaron looks at me like he's trying to solve an equation and I shift my weight, growing uncomfortable. Not only am I starting to lose circulation in my feet from the shoes Bianca let me wear, but I didn't mean to say those last few words out loud.

Aaron's face relaxes as soon as the realization hits. "You think it's weird I'm talking to you."

I nod.

"Because you –"

"Yes." I cut him off before he can say Cody's name. I never imagined talking to him about what happened.

Ever.

A look I can only describe as understanding crosses Aaron's features as he takes another long drink. I'm glad he gets it, so we don't have to vocalize my actions.

When he lowers his cup again, he surprises me by asking, "So, you're saying you didn't vote for me for homecoming king?"

My face scrunches. "What?"

"You think it's weird I'm talking to you because you didn't vote for me. It's okay; you can admit it."

Is he serious? I didn't think it was true what they said about athletes, but he can't be this slow. I glance over my shoulder to make sure I'm not being pranked, then ask, "Can you get concussions playing lacrosse?"

He lets a smile escape before he snickers. "Yeah. I've only had one in six years, though."

I open my mouth to speak, but nothing comes out. Now would probably be a good time to walk away, before I say or do something else to embarrass myself. I have to see Aaron every day in fourth period for the rest of the school year; now would not be the time to look like more of an idiot.

"Lucy."

I didn't realize I was looking down until I hear my name and my head pops up. "What?"

"You can breathe."

"I am breathing." *I'm just trying to figure you out, too.*

Shuffling his feet back, he stands up straight. He takes two steps forward and stops when his toes are directly in front of mine. Looking down at me, he says, "Hey."

I meet his eyes. They're much more green than I had realized. Then again, this is the first time I've ever stood an inch away from him.

"I was trying to lighten things up," he says. "I don't care about homecoming. I know you think it's weird I'm talking to you because of Cody."

I flinch. I wasn't expecting him to throw Cody's name out there like that. My reaction doesn't go unnoticed, and Aaron's eyes cloud over.

"I don't blame you for what happened," he says. "And I don't hate you."

His words sound sincere and take a moment to register. After what seems like an eternity filled with background voices and thumping bass, all I can come up with is an uncertain, "Good to know."

"Cops!"

Both Aaron and I jump as people around us start to shriek and scatter.

"Cops!" Someone yells again, and the music comes to an abrupt stop.

Bodies start to hemorrhage from the house faster than I thought physically possible. Some exit through ground floor windows, falling into bushes, but most rush through the sliding patio doors and bounce off one another. Chairs around us are shoved and tipped over as people run past. I spin around looking for Izzy.

"C'mon." Aaron tosses his cup aside.

"What about Izzy?"

"She's with her sister, right?"

"Yes, but –"

He grabs my hand. "I don't need a MIP. Do you?"

I shake my head. That would be a lovely addition to my record.

"Then let's go."

He starts to jog and I follow, gripping his hand and letting him lead the way. We make it off the patio, on to the lawn, and through the frat's dark backyard before I can fully process what's happening. I just ditched my best friend to run away from the police with Aaron Matthews. What alternate universe have I stepped into? Whatever it is, the Phi Nu patio door is the portal.

I quickly discover the frat's yard backs up to another street of homes, and it's not long before we're trespassing on someone else's property. Party goers who ran the same way as us split off in all different directions while Aaron pulls me to the right to creep along a fence line.

"Do you have a plan?" I whisper, realizing we're feet away from someone's back deck. A light flips on inside their home, and I can see through a small window into their kitchen.

"No," he glances from side to side, "unless not getting caught counts."

I think it does.

Crouched down and speed-shuffling through the grass, we make it to the front yard of the house and out onto the sidewalk in a matter of seconds. Thankful to be somewhere legal, my sigh of relief is cut short when Aaron keeps moving with my hand clasped in his. "Where are we going?"

"Away," he says. "They know a bunch of people ran, and they'll come looking. Downtown is up ahead. It should be busy, and we can blend in."

My eyes dart around the deserted street we're standing on. We definitely stick out here. I think I can get us to Bianca's from the main road; I should remember some of the landmarks from when we drove in. If not, I'll text Izzy for the address.

Aaron and I make it about two blocks in silence before my cell rings. Using my free hand, I pull it from my pocket and swipe the screen with my thumb. "Hello?"

"Lucy!" Izzy whisper-yells. "Where are you? Are you okay?"

"I'm fine. I'm …" We're coming up on a street sign. "… On Wilson Street, behind the house. Where are you?"

"With Bianca hiding in her man's bedroom closet. It smells like a sweat sock in here."

I want to laugh, but her situation isn't funny. "Are the police still there?"

"Downstairs," she says. "The guys who live here are trying to diffuse the situation. Apparently, this has happened before." She sounds annoyed, and I hear a muffled voice.

"Who is that?"

"B. She says she didn't force us to come to the party." I can sense Izzy's sarcastic eye roll. "She just doesn't want me to tell mom and dad."

Bianca says something again and is quickly shushed. I don't know if Izzy told her to be quiet or someone else; regardless she needs to get off the phone and stop talking.

"You need to hang up," I say. "I'll meet you at your sister's. What street does she live on?"

"Ferguson," Izzy whispers. "Are you sure you're okay?"

Out of the corner of my eye, I look at Aaron. "Yes. I'm not alone. Text me when you're on your way to B's."

"Not alone?" Izzy sounds worried. "Luce. Who are you with? Carson? Please tell me it's not some stranger."

He's definitely not. "I promise I'm safe. Now hang up before someone hears you."

"Lucy –"

I end the call before she can grill me. She's not in a situation where I can give her all the details, and I don't want to discuss things in front of Aaron.

Speaking of, we make it to the stop sign and turn the corner when my phone sounds again, this time with a text message: ***Don't make me freak out. Who are you with??***

Aaron asks, "Izzy?"

I sigh. "She needs to stop making noise. She's hiding in a closet."

He laughs. "I'd say we're better off. What does she want?"

"To know who you are."

"Here." He reaches for my phone, and I let him take it. When he can't get it to do what he wants with one hand, he lets go of mine. It's then I realize we were still connected. Did he forget he was still holding on to me? Because I somehow did.

Aaron swipes up the screen, which opens the camera, and flips around the view. He leans in toward me to capture us both in the frame. "Smile."

He hits the shutter before I can react, and then we look at the picture. His crooked smile looks perfect while I just look baffled.

"Want to try again?" he asks.

"No." I yank my phone from him with a little more force than intended. My look on the screen sums up my mood: tired and jittery with a hint of disbelief.

I quickly send the picture to Izzy with the words ***Ask questions later***. I should have known better than to think she'd listen, because immediately I receive a reply: ***WTF?!***

Ignoring her, I silence my phone and look up the street. There's a Coney Island restaurant that looks familiar. "I think I recognize that diner. Izzy said Bianca's place is on Ferguson. Ring any bells?"

Aaron's expression twists. I'll take that as a no.

He pulls out his phone, opening an app. "My car is parked a few blocks from the frat house, on Celotto." He studies the map. "Ferguson is only a half mile from there."

"Which way?"

He points ahead of us.

We start to follow the sidewalk along the road. Aaron shoves his hands in his pockets, and I wrap my arms around myself. It's chilly now that I'm not surrounded by a bunch of bodies. Despite the time, it is busier on this street like Aaron said. There's no shortage of cars, and I even see a few people riding bikes. Students, I assume. I guess that's one thing about a college town on a Saturday night – it doesn't really sleep.

"Are you cold?"

My eyes meet Aaron's. "Yeah, but it's okay. I've suffered through worse."

He nods, but when we reach the restaurant I mentioned, he pauses outside the door. "Do you want to stop and get a coffee?"

It takes me a second to process his question. I still can't shake the alternate universe feeling. "Oh, no. I don't like coffee."

Just then, three guys exit. Aaron catches the open door and looks at me. "Hot chocolate then?"

The light dawns. He must need caffeine because he's been drinking. I only saw him put away one beer, but who knows what else he had before he found me. He must need something else in his system.

"Sure," I say and walk past him into the place. It should only take us a minute or two.

Once inside, we take a seat on two stools in front of a long counter that sits directly in front of the kitchen. After sliding an order to one of the cooks, a waitress spots us and walks over. "Hey, there. What'll it be?"

Aaron gestures toward me and I say, "A hot chocolate, please."

She looks at Aaron. "And for you?"

"The same."

"Are these for here or to go?"

Aaron defers to me instead of answering her question. My brow jumps. For one, I thought he wanted coffee. And for two … does he want to stay?

"To go," I end up saying. I'd like to reunite with Izzy sooner rather than later to make sure everything is okay.

Despite my best efforts, Aaron pays for both of us and we leave with Styrofoam cups in our hands. The farther we get up the street, the more I'm glad he suggested we stop. Not only does the hot chocolate warm my insides, but it occupies my mouth so I don't have to think of things to say. I will, however, find a way to slip him the two dollars he paid for my drink. Sometime during yearbook will probably be my best bet.

Eventually we arrive at the corner of Ferguson, Bianca's street. Ready to finish this odd adventure, I pick up my pace.

"Whoa." Aaron catches up with me. "Why are you walking so fast?"

"I want to sit down. We left early for the party, and it's after midnight. I'm tire – ahhh!"

My cup goes flying as I catch myself against a tree lining the sidewalk. What the –? What did I just trip over?

Aaron is instantly by my side. "What happened?"

I look at the ground behind me and feel my cheeks begin to burn. There's an uneven dip in the cement. "Apparently I can't walk," I mutter. I can't believe this is the second time I've fallen in front of him.

He looks concerned. "Are you all right?"

"Yes." I'm embarrassed, but I'm fine.

As he leans over to check out the sidewalk, I stand up straight. Brushing crumbled tree bark off my hands, I take a step, which sends an unexpected shooting pain through my ankle. *Ouch.* I internally groan and hope it's a one-time thing.

"Someone should fix that," Aaron comments when he stands. "I'm surprised you didn't fall into the street."

"Saved by a tree," I say, trying to be funny. Spying my spilled drink feet away, I feel bad about wasting it. I'd like to go hide now. "Can we forget this happened?"

Aaron smiles and waits for a moment before he answers. "No."

My mouth falls open. "Please?"

He chuckles and starts to walk. I follow, picking up my litter in the process. Unfortunately, my ankle throbs and I try to hide my limp. Bianca's place is only up the street; I can fake it until I make it. Of course, Aaron notices.

"You hurt yourself."

"No, I didn't."

"Yes, you did."

"No, I didn't."

"Yes, you did."

"No, I – hey."

My body jerks to a stop as he steps in front of me and blocks my path. I shift my weight to my good foot as he closes the space between us and assesses me. Finally, he turns around and crouches low to the ground. "Get on."

"Huh?"

He looks over his shoulder. "Get on. I'll carry you."

"Like a piggy-back ride? No. I'm fine. Let's just go."

"You probably rolled your ankle."

"It's really okay."

He sighs. "Have you ever injured a joint? It's going to swell. You need to stay off of it and ice it as soon as possible."

"Lucy!"

My head snaps up. A voice that sounds a whole lot like Izzy just yelled at me from the general direction of Bianca's place.

"Would you get on the pretty boy already?!"

Oh my god. My face turns crimson. As embarrassment sets in yet again, I look down at Aaron who doesn't seem fazed at all.

"You heard the girl," he says. "Let me help you."

CHAPTER TEN

Aaron

"You can put her down over there."

My eyes follow Izzy's pointing finger to a futon set up in the tiniest living room I've ever seen. I only take one step before Lucy is trying to wiggle out of my hold and slide off my back.

"I'm good," she protests. "I can walk."

No, you can't, I think. I've never had a girl try so hard to resist my help. I grip the back of her legs and pull them tight against my waist. "Just hang on two more seconds. I've already brought you this far."

"Which is ridiculous," she mutters.

When we reach the couch, I turn around and release her, setting her on the cushion with a small plop. "There." I smile. "Was that so bad?"

All I get is a sigh. It's not the typical response I get from most girls. Usually I get a laugh or a shy smile, or that peek-at-you-from-under-the-eyelashes-I'm-trying-to-be-sexy thing. Lucy gives me none of those.

"Well, if she won't thank you, I will," Izzy says as she walks across the room. She sits down next to Lucy and asks, "Which foot did you hurt?"

"The left." Lucy wrestles with the strap on her shoe growing frustrated. "Ugh. Why won't this come off?"

"Here." Izzy grabs her foot which forces Lucy to lean back and rest her upper body on her elbows. Looking up at me, Izzy asks, "What else do we need to do here?"

"Elevate it. And ice wouldn't hurt."

"I'm on it," says a voice I don't recognize.

"Thanks, B," Izzy says as she removes Lucy's shoe. "Bianca, Aaron. Aaron, my sister," she introduces us.

"Hi." Bianca smiles as she brushes past me. She looks almost identical to Izzy except her face is more made up, and she has blue eyes instead of brown. "Our little fridge doesn't make much ice, but I have a freezer pack I use for my lunches. Will that work?"

"It should," I say and follow her.

Just off the living room is an extremely small kitchen which holds a sink, a skinny refrigerator, and enough counter space for two stove burners, a microwave, and a toaster.

"Is this a typical dorm room?" I ask. I'm used to the much bigger frat house.

"It's technically an upperclassmen *suite*." She uses air quotes. "Two bedrooms and a shared living space. The freshman dorms are different; they have one room with a bunk bed and two desks. Community bathrooms. You know."

No, I don't know, but it sounds kind of claustrophobic. I mentally add checking out the living conditions to my upcoming campus tours when I hear back from U of M and, hopefully, Notre Dame.

Bianca opens the freezer and finds a flexible blue ice pack. She grabs a dish towel, wraps it up, and hands it to me. "Ta-dah."

"Thanks."

As I start to make my way back to Lucy, I overhear heated whispering and stop in my tracks. Bianca does the same.

"Would you stop treating me like a patient?" Lucy tries to pull her foot away from Izzy. "I don't need a doctor."

"I think you do. Are you sure you didn't hit your head? Aaron-freaking-Matthews saved you."

"I didn't need saving."

"Would you just let him take care of you? The likelihood of this happening again is … is …"

"Slim," Lucy cuts her off. "Do you know how awkward this is for me? I'm dying here."

"I'm going to ask him to stay."

Lucy's voice drops even lower. "Don't you dare."

"Do you want him to drive all the way home alone? It's late, and he's been drinking."

"I'm sure he came out here with friends. He knows someone named Ben at the house."

Izzy's eyes roll. "Is it really a good idea for him to go back there? It's better if he stays with us."

Lucy sits up and leans as close to Izzy as she can. "Stop it. You're supposed to be my best friend."

Izzy's eyes light up. "I am your best friend. And I know when my duty calls."

Their conversation amuses me, and I find myself hiding a smile. I know Izzy's trying to force Lucy to be more comfortable around me, and I find myself wanting that, too. I understand Lucy has reservations, but I already told her I don't blame her for Cody. What more can I do to convince her she shouldn't feel weird around me?

Bianca nudges my arm with her elbow. "Should we interrupt them?"

It looks like Lucy might try to smack the grin off Izzy's face. "Probably."

We step into the room, and both girls' attention falls on us. "Oh, good." Izzy stands. "Aaron. C'mere." She hands me Lucy's ankle. "Do your magic while I find something to prop this up with."

Lucy exhales with a huff and flops on her back as I sit down and take Izzy's place. Setting her foot on my lap, I examine it. "It doesn't look too bad."

She ignores me and stares at the ceiling.

"And your toes are cute."

Her head snaps up.

Happy I got a reaction, I place the ice pack against her skin and she flinches. "Does it hurt?"

"No. It's cold."

"Here. Use these when you're done." Izzy sets a couple of fuzzy pillows from a nearby bean bag chair at my feet. "You're staying the night, right? I mean, you can if you want to. Right, B?"

Bianca shrugs. "Doesn't bother me any."

I look at Lucy. Her opinion is the only one that matters to me. "Does it bother you?"

She closes her eyes and waits a moment before saying "no" as if admitting defeat. Then, she glances over at Izzy's sister. "What about Deb?"

"As long as we stay out of her room, she's fine with anything," Bianca explains. Deb must be her roommate.

"Great!" Izzy seems happy she got her way. "Lucy, I'll go get your stuff so it's close by, so you won't have to move much. I'll bunk with my sister, and you and Aaron can figure out sleeping arrangements."

"The futon lays down flat," Bianca says. "I'm sure you can figure it out. I'll go get a blanket."

"Two, please," Lucy says and then looks at me. "I'll sleep on the floor."

I frown.

Once the sisters leave the room, I turn on her. "Do you honestly think I'd let you sleep on the floor?"

She shrugs. "I figured I'd give you an out. I'm sure I'm the last person on earth you want to spend the night with."

No, I think. That honor would belong to June. Or Allie. Or maybe they're tied for first place.

"Well, you're wrong," I say. "Besides, you don't have to worry. I'm not going to stay. I'm tired, but I'm not even buzzed. I'll go sleep in my truck for a few hours and then I'll get on the road."

She immediately looks concerned. "Sleeping in your parked car on some random street doesn't sound safe."

"I'll lock the doors."

She shakes her head. "No. You'll stay here. It's fine."

"Not if it makes you uncomfortable."

Lucy stares at me, and I stare at her. Then, slowly, she sits up straight. When her body moves her leg slides back, so I adjust the ice pack against her ankle. As her eyes comb over my face, she looks curious and confused, as if she's legitimately concerned there's something wrong with me. I can't help but notice she looks just as good after our escape and her stumble as she did on the frat house dance floor. I know it shouldn't surprise me, but it does. It's not like she's invisible at school. How can you look at someone every damn day but never really see them?

After a few quiet seconds she looks down, twisting her fingers in her lap. "Can I ..." Her voice is hesitant. "Can I ask you an honest question?"

"Sure."

Her eyes meet mine again. "Why are you being so nice to me? It doesn't make any sense."

Do I have a reputation I don't know about? "Am I supposed to be mean? I'm not normally an asshole."

"Please don't play dumb." She lets out a heavy breath. "Out of all the people who should hate me the most, you're at the top of the list. Right next to June and Co –" She stops short of saying Cody's name and looks away. "Right next to June and his parents."

I blink. What she says is true. Anyone looking at us would expect the dead guy's best friend to be upset he's gone and pissed at the person responsible. What they don't understand is I am mad and pissed, just not at Lucy. Never at her. At Cody, yes. At Allie, hell yes. And most definitely at myself, for not being there when Cody needed me the most. I'll carry that with me for the rest of my life, and I know Lucy feels guilty, too. I'm being nice to her because I know how she feels. I wish she didn't have to pay for Cody's mistakes, but my hands are tied. I promised I wouldn't tell his secrets, and I meant it.

"So?" Lucy asks. "Are you going to tell me why you're acting like what happened never did?"

"It's not an act. I just …" I run my free hand through my hair as I think of something to say. "I'm being nice because I understand what you're going through. That's all."

Lucy's brow furrows. "Thanks, but … there's no way you could."

She wraps her arms around her waist. It's obvious she doesn't believe what I said, and it bothers me. I really suck at vague explanations, but I want to make her feel better.

"Have you ever heard the saying 'things aren't always what they seem?'"

She gives me a look that screams *duh*.

"When what happened haunts you …" How do I put this? "Think of those words. Okay?"

She looks like she has questions, but before she can ask them, Izzy appears from around the corner. "Here's your stuff." She sets a duffle bag, two blankets, and two pillows on the floor. "Did you guys figure things out?"

I wait for Lucy to answer. If she says yes, then I'll stay for a little while. If she says no, then at least the cab of my truck is comfy.

"Yeah," she says.

Unexpected relief courses through me.

Lucy eyes me before swinging her leg off my lap. "I'm going to hobble to the bathroom and brush my teeth."

As she picks up her bag, I stand and look at the futon. How does this thing unfold?

"I think there's a button." Izzy reads my mind. She walks to the opposite side. "Yep. Here." She adjusts something, and I help her lower the back of the couch.

"Thanks," I say. "I didn't mean to crash your party."

"No worries. I'm glad Lucy wasn't alone when everything went down, including her own body. I wish I could have seen her fall." She laughs. "I'm a horrible friend."

I'll never admit it, but it was pretty funny.

"You're not a bad friend." Grabbing a pillow, I walk around to the opposite side of the couch. "You skipped homecoming with her."

"Of course. Lucy's not big on school functions right now," Izzy says. "Plus, I owed her. I kinda tattled on Ms. Wright, and she didn't appreciate it when the principal got involved."

I freeze. "Tattled on Ms. Wright?"

"She kicked Lucy off the student council for absolutely no reason." Izzy looks disgusted. "It was a gross misuse of authority. I mean, what the hell? I had to tell someone, even if Lucy didn't want me to."

What the hell is right. "She didn't get an explanation?"

"Wright fed her some BS about not being good enough because June screamed at her in the hallway. And then, you know, what happened last spring."

My entire body tenses. "She actually brought up Cody?"

Izzy nods and then looks uncertain. "Well, I'm not sure if she specifically used his name, but I know the accident was mentioned. I didn't overhear the conversation."

"Speaking of eavesdropping," Lucy sticks her head out from the bathroom, "this place isn't big. I can hear everything you're saying."

Izzy's eyes widen, and she bites her bottom lip. "Whoops."

My mind spins. I had no idea Lucy was catching crap from all sides.

"Are you finished?" Lucy reappears from the bathroom. "Are you done spilling the sordid details of my life?"

"Nope." Izzy sticks her tongue out at her friend. "I haven't even started on Hunter."

"Oh, please." Lucy rolls her eyes and then looks at me. "Ex-boyfriend. Big douche. That's all you need to know."

The two of them start to bicker back and forth, and my ears tune them out. Lucy's changed. What little make up she had on is gone, and her hair looks like she brushed it. I just now notice the shirt she's wearing has "Off Duty Mermaid" scribbled across the front. The saying fits her. She's not at school, the place I normally see her, and she's revealing herself to be more than what I knew existed.

"Good *night*, Isabel."

I refocus in time to hear Lucy try to dismiss Izzy. She grabs a blanket and a pillow and tosses them on the couch, arranging her space. I do the same on the other side, while reminding her to use one of the smaller pillows to prop up her ankle.

"Aww," Izzy says and walks over. "I have to get a picture of this."

"Why?" Both Lucy and I ask in unison.

"Because we all wound up here together. Say what you want about fate or whatever, but I say this is the official start of a brand-new friendship."

Lucy pokes Izzy in the shoulder. "You're only saying that because I threatened to cut you off."

"Just smile."

The two girls tip their heads together as Izzy holds up her phone. "Aaron, where are you? Get in the frame."

I walk around the couch and stand next to Lucy.

"Say cheese!"

I comply.

"You're a dork," Lucy says through a forced grin. I don't know if she's talking to me or Izzy.

Once the picture is taken, Izzy says goodnight and skips out of the room, leaving us to lay in the dark as far apart as possible. I have to admit the situation is more awkward than I thought it would be. I thought staying would be no big deal and I would be able to fall asleep, but in reality, it's not working out that way. My mind keeps going back to what I learned about the student council, and it makes me want to ask her what else she's had to put up with.

It makes me wonder what else I could potentially protect her from.

Minutes pass. After what feels like an eternity, Lucy whispers, "Are you still awake?"

Thankful she said something, I look over my shoulder. "Yeah."

She shifts her weight, and I can tell from her silhouette she's rolled onto her back. "You think this is weird too, right?"

I nod, even though I'm not sure if she can see me.

"Please don't feel obligated by what Izzy said. We're not ... we don't have to be friends. Sometimes her optimism gets out of control. Like her mouth."

I chuckle. "She reminds me of Cody."

"How so?"

"She's a little pushy, but because she understands you and knows all your secrets, you love her anyway. She's the definition of a best friend."

I think I hear her swallow. "You must miss him."

"All the time. Cody is in every memory I have since the second grade." There are so many stories I could share with her. "He was my partner in crime since his frog tied mine during the bullfrog race at Cub Scout camp."

It's been so long since I've talked to anyone about him, I keep going. "This one time, in middle school, Cody found a blow torch in his garage and thought it would be cool if we lit stuff on fire."

"And you agreed?"

"Heck yes. We scavenged through the recycling and found all these cardboard boxes, then took them into the woods behind his house so we wouldn't get caught. We brought a bucket of water with us, but failed to realize it hadn't rained in days and there was a drought. His mom saw the flames and came running; we could've burned down the whole subdivision," I half-laugh.

Lucy doesn't say anything, so I lace my fingers behind my head and continue. "And then, this one birthday, he had his party at the Holton pool. We had just seen *Guardians of the Galaxy* and would only say "I am Groot" to each other. The lifeguard tried to tell us to stop horsing around because, you know, we were re-enacting the movie. All we'd say to her was "I am Groot," so she eventually kicked us out." I sigh. "Man, I miss those days."

Lucy's voice is a whisper. "I'm sure you do."

It's then I know I've said something wrong. After an uncomfortable silence, I feel the couch move with her rolling over, away from me. "I'm sorry he's gone," she says, her voice cracking.

I close my eyes and hold my breath. Shit. I should've stopped talking. *Things aren't always what they seem*, I want to remind her. *Don't cry.*

Instead, I keep my mouth shut and my thoughts to myself. I have no idea how to console her without it being awkward and weird.

If only she knew how sorry I was, too.

CHAPTER ELEVEN

Lucy

"I still can't believe he left without saying anything."

I stare out Izzy's passenger side window as she drives us to school. It's an overcast and chilly September morning. Fall is definitely here. "Well, that's what happened."

Izzy's tone turns sarcastic. "Um, yeah. I was there. Are you sure you don't know why he snuck out in the middle of the night?"

Of course I know why Aaron decided to leave before sunrise. I nearly burst into tears beside him during his walk down memory lane. I tried to hide it, but I know I failed. The situation was already uncomfortable, and I made it unbearable. If I were Aaron, I would have run far away from the emotional girl, too.

"Nope, no idea," I say. I'm not going to relive the humiliation with Izzy. It will be hard enough seeing Aaron in class today.

"With the way he was acting ..." Izzy drifts off as she turns into the parking lot. "I just didn't expect that from him."

"He probably realized he made a huge mistake."

"What mistake?"

I blink at her. For a smart girl, she's not acting too bright. "The homecoming king spent half the night with me. He probably realized if anyone found out it would be social suicide." Yeah, I discovered that fun development when I opened Snapchat yesterday morning. Of the few people I still follow, both Willow and Brooke posted pictures from the dance. Aaron and June looked perfect on stage together.

Izzy grimaces. "I don't think he's into the popularity thing as much as you think he is."

I'm skeptical, and she knows it.

"You have to admit he doesn't come across as arrogant as his friends."

She pulls into a parking space, and I reach for my bag. "He did before he was forced into our yearbook class."

"I know, but we were wrong." She cuts the engine, pulls her keys from the ignition, and meets my eyes. "Fess up. He's nice."

My shoulders sag. "I never thought he was evil." Just way out of my league and someone I never thought I'd interact with.

"See?" Izzy reaches for the door handle. "He must have had a reason to leave. Maybe his parents called or something."

Or something, I think.

As we walk toward the school, I stare at the ground. I can't shake this uneasy feeling. For the last twenty-four hours I've tried to convince myself I don't care about Aaron or his opinion of me. So what if he thinks I'm an unstable klutz? It's the truth. And, in the grand scheme of things, it really doesn't matter. He came to his senses and left Bianca's to avoid me. I should have expected nothing less.

Then why do I feel so conflicted about it?

I'm so focused on my footsteps and my thoughts I don't realize something is off until Izzy and I are halfway to our lockers. It's too quiet, and when I look up, every pair of eyes is on me. Okay, maybe that's an over exaggeration, but at least one out of every two people we pass are staring in our direction. Nervous energy starts to course through my veins as Izzy nudges my arm with her elbow.

"Like Mondays aren't bad enough," she whispers. "Who peed in everyone's Cheerios?"

"Apparently I did," I mutter and suddenly become very interested in examining my backpack strap. Logically everyone is looking at Izzy too, but my gut tells me she's not the center of attention.

"Whatever," she says. "You didn't do anything."

I shoot her a sarcastic look.

"I meant recently," she clarifies.

As we pass the next group of staring students, Izzy throws her hands in the air and gets loud. "What? You've never seen two people walk down a hallway before? I know we're killin' it, but *come on.*"

Their eyes grow wide at being called out, and they quickly turn to face their open lockers. I bite my lip to suppress a smile, but one corner of my mouth still twitches. Sometimes I love that my best friend doesn't have a filter.

"Hey."

My body jerks to a stop as Nick suddenly appears in front of me. "Oh. Hey."

"Have you been to your locker yet?"

My eyes meet Izzy's before shaking my head no.

His expression falls. "I think you should know ... someone messed with it."

"Messed with it?"

He nods. "I noticed – a lot of people noticed – this morning."

Well, that explains all the staring. I sigh. "How bad is it?"

"It'll take some time to clean up."

Great. My mind automatically jumps to paint, permanent marker, nasty messages, the possibility of serving detention for destruction of school property ...

"C'mon." Izzy starts to march down the hallway. "Let's see what these morons did."

Reluctantly I follow her, and Nick follows me. When my locker comes into view, the first thing I notice is it's no longer painted the same shade of deep blue as all the others. It's now neon yellow. As I get closer, I realize the yellow isn't paint. It's plastic tape.

Yellow crime scene tape.

"Seriously?" Izzy scowls when we stop directly in front of our lockers. Hers is untouched.

Reaching out, I run my fingers over my new "decorations." The words CRIME SCENE are bold and black, and they scream at me from a million different angles. The yellow tape is perfectly plastered to the exact dimensions of my locker door with clear, super sticky packing tape. Not only will this take time to rip off, it will probably ruin the paint underneath. I close my eyes and concentrate on my next few breaths.

"Do you know who would do this?" Nick asks.

"June." Izzy doesn't hesitate. "The question is why."

That's easy. My eyes pop open. "She found out."

"About what? This weekend?"

I glance between Nick and Izzy, wondering if it's safe to say anything with him around. I decide to nod yes, since 'this weekend' is a pretty generic statement.

"Are you talking about this?" Nick pulls his cell out of his pocket and touches the screen with his thumb. After scrolling, he holds it up. There, plain as day, is the picture Izzy took of the two of us and Aaron at Bianca's Saturday night.

"When did you start following me on Snapchat?" Izzy reaches for his phone. "I don't remember approving you."

"You didn't," he says, handing it over. "It looks like a screen shot. Someone who follows you must have taken it and shared it. Then others did, too. I thought it was weird that it ended up in my feed from Shawn, but then one of the hashtags says "Pass it on."

"Idiot sheeple," Izzy mutters and then looks at me. "I'm sorry, Luce. I thought only my followers would see it. I didn't think any of them were friends with June or her flying monkeys."

"I know," I sigh and start to pry the tape off my padlock so I can open my locker. I know Izzy's account is set to private like mine, but then again, we should both know better than to think anything posted online is safe.

While Izzy effortlessly stows her bag and grabs her stuff for English, I wrestle with layers of stuck plastic. If June did this all by herself, she took her time and did it right. There's no way I'll get all of this off before a teacher or someone with authority sees it. I wish I had some scissors or at least something sharp.

"Lucy."

All three of our heads turn. Naturally Aaron would appear. He's wearing an expression that morphs from anger to concern. I silently hope he'll keep walking. I feel exposed enough as it is.

"Let me help you," he says and steps between Nick and me. Reaching into his pocket, he finds his keys and flips open a small Swiss Army knife attached to the ring. He slices the tape over my lock and cuts it back.

"Thanks," I say just as the warning bell sounds. I quickly grab the dial and enter my com to avoid eye contact. "You should go so you're not late."

"I think I'll stay."

Why? It's obviously not a good idea to be seen together. "I don't think –" I try to yank open my locker, but the door barely budges. "I don't think you should do that."

"I want to." He invades my space by leaning close. The smell of his body wash distracts me, causing me to look up directly into his face. I notice his hair is damp. "I'm not afraid," he says. "I want to talk to you."

My mouth falls open a tiny bit. What am I supposed to say?

"C'mon, Nick."

I refocus on Izzy as she drapes her arm over Nick's shoulders. "I think Lucy's all set with her Boy Scout here." She winks her goodbye as she turns our confused-looking friend around. "So, how was the football game?" I overhear her ask as they walk away.

Once they're out of earshot, Aaron says, "I see your ankle is better."

"Um, yeah," I manage to expertly stutter before adjusting my backpack on my shoulder. "The ice helped. I just banged it up a little. No sprain or anything."

"That's good," he says as he concentrates on my locker by cutting a line through the tape between the door and the frame. When he completes three sides, he pulls on the handle and the door pops open. "There."

"Thank you," I say as I rush forward to throw my stuff inside. He steps back but doesn't leave as I grab what I need for class.

"Listen," he says as the final bell rings. "About this weekend –"

"Forget about it," I say with my head still in my locker. "If anyone brings it up, I'll fake amnesia." I'm sure he doesn't want me running around telling everyone how we kinda spent the night together.

"That's not what I was going to say."

My face scrunches, and I meet his eyes.

"I know I upset you, and I want to apologize." He shoves his hands in the front pockets of his jeans, giving me the impression he's uncomfortable. "I left when you were sleeping so I wouldn't make things worse. I shouldn't have brought up my past with Cody. I'm sorry."

He's sorry? I'm dumbfounded.

"What is going on?"

Our attention snaps from each other to Ms. Wright. She must have stepped out of her classroom because she's walking from that direction. It would figure the one teacher who doesn't like me would see this mess.

"Terrific," Aaron grumbles under his breath.

When Ms. Wright gets close enough, she grabs my open locker door and moves it back and forth, examining it. "What is this?"

I shrug. "Someone's idea of a bad joke, I guess."

"Well, it's definitely not funny," she says.

We stand there in silence until Ms. Wright stops her vandalism inspection to lock eyes with me. "You're going to have to clean this up."

"Wait a minute," Aaron interrupts. "Shouldn't the person responsible clean it up?"

Ms. Wright's hands land on her hips which draws my attention to her cute skirt. "Do you know who did this?"

Aaron opens his mouth, but before he can say anything I half-step, half-skip in front of him, bumping off his chest in the process. "We don't know," I say. The last thing I need is June coming down harder on me because Aaron ratted her out. Or, if it wasn't her, I don't need the people involved getting angry.

Ms. Wright narrows her eyes. It couldn't be more obvious I'm lying. "If you're not going to tell me, then I'm making it your responsibility to get rid of this. It's not fair to make an innocent janitor do it."

"I already planned to take it down," I say. I'll just have to skip lunch to get it done. I don't have any other free time, other than ditching yearbook, and I'm not going to make Izzy wait for me after school. She would, but I'd feel like crap for asking. Plus, I know she'd help me clean and this isn't her problem.

"Okay." Ms. Wright shuts my locker. "The two of you are late."

"Let's go," Aaron says, pulling me by my elbow to get me to follow him. I do and I don't know why; English is the opposite way.

"Try to have this gone by the end of the day," Ms. Wright calls to our backs.

When we turn a corner, Aaron stops walking. "You know June's behind this, right?"

"I assumed."

"Then why wouldn't you let me say anything?" He looks at me in disbelief. "Just because she's pissed about where I spend my time doesn't mean she gets to take it out on you."

"You've talked to her?"

"She's been blowing up my phone since she saw Izzy's picture."

"Awesome." Despite my sarcasm, I hug my book and my folder to my chest.

"Don't worry," Aaron says. "I'll take care of it. She just doesn't know how to take no for an answer."

My brow furrows. "What's the question?"

He looks at the floor and then up at me again. "The queen wants to date the king." He crosses his arms and leans against the wall. "It's wrong on so many levels."

I can imagine why. "About that," I change the subject, "I thought you were kidding when you brought up voting for you at the party. Congratulations."

Aaron makes a face. "Eh … no congrats necessary. Is there any way we could keep my humiliation out of the yearbook? I looked like an idiot wearing that crown."

I smirk. "Not possible. Homecoming is always a two-page spread."

"Ugh." He groans. "The king is not happy."

I unexpectedly laugh. "Well, the *king* is going to have to suck it up."

Just then, a door to a nearby classroom opens. Kids spill into the hallway, headed toward the library. None of them pay us any attention, until a small group of four or five guys notices Aaron. One of them hits another on the arm, and they all turn to look.

"Do you know them?" I ask.

Aaron nods. "Lacrosse." He raises one hand in a wave.

"Dude," one of them says loudly. His eyes dart back and forth between me and their teammate, and he throws his hands out in a "What the fuck?" gesture. If it wasn't clear earlier, it's blatant now. None of Aaron's friends want him around me.

None.

I don't know why my heart sinks, but it does. Shuffling backward, I turn and walk away.

"Lucy." Aaron calls behind me. "Lucy. Wait."

I don't turn around.

"SALAD BAR?"

"No."

"Fries?"

"No."

"Chicken sandwich?"

"Maybe."

"Sundae?"

"Definitely."

Izzy nods her approval and leads the way through the cafeteria. As we wait in line for the frozen yogurt machine, I peer through a glass case that protects other sugary selections. Slices of pie, chocolate pudding, and little cups of red Jell-O topped with whipped cream tempt me. Our school gives us plenty of other so-called nutritious choices for lunch, but today I'm opting out. With the way things have been going, I think I've earned some empty calories.

"So," Izzy says as she steps up to fill her bowl with vanilla-chocolate swirl, "when we walk back to our table, you'll have to point out your knights in shining armor."

I roll my eyes. "I told you I don't remember what they looked like. Plus, they're not heroes. They had to be forced or at least threatened." With what, I don't know. But it's the only thing that makes sense.

"Aaron must have a lot of pull," Izzy muses as she moves on to the bin of toppings. "I have to admit, I'm impressed."

"You and me both."

Frowning, I lower the yogurt lever and watch my cold lunch slide out. Earlier, after I left Aaron, I tried to sneak into English when the teacher's back was turned. It didn't work, and she was sure to make it known I'd received a tardy. Then, between classes, I started to notice some of the tape on my locker was missing. Confused, I went on with my day. Little by little the mess disappeared. Now everything is gone and with very little damage to the paint underneath. I realized whoever took care of my problem did so carefully, and as I opened my locker before lunch, a note fell out:

To prove we're not really assholes
Micah, Chris, Elijah, and TJ
JV lacrosse

I KNOW Aaron made the guys do it, probably because they're the same ones who caused me walk away from him this morning. Now they're involved in something that doesn't pertain to them, and I'm sure they resent me even more for it. I don't think Aaron realizes his actions could backfire on both of us.

"Whoa," Izzy says. "I know you're stress eating, but you might want to let go."

Startled, I focus and release the lever. Frozen yogurt is oozing over the sides of my bowl and all over my hand. "Great."

"Here." Izzy hands me some napkins.

Once I clean myself up and we pay, we make it to our seats. Izzy and I have sat at the same table since we were freshman. I don't know why we never moved; we just started here and it stuck. Tucked next to the stage in the cafeteria, we're out of the way but have a good view of both entrances, plus whatever happens on the stage. Sometimes it's a performance from the current musical to get us to buy tickets, other times it's spirit wear or fundraising sales. Today students are lining up to pick up their photo packages from the dance Saturday night.

Licking my spoon, I ask, "You talked to the photographer, right? He's sending us the digital copies of any group pics?"

"Yes, ma'am," Izzy responds.

Nodding, I look down and concentrate on mixing my frozen yogurt into soup. My mind drifts, hoping to get a nap in after I finish my Spanish homework and before dinner.

"Well, well, well. If it isn't Lethal Lucy."

A tray of food is smacked down on the table directly across from me. My body jumps, and my eyes land on the last person I ever thought I'd see here. She's grinning at me and looks just as Goth goddess at the day I met her.

"Delinquent Delaney?"

She crosses her arms and arches an eyebrow. "The one and only."

CHAPTER TWELVE

Aaron

L ucy is ignoring me.

I've been trying to get her attention since I sat down in yearbook class. Granted, I didn't sit right next to her, which would have been the easy thing to do. No, I figured she's had enough of me and everyone who associates with me today. Still, I want to make sure she got the message about her locker. I told the guys who decided to be jerks earlier they had to take care of it. There are perks to being the captain of the team they aspire to make one day, especially when they know how well I get along with Coach.

As time ticks by, I start to run out of indiscrete ways to get her to notice me. I've already dropped my pencil and some papers on the floor. I've pretended to stretch. I even used the hall pass for the bathroom. She's avoided eye contact with me eight times – not that I'm counting. As I tap my pencil eraser against the notebook in front of me, I realize my leg is bouncing to the same rhythm. I can't sit still. I'm going to have to make up a question to go talk to her.

Instead of brainstorming a list of businesses to solicit for yearbook ads, which is what I'm supposed to be doing, I lean over my notebook and start to write down question ideas. I'm no further than the weather and the upcoming Fall Fest, when out of the corner of my eye I see one of our staff photographers restrain herself from slamming down her camera. Lucy must notice too, because she's up out of her seat and by the girl's side in seconds.

"Uh, Alex?" She taps her on the shoulder. "Is there a problem?"

"All my pictures are way too dark," the girl complains. "I've messed with every setting and nothing works. I think this camera is broken."

Lucy frowns. "Lemme see."

Alex hands over the Nikon, and Lucy immediately starts pushing buttons on the back. Well, I assume it's a Nikon. It's the only brand that popped into my head. What other brands are there? I know it's not a Polaroid.

"Your f stop is set way too high," Lucy explains. "See? Lower number, more light."

"But then they'll be blurry," Alex says. "Lower number, slower shutter speed."

"Then just adjust your ISO. Here."

As Lucy sits down to demonstrate, I notice she looks completely confident and in her element. I also notice, as she folds one leg beneath her butt, her long sweater gets pulled off one of her shoulders. Seconds pass before she realizes, and when she covers it up, I'm disappointed.

"Earth to Aaron."

My eyes land on Izzy, who has silently slid into the empty seat in front of mine. Propping her elbow on my desk, she sets her chin on the heel of her hand and bats her eyelashes. "What'cha lookin' at?"

Clearly caught, I lean back in my seat. "Nothing. I mean, I didn't know Lucy knew so much about cameras."

She smiles. "Photography is one of her hobbies."

"Really? Then why doesn't she take pictures for the yearbook?"

"She used to." Izzy glances in her friend's direction. "You know. Before she stopped attending school events."

My face falls. Unfortunately, I know why she made that decision.

"Anyway," Izzy continues, "I came over here to tell you I think it's cool what you did about her locker. I know she appreciates it even though she's worried."

So the guys did leave a note. "She shouldn't worry. It's over and done with."

"For now." Izzy looks at me like I've bumped my head. "C'mon. You know June's not going to drop this. That's why Lucy's avoiding you. So no one can say they saw you two talk."

My jaw tenses. "It shouldn't matter."

"But it does."

I sigh. I get what's she's saying, but it's stupid. My eyes swing to Lucy. No one knows the truth about what went down with Cody that night, not even her. It's me and me alone; therefore my opinion should be the only one that counts. If I tell June or anyone else to back off, they should.

"You're staring again."

Izzy pulls me out of my thoughts. "Sorry."

She gives me a curious side-eye. "You really like her, don't you?"

Her question takes me off guard. "Huh?"

"Lucy." She starts to grin. "You like her."

Define like, I think. "If you mean she's a nice person who shouldn't be going through any Cody-related crap, then yeah. I like her." Not to mention I've decided she's pretty damn cute.

Izzy's eyes light up as if she read my mind.

"Let me see this." Izzy grabs my notebook, spinning it around. She scowls. "Weather? Fall Fest? This is an interesting business list."

"It's nothing," I say and scribble out the words. "I already know my dad will buy a full-page ad for his chiropractic office, and I can probably get the place where I buy all my lacrosse equipment to buy one, too. They know me by name."

"Impressive." Izzy nods. "Here's another person you should call." Stealing my pencil, she writes down a phone number.

"Who?"

She jerks her chin to the left. "Your girl."

"Lucy?"

"No, Cleopatra." She laughs. "Yes, Lucy."

The bell rings. Before I can say anything, Izzy jumps up and starts walking backward to her original seat. "Now you two can talk without anyone knowing." She winks. "You're welcome."

As she turns her back to me, I look down at Lucy's number and shake my head.

Izzy truly is the female version of Cody.

By the time the end of the school day rolls around, I still haven't used Lucy's number. I saved it in my phone under 'Cleopatra', and I was going to text her during lunch. Instead, I kept typing and deleting words. I found out what I wanted to know from Izzy during yearbook; Lucy knows who's responsible for cleaning up the mess. There's nothing more to say.

Except I have this nagging feeling I should say *something*.

Shaking it off, I resist the urge to look in her direction as I pull the books I need for homework out of my locker. I debate going to the gym to spend another hour or so in the weight room. I've been breaking up my work out time between the morning and the afternoon, since I can't use the equipment during PE anymore. I already went before school, but –

"Is it true?"

I turn around to see Harrison and two other guys from my team, Jason and Max, standing behind me. I frown. "Is what true?"

"You and Lucy," Harrison says, his voice low. "I've been texting you since yesterday. What's going on?"

All three guys lean forward like they're about to hear the juiciest gossip to ever hit Holton High.

"Dude," I say. "I answered you. Nothing's going on. I went to Central because Ben invited me. I didn't respond to your other messages because June's texts killed my battery."

"Come on," Jason presses. "You left the hottest girl in school to meet up with the chick who ran over your best friend. That's not nothing."

"You should have seen June go off at the dance," Max jumps in. "It took Kat at least a half hour to talk her down. And that's before she found out where you went."

My eyes roll. "June needs to learn she can't get her way all of the time. And – I'll say it again – I didn't leave to meet up with Lucy. I went to see our old teammates. She just happened to be there."

Max looks confused. "So … you had to hang out with her and take a selfie?"

This conversation is starting to irritate me. "No, I didn't. The cops showed up, and we ran. I couldn't go back to the frat house, so I ended up where Lucy was staying. To be honest, she helped me."

All three guys exchange glances. "What?" I get sarcastic. "Not the story you expected?"

"It's just …" Max shrugs. "It looks bad. Cody was a brother to all of us, and if it wasn't for her …"

No, I think. *If it wasn't for him.*

"All we're saying is its weird, man," Jason says. "She's the last person you should want to be around."

"Or help," Max adds. "Micah told us about the locker thing."

"Yeah. The girls aren't going to be happy." Jason looks at Max. "It took them like, what? Two hours to do what they did?"

My brow jumps. "Girls? I thought it was only June." Who, by the way, was noticeably absent today.

"Nah. It was her, Kat, and Casey."

My expression twists. The news Kat helped stings. She never struck me as that type of person.

"Look." I let out a heavy breath. "I hate thinking about what happened to Cody. Trust me. I miss him just as much as you do. His locker should be right here next to mine, but it's not. He should be co-captain of the team, but he won't be. We all feel bad, but taking it out on Lucy isn't going to make anything better. I talked to her this weekend. So what? We ended up helping each other out of a shitty situation."

The three of them are silent. Just when I think my words have sunk in, Jason busts out with, "But she still ran him over."

I want to bang my head against my locker. *Not on purpose, you idiot.*

Harrison must sense my frustration, because he says, "Hey, Max. Don't you have to be home when your brother and sister get off the bus?"

Max makes a face. "Yes, although they're in middle school. I don't know why I *have* to be there." He checks the time on his phone and takes a few steps back. "I guess I'll catch you guys later. Jason, you still need a ride?"

"Yeah." He fist bumps Harrison and then me. "I can't wait to get back on the field with you guys. Husk-*ies!*" He draws out the word.

When they're halfway down the hall, I expect Harrison to go, too. Instead, he has an odd look on his face, like his brain is stuck.

"Spit it out," I say.

"What?"

"Whatever's bugging you." I turn back to my locker and drop another notebook on the pile of stuff sitting on the ground at my feet. I didn't realize I had so much homework to do.

"I understand where you're coming from," he finally says. "What happened wasn't completely Lucy's fault. Cody was really, really drunk."

"Cody was shit-faced." No need to mince words.

"Still," Harrison hesitates, "you need to know not everyone shares our opinion. In case you haven't noticed, common sense seems to be rare among our friends."

I stop what I'm doing and look at him. If I had to name one person I'm closest to after Cody, it would be Harrison. He's obviously trying to tell me something, so I gesture for him to continue.

"You have to realize people are going to blame Lucy no matter what. It doesn't matter what we say or what the police said. They don't like her. Period."

Anger starts to build in my chest. I didn't realize all of our friends were such narrow-minded assholes. If they knew the truth, that Cody chose to die, they'd all be singing a different tune. Hell, they'd probably host a suicide awareness parade through town. But, since I can't share that information, they need to get a grip. An accident is called an accident for a reason.

"Anyway," Harrison continues, "what I'm trying to say is you should keep your reputation in mind. Especially when it comes to the team. You're the captain, and they need to trust you. Right or wrong, that trust takes a hit when they see you with Lucy."

I shake my head. "Let me get this straight. You think I should stand by and do nothing while she's being harassed? For the good of our season?"

"Yes and no. It's complicated."

I cross my arms. "Enlighten me, then."

Harrison steps closer. "Between you and me, I agree Lucy doesn't deserve all the hate. I hear a lot of it, and it sucks. All I'm saying is I think you need to think about things before you act on them. Everyone is watching. Things get seen, rumors spread, and people do stupid shit. You know how it is, man."

"So, what do you suggest?"

"Just ... I don't know. Pretend not to care?"

My eyes roll. "That doesn't help."

"What I mean is find a way to stand up for Lucy without everyone knowing. If there's less fuel for the fire, the fire should burn out, right? Pretend to play nice, and they should back off."

I didn't realize doing the right thing would cause an issue with anyone but June. Rubbing the back of my neck, I concede, "Maybe you're right." Maybe defending Lucy so publicly wasn't the way to go.

"Thanks," I say as I squat down to cram my books into my bag. "I'll think about what you said."

"No problem. And if you need to talk, you know where to find me."

I nod.

After Harrison takes off, I decide to head to the gym after all. I should probably go home and get started on homework, but I need to clear my mind first. I won't be able to process anything, let alone calculus or chemistry, unless I work the tension out of my system.

Some people read for an escape, or play video games, or binge Netflix. I need to move.

Approaching the gym, that's all I concentrate on. Moving. I need to change clothes, and as I round the corner to the men's locker room, the door to Coach's office opens ahead of me. Fully expecting a guy to walk out, I freeze when a girl does instead. And it's not just any girl.

It's Allie.

My adrenaline spikes. Why is she talking to Coach?

Never mind. I don't want to know.

Quickly, I turn and duck my head, then start to walk back the way I came. She didn't immediately look in my direction, so hopefully she didn't notice me. Not wanting to take any chances, I step into the doorway of a classroom and lean against the wall. When she walks by without so much as a glance, I think I'm in the clear.

As I try to sneak away in the opposite direction, her voice is loud enough to echo off the empty hallway walls. "Aaron."

I stop in my tracks but refuse to turn around. "Yeah?"

"Are you trying to hide from me?"

Yep. Without looking at her, I leave. Forget the weight room. Forget working out.

I need to get out of here.

FIFTY-SIX STEPS from where I parked my truck, I end up in the only place that makes sense to me.

Seventh section, tenth row, third plot.

Seven ten third.

As I crouch down in front of Cody's headstone, I remember when I committed the numbers to memory. It was right after we carried him from the hearse to the gravesite, when my vision started to blur as we set him down. The minister was droning on and on about a better place and seeing him again one day, and I needed to focus on anything but the scene in front of me. I was angry.

Angry at the minister and ready to tell him his recycled sermon was bullshit. Angry at Allie, who stood at the back of the crowd. Angry at June's attention-seeking sob fest; even Cody's mother wasn't crying that hard.

And angry at myself. I was on the verge of breaking down; my eyes burned with tears like they had been branded with white hot pokers.

My hazy vision cleared when it landed on a white section sign with the black number seven. Even though it was several feet away, it seemed to jump out and scream at me. Instantly I felt panicked, like when I came back here, I'd never find Cody again. So, I started counting. And I kept counting, until the numbers were ingrained in my brain and the service was over.

"Dude," I say out loud. "I could use a little help here."

Falling back on my butt, I sigh and prop my elbows on my knees. Staring out into space, I remember all the one-sided conversations I've had here in the past few months. I sit like that for a while, looking over the top of Cody's stone into the expanse of cemetery behind him. I pretend he can read my mind and silently rehash everything that went down today.

"I don't know what to do," I finally say. "Allie keeps finding me. June is a mess. Our friends are …" I run both hands through my hair in frustration. "I don't even know what to think about them. Do you think Harrison's right? Would the guys really throw a season because they don't approve of how I spend my personal time? That's some petty shit right there." Looking down at the ground, I kick at a clump of grass with my heel. There's a lot at stake if the season tanks. "Maybe I should stay away from Lucy," I mutter.

Just then, the wind blows, rustling the leaves of a dying flower arrangement. The sound draws my attention to a folded piece of paper hiding near the ground. What is that?

As if on cue, my mind conjures Cody out of thin air. He's sitting on top of his headstone sideways, casually, with one leg bent and the other foot touching the ground. He gestures toward the paper as if saying, "Well? Pick it up already."

Curious, I reach for it. Unfolding the note, I find only two words written inside: *I'm sorry.*

Immediately, it clicks. Lucy left this here. How do I know? I recognize her handwriting from yearbook class.

"She says she's sorry," I say aloud to imaginary ghost-Cody. He grimaces and shrugs, like the words hurt but there's nothing he can do. He stares at the ground, looking as apologetic as Lucy sounds.

If he had survived this, I know he wouldn't have blamed Lucy at all. He would've told her the truth about what he was trying to do. Probably not why, but he would've found a way to apologize for involving her. It was his decision to do what he did that night. Not hers.

Standing, I walk back to my truck and search the cab and the floor until I find a pen. When I do, I set the note against the frame of my truck and write *It's not your fault* under her words. Then, I fold the paper back the way I found it.

Returning to my best friend's grave, I watch him give me a thumbs up before disappearing into my imagination. Shaking my head, I slide Lucy's note back where I found it. Maybe I was supposed to find this and answer for Cody. Maybe, if she reads my response, it'll ease some of her guilt.

I want that for her. So bad.

There's only one way I'll know if she's feeling better – I need to stick around. I don't want to stay away from her, no matter what my teammates say. So, no.

Lucy and me, we're in this together.

CHAPTER THIRTEEN

Lucy

"Oh. My. God." Delaney's eyes roll back in her head.

"I told you it was the best mac 'n cheese ever," Izzy says before taking a bite. "Dig in, Lucy," she mumbles with her mouth full.

Stabbing my fork into the food we're sharing, I blow on the noodles while eyeing the best part of my scoop. I managed to snag a big chunk of the crunchy crust they put on top.

"This is a million times better than that frozen slop you two were eating for lunch," Delaney says as she reaches for her glass of water. "Why were you headed down the road to diabetes again?"

"We weren't headed down the road to diabetes," Izzy says. "Lucy just had a bad day, that's all. You can't tell me you've never eaten junk food before."

"Never touch the stuff." Delaney takes a drink from her straw. "I'm actually pretty healthy."

Izzy's skeptical. "Really?"

Delaney nods. "I've never smoked, I don't do drugs, and I won't touch alcohol. Lucy knows why."

As she takes another big bite of our dinner, Izzy looks to me for an explanation. My eyes jump to Delaney. "Jack, Jim, and Johnnie, right?"

"Bingo."

I wasn't sure if that was the real reason or not.

"How is everything here, ladies?" Our waitress stops by to check on us. "Can I get you anything else?"

We all look at each other before Izzy responds, "We're good, thanks."

She refills Delaney's water anyway, and we all stab more macaroni. "So, who are Jack, Jim, and Johnnie?" Izzy asks. "Ex-boyfriends?"

"No," I answer since Delaney is still chewing. "They're brands of whiskey. Delaney's parents are ..." How can I put it gently?

"Alcoholics," Delaney offers without hesitation.

Izzy's face falls. "Oh. I'm sorry."

"Don't be." Delaney shrugs one shoulder. "It's what landed me here with you guys."

Earlier today, at lunch, Delaney told us a move to her aunt and uncle's house brought her to Holton High. She didn't specify the reason behind it, but I had a hunch it had to do with her parents. We ended up spending a lot of time together over the summer completing our community service. Eventually I confessed to why I was there, earning me the nickname Lethal Lucy. She said she wanted a nickname too, so I came up with Delinquent Delaney.

"Speaking of here," Izzy says, "how do you like the tour of our little town so far?" It was her idea to show Delaney around once we found out she used to live thirty minutes away. I also think she used it as an excuse to get me out of the house.

"This restaurant is definitely cool," Delaney says. "Was it really a working fire station?"

"Yep. Until they built the new one around the corner."

"I could see myself working here," she says, eyeing the wood plank ceiling and exposed pipes. "I like the vintage vibe."

"Is that why you drew Marilyn?" I ask, pointing toward the ink on the inside of her forearm.

"Kinda. I drew Elvis, too. Well, part of him anyway."

She points to her other arm. I can barely make out a set of eyes; they're so tightly surrounded by exotic flowers. As usual, her artwork is amazing.

"I ran across one of his old movies before the cable got shut off again," Delaney explains. "It was set in Hawaii."

"How long does it take you to do this?" Izzy asks, setting her fork down and gesturing for Delaney to hand over her arm for inspection. "It would take me forever and look like blobs. I can't even draw a straight line."

"It usually takes me all day because I keep adding things until I run out of skin."

"Then you wipe it off?"

"When I'm ready." Delaney smiles. "It's permanent marker. Rubbing alcohol is required."

Izzy smirks. "I thought you never touched alcohol."

Delaney shoots her a sarcastic look.

The familiar sound of a phone vibrating against the table makes us all pause and look down at our cells. "Not me," Delaney says and spears more mac 'n cheese.

"Not me either." Izzy pushes her phone away. "Lucy?"

I don't know what to say. It's my message all right. But ...

"Luuuuucy," Izzy sings. "Is it your mom?"

No, that would be expected. Squashing my surprise, I turn to face my best friend with pursed lips. "Really? You gave him my number?"

Izzy grins, then leans over with wandering eyes. "Yep. What did he say? Let me see."

"No." I press my phone against my chest so she can't read the screen. "You're in trouble."

"C'mon." She pouts. "He was practically sending up smoke signals to get your attention in class today. I had to give the boy *something* to work with. You were being rude."

"No, I wasn't. I was being safe."

"Safe?" Delaney licks the back of her fork. "Are there other criminals at Holton besides us?"

I glance at her. "Not that I know of."

"June might qualify," Izzy muses, then looks across the table and meets Delaney's eyes. "We should probably warn you now. Stay away from June. She's the definition of the word biatch."

Delaney's brow jumps. "Do tell."

As Izzy starts to explain the situation that is June, I sneak a peek at my phone and Aaron's message: *Hey, Lucy. This is Aaron. Izzy gave me your number.*

It's as tame as tame could be. So why did my stomach flip when I first read it? And what am I supposed to say in return? *Okay, great. See you around. Bye!*

Looking up, I realize Izzy has gone off on a tangent. "Listen," I interrupt, focusing on Delaney. "Let me make this easy. June was Cody's girlfriend."

"The guy you –"

I nod.

"Ahhh. Say no more."

My phone vibrates again, and I glance down at the screen: *Are you there?*

"Is that him?" Izzy scoots closer to me. "What's he saying?"

"He wants to know if I'm getting his messages."

"So say yes," Izzy urges.

"What's the big deal about this guy?" Delaney asks. "Who is he?"

"*He* is Aaron Matthews," Izzy answers before I can. "He's captain of the lacrosse team and the recently crowned homecoming king. And," she wiggles her eyebrows, "he likes Lucy."

"He does not," I protest.

"Please." Izzy gives me a blank stare. "Did you forget what he did for you today? What he did for you at the party? What about your scholarship picture?"

"He's only being nice because he says he knows what I'm going through." At least that's what he told me at Bianca's. "And he wouldn't be texting me now if *you* didn't give him my personal information."

"How would he know what you're going through?" Delaney asks. "Is June being a wench to him, too?"

"Kind of," I say. "She wants to hook up with Aaron, but he doesn't like her."

"Why?"

"Because he was Cody's best friend."

Delaney's eyes grow wide. "Let me get this straight. The guy you bumped off with your car, Colton –"

"Cody," I correct her.

"Cody," she shakes her head, "his girlfriend was June. June's mad at you for what happened to her man, but she wants to get naked with his best friend? And the best friend, Aaron, wants you?"

"Right," Izzy says.

"Wrong," I say. "Aaron doesn't want me. He's just being polite. Honestly, I think he just feels some weird obligation to help." I neglect to mention what he said Saturday night, that things aren't always what they seem. Obviously, there's something I don't know, but the chances of me finding out what it is are slim. I doubt it has anything to do with him quote-unquote "liking" me.

"Well, whatever the reason, answer the guy," Izzy says. "If you don't, I will."

I frown. "How?"

"I know your password."

Ugh. She's right. I stare at the phone and then shoot back a quick response: *Sorry. I'm here. Eating dinner right now.*

"What did you say?"

Izzy is starting to annoy me. "I told him I'm having dinner."

"Argh," she groans and moves back to her plate. "You're failing at flirting."

I stare at her, confused. "Why on earth would I flirt with the hottest guy in school?"

Izzy bounces up and down on the bench seat. "I knew it. You think he's hot."

My eyes roll. "Everyone thinks he's hot."

"Wait, wait, wait." Delaney leans forward. "How good-looking are we talking here? GQ model material or just average high school kid who skipped the awkward acne stage?"

How do I describe Aaron? "Umm … you could say he skipped the awkward stage."

"Pffft," Izzy disagrees. "He didn't skip it, he leapt past it." She points her fork at Delaney. "Think Zac Efron after *High School Musical* but before *Neighbors 2.*"

"But with greener eyes," slips out of my mouth.

Both girls look at me with raised brows. "You have been paying attention," Izzy says with a smile.

My phone vibrates again, and this time Delaney looks just as invested as Izzy. "What'd he say now?"

Reluctantly, I read the message out loud: "Crap. Sorry to interrupt. I'll text you later."

"Nice." Izzy bumps my arm with hers. "I wonder what he wants to talk to you about."

Me, too, I think. Shrugging, I set my phone aside and turn my attention back to my food. I don't want to appear too curious; Izzy and Delaney don't need anything more to speculate. "I guess I'll find out later."

"You'll tell us what he wants, right?" Delaney's eyes light up. "This is kind of like the soap operas my aunt watches. Except its real life which makes it *way* more interesting."

I nod. I'm sure it's no big deal anyway.

Right?

LATER THAT NIGHT, as I get ready for bed, I check my phone for what seems like the hundredth time. Aaron hasn't messaged me again. I shouldn't be disappointed, but I kind of am. I tried to act nonchalant about it earlier, but I really want to know what he had to say. Was he just being friendly? Did he have a yearbook question? Or did he have something worse, like a warning about June?

Sighing, I plug my cell into the charger and leave it on my desk across the room. It has to stay over there, so when the alarm goes off, I have to physically get out of bed to snooze it. Otherwise, I'd sleep until noon and miss half a day of school ... which doesn't sound like a bad thing.

As I crawl beneath my blankets and flop back against the pillow, two faces pop into my head. Both Izzy and Delaney tell me to put my big girl pants on, text Aaron, and ask him what he wanted. My insecure mind responds and says that's not a good idea. He could be sleeping. He could be with friends. He could have forgotten all about me.

Ding.

Faster than I'll ever admit, my phone is in my hand.

Are you still awake?

It's him. I make myself wait a full sixty seconds before responding. I don't want him to think I was waiting around with bated breath or anything.

Yes I type and hit send. Channeling Izzy's earlier flirting comments, I start to overthink my one-word answer. Maybe I should have said, "Yeah. What's up?" or "Yes, but you almost missed me." Not that I'm trying to flirt, but I should at least appear interested.

How was dinner? he asks.

Good, I type. *Can't beat mac and cheese from the Fire Hall.* I'm proud I sent more than the word 'good.'

Lucky, he replies. *That stuff is the best.*

At least we agree on something.

I don't know what to say next, so I bite my lip and wander back over to my bed. Tucking one leg beneath me, I sit down and stare at his words. Are we going to discuss food? Should I tell him my favorite is homemade mashed potatoes?

Izzy told me you don't want people to see us talk, he sends.

Okay. So that's what this is about. *Yeah. I didn't think it was wise. At least for today, anyway.* Which reminds me, I need to thank him for taking care of my locker.

So, it's not a permanent thing?

I pause and wonder if it should be. Then I shake my head and type *No.*

Good, he sends. *You had me worried for a minute.*

I still think it's odd he cares. *Even so,* I say, *I think we should keep our conversations private. We're only a month into the school year, and it's not fun to be a target.*

I hope he realizes that statement applies to both of us. He may not have experienced anything negative yet, but I have a feeling it's going to happen if he keeps putting himself out there for me. There's no reason we should both suffer.

Yeah, he replies. *I received some flak from a pretty unexpected source today. Well, sources.*

My shoulders tense. *See?!*

It's okay.

How?

We'll just have to be more careful.

Instantly, I'm curious. Who said something and what did they say? I want to ask but doubt it's my place. Instead I opt for another question: *What does being careful mean?*

It takes him a minute to respond. *We can text each other. And make eye contact in yearbook.*

I smirk. I didn't realize avoiding him would be a big deal.

And we can acknowledge each other in the hall.

A tiny smile creeps across my face.

And at lunch.

I snicker.

And in the parking lot.

He can stop now. *Ok. Ok. I get it. If I see you, I won't ignore you. But I won't talk to you at school unless it's related to class. Deal?*

Deal, he sends.

After a minute of silence, I assume our conversation is over. I start to type "Have a nice night" when *What are you doing?* appears on my screen.

Deleting what I had, I send *Sitting on my bed texting a weirdo.*

I'm weird??

Yes.

In what universe?

My brow jumps. Someone's a little full of himself. *You're texting a girl you shouldn't be texting. And don't ask why because you know. That makes you weird.*

He shoots back *Is that all you've got?*

Yeah, unfortunately. I don't know him well enough to tease him about anything else. *Basically,* I send.

So you don't know about my obsession with Michael Bublé?

What? Is he kidding? *For real?*

Um ... His response is delayed. *I plead the fifth.*

Aaron Matthews has a thing for old timey music? Not that there's anything wrong with that. I'm sure he listens to other stuff too; you can't get pumped for a game listening to a crooner. *Huh,* I type. *I'll file that information away for a rainy day ;)*

Come on. You have to have some guilty pleasures. Name three.

Three? *What makes you think I have that many?*

Ha. You probably have more.

I don't, but he barely knows me. A lot of things I like may surprise him. After tapping my chin in thought, I settle on *Greta Van Fleet, singing in the shower, and scary movies.*

Immediately *Wait. You're a member of the Peaceful Army?* pops up on my phone.

He knows what that is? *Yes.*

I never would have guessed.

Back at ya, Bublé. Truth is, I didn't like GVF until I stumbled across a song Izzy added to our shared playlist. I wonder how Aaron discovered he liked big band music.

Tell me more about the movies, he sends. *Do you like the gory kind or the kind that mess with your head?*

I like them all. Monster movies, paranormal stuff, even slasher films. *All of the above.*

You must love this time of year.

I do. Ever since I can remember, I've loved the fall. The changing leaves, warm cinnamon sugar doughnuts, hot cider, hay rides. Halloween. *It's my favorite.*

You'll have to give me some recommendations then, he sends. *I don't usually watch scary movies.*

Why not?

Because it's not fun when you don't have a scared girl to jump into your lap.

Does he expect me to believe he has trouble finding a date? *Sorry about your luck,* I type. *Maybe you should ask out a freshman. They all looked frightened the first day of school. A horror movie might give them a heart attack and then you'd have to resuscitate them.*

He sends some crying laughter emoji's. *Like mouth to mouth?*

Of course. What else?

The little text bubble on my phone appears and disappears a few times, telling me he typed something and then changed his mind. Finally, *I wish we were having this conversation in person* shows up on my screen.

Why?

Because I can't imagine you talking about this without blushing.

My face turns red a lot lately, but it's not now. And it doesn't happen only around him. *For the record, I'm not blushing.*

That's too bad, he responds. *I like it when you do.*

I blink a few times. Autocorrect must have kicked in or something because … just … what?

Coherent thoughts refuse to form in my brain as I try to think of something to say. My mind jumps from *Ha ha funny* to *Liar* to *Has your phone been stolen?* I settle on the latter.

No, he sends. *You need to learn how to take a compliment.*

My heart skips a beat. I think it's best to end this conversation before I say something stupid. *I'll work on it but not now,* I send. *It's late, gotta go.*

Okay, he responds. *I'll talk to you later.*

Just as I'm typing "K, 'Night" he sends me one word: *Right?*

Erasing what I wrote, I start to type "Yes" when *Right?* appears again. And again. And again.

OMG stop, I send with a smile. *Yes, you're right. I'll talk to you later.*

Just wanted to be sure, he sends. *You're fun to mess with. Good night.*

Now I am blushing. *'Night.*

CHAPTER FOURTEEN

Aaron

"Can we talk?"

I stare at the ceiling before I slam my locker door shut. After I do, I meet June's wide, blue puppy-dog eyes and say, "No."

"C'mon, Aaron," she pleads. "Please?"

I lean against my locker. It's too early for this. "What do you want?"

"I know you're mad at me." June looks down and twists her fingers together. "I just wanted to say I'm sorry."

"You're sorry?"

She nods.

"For yesterday?"

She nods again.

I study her face, trying to figure her out. I doubt she's being sincere. If she were, she would be apologizing to Lucy, not me.

After a few silent seconds, she clears her throat. "Anyway, I was thinking we could spend some time together. You know. Hang out. So I can make it up to you." She steps closer. "Fall Fest is this weekend. I'll pick you up and everything. Do you want to go?"

"You're not serious."

"Why wouldn't I be serious?"

I can't believe I have to explain it to her. And I'm not going to. Shaking my head, I take a step. "No, June. I don't want to go to Fall Fest with you."

She grabs my arm. "Why not? I said I was sorry."

"Yeah. To the wrong person."

Her mouth falls open, and then her eyes narrow. "I don't get what you see in her."

I see a lot, I think, especially after last night. I got to know more about her, even if our conversation was short. I was kinda bummed when she had to go; I wasn't lying when I said I wished we were talking face to face.

"It doesn't matter what I see," I say. "There's right and there's wrong, and you should know the difference."

"You're not my mother," falls out of her mouth before she snaps it shut. Closing her eyes, she takes a deep breath before opening them again. "Look. I know what we – I – did was wrong. But you left me and wound up with her. I ... I didn't know what to do. I over-reacted."

"You think?" I'm not cutting her any slack. "Just leave her alone. It's not that hard."

She scowls. "I don't understand you. Like, at all. You should be standing up for Cody. Instead you're making friends with his killer."

It takes everything I have not to rip into June. I want to spill Cody's secret so bad. Instead, I lean in close to her. "It was an accident," I say with controlled calm. "Let it go."

"Hey, guys," Harrison appears by my side. "Are we going to class or what?"

"Yep," I say and take a step back.

He smiles at June. "Hey. Where were you yesterday?"

"I was sick." She starts to walk away, even though her attention stays focused on me. "Sick to my stomach."

"That's not cool," Harrison says. "Did you have the flu?"

June leaves without bothering to answer. "Glad you're feeling better!" Harrison calls to her back. He looks at me. "What's her problem?"

I smirk.

"Dude," Harrison says. "I told you you've got to start playing nice."

"I know," I sigh. It's harder to fake than I thought.

As we start to head to class, my eyes stay on June long enough to kick myself. Between the faces her friends are making, her scowl, and her gestures, today might be an interesting day.

———

BY THE TIME lunch rolls around, I haven't seen or heard anything out of the ordinary. I'm glad; maybe I misread the girls.

After dodging a flying piece of pizza crust meant for Jason's face, I take a bite out of my apple and look around. June and her friends are sitting at the end of the table as usual, talking and pointing to something on a phone. Since they seem harmless, and I'm not interested in the food fight, my eyes bounce through the cafeteria to find Lucy. We've only shared one glance today when we passed in the hall.

I'd like another.

It takes me a minute to find her. When I do, she's sitting almost hidden on the opposite side of the cafeteria by the stage. As I take another bite, I watch Izzy and a girl I don't recognize burst into laughter. Lucy only sort of smiles. I frown as I chew. It would be nice if she could just relax once and a while.

Then, as if she senses me, Lucy glances in my direction. Our eyes lock, and I wink behind my apple. She shakes her head, but tries to hide a bigger smile as she looks away. I feel like I won the lottery.

An elbow to the ribs shifts my focus. "Ow. What was that for?"

"Too obvious," Harrison says quietly before shoving chips in his mouth.

"Sorry," I mutter. "Are there places I'm allowed to look?"

He swallows. "I'd start down there."

He nods to his right, and my eyes follow. All of the girls have moved closer to June. Their body language is tense and not at all like it was a minute ago. Suspicious, I decide now is a good time to throw away my garbage. Taking the long way around the table, I toss my tray in the trash closest to them, then kneel behind the barrel and pretend to tie my shoe.

"Casey," June says. "Just go over there and do it."

"Why me?"

"Because you're eating soup. Dump it quick and go."

"Over her head? No way," Casey says. "Everyone will see me. I can't get another detention."

"Ugh," June groans. "Jessie? What about you? How many detentions have you had?"

"I'm not pouring Casey's lunch over Lucy's head." Jessie sounds bored. "This is your hang up, not mine."

"Guys," June whines. "I've been humiliated twice because of her. It's not fair."

"Who said life was fair?"

"Look," Kat interrupts. "None of us want to get in trouble. If you really need our help, we'll have to plan things out like before. We can all go to my house after Fall Fest and come up with ideas."

"I'm not going to Fall Fest if Aaron isn't taking me."

"Why not?" Kat sounds irritated. "We'll all go together. It'll be just as fun as it is every year."

"You don't get it," June says. "He's the best. I'm the best. The *best* go together."

"You're such a spoiled brat."

The group falls silent for a quick second, and all eyes land on Kat before she says, "You know I'm only kidding."

"Then you should do it." June's voice sounds lighter. "Here. Take my drink. It's red; it'll ruin that ugly shirt she's wearing. You'll be doing her a favor."

I can't believe I'm hearing this. *Say no, Kat.*

"I'd rather make plans for other things this weekend," she says. "My parents will ground me if I get caught."

"Fine," June huffs, and I hear feet shuffle. "If none of you will stand up for me, I'll do it myself."

My pulse races. I can't let this happen. I can't let this weekend's "planning" happen, either.

Staying low so they won't see me, I walk away from the table and pull my phone out of my back pocket. Forcing my fingers to type a text I don't want to send, I make it to the cafeteria doors, slip out into the hallway, and find a spot to lean against the wall. My insides sink, but I don't know what else to do.

It only takes a minute for June to find me. "Aaron?"

She's holding her phone in one hand and her drink in the other, which is good news for Lucy. I was pretty sure her plans would change as soon as she read my message: **Meet me in the hall.**

"You wanted to see me?" She asks the question innocently, but the tone doesn't fit her.

"Yeah," I say, pulling together as much remorse as I can. "I've been thinking. I was pretty hard on you this morning."

June tips her head and gives me a sly grin. "Maybe I'll forgive you."

I didn't apologize, I think.

Forcing a smile, I end up with a lame lip twitch instead. She doesn't seem to notice. "Well, if you're still interested, I changed my mind. I'll go with you this weekend, if you want."

"Really?"

"Yes."

She throws herself against me, tossing her arms around my neck and knocking us off balance. Some passing students see us and whistle.

"Let's start over, okay?" She grins up at me. "I meant what I said. I'll pick you up on Saturday. Does five sound good?"

"Yeah." *No.*

"You won't regret this, I promise."

I already do.

"LET'S TRY FOR THE PANDA."

June turns to face me, sliding her arms inside my jacket and winding them around my waist. She shoots me a smile. "He's big enough to snuggle with. If I win him, I'll name him after you."

My jaw tenses. "Please don't."

"Why are you so grumpy?"

"I'm not." Stepping back, I remove her hands. "You seem to keep forgetting we're not dating."

We've been at Fall Fest for less than an hour. So far, I've shrugged off a hug when she picked me up, avoided a kiss when I paid to get in, and pulled my hand out of hers too many times to count. Now this.

"I'm just trying to have a good time." June pouts. "If you didn't want to come, why did you ask me?"

She won't like the truth, so my brain comes up with something basic. "I'm sorry. I have a lot on my mind."

"Like?"

"College."

It's not a total lie. A few days ago, I got a letter from Notre Dame. They said they liked what they saw last season and are looking forward to watching me this spring. Depending on my skills and my grades, I could possibly be offered a spot on their team. In the meantime, I need to get two letters of recommendation and send them my unofficial transcripts plus my SAT scores.

"What's the problem with college?" June's brow furrows. "I thought you had things wrapped up with lacrosse."

"Not yet. I have decisions to make."

"Such as?"

"Where to go, for starters."

June looks like she's dealing with a toddler. "Let me help you. Pick the school that offers you the most money. Problem solved."

"What if their team has a crappy record?" Not that either of my choices do.

"Then go there anyway and save the day." She steps closer and meets my eyes. "Be their hero."

I fight the sarcasm on my tongue. "So, nothing matters but free money?" Although it's a huge bonus.

"Why do you think I'm going to be a Golden Gopher?" Her expression turns serious. "I mean, their team is highly ranked, but can you imagine *me* living in Minnesota? Not my first choice."

Frowning, I forget how to keep my mouth shut. "Then why settle?"

"Because they gave me a full ride to play volleyball."

Makes sense. "Well, that doesn't sound so bad."

"Have you heard about the winters out there?" She shudders. "I don't know how I'm going to look cute bundled up all the time. Maybe you'll have to come visit and keep me warm."

She gives me a flirty smile, but when I don't react, she switches gears. She steps to my side and loops her arm through mine. "Let's forget about college stuff. I need to win that panda. He's *so* adorable."

Reluctantly, I let June lead me over to the nearest midway game, one where you roll a golf ball into different colored holes to move a plastic dog along a race track. Ten people can compete at a time, so while we wait our turn to pay three bucks, I look around the festival to avoid talking to her.

Set up next to a working orchard, Fall Fest has been a town tradition for years. It combines seasonal things like hayrides, corn mazes, cider, and apple pies with a carnival lit up like Vegas. Every year the Ferris wheel is set up next to the Gravitron, which is next to the bumper cars and the Tilt-A-Whirl. The Scrambler and the Fire Ball challenge you to keep down the last thing you ate, while music from local bands fills the air from the beer tent. My stomach always growls as soon as I see the cotton candy, smell the popcorn, and read the signs for deep-fried elephant ears.

"Aaron." I feel a nudge. "Pay the guy."

After the first game, we quickly learn you don't automatically get the big prize when you win. You have to win several smaller prizes and trade up. By the time June finally gets her damn panda, I'm just about bankrupt.

"Thank you so much!" she gushes as she squeezes the stuffing out of the thing. "I have to name him Aaron now."

Can a stuffed animal mock you? Because as June holds him on her hip, I could swear his crooked smile is laughing at me.

"Hey, guys."

Both of us turn around to find Kat, Casey, and the other girls from school.

June's face lights up. "Hi! Look what Aaron won for me. Isn't it the cutest?"

I watch the group "ooo" and "ahh" over the panda. You'd have thought I'd given her a real kitten or something.

"That was nice of you." Kat smiles at me. "I'm too cheap to play any of these games."

"I used to be," I say, meaning I had no choice. One look at June's expression makes me realize she took my words the wrong way. I didn't spend all my money because I like her.

"Where are you going next?" Kat looks between us. "We were going to wait in line for the Fire Ball."

"We'll go with you," June says before her face falls. "Shoot. I didn't really think about rides." She looks at me and then the panda. "What are we going to do with little Aaron? I don't want him to get stolen."

What?! She did not just say that in front of people we know. She makes it sound like we hooked up and had a panda baby.

"Give me your keys," I say quickly. "I'll put him in the car."

"You will?"

"Then I'll come find you." *After I take the longest way there and the slowest way back.*

"You're such a gentleman," June flirts as she hands me the bear.

Temporarily free, I head to the parking lot, crisscrossing a path through the midway because it takes more time. When I drop off the panda, I contemplate taking June's black BMW for a joy ride.

"Probably not a good idea." Cody materializes in my head. He's leaning against the hood of June's car with his arms crossed. "You won't get the same parking spot. How are you going to 'xplain that?"

Groaning, I realize my last resort to stall is to take the opposite way back to June. Cody laughs.

Despite being as crowded as the carnival, the orchard side of Fall Fest is a lot less bright and a lot less noisy. That's why, when I'm smack in the middle of it, the loud sound of a tractor returning from its latest hayride catches my attention. Pausing, I watch the passengers hop off the trailer. One by one they jump to the ground, kids, parents, a dog ... and Lucy.

A smile creeps across my face as I watch her. She follows a group of people I assume are her family as they make their way over to a nearby stand selling donuts. Lucy ends up last in line and suddenly, I'm starving. I only have five dollars left on me, but it's going to be spent on fried dough covered in sugar.

"Having fun?"

Lucy jumps and turns around. "What are you doing?"

"Um ... getting donuts."

She shakes her head and then looks over my shoulder. "Is anyone–?"

"They're all over by the rides," I say, then lean in and whisper, "We're safe."

"Oh. Okay." Her body relaxes, and she shoves her hands in the pockets of her big chunky sweater. "Why are you over here then?"

You don't want to know. "I needed donuts."

She gives me a suspicious look out of the corner of her eye. "I'm pretty sure they sell them by the rides, too."

I shrug, and we move up in the line. "So, are you here with your family?"

She nods. "My parents and grandparents and my brother. We come every year."

"I'm surprised Izzy isn't with you."

"Don't worry. I'm sure she'll try to drag me here tomorrow."

"You don't want to come back?"

Now it's her turn to shrug. "It's ... I'm just ..." She looks at her shoes, then at me. "No. I don't."

I smile. "I always like an honest answer."

"Lucy? Who's your friend?"

We both look at a woman who has to be Lucy's mom. Her hair is the same shade as her daughter's but short, and they look alike despite the age difference. I sense Lucy tense a little beside me.

"Aaron, this is my mom. Mom, Aaron. He's a friend from school."

"Hello, Aaron." Lucy's mother extends her free hand. "I'm Gayle."

"Nice to meet you," I say as I shake it. I feel like I should say something else, so I add, "Your daughter got me interested in yearbook."

"Did she now?" Her smile gets big. "And here I've been told nothing exciting ever happens at school."

"Mom." Lucy shoots her mother a look.

"Would you like a donut?" Gayle reaches into the bag she has tucked under her arm. "We bought a few dozen."

"Oh, no. I was going to get my own."

"Nonsense." She hands me one and gives another to Lucy. "We're going to head over to the corn maze with Will. Meet you back here in, say, half an hour?"

"Meet you?" Lucy looks confused.

"I'm sure you'd rather spend time with your friend." Gayle starts to walk away. "You two have fun."

Lucy opens her mouth to protest, but nothing comes out. As her family leaves her behind, she apologizes. "I'm sorry."

"For what?"

"For getting stuck with me."

Grinning, I say, "I'll survive. You know why?"

"Why?"

"Because I got a free donut."

She smacks my arm as I take a big bite.

We start to walk along the outer edge of the orchard, passing stands for cider and lemonade, baked goods, and homemade crafts. "For real," Lucy finally says. "Your friends will miss you. You should go."

I don't like that she's trying to push me away. I'd rather spend the rest of the night here with her, but I see what she's saying. I'm sure June is freaking out, although I haven't felt my phone vibrate in my pocket. "How about this?" I suggest. "How about you walk with me to where the orchard meets the carnival, and then we go our separate ways?"

She mulls it over for a second. "Okay."

During our walk, we stop to look at different booths, and Lucy tries on some knitted, floppy gloves. "What do you think?" She holds up her hands. "Are they me?"

"Totally." They are her. I don't know why I think so, I just do. The yarn is multicolored but mostly blue, and they look fuzzy and warm. "You should get them," I say.

She shrugs and puts them back. "Maybe." She moves on to a hat that looks like an owl. "I bet Izzy would wear this."

"You wouldn't?"

"Nah. I'm not that brave."

"What about this one?" I hold up a hat that matches the gloves and then put it on. It's plain but lopsided and oversized; it almost covers my eyes.

"Oh, yeah. Definitely. I think it would swallow my head."

"You could use it to go undercover," I say.

She laughs.

We move around the booth looking at things until we get separated on either side. I can still see her across the way, so when a guy I recognize from school finds her, I notice.

"Oh, hey Nick," I hear her say.

"I saw you over here and thought I'd say hi," he says. "Are you all by yourself?"

Her eyes dart to mine, then quickly to Nick. "No, I'm here with my parents. They took my brother to the maze, so I thought I'd look around."

"Gotcha."

Lucy turns her attention back to the scarf in front of her, and Nick clears his throat before asking her about it. "That would be a good color on you."

"You think?"

"Here." He holds out his hands. "Let's see."

Lucy gives him the scarf, and he loops it around her neck. She adjusts it and he helps, his finger getting caught in her hair in the process. They awkwardly laugh it off, and Lucy looks embarrassed when he starts to tell her how right he was.

He likes her.

The realization bothers me. I know it shouldn't; Lucy can be friends with whomever she wants. Still, the longer they talk, the more I don't like what I see. I fight the urge to interrupt them, to make him aware I'm here, but I don't think she wants anyone to know.

Finally, after a few minutes, Nick gets pulled away by some other people from school. He asks Lucy, "Do you want to come with us?"

"Thanks, but I can't," she says. "I have to meet up with my family soon."

"Oh. Well, see you Monday."

"'Kay."

Her refusal makes me smile. It makes me think, in some convoluted way, she'd rather spend her time with me.

Suddenly, an idea to test that theory jumps into my head. It'll probably backfire, but I can't stop myself. Once I make it over to Lucy's side, I ask, "Friend of yours?"

"I guess so. We hung out a few times before … you know. Last spring."

"Were you two …?"

"Together?" Her brow jumps. "No. Not even close."

That makes me feel better. "So, since you don't want to come back to Fall Fest tomorrow, did you hear about the scary movie marathon?"

"There's a marathon?"

"Yep. All day. Do you want to go?"

She looks surprised. "With you?"

I nod.

"To watch scary movies?"

I nod again.

"Where is it?"

"My house." I try to act casual. "What do you say?"

CHAPTER FIFTEEN

Lucy

I said yes.

I freaking said yes.

Why did I say yes?

With the exception of the radio, silence fills the cab of Aaron's truck. Last night, after I got home from Fall Fest, I thought he'd come to his senses and cancel the movies. He didn't. Instead, he picked me up at noon just like he said he would. Now, I'm on my way to his house, questioning my sanity.

My cell buzzes in my hand, earning me a curious look from Aaron. "Sorry," I say. "It's just Izzy."

He smiles. "She's losing her mind, isn't she?"

"How'd you know?"

"My gut instincts are rarely wrong."

I glance down at my phone. I want to ask him what his instincts say about me. I keep quiet though, because I don't want him to ask me the same thing. My gut isn't being very clear. The ball of nerves in my stomach is a weird mix of anxiety and butterflies.

"What does she want?" Aaron asks as we stop at a light.

"It's her and Delaney, actually," I say. "You know, the new girl."

He nods. "With the tattoos."

"They're not real."

"I remember."

Aaron asked me who Delaney was a few days ago, after he saw us sitting together at lunch. True to our deal, we only talk in school about class-related things, so when he messaged me about her, I responded.

Aaron taps his thumbs on the steering wheel in time with the music. "So, what do they want?"

"They want to know what I decided to wear."

"You had choices?"

"No, I had opinions." My nose scrunches. "They wanted me to dress up." Among other things. They also tried to get me to admit I was secretly crushing on Aaron.

"Dress up?" Aaron frowns as the light turns green. "We're watching movies, not going to prom."

"That's what I said." Really. It's exactly what I told them. I type *Skinny jeans for the win* and imagine their sad faces.

After we turn a few corners, I realize where we're headed. "You live on Holton Lake?"

"Yes. Is that a problem?"

"No, it's just ..."

"It's just what?"

What word can I use? "Swanky." It's true. The biggest houses in this town are on Holton Lake.

"Swanky?" Aaron scoffs. "Says the girl with the classic Corvette parked in her driveway."

Now it's my turn to snicker. "My dad likes to fix up old cars."

"It's a pretty sweet ride. Do you ever get to drive it?"

"Heck no. I don't drive anything anymore." Especially my dad's baby.

We don't say much else until Aaron pulls into his driveway and parks in front of a small mansion. Looking out my side window, I stare up at two stories of beige brick with a massive front porch. Martha Stewart must have just left. I've never seen so many hay bales, cornstalks, grapevine garlands, and colorful gourds in one place. If their fall decorations look like this, Christmas must be an extravaganza.

"What did you mean?"

I peel my eyes away. "About what?"

"You said you don't drive anything anymore."

Crap. I didn't mean to confess that. "Um … it means …" I turn my phone over and pick at the corner of the case. "It means I don't drive. Since … you know."

I hear the rattle of Aaron's keys as he takes them out of the ignition. "Ever? Not even to school?"

My shoulders shrug. "Izzy picks me up."

"Every day?"

His voice betrays his thoughts, so I look at him. Yep. He thinks I'm nuts. "She's cool with it," I explain. "She knows things will go back to normal eventually."

Aaron looks as if what I said makes zero sense. After a second or two, he rearranges his features. "If you ever need a ride, let me know."

"Oh, that would go over real well." I get sarcastic. "We can't even look at each other in the hallway without causing chaos."

"We look at each other." He gets defensive, then admits, "Secretly."

"Exactly my point."

Aaron opens the truck door. "Well, you could always hide when we pull into school. I'll walk in first, and you can sneak in later."

"Now that," I point at him, "*does not* sound like fun."

He grins as he jumps out of the cab. "C'mon."

Walking beside each other, we make our way through the garage and into his house. As soon as we step inside, I'm standing in a mud room connected to the kitchen. Aaron takes off his shoes, so I do, too.

"Let me give you the quick tour," he says, walking backward. "This is where we keep the food."

My eyes bounce around the kitchen, from the stainless-steel appliances, to the white cupboards, to the breakfast nook. There's a pile of mail sitting on the counter next to a bowl of oranges and bananas, and small pots of labeled herbs sit on the windowsill over the sink.

"Up there," Aaron points to a wide staircase, "are the bedrooms, and over here," we round the stairs, "is the living room."

My jaw drops. Not only does every piece of furniture in here look soft and cozy, huge windows cover the back wall of the room. From the cream-colored carpeting all the way up to the vaulted ceiling, they have an almost panoramic view of the lake.

"Wow," I say and walk forward to get a closer look. Glancing down, I see a stone patio scattered with dry leaves a floor below us. Matching stone steps lead to the lake shore where there's a dock, but no boat. The sun reflecting off the water catches my eye. If I lived here, I would waste a lot of time looking out these windows.

Aaron walks up behind me. "Do you see something?"

"Water. Trees. Sun." I look over my shoulder. "Does this view ever hypnotize you?"

"Sometimes." He shrugs. "I like it when the sun goes down. The colors can be cool."

"You're into sunsets?"

"Isn't everyone?"

"Look out!"

Both of us turn to see a soccer ball bounce over the staircase railing and fly in the direction of our heads. I duck as Aaron swats it away. "What did mom say about kicking balls down the stairs?"

A younger girl practically slides down the steps. "Sorry! I thought I could stop it."

"Well, you didn't." Aaron leans over and grabs the ball off the floor. He bounces it back in the girl's direction, and she catches it. "Go outside with that. You're going to break something."

"I won't," she protests.

"Really? You almost broke Lucy's nose."

"The worst she would have gotten was a bruise." The girl gives Aaron an irritated glance and stops walking in front of me. "Even though that wouldn't have been cool."

Aaron sighs. "Lucy, meet my sister, Ayden."

"Hey," we both say at the same time.

Aaron puts his hand against my lower back and nudges me forward. "We'll be downstairs. Don't let anyone bug us, okay?"

"Fine." Ayden drops the soccer ball on the carpet and catches it under her foot. "Since when do you have a girlfriend?"

My eyes jump to Aaron, expecting him to correct her. Instead, he says, "Since it's none of your business."

My heart skips, which I didn't expect. I let him show me to a door off the living room which hides stairs to the lower level of the house. When we reach the bottom, I step into a more relaxed, yet completely tricked out living area.

"Sorry about my sister," he says. "What do you want to drink?"

"Ah ..." I'm still trying to figure out his last comment. "I'm not your girlfriend."

"I don't think we have that." His expression twists. "Does it come in bottles or cans?"

"Very funny."

He smiles as I look around, taking in the theater seating in front of the huge TV, the foosball and ping pong tables, the dart board next to a pinball machine, the glass doors leading to the patio I saw from above, and the bar standing in front of a mini-kitchen.

"What did you want me to tell her?" Aaron asks as he walks away. He opens the fridge and leans inside. "She's thirteen; she doesn't need details. You're a girl, and you're a friend. End of story."

I nod, even though he's not looking at me. It makes sense ... I guess.

While Aaron grabs drinks, pictures on the wall catch my eye. There are two almost life-size decals, one of Aaron mid-run in his lacrosse gear and one of Ayden mid-kick in her soccer uniform. Hanging in between them are a bunch of framed photos, so I shove my hands in my back pockets and wander over to take a look. There's an adorable one of both kids when they were little, hugging on the beach.

"I bet your friends love looking at these when they come over," I say, spotting one where diapers are involved.

"Yeah, yeah," Aaron says as I hear the refrigerator door shut. "They're used to them by now, thankfully."

I take a few steps and my eyes land on another picture, one of two boys wearing different Little League uniforms and making faces at each other. They look like they could be related, and I find another one of the same two kids, this time decked out for Scouts and holding birdhouses. And then there's another, both boys flexing their pre-teen muscles wearing swim shorts.

"Is this a cousin of yours?"

As soon as the question is out of my mouth, my stomach drops. I know who it is. My eyes bounce from frame to frame, finding Cody practically everywhere.

"Shit." Aaron suddenly appears by my side. He starts reaching for pictures. "I'm sorry; I meant to take these down."

I'm frozen for a second while he collects a stack of frames in his hands. "No." I reach out and touch his arm. "Stop. You don't have to rearrange your house for me."

"But –"

"It's okay."

He frowns. "Are you sure?"

"Yeah." Now that I know they're here, I just won't look at them. "Pictures don't ... they don't really bother me. It's ... other things." I don't want him to think I'm lying, so I reach for the last frame he took down and hang it back on the wall. "See?"

Aaron blinks, then nods. As we work together to put back the photos, he quietly asks, "What other things?"

"Hmm?"

"What other things bother you?"

I hesitate, biting my lip. I'm not sure I want him to know. I already told him one secret when I said I didn't drive; I'd rather not discuss everything that's wrong with me.

After he hangs the last picture, Aaron meets my eyes. "I have nightmares," he quietly confesses. "Almost every night. I wake up in a cold sweat, and my heart wants to explode." He pauses and runs his hand through his hair. "So ... that's what bothers me."

My forehead creases. "Have you talked to anyone about it?"

"Like who?"

"Like a doctor."

"No." He shakes his head. "Have you talked to anyone about what bothers you?"

Again, I hesitate. Do I want to tell him? He shared something personal with me. I open my mouth, but the words get stuck. "I – I – yes."

His brow jumps. "Izzy?"

"Well, yeah." I wrap my arms around my waist and look at the ground. "And Dr. Marie."

"Who?"

"My … therapist." I cannot believe those words came out of my mouth.

I look up to gauge his reaction. I'm sure he's ready to take me home now, scary movies be damned. If I really wanted to freak him out, I'd also tell him I have meds I don't take and I sometimes leave letters on his best friend's grave.

Instead of slowly backing away from me, he moves closer. "Does it help?"

I shrug. "She asks a lot of questions, and I usually don't have any answers. But we talk, so I guess that's a good thing."

We're quiet for a minute and he studies my face, concern written all over his. It's awkward, and my thoughts jump back to what he told me. I feel awful, knowing I'm probably featured in his bad dreams. Why would he want to be around me if that's true?

"I'm sorry about your nightmares," I say. "If it weren't for me–"

"They're not your fault."

"But they kinda are."

Aaron tenses before he sighs. "Don't you remember what I told you? Things aren't always what they seem."

I do remember, but I'm still confused. "So … you're telling me your dreams are about rabid bunnies and not that night at the Field?"

He smirks. "Did you just say rabid bunnies?"

"I did."

"Does that mean we're watching *Pet Sematary* first?"

Now it's my turn to sigh. "Does that mean you're avoiding my question?"

It takes him a moment to respond. "No."

Aaron walks over to the bar and picks up the two cans he had set down before he ran over to my side. Returning to me, he gives me one. "My nightmares are about a guy who should've done more and didn't."

Before I can say anything, he walks past me and toward the TV. "I figured we could search for movies."

Okay. Apparently, we're changing the subject.

I follow behind him, grateful we've moved on. I'm also a little surprised he still wants to go through with this. I watch as he picks up various remotes and controllers, turning on the entertainment system and navigating to Netflix.

"So, I checked, and they have this whole horror section," he says and looks at me. "What are you in the mood to watch?"

I really don't know. "How about we randomly choose? Just scroll and stop."

"Okay. We'll close our eyes, and you say when."

I nod and play along. After he says, "'Kay, go," I count to ten in my head and say, "Stop."

We open our eyes and see we've landed on the original *Scream* from 1996. It's older than we are, but still a good movie.

I turn around to sit down and notice four seats make up the row of theater seating – two recliners on the end are connected by consoles to a loveseat in the middle. I opt for the recliner closest to me, setting my drink in the built-in cup holder. I expect Aaron to take the other end, but instead he sits in the middle on the loveseat, leaving a console and a cushion between us. He looks over at me, kind of smiles, and hits play.

"Oh, wait," he says as the opening begins. He jumps up, runs to the wall, and dims the lights. Then, he closes the blinds over the patio doors. "Scary movies and bright light don't go together."

He returns but not to his original seat. I swallow as he moves one closer, and now we're only separated by the console. *You know what else doesn't go together?* I think. *Us.* I can't describe this situation; I can't wrap my head around it. On what planet is this my life?

"Is it too loud?" Aaron asks after the first bloody, screaming scene is over.

"No." It's definitely loud, but I chalk it up to the expensive sound system hooked up to the TV. "I hope your sister doesn't think we're the ones killing each other down here, though."

"Nah." He shakes his head. "I doubt she's even paying attention. She's either outside practicing or up in her room."

Speaking of his family ... "Where are your parents?"

"My dad left this morning for a work conference, and my mom went with her friends to check out the craft stuff at Fall Fest. I'm sure they're shopping or brunching, or whatever it is they do."

"Oh. That sounds nice." I mentally kick myself for sounding lame.

We fall silent, getting pulled into the movie. After a while, I sneak a look at Aaron. I know I shouldn't, but I let my mind wonder what it would be like to be a normal girl on a real date with him. There's no question he's cute, he's nice, he's smart ... if he had legit asked me out the same time last year, I probably would have fainted.

"Are you staring at me?"

Oh shit. "No – no. Nope."

Aaron grins. "Methinks the girl protests too much."

My expression twists. "Did you just try to quote Shakespeare?"

"Yeah," he laughs. "I think I screwed it up."

"You did screw it up."

I shift my weight and focus back on the movie, trying to pretend nothing happened.

"You were totally staring at me."

My jaw drops. "How are you going to call me out like that? I wasn't staring. I was ... I was checking to see if you were awake."

He leans toward me. "It's okay. I ...," he hesitates, "I was checking you out upstairs when you were looking out the windows."

Oh my god. "Seriously?"

"And before you ask, yes I'm being honest and no, I don't know what I'm doing."

He looks sincere. I blink, then mumble, "Same."

He looks back at the TV, so I do too, although I don't think either of us are really watching what's on the screen. My thoughts bounce to a million different places. Did we just accidentally admit something to each other?

We don't speak for the rest of the movie. As the end credits begin to roll, I'm willing to bet our "marathon" has turned into a "one-a-thon." I wonder what excuse he'll use to take me home, not that I'll argue. Maybe I should volunteer to go and save him the headache.

Aaron grabs the remote and pauses the TV. Turning to me, he asks, "Are you hungry?"

"What?"

"Are you hungry? I need to eat before the next movie."

He stands and stretches, then his stomach growls. I can hear it because it's only a few feet from my face.

"Um, sure." I guess I'm not leaving. "What did you have in mind?"

"Pizza?" he suggests. "We could have it delivered."

"Okay." I start to push myself out of the chair, but I've sunken into it after two hours. Aaron holds out his hand to help me, and I grab it. "Thanks."

Once he pulls me to stand, he laces his fingers through mine and starts to walk toward the stairs without letting me go. I'm surprised, but I roll with it. I don't want to yank my hand away. Besides, it's kind of nice.

We're halfway up the stairs when we hear Ayden yell, "He said he didn't want to be bothered!"

The door is flung open, and both Aaron and I freeze. June sprints down two steps before she stops and sees us. My heart starts to pound as her eyes flash, landing on our joined hands.

"You have *got* to be kidding me," she snaps. "I thought your sister was lying."

"What are you doing here?" Aaron sounds annoyed.

"What am *I* doing here?" June points at her chest. "What is *she* doing here?"

"That's none of your business. You can't just come over whenever you feel like it."

"Oh, really?" She pulls out her phone and starts rapidly texting. "Did you forget we went out last night?"

Whoa. Wait. What?

Aaron's eyes widen. "You know it wasn't like that."

"Could've fooled me."

Before he can react, June takes a picture of us with her cell. "Now everyone's going to know what an asshole you are."

"June –"

"Don't talk to me!" She starts to leave but turns around when she reaches the top step. Her eyes bore into mine. "You have no idea what's coming."

"Wait," Aaron says just as June runs up the remaining steps. He lets go of my hand and sprints after her, leaving me alone in his basement stairwell.

Did I hear her right? The two of them went out last night? Fall Fest was a *date*?

Feeling like the biggest idiot, I cross my arms and slowly walk to the top of the stairs, peeking around the door awkwardly. I can hear Aaron and June arguing; it sounds like they're outside. I take a few measured steps into the living room. How am I going to get out of here? Is there a back door I can sneak out of?

"He doesn't like her, you know."

Startled, I look over to see Aaron's sister standing between the living room and the kitchen, bouncing her soccer ball from knee to knee while watching her brother out the window.

"Whenever she used to come over with Cody, Aaron was always making faces behind her back." Ayden catches her ball and looks at me. "Everyone ignored me, but I saw things. She's not his favorite person."

Well, that makes me feel a little better. I barely get out the word "Thanks" before Aaron comes marching back in the house. He pauses when he sees me, then comes closer.

"Please don't listen to her," he says. "June has some twisted ideas about us, but none of it is true. She had no right to threaten you like that."

It's kind of her MO. "What would be weird is if she didn't threaten me," I say.

"Still ..." Aaron looks frustrated. "I'm sorry."

I shrug. "So ... did you take her to Fall Fest last night?"

He closes his eyes for a few seconds, then opens them again. "Technically, she took me. And I kept telling her it meant nothing."

I look down. Why does this disappoint me? It shouldn't. He doesn't owe me an explanation. Who am I to him?

"So," Aaron sounds uncertain. "Do you still want to hang out? I can order that pizza."

"I want pizza!" Ayden speaks up from behind us.

He shoots his sister a look before directing his attention back to me. "Lucy?"

It would be easier to just go, but I don't want to disappoint Ayden. "Sure," I say with a weak smile.

From the look on Aaron's face, I can tell he knows I'm only staying for her.

CHAPTER SIXTEEN

Aaron

Looking over my shoulder, I'm suspicious of everyone and everything. It's Monday morning, and locker doors open and slam shut around me. I'm waiting for June's threat to drop. I don't know what it is or when it will happen, but I'd like to intercept it if I can.

"I've got nothing," Harrison says, walking up beside me. He pulls out his phone. "No one is talking."

I grab my stuff for first period, then lean against my locker. "That's what bothers me."

The two of us stand side by side as our eyes sweep the hallway. When June got pissed after homecoming, she let anyone and everyone know about it. Now, she's silent.

"Have you talked to Lucy?" Harrison asks.

"No."

June's visit brought an abrupt end to our movie marathon. Lucy asked me to take her home after we ate and I understood why, even though I didn't want her to go. She even tried to call Izzy to pick her up, but I managed to convince her to let me take her home. The drive was pretty quiet, and I have no idea what she thinks about me. It wasn't the way I wanted the day to end – not by a long shot.

"Thanks for looking out," I tell Harrison. "You're the only eyes and ears I trust right now."

He claps me on the shoulder. "I've got you, man. You know how I feel about things."

I nod. After I dropped Lucy off, I remembered my conversation with Harrison and recruited him for recon. It's a given Izzy and Delaney will be looking out for Lucy too, so hopefully the four of us will be able to head off any June-related bullshit without anyone really knowing.

"I'd better get moving," Harrison says. "We shouldn't be seen together much if our friends decide to be honest with me."

I agree. "Talk to you later."

He blends in with a group of people before casually walking over to where most of our team is standing. I shift my attention down the hall toward Lucy's locker and see her there with Izzy and Delaney. I admire the fact she showed up today. I would have skipped, even though there's no telling when June will make good on her words.

The warning bell rings, and everyone starts to shuffle to class. As I head to chemistry, I catch June and Kat, along with Jessie and Casey, come out of the girl's bathroom at the same time. They aren't talking, which hits me as strange. I turn my back as they pass by, then walk around the nearest corner once they're gone. My subconscious tells me I need to check out that bathroom.

When the final bell rings, I wait a few extra seconds and then look both ways to see if the hall is clear. Quickly, I walk to the bathroom and sneak inside; I just need to see if there's anything there. Taking a few steps down the row of stalls, the squeak from my sneakers is the only sound in the empty space. I see doors, mirrors, sinks – but nothing about Lucy.

Relieved, I turn to go to class when the bathroom door starts to open in front of me. I'm frozen for a quick second before I try to hide in one of the stalls. I don't make it.

"I thought I saw you come in here."

Taking a deep breath, I let out an annoyed sigh. Of course Allie would show up.

Cody materializes beside me, looking just as annoyed. *You know this is all your fault, right?* I ask him silently. His imaginary eyes dart to mine, then back to the door.

She squints. "Why are you in the girl's bathroom?"

"I took a wrong turn."

"Really? How many years have you gone to this school?"

I start to walk past her. "I wasn't paying attention."

She backs up and stands just outside the door, enough for me to exit but not walk away.

"I'm late," I say.

"Why were you in there?" She tips her head. "I'd think you would know it's wrong."

I sigh. "I saw someone leave who threatened one of my friends. I wanted to make sure she didn't do anything."

"Who was threatened? If it's serious, you should report it."

Frustrated, I rub my face with the palm of my hand. "If I told you, you wouldn't care."

Her expression twists. "Of course I would."

We're silent as we stare at each other. She won't let me leave, and I'm not going to push her aside. Should I tell her who it is? Or text someone for help? Unfortunately, the only one who could help me would be Cody. Anyone else would be confused as hell.

"Seriously, I'm missing chem–"

"It's Lucy, isn't it?" she asks.

I don't answer.

"It has to be. Someone messed with her locker last week."

"Great detective work. Happy now?"

"You're friends with her?"

I can't place her expression. Is it surprise? Or is she annoyed? "Yes. Is that a crime?"

"Well, no, but –"

My eyes narrow. "Don't go there."

Allie steps back a little. "I'm sorry. I didn't mean ... it just seems ..."

"Weird? You know what else is weird? You holding me hostage outside this bathroom."

"I'm not–"

"You are."

She scowls and sarcastically gestures to the side. "You're free to go."

I step around her and don't look back.

We have a problem.

My phone vibrates with five minutes left in second period. Holding it beneath my desk, I'm in the middle of typing *What?* when Harrison sends a picture. It's of Lucy wearing next to nothing with the word "SLUT" scrawled across the bottom. It's obviously been photo-shopped. Anger makes my pulse race.

I'll find you after class, Harrison sends.

Once I'm out of English, I scan the hallway looking for him. As I do, I notice a lot of people looking at their phones. I didn't get Lucy's picture directly, so it's obvious I was skipped on purpose. How did June get everyone's number? Harrison appears out of the crowd and jerks his chin. "C'mon."

We walk to a smaller, less crowded area where there is only one row of lockers. He pulls out his cell. "My phone started blowing up with notifications that people were liking a new post."

He shows me the screen. It's the @RIPCodyC Instagram account started back in May. I have no idea who created it because back then I didn't care; I deleted the app and stopped looking at that stuff.

"Can I see?"

Harrison lets me take his phone and scroll through the pictures posted. The only shitty one is of Lucy; all the others are of Cody. There are posed team pictures, most likely taken from past yearbooks, action lacrosse shots, and candid photos with friends. I'm in a bunch of them.

"Whose account is this?"

"I thought some guys from the team started it, but anyone with the password can sign in."

"Aaron."

I turn around at the sound of Izzy's voice and see her standing behind me with Delaney. "Have you seen this?" she asks, irritated and holding out her phone.

"Unfortunately," I say. "Where's Lucy?"

"I don't know. She walked out of class and disappeared." Izzy looks around. "She hasn't answered my messages, although it's only been maybe ten minutes since she saw this."

"Do you know where she could have gone?"

"Not far. She doesn't have a car."

I give Harrison his phone back, pull out mine, and send *Where are you?* to Lucy.

Delaney steps ahead of Izzy, anger in her eyes. "June is behind this, right?"

"I think that's safe to assume," I answer.

"So, what are we going to do about it?"

"Do?" Harrison squints.

"Yes; we can't let her get away with this." Delaney looks at Izzy. "We need to stand up for her."

"I'm in," Izzy says without hesitation. "Do you have something in mind?"

"Oh, yeah." Delaney looks from me to Harrison. "Will you two help?"

I nod, answering for my friend. "What do you need?"

"A place where I can be left alone for few minutes. We'll take care of the rest."

Harrison and I look at each the other. "The weight room?" I suggest.

"We could stand guard," he says.

The bell rings, reminding us we need to get to third period, and we all start walking. When we need to split off in different directions, Delaney says, "Wait about twenty minutes and then ask to use the hall pass. I'll meet you all there."

We agree, and I rush to my locker to trade my English stuff for calculus. Once I'm in my seat, I check my phone. No answer from Lucy.

At least tell me you're okay, I send. *Please.*

The next twenty minutes tick by slowly, but when they're up, so am I. Headed to the weight room holding the ancient calculator pass, I run into Harrison halfway.

"What do you think Delaney is up to?" he asks.

"Whatever it is, I'm down. June needs a kick in the ass."

Harrison nods. "The comments on Lucy's picture are all over the place."

What? That didn't even cross my mind. Frowning, I gesture for him to hand over his phone again, and he does. The reactions to Lucy being called a slut are adding up. They range from the innocent "Yeah, right" and "LOL whatever" to "Whoever posted this should take it down" and "What does this have to do with Cody?" Then there are the ones that make my blood boil.

"I'd get with that."

"What's her number?"

"I knew it."

"Bad girls turn me on."

Are these people for real?

When we arrive at the weight room, Delaney and Izzy are rounding the opposite corner. Delaney is carrying a backpack, and Izzy has a big roll of paper tucked under her arm. I arch an eyebrow in question.

"It was left over from making yearbook signs," she explains.

"Let me make sure there's no one in here," Harrison says and disappears through the weight room door. He reappears moments later. "All clear."

As the girls walk by us, I stop Izzy. "Have you heard from Lucy?"

She shakes her head. "If she doesn't answer, I'm going to leave and look for her."

I nod. I might do that, too.

Leaning against the wall, I drum my fingers against my leg while Harrison paces. It's obvious Delaney is making a sign, but of what? As time passes, I start to fidget. I have no idea what excuse we'll use if a teacher walks by. I suppose we could all hide in the weight room–

"So," Harrison interrupts my evacuation planning. "She's cute, huh?"

"Who?"

"Delaney." He wiggles his eyebrows. "I've never talked to her before. She's got that whole badass-with-a-good-heart-thing going on."

I have to agree she has a take-no-prisoner's attitude, which is kinda hot. "Yeah. You should ask her out."

"You think?"

My phone buzzes, distracting me. When I look at the screen, I'm relieved. Lucy finally texted back: *You guys are going to get into trouble. Tell Izzy to stop her.*

A picture appears beneath the words, and I see Delaney in the weight room smirking next to her drawing. As I make the picture bigger, I smile. Lucy told me Delaney's artwork was good, and this is awesome. She's drawn a huge caricature of June, lying on her stomach kicking and screaming. There's a laptop and a cell phone in front of her, and the thought bubble above her head reads, "Someone pay attention to me!"

Shrinking the picture, I type *Nope* back to Lucy. *June deserves this.*

I agree, she sends, *but my friends don't need detention.*

Who says they're going to get caught?

I do.

Not if we're fast enough, I think.

"What's up?" Harrison asks. "Is that Lucy?"

I nod and show him my screen. Judging from the picture she sent, Delaney has to be almost done, if not finished, with her drawing. Using my elbow, I crack open the weight room door. "You guys ready?"

"We're coming," I hear Izzy say, then see her and Delaney round the tiled half-wall that blocks the view into the room from the door. "Did you hear from Lucy?" she asks.

"Yep. She wants me to stop you."

"Not on her life," Delaney says as they step out into the hallway. "This masterpiece deserves to be seen. Where's June's locker?"

Harrison wastes no time volunteering to help. "Follow me."

As they take off down the hallway, Izzy and I fall into step behind them. "I knew she'd get ahold of us if she saw what we were doing," she says. "Did she tell you where she was?"

"No."

"You should find out." Izzy gives me a knowing smile. "I bet she'd like some company, if you know what I mean."

I don't know what she means. I shoot her a confused look, and she sighs.

"She likes you, Aaron. Even if she won't admit it."

I feel my brow jump. She likes me even after what happened yesterday? I like this news. "How do you know?"

"Because girls know these things." She holds up her hand like it's obvious. "Just like Lucy knew I liked Wes before I knew I liked Wes. As far as I was concerned, I just really liked the way his butt looked in his jeans."

I try not to laugh. "Wes as in Wes Mendes on my lacrosse team?"

"Are there any other Wes' who go to Holton?"

I shake my head. "Does he know this?"

"Yeah." She scrunches her nose. "He asked me to homecoming, but I said no so Lucy wouldn't be alone. He hasn't really talked to me since."

The weight of what she did settles over me. I stop walking, so Izzy does, too. "You're a really good friend. I mean it. I'll talk to Wes."

Her eyes get big. "What are you going to say?"

"That he's an ass, and you didn't blow him off; you had a good reason."

She looks a little panicked. "Don't make it sound like I'm mad. I'm just curious if he's still interested."

I smile. "I'll find out for you."

She grins back, and we start walking again. Delaney and Harrison are way ahead of us, almost to June's locker.

"So, what's the plan? Hang the sign and go?"

"*We're* going to hang the sign up really high and go," she says. "Harrison's tall, and Delaney can sit on his shoulders. I've got the tape." She pats the backpack she's carrying.

Harrison will like that, I think. "What do you mean 'we're'?"

Izzy looks at my hand. "You're going to return that hall pass, pretend to be sick, and find Lucy."

"I am?"

She gets sarcastic. "Please. You'd rather stay here?"

She's right.

"Besides, someone should be with her. After me, you're the next best choice. I'll stick around and rein in the yearbook staff."

Sounds logical. When we get to my math class, I pause outside the door as Izzy joins Harrison and Delaney who have stopped walking. They're pointing to an open area between the top of June's locker and the ceiling. Izzy turns around and gestures, shooing me back into class. "Get going," she mouths.

Holding my side, I try to will my skin to look pale and open the door.

IT DIDN'T TAKE much to convince Mrs. Moreno I wasn't feeling well. I've never tried to fake sick before, so I think my past record worked in my favor.

On my way out of school, the empty hallway displayed Delaney's sign like a huge billboard above June's locker. There was no evidence of who put it there, so I was pretty sure we'd gotten away with it. Unless, of course, the other three were already sitting in Mr. Hughes' office. I kind of wished I'd been around to see June's reaction, but then again, no. I was positive I knew what it would be.

Now, sitting outside in the parking lot, I'm waiting for Lucy to respond to my message: *I couldn't stop them.* I figured it would get her attention. I can see the message was delivered, but she hasn't read it yet.

Starting my truck, I mess with the radio while I debate driving around town without any real destination. What Izzy said replays in my head; she said she thinks Lucy likes me. I wonder what that means. Am I just growing on her, or is it more? Could she be into me? She's so cautious when we're together. I mean, I get it; I know why. And I haven't exactly been forward with her, either.

My phone buzzes in my lap. *You didn't even try to stop them, did you?*

Guilty as charged. *It's fine. No one suspects anything.*

Has anyone seen it yet?

Not that I know of. Third period ends soon, though.

Seconds pass while I wait for another response. How am I going to get her to tell me where she is?

Just ask, dumbass.

As I start typing, another message comes through. *I know I shouldn't care but ... tell me what happens.*

I erase what I started and type *Can't. I'm not at school anymore.*

What? Why?

I faked sick so I could find you.

There. Now she should tell me –

Seriously? Now I have that guilt, too? Thanks a lot.

I frown. She doesn't sound close to liking me *at all* right now. *It was my choice,* I send. *Don't get crabby.*

Staring at my phone, I curse and wish for an undo button. I sent that last sentence without thinking. She's already upset; why not call her names, too? I meant it in a joking way, but –

Really? Crabby? You haven't even SEEN crabby.

A smile creeps across my face. Okay, she's irritated but not completely mad. How can I ...

I'd like to see it, I send. *Where are you?*

She types, then stops, types, then stops. Finally, *Nice try. You'll never find me* appears on my screen.

Fine. I'll just go to your house and wait there. Gayle and I can have a nice chat if she's home. Did I just remember her mom's name and use the word 'chat'?

Lucy sends me a mad, red-face emoji. *I don't understand what the big deal is. Can't I just be alone?*

No, I think. My mind jumps to Cody. I left him alone. Not that Lucy is in the same mindset he was … or is she? I never knew how Cody felt.

What if I'm the one who doesn't want to be alone? I send.

After a few moments, I finally get *Okay. I'll send you one clue. If you don't figure it out, I'll see you tomorrow. Maybe.*

Got it.

You won't guess.

Try me.

The next words that appear mess with my head completely. I know exactly where she is.

Seven ten third.

CHAPTER SEVENTEEN

Lucy

I hear the sound of an engine and the slow crunch of tires on gravel. When I look over and see Aaron's truck, my heart stops. How in the hell ...?

I'm frozen in place in front of Cody's grave, sitting with my knees pulled to my chest. When Aaron's feet hit the ground after he opens the door, I manage to pry my eyes away from him and glue them to Cody's headstone. It's not helping. How am I going to explain why I'm here? *I* don't even know why I'm here.

It seems like an eternity before I see Aaron's legs out of the corner of my eye. He sits down beside me and mirrors my pose. After a few uncomfortable seconds, he says, "Fifty-six steps."

I look at him. "What?"

"It takes fifty-six steps to get from there," he looks back at his truck, "to here."

"You counted?"

He shrugs. "I do every time."

I swallow and go back to staring at Cody's name. How often does he visit? I should have lied about where I was. I honestly thought I was being vague.

Resting my chin on my knees, I ask, "How did you find me?"

"This spot is committed to memory." Aaron moves and rests his elbows on his legs. "I never want to forget where he is." He looks at the ground before giving me a resigned glance. "What about you? How'd you come up with the numbers?"

"My ther – Dr. Marie, she wrote them down."

He nods. "So you could leave the note?"

My mouth falls open. He stares at me as I stare at him; he doesn't even bat an eye. "You ..." I open my clenched fist to reveal the paper I picked up when I got here. "You answered my letter?"

Now he looks a little embarrassed. "Well, two words really isn't a letter, but ... yeah."

"Why?"

When I wound up here and saw it hadn't disappeared, I slid it from beneath the dry flower stems to read someone else had found it, too. In between fending off messages from my friends, I couldn't comprehend who had written me back. I started to think I was imagining the words.

Aaron pulls a blade of grass out of the ground and plays with it. "I answered it because it's what Cody would have said to you, if he could." His eyes meet mine. "Honest."

Really?

He must read the question on my face, because he adds, "Things aren't always what they seem, remember?"

I'm kind of stunned. "How did you know it was from me?"

"Yearbook class." He tilts his head. "I tend to get a lot of editor's notes."

My cheeks start to feel hot. Do I subconsciously pay more attention to him? "So ..." I hesitate. "You don't think I'm crazy?"

He gives me a lopsided smile. "If you're crazy, then so am I."

Tension leaves my body at his words.

"Wow," Aaron says. "You finally let go of the death grip on your legs."

I look down and realize I'm not hunched into such a tight ball. "Oh ... I guess I feel more comfortable now."

He shoots me a questioning look, so I elaborate. "When you pulled up, I froze. I wasn't sure how you would react to me being here."

"Last I knew this was a public place."

"And last I knew, the three of us aren't the best combination." I nod toward Cody's stone. If anyone from school saw us here, they'd freak.

"We should take a picture and put it in the yearbook." Aaron's eyes light up. "I know Cody wouldn't mind. He loved to mess with people." He leans forward and makes a sideways peace sign in front of his face. "We could caption it *thug life.*"

I bite my lip to suppress a smile. It's so inappropriate, it's funny. Still, the thought of advertising our current location makes my palms itch. "Sorry, but I think I'll pass."

Aaron smirks as he shakes his head. "You shouldn't care what other people think."

I give him a blank stare. "Says the person whose face is *not* pasted on the naked body of some random model."

His brow jumps. "You mean that's not you?"

"No, it's not."

"Damn," he sighs. "That's disappointing."

My eyes roll.

"Speaking of stupid things," Aaron reaches for his back pocket, "I wonder if the school imploded yet."

Good question. I check my phone, and I only have one old message from Izzy that arrived just before Aaron did: *Someone is looking for you.* Well, he found me.

Aaron stands, patting around his jeans. "I think I left my phone in the truck." He reaches for me. "C'mon."

I let him help me to my feet. As we walk side by side, I realize my blood pressure has returned to normal. When Izzy showed me the picture, I didn't think twice. I bolted out the door before I had to look anyone in the eye. I know it's not me and I know it's a lie, but people are gullible. June warned me; she said I had no idea what was coming.

Unfortunately, I'm sure there's more in store. How can I get her off my back? Is she that hard up for something to do?

When Aaron opens his truck door for me, I hop up into the cab. After he climbs into the driver's seat, it hits me we were in these exact same spots yesterday. Surprisingly, it feels natural, even with the way things ended.

Aaron finds his cell on the dash. "Let's see what the damage is." He scrutinizes his phone, then lets out a laugh. "Harrison says June's head spun around."

I smile. "How very *Exorcist* of her. Do you think she's into scary movies, too? Maybe we should invite her over."

He doesn't look amused. "No," he says and goes back to scrolling. He leans over the center console toward me. "Here. Check this out."

I move closer so I can read the screen; all the messages are from his friend, Harrison.

The sign worked, I guess.

I think June's head starting spinning around when she realized what everyone was looking at.

She had couple of guys rip it down, then stormed to the office.

I'll keep you updated. Hope you found Lucy.

The last sentence takes me by surprise. "He knows about me?"

"Not everyone hates the idea of us."

I turn to look at him, and it's then I realize our faces are inches apart. My breath catches. He really did win the lottery in the looks department. I think his eyelashes are longer than mine.

"Lucy?"

I blink. "What?"

"Did you hear what I said?"

He said something? "Uh, no."

"I asked if we're okay." He sits back a little. "I didn't want you to leave yesterday."

I know he didn't, but it felt like I should. It was obvious June thought their time together meant something, whether he realized it or not.

"I'm not mad at you," I say. "June threw a wench in the day and being there felt icky."

Aaron shoots me a questioning smile. "Icky? I don't think I've heard that word since I was three."

"Well," I lean back in my seat, "would you rather I said it felt like the seventh circle of hell?"

"Geez." Aaron holds his hands up. "Fine. Icky it is."

I almost laugh.

Pulling out his keys, Aaron starts the truck. "Since the movies didn't work out, let me make it up to you. Where do you want to go?"

"Oh. Home is fine, I guess."

"Home?" His expression twists. "We're skipping school, and you want to go home?"

"Where else would we go?"

He thinks for a minute, then looks at the time on his dash. "Bread-sticks," he says.

"What?"

"Holton House starts serving lunch at eleven thirty. Let's get something to eat; I'm starving."

I silently agree. The little restaurant does serve the best bread-sticks in town. They're just the right combination of soft garlic buttery goodness, and you can get a bag for only a couple of bucks. "Only if we get the cream cheese dip," I say, just to be complicated.

"Is there any other kind?" He glances at me as he starts to drive. "I tried the marinara once. Ruined the whole experience for me."

It's not long before we're standing in line, ordering our breadsticks and something to drink. I try to pay for half of the food, but Aaron won't let me. This is the second time he's bought me something; I still owe him for the homecoming hot chocolate.

"Listen," I say after I sit down across from him at a table for two, "you have to let me buy once and awhile. This isn't 1945."

"It's not?" He opens up the bag of bread and reaches for a piece. "I thought you were a pin-up girl." He winks.

"So not funny," I say with a straight face. Reaching for the dip, I steal it before he can have any. "This is mine."

He actually looks sad. "What?"

"Say stupid shit and forfeit the dip." I pause. "Hey, that kinda rhymed."

Aaron laughs and starts to stand. "Sorry. I'll go buy another one."

"Sit down." I sigh and push the cream cheese toward him but don't take my hand off the container. "Be nice, and I'll share."

His hand lands on top of mine. "I make no promises."

He tries to slide the dip toward him from beneath my fingers, but I tighten my grip and pull it back. His brow jumps at the challenge, and he tries to steal it again. I smile and hang on. It's not long before we're laughing and having a dip war.

"Let go."

"You let go."

"You're wrecking the tablecloth!"

"It's plastic."

"Just give it to me."

"No; this was my idea."

"You suck."

"Is that all you've got?"

A deep voice speaks from behind me. "Aaron? Is that you?"

Aaron looks up, and his smile fades. He drops the dip like it's a hot potato.

"Hey, Mr. Cunningham."

Goose bumps immediately break out over my skin. Suddenly, I feel like I'm running a fever. I look down, hoping to hide behind my hair. I've never met Cody's father – or his mother. I know they know my name, but I don't know if they know my face.

"Long time, no see, kid." Cody's dad extends his hand, and Aaron shakes it. "How've you been?"

"Um, good ... I guess."

"That's good to hear. Coach been working you hard?"

"No, sir. Not yet."

"Well, you've got a big season ahead of you. I hope you're at least in the weight room."

"Oh, definitely. Yeah."

I can hear the unease in Aaron's voice, and I sneak a peek at him. I've never heard him so unsure of himself. He even looks a little pale.

"Who's your friend here?"

Oh god. Oh no.

"This is ... ah ..." Aaron clears his throat. "Cleo."

My head snaps up. Where did he get that name?

"Hello, Cleo."

I'm forced to look at Cody's dad. He's tall, but then again, I'm sitting. He's wearing a blue button down and khaki's, and the watch on his wrist looks expensive. He gives me a polite smile, but I could swear his eyes spark with recognition.

"Hi," I half mumble and force a smile of my own. "It's nice to meet you."

He nods. "Do you ... go to Holton?"

"Yes."

"You look familiar. Did you know my son?"

I think I might puke. The once appetizing smell of garlic overwhelms my senses and suffocates my nose and throat. My pulse starts to race and I can picture the scene, vomit all over Mr. Cunningham's brown loafers.

"Cleo only knew Cody by name," Aaron says. "She's kinda new to our group of friends."

Thank you, I silently say.

"Oh, well. He always had so many kids in and out ..." Mr. Cunningham drifts off. "Everything becomes a blur after a while, you know?"

I can tell he's talking about more than a revolving door of Cody's acquaintances. "I'm so sorry," I whisper.

Mr. Cunningham puts his hands in his pockets, and his face falls. "Me, too."

"John? You ready?"

I look over, and it appears Cody's dad has coworkers waiting; three other men are standing at the counter dressed in a similar way. They're all holding carryout bags.

"Yep." Mr. Cunningham nods. "We just stepped out to grab lunch," he tells us. "Aaron," he looks at him, "it was good to see you. I know it might seem odd, but don't be a stranger. Claudia and I ... our door is always open."

"Yes, sir."

"And Cleo –"

My heart stops beating.

"Take care."

Sympathy is written all over his face, and all I can do is nod as he walks away. My turning insides tell me he has to know who I am.

When he leaves the restaurant, I finally look at Aaron. I'm speechless. "I ... I ..."

"Do you want to get out of here?"

I jump to my feet.

Aaron picks up the food while I grab our drinks. With a disposable cup in each hand, I follow him to the rear exit of the restaurant, which takes us away from the main street and in the opposite direction of Cody's dad. Once our shoes hit the sidewalk, I feel like I can breathe again.

We head up the road, passing one block, then two. "That was ..." Aaron hesitates. "Different."

Different? I can think of a million other words to describe what just happened. Paralyzing and horrifying immediately jump to mind. I never want it to happen again.

"I didn't know he would be there. Honest," Aaron says. "It kind of threw me off."

It sounds like he's apologizing. "It's not your fault." *Not at all.*

A small park comes into view and, without talking about it, we walk in that direction. When we come up to a picnic table next to some swings, we set down our lunch.

Aaron starts to open the bag but stops. "We're never going to escape this, are we?"

Meeting his eyes, I know I look defeated. "I don't think so," I say quietly.

He takes an irritated breath. Grabbing a breadstick, he takes a huge bite without the coveted dip. "You know," he says as he chews, "I wish –"

He doesn't finish his sentence. It could end in any number of ways. *I wish I stayed at school. I wish Cody were alive. I wish this bread were warmer.*

"I wish none of it had ever happened."

He's preaching to the choir. "Same," I say before I take a sip of my root beer.

Aaron slams another breadstick, and I realize I'm not the only one who stress eats. It's okay; he can have them all. I lost my appetite after the vomit vision.

Slowly, I walk over to the swings and sit down. With my feet still on the ground, I push myself back and forth, looking at the bare trees and fallen leaves. Apparently, I can't show my face anywhere today. Would it be possible to impersonate someone else? At least until graduation? I could dye my hair, and Delaney could tattoo me up.

A name jumps in my head – Cleo. She sounds like a mysterious, inked lady. I look over at Aaron, who's brushing off his hands. "Who's Cleo?"

He smiles a little. "You."

"No. I mean the real Cleo."

He walks over and stands behind me, reaching for the chains of my swing. He stops my movement, then gives me a push. "It really is you. Your name is Cleopatra in my phone."

I look over my shoulder. "Why?"

"Izzy. When she gave me your number, she made a joke."

That makes no sense, but then again, we're talking about my best friend. I love her, but sometimes I don't understand her.

"Well, you're just Aaron in my phone," I say. "Should I change it to Marc?"

He gives me another push. "As in Antony?"

I nod.

"That depends. Will we be lovers?"

What? My face flushes. "No! I just meant the two names go together. Like Bert and Ernie."

Aaron stops my swing and looks at me. "There it is." He gives me a cocky grin. "I haven't seen the blush in a while."

I close my eyes and take a deep breath. "Sometimes I hate you."

He laughs. "Hate is a passionate emotion."

"Just push the swing."

He does as he's told. Aaron helps me relive my elementary recess days for a few moments longer, then sits down on the swing beside mine. "Can I ask you a question?"

"Sure," I say, slowing down.

"What do you think about me?"

Dragging my feet through the dirt, I stop moving completely. "Do you mean now or before?"

"Doesn't matter."

"At first I didn't know you at all." I shrug. "I only had an impression of you, and your kind didn't mix with mine."

He frowns. "My kind?"

"Yeah. Jerky popular jock guy. I'm a quiet-ish yearbook girl."

His eyebrows jump. "You thought I was a jerk? Did I do something?"

"No. You just hung out with all the pretty people." I feel a little stupid saying it. "You know how high school hierarchy works."

He looks surprised. "And now? You realize I'm not a jerk, right?"

"I do." It's the truth.

Before he can ask another question, I come up with one of my own. "What about me? You didn't know my name until that night at the Field, right?"

"Wrong." Aaron sways back and forth on his swing. "I did know your name. I just didn't know you."

Oh. "So, once you got to know me, you decided you liked the whole damsel in distress thing?" I snicker. "Because that's about all I've got going on right now."

"Wrong again." He meets my eyes. "You're the only other person who knows what it feels like when someone says Cody's name."

My heart unexpectedly stops. It's sad our only real connection is the sick, twisted feeling I wouldn't wish on anyone in the world – not even June.

"I get it," I say, staring at my now dust-covered sneakers. "We're connected by him."

Aaron's silent. I can feel him looking at me, but I can't return his stare. Twenty bucks says it's because he said Cody's name without warning, which sucks. Why does the weight of it hit me some times and not others?

After quiet seconds, he says, "Hey."

I still can't look at him, so I focus on the far side of the park. "Yeah?"

He reaches over, grabs the chain on my swing, and pulls us closer. The sudden movement forces me to face him. "What I said came out wrong."

"No." I shake my head. "It came out honest."

He concedes with a nod. "Still … it wasn't what I meant to say." He pulls me a little closer. "I think there's more to us than my best friend, don't you?"

Just like my heart stopped without warning, my stomach surprises me by twisting into a knot. "I …"

"Remember, I'm not jerk off jock guy."

"But I *am* quiet-ish yearbook girl."

Aaron throws me a tiny smile. "And I think I could like hanging out with her. A lot."

My mouth falls open a bit. I don't know what to say. In the back of my mind, a little voice that sounds a lot like Izzy says I'm screwing this up. *Speak!*

"I like hanging out with you, too," I finally confess.

"But?"

"But the people around you make it hard." I pause. "I do like you, it's just …"

"You don't want to get harassed."

"And I don't want it to affect you, either."

Aaron looks lost in thought for a moment before a sly look crosses his face. "First of all, seeing you would *definitely* affect me."

He wags his eyebrows and he looks so ridiculous, I snort.

"What if ..." He pauses. "What if we just took it slow?"

My brow jumps. "You really want to date me?"

"Why not? It sounds fun, yet dangerous."

I can't believe we're having this conversation. I can't agree to see him ... can I? I've changed so much since that night at the Field; I'm not the same Lucy I once was. He didn't know her, and it makes me wonder what he sees in me now.

Using his elbow, Aaron nudges my arm. "So, what do you say?"

An immediate wave of disappointment washes over me at the thought of saying no. The feeling has to mean something, so I slowly nod yes.

Aaron grins, and a little sarcasm escapes me. "I mean, fun and dangerous are my middle names."

He laughs. "Funny, so are mine."

I shake my head, and he releases my swing. We sway apart, and then he starts to swing normally, as if we didn't just make a game-changing decision.

"Bet I can go higher than you," he taunts.

Challenge accepted. I start pumping my legs. *Is this really happening?*

It's not long before we're side by side, swinging as high as we possibly can. I've kinda grown since the last time I did this, and I start to worry if the playground equipment can handle the weight of both of us.

"What do I get if I win?" I ask on our downswing.

"What do you want?"

I want to travel back to a certain night in May, but he can't give me that. Mulling it over, I say, "I want a dozen roses. A hot fudge sundae, dancing under the stars, and my toenails painted blue."

"What?" Aaron looks confused, and his momentum falters. "All at once?"

"I hadn't considered that, but ... no." I smirk as his rhythm slows. "You didn't realize I was so high maintenance, did you?" I'm joking, of course. There's no way I would make him do all of those things.

Aaron's eyes question me as we fall out of sync and my legs reach higher than his.

"Hey ... looks like I win," I say over my shoulder with a grin. "Go me."

He shakes his head with a laugh. "And all I was going to ask for was a kiss."

Now my swinging slows. Are we already there? *No, no we're not.* "Nice try," I tease. I keep swinging as my pulse perks up at the idea. Maybe we will get there.

Eventually.

CHAPTER EIGHTEEN

Aaron

Thirteen ... *a dozen roses* ... fourteen ... *hot fudge sundae* ... fifteen ... *stars and dancing* ... sixteen ... *blue toe nails* ...

In between reps, I commit Lucy's list of demands to memory. She confessed she was only kidding, but I'd like to surprise her anyway. I'm pretty stoked over the whole dating thing, even though I don't care if we're slow about it or not.

Seventeen ... *roses* ... eighteen ... *ice cream* ... nineteen ... *dancing* ... twenty ...

"Hey."

Harrison's face appears upside down over mine as I use the bench press. "Hey," I huff.

He catches the weight bar and helps me rack it. "I'm having a party."

"What?" I sit up. "Since when?"

"Since I need an excuse to see Delaney." He walks over to our water bottles and tosses mine at me. "Her aunt won't let her date until she's eighteen."

People still do that? "When is the big birthday?"

"In two weeks."

I take a long drink, then smile. "Are you sure she's telling the truth? Maybe she just doesn't want to go out with you." I can't help but mess with him.

"Very funny." He smirks. "She told me to keep that day open."

I laugh. "So, what are we talking about? Intimate gathering or full-on frat?"

"I figured I might as well invite everybody. If they find out, they'll just show up anyway. There hasn't been a big party since ... well, you know."

Yeah, I know. I down more water. "You remember the curfew is still a thing, right?"

"Only for public places," Harrison says. "We'll stay downstairs so we won't piss off the neighbors. And I'm not providing alcohol. If people bring it, that's on them."

"You know it's gonna happen, man."

He shrugs. "Can I count on you to help me with crowd control?"

"Sure." There's no way I'd let my friend down, even if I'd rather spend my time with Lucy. He's been my only ally when it comes to her. Speaking of, I wonder if I can convince her to go. She avoids things like this for good reason, but –

"Hey," I say. "Why don't you make it a costume party? It's almost Halloween." *And I know someone who could disguise herself.*

"You think people would go for that?"

"They dress up for spirit week, don't they? Besides, if they don't play along, it might end up a party for two – you and Delaney." *Quick thinking there,* I silently pat myself on the back.

Harrison grins. "All right. I'll start spreading the word. It'll be this Saturday, since my parents are headed up north."

"Aw, man," I fake groan. "You mean Jim and Loretta won't be there?"

Harrison makes a face. "Jim and Loretta need to go to their high school reunion."

Both of us glance at the clock and realize we need to get moving if we're not going to be late. I told Harrison I'd been working out before and after school, and today he decided to join me. Once we shower and change, we head toward the door. I hope to catch a glimpse of Lucy before first period; it would make sitting through chemistry a little more bearable.

Just as we enter the hallway, Coach comes around the corner. "Good morning, boys. Aaron, I need to speak with you."

I wonder why. I exchange a look with Harrison before I follow Coach to his office. The bell for first period rings as I take a seat across from him like I did about two months ago. "I hope this isn't about my schedule again," I half-heartedly joke.

"No," he says, leaning back in his chair and crossing his arms. "I had a visit from some of your teammates yesterday."

"And?"

"They're concerned your head might be in the wrong place."

My expression twists. "In regard to what? Practice hasn't even started yet, and I don't see any of them in the weight room."

Coach lets out a tired sigh and sits up straight. He flips over a piece of paper and pushes it toward me. My face falls when I see it's a picture – the same one June took at my house when I was walking up the stairs holding hands with Lucy.

I shake my head, irritated. "What did they tell you?"

"That you're hanging out with the wrong crowd."

I let out a sarcastic laugh. "One person is a crowd?"

"They said she's the one who–"

"Yes," I cut him off. "She … Cody … yeah." Everyone knows what happened – mostly. I shouldn't have to explain it. "I don't see what my personal life has to do with lacrosse."

"It doesn't have anything to do with it, unless you're not focused." Coach moves forward in his seat. "Do you want to tell me what's going on?"

I let out a heavy breath. How do I explain stupidity? "They're mad because I'm friends with Lucy. They don't like her, so they think I should hate her, too."

Coach's eyes move from me, to the picture, and back again. "It looks like you might be more than friends."

SARA MACK

"We're working on it," I concede. "It's new."

Coach is silent for a moment. "And she's not distracting you in any way?"

"Like how?" I'm not following. "I'm passing all of my classes, if that's what you mean. My mid-term grades will be stellar, I promise."

He gives me an understanding nod. "Good. I've known you for close to four years now, and I trust you. Believe me, I don't know what the guys were trying to prove with this," he gestures toward the picture, "but they're too old for kid games. Or at least I thought they were."

I glance down at the photo, at the look of shock on Lucy's face. "They're just trying to shake me. It won't change anything. They can have their opinion, but I can have mine, too."

The more I think about what the guys did, the more it pisses me off. I can't believe they would go behind my back and try to hurt my reputation with *our* coach.

"I don't know how this season is going to go," I say and flop back in my chair. "It's very possible they'll vote me out as captain." The reality of the thought hits me. If that happened, it would screw with all my college plans.

"No; the decision from last year stands," Coach says. "As long as your performance is up to par, there's nothing they can do."

"Thank you," I say and mean it.

"So, tell me," Coach relaxes into his chair, "there must be something special about this girl. It seems your mind is made up despite what your team thinks."

"I ..." Are we really going to have this talk? "I'd like to get to know her better, yeah. She's ..." I don't know what to say. Funny? Smart? Cute? Broken? "There's more to her than meets the eye."

"Spoken like a true leader. Someone who doesn't take things at face value or fall in line like a lemming." Coach smiles. "How did the two of you get mixed up together? I have to admit when I found out who she was I did a double take."

Of course he did. "Yearbook," I say.

174

Coach chuckles. "Didn't I tell you that class would be good for something?"

Slowly, I smile. "Yeah. Yeah, you did."

By the time we finish talking, first period is almost over. When I'm at my locker, I lean against it to wait for my teammates to show up at theirs. There's no way I'm going to let what they did slide.

The first people I see are Max and Jason, and I make a beeline straight for them through the crowded hallway. By the time I get there, a few of the other guys have also shown up.

"Aaron." Jason smiles and raises his hand for a high-five. "What's up?"

I slam the picture I took from Coach's office flat against his chest and get in his face. "I don't know what you're trying to pull, but it didn't work."

"Whoa, dude. Chill." He raises his hands and takes a step back. "We're just trying to help."

"I don't need your help."

"Hey." Max tries to intervene by putting his arm between us. "It's true. We just want what's best for you, man."

"By going behind my back with Coach? That makes no sense."

"What's going on?" Harrison appears.

"Our teammates think they know everything," I say through gritted teeth. I toss the picture at Harrison. "They paid a little visit to Coach, telling him I've lost my mind."

"That's not what we said." Max steps in between me and Jason, lowering his voice. "We're just looking out for our captain. What if Lucy offs you, too?"

Every muscle in my body tenses. This might get more physical than I planned.

"Don't you think that's a little harsh?" Harrison asks. "You act like she's is some sort of serial killer."

Max shrugs. "You never know."

I lunge forward, and Harrison holds me back. "Okay, okay! Let's not do anything we'll regret."

We're starting to attract attention, and I close my eyes to avoid hitting my so-called friend. Harrison steps around me and in front of Max. "Lucy isn't out to murder the entire lacrosse team," he says. "You sound like an idiot."

Max crosses his arms and looks around with a smartass expression.

"Listen. I'm having a party on Saturday. Everyone is invited. Let's forget this happened and hang out like old times. Okay?" Harrison looks at me. "Okay?"

It takes everything I have in me to nod yes. It's the furthest thing from okay; I won't forget what he said.

Max relaxes his shoulders. "Fine."

Everyone around me starts to talk about the party, and when the warning bell rings, I turn to leave. As I do, I catch a glimpse of Lucy down the hall. She's staring straight at me with a worried look. I subtly shake my head, meaning "don't worry about it." Frowning, she walks away with Izzy.

———

"HELLO." I smile, sliding into the empty seat in front of Lucy. This is the first chance I've had to talk to her all day. "Can you approve this layout?"

"Can you tell me what happened this morning?"

She doesn't look up from the copy she's proofing. Instead, she draws a line through a sentence with a red pen and writes "rework" in the margin. Is she mad?

"If it was bothering you, why didn't you text me?" I ask.

"Because you can lie behind a phone."

Her eyes meet mine, and she looks more anxious than anything. I don't want to tell her the whole truth; I'd rather see her nervous than upset.

"It was about lacrosse," I say and try to play it off. "It's me and Coach against my team. They'll get over it."

She's skeptical. "For real?"

"Scout's honor." I hold up three fingers near my face.

She lets out a breath and appears to relax a little. Her eyes land on my other hand. "What did you want me to see?"

I set the paper I printed off in front of her, and she squints. "Didn't I already approve this online?"

"Yeah, but I made a change." I'm trying to tell her about Harrison's party while pretending to talk about yearbook business. "Check out the bottom."

She finds what I added. "Why didn't you just text me this?"

Hmm … sounds familiar. "Because this way you can't refuse behind a phone." I smile innocently, and she rolls her eyes. "So, thoughts?"

"Things will be obvious if we're at a party together," she whispers. "How is that going slow?"

"That's why it's a costume party," I whisper back. "You can hide in plain sight."

"I can't." She shakes her head. "Your friends won't believe you're hanging out with some stranger."

Thankfully, I've already thought about this. "Let me worry about who sees us," I say. "Izzy and Delaney –"

"Are totally going and you're coming with us."

I turn around to see Izzy with her hands on her hips. She's focused on Lucy.

"We'll all be there with you." Her tone softens. "Plus, we have more people on our side now."

Lucy doesn't look convinced.

"If you're worried about June, don't make things convenient for her," I say. "Staying home would do that. Harrison invited me, and I'm inviting you. I think we could have fun."

Izzy nods enthusiastically and I give Lucy a small smile, but she still looks like she'd rather swallow shards of glass. The truth is I want to spend time with her, and I don't care where that takes place. But I promised Harrison I would be at his party, and I'd like Lucy to be there, too.

Izzy crouches down between us and looks up at her friend. "Luce," she says. "You know how good Delaney is with makeup. No one will recognize you. I promise. And if anyone says anything, you know we'll have your back. You should be able to do regular high school things."

Lucy shoots Izzy an annoyed look. "You know you're defining peer pressure right now."

"No." Izzy pouts. "Peer pressure is negative. I'm being positive."

Lucy looks exasperated. She sighs, then meets my eyes. "I'll think about it," she says. "That's the best answer I can give you."

"I'll take it," I say. At least it's not a no.

Izzy seems satisfied too, and once she leaves, Lucy says, "You're going to have to fix this layout." She hands me the paper. "'Party at Harrison's this Saturday. Wanna go?' doesn't look right above 'Caught in the Act Photography Studio for all your senior portrait needs.'"

I laugh. "It was a creative way to ask you, right?"

She scoffs but smiles.

"Besides, I thought your middle names were fun and dangerous. What's more dangerous than messing with the yearbook?"

She doesn't hesitate. "Going to Harrison's party."

"DUDE. WHAT ARE YOU WEARING?"

I sigh and turn around. This is at least the tenth time I've answered this question tonight. Have none of these people seen *Gladiator*?

"Is that a skirt?"

"No, Jason. It's not a skirt."

I pull at the neck of my white tunic which is covered in plastic body armor and connected to a red cape. Harrison, my wing man, appears beside me. "Aaron lost a bet. Didn't you?" He grins.

I nod. This is the story we came up with, when I told him I wanted to show up as Marc Antony to his party. He looked at me like I was crazy, but after I explained why, he understood. I figured if Lucy decided to come, she'd choose to be Cleopatra. I assumed no one would know who Marc Antony was so they wouldn't connect the two of us, but I also assumed they paid at least a little attention in world history. I'm starting to second guess a lot of things about my friends.

"Yeah, I lost a bet," I say. "Harrison failed his test."

"What test?"

Harrison wiggles his eyebrows. "A pregnancy test."

My drink nearly shoots out my nose. Every time someone asks about the "bet," Harrison changes the test. This is the most insane one yet.

As I try to swallow without choking and Harrison laughs, Jason looks at us like we've grown three heads. "Okaaaaay ..." he says slowly as he lowers his storm trooper mask and walks away.

Once he's gone, Harrison checks his phone. "Where are they?" he asks impatiently. "It's been an hour already."

He scans his crowded basement for the girls. There has to be at least fifty people from school here, and they're all dressed up just like he asked. As music pumps through his parents' sound system, my eyes jump from some sort of sexy zombie girl to a scary-looking clown to an inflatable T-Rex. I haven't heard from Lucy. I didn't want to annoy her, so I limited myself to three text messages about the party – all of which went unanswered.

"She'll be here, bro," Cody's voice sounds in my mind. "Just be patient."

Like Cody was ever patient. I'm starting to wonder if my subconscious has decided to sound like my best friend as some form of karma.

Commotion from the stairs pulls our attention that way, and my eyes roll as June and her entourage arrive. I try to ignore them until I realize they're all wearing the same thing – bright orange jumpsuits. I find Kat and focus on her, because I really don't get why she continues to sink to June's level. How is it possible I've misread so many people for so long?

When she turns around, I do a double take before I can stop my legs from walking in her direction. Anger rises in my chest. Are you fucking kidding me?

"Kat." I reach for her elbow, and she faces me when she feels my hand. "What the hell?"

To her benefit, her cheeks turn red. She looks at her feet before meeting my eyes. "It ... wasn't my idea."

"But you had to go along with it?" I raise my hands, exasperated. "What kind of weird hold does June have over you?"

"She wanted to get back at Lucy for the sign."

"Who says she had anything to do with the sign?" I run my hand through my hair. "Jesus Christ, it wasn't her."

Kat looks surprised. "But ..."

"But nothing. I can't believe you'd think this was okay."

I look around at the three other girls moving through the room. They're easy to spot wearing their bright costumes–jumpsuits made to look like prison uniforms with "Lucy Anderson #051417" stenciled across the back with black spray paint.

"Aaron, I'm sorry."

"I don't care what you are," I say, backing away. "Just ... never mind."

I head across the room, putting as much distance between us as I can. Placing my hands behind my head, I let out a frustrated breath. Lucy was right. She's always right. When am I going to start believing her? I guess it's a good thing she decided not to –

Movement from the stairway catches my eye. As three new party-goers enter the room, I can clearly pick out Izzy and Delaney. The person walking behind them isn't Cleopatra.

But I know it's Lucy.

CHAPTER NINETEEN

Lucy

I'm glad my mask hides my slack-jawed expression.

My eyes instantly find Aaron among the crowd in Harrison's basement. As Izzy, Delaney, and I get closer to him, my stomach does a little flip-flop, fluttery thing. Out of all of his costume choices, I never dreamed he would show up as Marc Antony.

"Nice legs," Delaney comments when she steps up beside him.

"Nice face," he replies with a smile.

Watching through my mesh-covered eye holes, I decide to stay off the side and back a bit from my friends, since they're both identifiable and I'm not. Izzy decided she wanted to be a hippie, so Delaney painted intricate daisies on a vine across her forehead and around her temples. She looks like she wearing a crown of flowers without any real flowers. Delaney transformed her own skin into feathers to become a peacock. The iridescent blues, greens, and purples would make her look almost alien if not for the jacket she's wearing. It's covered in real peacock feathers, and when I asked where she found it, she told me her aunt was "eccentric."

As for me, I wasn't brave enough to show my real face. It wasn't until I was flipping through Netflix this afternoon that an idea struck. During my friend's relentless text messages, I told them the only way I'd come tonight is if they could make my costume happen – and now here I am, covered from head to toe, still against my better judgement.

Aaron's eyes bounce to me and then back to Delaney. "Harrison's been waiting for you." He then wiggles his eyebrows at Izzy. "And I kind of told Wes you'd be here. You might want to find him and say hi."

"Really?" Izzy grins at me over her shoulder and pulls Delaney away.

No sooner do my friends disappear than Aaron is standing right in front of me. "Want to get out of here?"

"Is that an option?" I ask. I thought I *had* to attend.

"Wait a few seconds, then follow me."

"Okay."

Aaron leaves and heads up the stairs I just came down. Once I count to thirty in my head, I follow him. At the top of the stairs, I find an empty living room but an open front door.

"Well, hello," he says when I peer outside.

"Aren't you cold?" His arms, legs, and even his feet are exposed.

"What was that?" He puts his hand to his ear and steps closer. "You're a little muffled."

"And you're a little naked." I know he heard that, because he gives me a crooked smile. Pushing open the door, I join him on the porch and push my mask up so it sits on top of my head. "I asked if you were cold."

"It's almost fifty degrees." He rubs his arms. "I wasn't cold in the house."

"Then why are we out here?"

He doesn't answer me. Instead, he walks over and leans against the porch railing. "So, you went with Ghostface from *Scream*, huh?"

"Yeah." I lean my black robe-covered butt on the railing next to him. "Obviously not what you were expecting."

"I didn't know what to expect. I knew what I was wearing regardless. If you showed up, I thought it could be our inside joke." Aaron bumps his shoulder against mine.

"That's what I thought, too." I bump him back. "I figured you'd know it was me even if you couldn't see my face."

"Great minds think alike, I guess."

"I guess."

We fall silent, so I look around. Harrison lives on the historic side of town but his house is more modern, like it was built to look old. Despite the fact we're outside, I can hear the dull thump of the music from the party.

"Hey."

I turn, and Aaron offers me his hand like he wants to hold mine.

"Thanks for coming," he says. "I know it wasn't easy for you."

I almost tell him I wasn't going to come. If it wasn't for Izzy finding this robe in her basement, and Delaney finding the mask at the dollar store, I probably wouldn't be here. But his serious expression makes me pause; he seems moved I stepped out of my comfort zone. I take another look at what he's wearing and realize what a sweet gesture it is. I'm sure his friends questioned his fake armor and cape. How did he explain without giving anything away?

Slowly, I wind my fingers through his and squeeze. "I'm glad I made the right choice."

A smile teases at the corner of Aaron's mouth before he reaches out with his free hand and pushes some tangled hair behind my ear. With the mask sitting on top of my head, I'm sure it's a mess under there.

Quickly, I swipe it off and shake my head, hoping it will help. Aaron's fingers linger on my chin though, and the fluttery feeling I felt earlier instantly returns. His eyes look intensely green as they stay locked on mine. He leans a fraction of an inch closer, and I internally start to panic. Is he doing what I think he's doing? Right here? Right now?

Despite my racing thoughts, I'm drawn toward him. As I close my eyes, I feel his breath on my lips before I hear distant voices. My eyes pop open, and our attention snaps to the front door.

"C'mon," Aaron says and pulls me to my feet. He sprints off the porch, and I follow. We round the side of Harrison's house, finding nothing but moonlight and tall shrubs.

"Here," he says and jumps in between two of the bushes. It looks like a row of them is planted against the house. Aaron presses his back to the siding while he wraps his arms around me and holds me against his chest.

"Are we seriously hiding in the landscaping?" I whisper.

He holds back a laugh, but I can feel it under my cheek. "Yes. And we're running away from another party. I sense a pattern here."

My mind flashes back to homecoming night at Phi Nu. I've gone from wary to cozy with Aaron. Who knew?

Standing there, we listen as people leave. Loud and laughing, I have no idea who they are. When we hear car doors slam, Aaron relaxes his hold but doesn't let me go.

"I think," he says as he looks down at me, "I like how this escape is going a lot more than the last one."

I have to admit I do, too. "Yes. No rolled ankles or forced awkward sleepovers."

Aaron's expression falls. "It wasn't awkward until I made it that way."

"No ... I think I managed that all on my own."

"If I hadn't said what I said–"

"Not your fault," I cut him off.

He leans back a tiny bit to study me, and to prove I don't blame him, I move my arms from between us and wrap them around his waist. He doesn't say anything, so I look up at the clear sky and the bright moon. "Look at all the stars," I say to fill the silence.

His gaze follows mine. "No way," he says with a smile in his voice.

"No way what?"

Reaching under his costume at his hip, he pulls out his phone.

"That thing has pockets?" I ask in awe.

He nods, then opens an app on his cell. He scrolls, selects something, and soon the crooning sounds of Michael Bublé fill our little space in the bushes.

"Dancing under the stars as requested." He grins and moves my hands from his waist to his shoulders.

"Really?" I ask as we start to move in a slow circle. "I told you I was kidding. You don't have to do this."

"I have your demands memorized," he says. "You won. I don't mind paying up."

"I think you're just using my body for warmth at this point." What guy in his right mind wants to dance while potentially freezing in shrubbery?

"I won't deny it's a bonus," he says. "Just enjoy it. I plan to."

He pulls me close and I cave, resting my head on his shoulder. As we barely move, his hands brush against my back, and I find mine moving to his neck. Alone like this, it's easy to imagine things aren't so complicated. I let my mind wander, and by the end of the song my bones are like mush. I haven't felt this calm in a long time. If he asked, I would stay like this all night.

"Lucy?"

I lift my head and open my eyes. "Hmm?"

"Thanks for putting this on your list."

His voice is a whisper, and it's then I realize how close his mouth is to mine. "You're welcome," I say quietly.

His lips brush mine before I can think. His kiss is timid at first, probably because I tensed up in surprise. He doesn't give up on me though, and it only takes a few seconds for me to box up everything that makes us us and shove it in the back of my mind. My racing heart takes over, and through the haze and disbelief and butterflies, as our kiss grows deeper, one thought becomes crystal clear – kissing Aaron feels like I've been kissing him my entire life. We fit together; it feels *right*. It feels like I just discovered my new favorite thing.

When we separate, he gives me a hint of a smile after fighting a bigger grin. "We should do that more often."

I bite my bottom lip and nod.

"Do you want to go somewhere else?" he asks. "We could stop at home and change first."

"Okay. Let me tell the girls I'm leaving." I reach into my robe for my phone.

"What?! That thing has pockets?" he teases me.

I whap him against the arm with my mask. "I was impressed, okay? Your outfit doesn't look like it has a lot of extra room."

He laughs and then drapes his arm around me as we head back toward the house. "So, you've been checking me out?"

"Stop." I concentrate on my phone and type as we walk. "You know everyone's been checking you out since the seventh grade."

"Including you?"

I sigh. "Unfortunately, yes."

"Why unfortunately?"

My phone dings with a message, and I avoid answering his question by reading it. **Good,** Izzy sends. **Don't come down here.**

What? I stop walking. "Why is Izzy telling me not to come in the house?"

"Probably because of June and her friends."

I turn to face him. "Care to elaborate?"

Aaron's arm falls from my shoulders, but he hangs on to my elbow. "That's why I wanted to come outside. I wanted to warn you, but then we got distracted." He sighs. "The girls wanted to get back at you for the sign. They got creative with their costumes."

My brow jumps.

"And you were right," he rushes to add. "You knew coming here might be an issue."

My stomach sinks. I told them not to make that stupid sign. But no, nobody listens to me. And they got creative with their costumes? What does that mean?

My phone dings, this time with a picture. Oh.

"A yellow reflective vest would have been more accurate," I say, irritated.

"I just need to run inside and get my keys," Aaron says. "Harrison wanted everyone to drop them in a bucket to be safe, so no one left who wasn't sober."

I purse my lips, annoyed. I don't know why this bothers me so much. I mean, I expected something to happen. There was no logical way it wouldn't. Still, I almost forgot about things for a whole what? Half hour? It was nice. Every time I turn around the biggest mistake I've made in my entire life gets thrown in my face. Every. Single. Time.

"I don't want to leave you alone out here," Aaron says as he takes a step. "Come with me and stay upstairs by the door. I'll be fast; I promise."

I nod but remain silent. The quicker we can leave, the better.

We make our way up the porch stairs and into the house, but as soon as Aaron closes the door, we both sense something is off. We don't hear any music, just loud voices. I look at him, and he looks at me, until someone yells, "Enough!"

Aaron takes off, and I follow without any sense of self-preservation. My friends are down there, and I have no idea what's going on.

When we reach the bottom step, it's as if someone drew a physical line down the center of the room. Izzy, Wes, Harrison, Brooke, Willow, Nick, and a handful of other kids stand on the one side behind Delaney. June and her crew, most of Aaron's teammates, and basically everyone else stand on the other.

"Well, well. Look who finally decided to make an appearance," June snarks as she pulls her attention away from Delaney. "Are you done saving your Juliet, Romeo?"

A few chuckles echo through the room as Harrison steps forward. "I said he lost a bet."

"Whatever." June crosses her arms and tries to look around Aaron at me. "What are you supposed to be? The Grim Reaper? How fitting."

The laughter seems a little louder now. Aaron's teammates don't look amused though, and he tries to walk forward but I grab his arm to stop him.

"Hey." Delaney's tone is sharp as she crosses her arms and moves closer to June. "Eyes over here, sweetie. We're not done."

"'Lane," Harrison warns. "Don't."

"Relax, Harry," she suddenly turns sweet. "I've got this, baby."

Huh? When did they give each other nicknames and start calling each other baby?

"Dude. You're seeing this chick?"

Some guy directs his angry comment at Harrison. Before he can answer, Aaron snaps, "Shut up, Max."

"What are you going to do about it, *captain?*" He twists the word.

Delaney snaps her fingers, bringing everyone's focus back to her and June. "I asked you a question," she continues, staring a hole through June's face. "Are you going to give me an answer?"

"I don't owe you anything, freak." June looks Delaney up and down like she's contagious. "What in the hell have you got on anyway? If you're so worried about what I'm wearing, maybe you should take a look in a mirror." She looks over her shoulder. "Anyone have a mirror they can loan this bitch?"

The room erupts with both gasps and snickers as blood starts to pound in my ears. They can pick on me all day long but not my friends. Never them.

Izzy must feel the same way because Wes has to hold her back as she tries to rush forward. Delaney doesn't look the least bit fazed, however. Her tone stays calm and even.

"You have no idea who I am or where I'm from," she says. "You have no idea what I've done, so you may want to check yourself."

"Oh, right. You met Lucy at criminal camp." June's narrowed eyes land on me again. "Right after she killed Cody."

"No."

Aaron's voice nearly shakes the room. I can't hold him back, and he marches up to June and Delaney. "It was an accident," he seethes. "Stop spreading lies."

"How can you defend her?" June points at me and then at those who are apparently on my side. "How can *any* of you defend her?"

"Easy," Aaron says. "She's human. And a good person."

"Really?" She fakes a laugh. "Does a good person run over someone with their car?"

"Does a good person do what you're doing?" Aaron fires back. "All Lucy wants is to be left alone. Why is that so hard for you?"

"Because she ruined my life!"

"Do you think hers is perfect?"

Oh my god. I can't take this anymore. My pulse continues to race, and their voices start to sound fuzzy. No one should have to put up with this but me. No one should have to defend me but me.

"Stop."

My throat is dry and scratchy, and my voice doesn't come out loud enough.

"Stop."

They're still arguing.

"Stop!" I finally yell loud enough for everyone to turn and stare. I blink to focus, my eyes darting around the room. It seems half the senior class is here. Kids I know. Kids I barely know. People I care about. People I don't.

"If you're going to scream at someone, scream at me," I say and will my legs to carry me to the center of the room. "There's nothing you can say to make me hate myself more than I already do."

"Lucy–" Aaron starts, but I shake my head to keep him quiet. When I focus back on June, she seems a little stunned I'm talking to her.

"So?" I ask. "Do you want to tell me how I ruined your life?"

She glares at me but remains silent.

"This is your chance," I say, growing a little more defiant. "In front of all these people. Tell me what you really think, and then we can compare our trashed lives. Because I can take it. Well, I can't, but I'll just add it to my next therapy session."

The room goes so quiet, you could hear a pin drop.

"Oh. You didn't know?" I look around. No one behind June will meet my eyes as words I didn't know I was capable of saying start to spill from my lips. "I go every Friday. We can talk about how bad your life sucks after we discuss how I can't drive anymore. Or how I got kicked off the student council. Or how I can't smell a fire, or have anything the color red on my hands–"

"I don't care," June interrupts.

"Jesus," Delaney says. "Could you be a bigger –"

"She took Cody away from me!"

"Cody took himself away from you!"

Aaron's outburst makes me jump and surprises us all. I look up at him, and he looks furious.

"Don't pretend your relationship was perfect because it wasn't." He points at June. "Between you and Allie–"

He suddenly stops speaking, his eyes growing wide. He looks like he's been slapped except no one touched him. I glance at June, and she looks the same way. Obviously, I missed something.

"How do you know about that?" she whispers.

Aaron frowns. "How do you?"

The next thing I know, Harrison appears between us. He spreads his arms wide and forces us to step away from one another.

"That's it. My house, my party. If you can't pull your shit together, get out."

He doesn't have to tell me twice. I haven't had my poop in a group since last May.

I turn to leave and feel Aaron's hand at the small of my back. He follows me, and when we make it outside and to his truck, I'm impressed by the number of people who also chose to go.

Maybe there's a little hope for Holton High after all.

CHAPTER TWENTY

Aaron

Lucy's eyes fill her face when she sees me sitting in her driveway Monday morning. I roll down my window and wave. I know what she's thinking, which is why I didn't warn her I'd be here. I need her to ride with me to school today.

"Where's Izzy?" she asks as she walks toward me.

"Good morning to you, too," I tease. "Change of plans. Hop in."

She narrows her eyes before slowly rounding the front of my truck and climbing inside. "What's going on?" she asks as she settles in the seat.

I wiggle my eyebrows. "Izzy said she was tired of hauling you around."

"That's a lie," she says with a straight face.

Conceding with a nod, I put the truck in reverse and back down the drive. When I stop to wait for traffic, I hand her my phone. "Someone has requested our presence."

While she reads the message from June, I recall the words in my head: *Can you meet me behind the gym before school? Bring Lucy. It's important.*

"What?" Lucy's mouth falls open. "Why would you ... this isn't a good idea."

"Probably not," I say as I pull out onto the road. But I can't help my curiosity. After we left Harrison's party, my thoughts were consumed with the fact she knew about Allie. She *knew*. How? How was that possible? Did Cody tell someone other than me? Who?

"It's an ambush," Lucy says. "Her friends are going to jump us and tie us up in her basement."

I chuckle. "I think you've been watching too many movies."

She shakes her head. "Art imitates life. Besides, after what happened this weekend ... she has to hate me more than ever." She lets out a breath. "I can't believe I did that."

"Like I told you, what you did was awesome." I reach over and squeeze her knee. "June needed to be put in her place, and the last person anyone expected to do it was you."

She looks uncertain. "Everyone knows my secrets now, and they can use them against me."

"Not if I have anything to say about it."

"Ugh." She groans and leans her head back against the headrest. "It's not your job to defend me. I should just home school the second semester. It would be easier for everyone."

It wouldn't be for me. She's the first thing on my mind when I wake up and one of the two reasons I pull my ass out of bed every morning. Seeing her is my first priority with graduating a close second. I don't know if that makes me a good person or if it means I'm completely whipped. Honestly, I'd be okay with both.

We're quiet the rest of the way to school. From our conversations over the weekend, I know if I keep disputing her worries she'll only come up with more reasons to be anxious. I'm figuring out Lucy is a "show me or didn't happen" type of girl, so I'm hoping by meeting June we can put something to rest. I don't know what June wants, but my gut tells me it's about the secret I thought only I knew.

As I turn into the parking lot and head toward the gym, I can feel Lucy tense up beside me. "I really think this is a bad idea," she says quietly.

Guilt washes over me. I'm putting her in an uncomfortable situation to get answers to my own questions. "If that's true," I say, "you can hold it over my head forever." My mind races. "And you don't have to do anything you don't want to do. You can stay in the truck, if you want."

She nods.

When we round the corner of the building, I spot June sitting in her BMW. She's parked as far away as possible from the few cars in the lot. I park two empty spaces down from her, so she can see Lucy but Lucy doesn't have to be close.

"Okay." I put my hand on the door handle and look at her. "I'm going in."

She half smiles at my mock-serious tone.

Shoving my hands in my pockets, I walk toward June as she gets out of her car. "Thanks for coming," she says when I reach her.

I purse my lips and nod as she crosses her arms and looks around, as if she's just as nervous as Lucy.

"So ..." She looks at her feet. "About Saturday. What you said."

"Which part?" I'm not going to let her get off that easy.

"About," she looks around again, "Allie," she whispers.

My brow shoots up.

"How do you know about that?"

Now it's my turn to cross my arms. "How else? Cody."

She hugs herself a little tighter. "Does anyone else know? Did you tell Lucy?"

"No." I scowl. "Cody swore me to–"

"Because I can't have it getting out. You understand that, right?"

Her eyes plead with mine. It's the most sincere I've ever seen her. Of course I wouldn't tell anyone; I get that it would be embarrassing for people to find out she was cheated on. But, an idea dawns. I can use this to my advantage.

"I need you to lay off Lucy," I say. "Leave her alone, and tell your friends. Whatever made up thing you have against her is over. Got it?"

June closes her eyes and takes a deep breath. When she opens them again, she says, "Yeah. That's one of the things I wanted to say to you both. I'll ... stop."

I want to believe her. Maybe now I can.

She looks around me toward Lucy. "Is she going to come out or ...?"

"She doesn't trust you," I say.

June sighs, annoyed. "I'm trying to be the bigger person here."

There's the attitude I was expecting. "Maybe you should try harder," I say and gesture toward the truck.

Her head falls back in annoyance, then she starts to walk, so I follow. This Allie secret must be huge to her. Lucy notices us coming, and I give her a look to let her know everything is okay.

When we make it to her window, she rolls it down since I left the truck running. No one says anything, so I nudge June with my elbow.

"I'm ... done," she searches for words. "You won't have to worry about me anymore. Or anyone else."

Lucy looks surprised but doesn't say anything. After a few seconds, June turns to me. "Okay, well, I told her. Gotta go; I don't want to be late." She takes a step but stops. "Remember you promised."

I meet her eyes. "Only if you hold up your end of the deal."

She gives me a curt nod before walking away.

I watch as she gets into her car, then set both hands on the truck door and lean into Lucy's window with a smile. "See? She didn't kidnap us."

Lucy looks doubtful. "What happened? Why did she change her mind?"

I want to say it doesn't matter, but I'm getting sick of all the lies. "I wish I could tell you, but it's a secret I can't share."

She searches my face. "Are you in trouble?"

"No, no," I reassure her. "It's not my secret. It's Cody's."

She blinks and looks away. "Oh, okay. Never mind."

"Hey." I stand on my toes, leaning forward and ducking down as far as I can so she'll see me. "What happened wasn't your fault."

She turns her head. "It kinda was."

"No. Not entirely." How many times do we have to have this

conversation?

She's quiet and winds her fingers through her backpack straps before her expression twists. "Well, duh."

I chuckle at her sarcasm.

We faintly hear the warning bell, and Lucy looks toward the school. "We should get going."

"Yep." Walking around the hood of my truck, I climb in the driver's seat. Before I pull out of the parking spot, I look at her. "Do you think we should walk in together?"

Her eyes grow wide like when I first saw her this morning. "People's heads might explode."

"It could be worth it."

She pretends to think it over. "Nah," she decides. "I wouldn't want the janitor to have to clean that up. Let's give June some time to talk to her friends."

I don't argue.

"Hi."

Lucy jumps. "What are you doing here?"

"I'm walking down the hall."

"Yeah, but," she looks around, "you're at my locker."

I am. It's the end of the day, and since I picked her up this morning, I thought I'd offer to take her home, too. Smiling, I lean my shoulder against the locker next to hers. "This is the senior hallway, right?"

"Damn straight," Izzy says as she stacks books in her bag. "Are you here to collect your woman?"

"Izzy!" Lucy shushes her.

"Oh, please." She rolls her eyes. "It's obvious you two have a thing for each other. Why deny it?"

"Yeah, why deny it?" I say with a grin. I know she's probably going to be annoyed with me, but our earlier conversation with June has me optimistic.

A blush creeps over Lucy's cheeks. Instead of answering me, she sticks her head back behind her locker door.

"Anyway," I say, "I was wondering if you wanted a ride home."

"She does," Izzy says, tossing her bag over her shoulder and slamming her locker shut. "See ya tomorrow." She wiggles her fingers at us as she walks away.

After Lucy grabs her things, she pins me with narrow eyes. "I thought we weren't being obvious."

"Does it matter if no one cares?"

"I'm not sure it's safe to say no one cares just yet."

I follow her gaze to see a few of my teammates staring at us from down the hall. When they see me looking at them, they quickly pretend to be interested in different parts of the ceiling.

"Hmm. Their heads haven't exploded," I joke. "How disappointing."

She playfully shoves my arm.

"Oh, now you've done it. You've initiated physical contact. Let's watch them now and see what happens."

She turns away from me while trying not to laugh.

"C'mon," I say and take a step. "Let's get out of here. I need some help with my chemistry homework."

"Really?" she asks. "You expect me to tutor you?"

"No, but it'd be nice."

She shakes her head like she doesn't understand me but leads the way out the exit door near us. We'll have to take the long way to the parking lot, but I don't care. Should I tell her now or later that when I said chemistry, I meant *our* chemistry? The kiss we shared two days ago was, without a doubt, my best first kiss ever.

We fight over the radio station on the way to her house, and when we pull up, I slam on the brakes in surprise. There's a police car sitting in her driveway.

"Is everything okay?" I ask.

"Oh, yeah. That's just my uncle. He's probably here to see my mom."

Her uncle the cop is visiting? Damn. My hopes of making out

while we study suddenly fly out the window.

Once we're inside, we find Lucy's mom and her uncle talking in the kitchen.

"Hey, sweetie. How was school?" her mom asks.

"Same 'ole, same 'ole," she answers. "Mom, you remember Aaron, right?"

She smiles. "Yes, from the festival. How are you, Aaron?"

"Good, thanks Mrs. Anderson."

"We're going to study for a little bit, if that's okay," Lucy says as she walks closer to her family. "Hey, Uncle Tony."

"Hiya, kid." They bump fists. "How's life treating you?"

Lucy shoots me a quick glance. "Better."

Her uncle smirks and meets my eyes as her mom's grin lights up the room.

"Well, make yourself at home, Aaron," she says. "The fridge is yours and snacks are in the pantry."

"But stay away from the cinnamon rolls," her uncle warns, and I notice he's eating one. "Those are mine."

Message received, I think as I nod, wondering if Lucy's dad is as intimidating.

"This way," she says and I follow her into the living room. She keeps walking, and we end up in a den off to the side where there's a big desk, two arm chairs, and tons of books on shelves from the ceiling to the floor. Two oversized windows overlook a wooded backyard.

"I feel like I'm in a library," I say as I drop my backpack next to a chair.

"My dad teaches literature at U of M," Lucy says, "and writes mystery novels on the side. My mom is also a freelance writer. You know, magazine articles and stuff."

No, I don't know, but I say "Nice" anyway. "Does your dad have any pull at Michigan?" I smile. "They're one of the schools looking at me for lacrosse."

She looks impressed. "Not unless you take one of his classes. The athletic office doesn't exactly consult with the English department."

"Makes sense," I say and sit down.

Lucy sits opposite me and tucks one leg beneath her while she hauls her bag onto her lap. Looking around, I ask, "So, does that mean Michigan is in your future, too?"

"I do get the friends and family discount," she jokes. "So, most likely yes."

"Most likely?"

She pulls a notebook out of her backpack. "I've thought a lot about moving out of state, to get away from here." She pauses. "I've been accepted to Northwestern, but it's a lot of money."

"But you haven't made up your mind yet?"

"No."

My stomach sinks at the thought of her moving away. I don't know why; Illinois is right next door to both Michigan and Indiana, if Notre Dame works out of me.

"So, where do we want to start?" she asks.

I haven't even pulled a book out of my backpack.

When I don't answer, she gives me a questioning look. "Aaron? What are you stuck on?"

I decide to be honest. "You."

"Excuse me?"

"I don't need any chemistry help. I just wanted to hang out."

She stares at me with disbelief, and I grin.

Standing, I wander over to a picture hanging on the wall. It's a newspaper article that includes a photo of a very studious-looking man sitting at the same desk in this room.

"I take it this is your dad?"

"Yes," she says and joins me. "I took his picture for the Holton paper; they needed one for their article about local authors. He liked it, so he uses it for his book covers now."

My mind flashes back to Izzy saying something about Lucy's photography hobby.

"Why don't you take pictures for the yearbook?"

She shrugs. "Because I don't go to school events anymore."

"But you still take pictures, right?"

"Of course."

Looking around, I see other photos in frames, but I have no idea if she took them. "Show me," I say.

"Show you what?"

"Your pictures."

She tilts her head in thought for a second, then says, "I have a better idea. Follow me."

I end up standing outside her bedroom as she walks up to a dresser. While she grabs a complicated-looking camera, I try to learn a little more about her. Her room is clean, unlike mine, and I can see a puffy bedspread, a bean bag chair, pictures stuck all over the walls, and a lava lamp. I also spy a laptop, headphones, and some state-of-the-art wireless speakers that make me a little jealous.

After grabbing what I assume is a rechargeable battery, Lucy pushes it into the side of her camera and walks back to me. "Welcome to Photography 101," she says and hands me the equipment.

"Oh no," I say and try to give it back.

"Take it."

"No, seriously. I'll screw something up."

"Not if I'm helping you," she says and leans against me to get me moving. "I think you'll surprise yourself."

My expression twists.

After we make our way downstairs, we grab our coats before I follow Lucy outside into the yard I saw from the office windows. Walking a few feet into the trees, she says, "Okay," and loops the camera strap over my head. "Hold it up. What do you see?"

I look through the little window and move the camera around. "Cloudy sky. Bare tree branches. Dead leaves. Some pinecones." I turn toward her. "Your nose."

She half-laughs and puts her hand in front of the lens, but not before I hit the shutter button. Pulling the camera away from my face, I see the picture I just took displayed on the screen. It's mostly blurry palm, but I also got her forehead and one eye. "I *am* good at this," I joke.

She looks over my shoulder. "Try again, Leibovitz."

"Who?"

"Never mind," she says. "Let's practice on things that don't move for now."

She really wants me to do this, so I listen to her and focus. Several nature shots later, I say, "This one turned out pretty cool." It's just a bunch of tangled tree branches, but I think it's artistic in a rock album cover kind of way.

"See? You're a natural."

"I'm not so sure about that," I say as I start flipping through the pictures. "Just so you know, I get to teach you how to play lacrosse next."

"Um ..." She looks doubtful. "You may want to rethink that."

"Hey, I used your $500 camera."

"And lacrosse can cause bodily harm."

"I'll wear my cup." I wink.

She tries to look shocked but ends up laughing. "I meant harm to me, but okay."

Shoving her hands in her jacket pockets, she walks farther into the woods while I trail behind her taking meaningless photos. Pine tree. Click. A hollowed-out log. Click. Squirrel. Zoom, click. I glance at the screen. Yep, he's a blur.

When I look up, Lucy has stopped in front of a huge rock. She tilts her head, stares at it for a second, then crawls up the side. When she's sitting on the top, she brushes off her hands and says, "I used to sit up here when I was little and pretend I was riding a horse."

"Well, move over, cowgirl," I say and join her, careful not to bump her camera against the stone. When we're sitting shoulder to shoulder and hip to hip with our legs stretched out in front of us, she reaches for her equipment and I hand it over. She reviews the pictures with me.

"I like this one." She nods toward the picture of the rotting log. "This one is good, too," she stops at another. "I can print the ones you like, if you want."

"Then I'll need to take a picture of you."

"Why?"

"Because it would be the one I like the most."

She shakes her head like she doesn't believe me, and I realize now would be the perfect time to kiss her. Should I? I mean, it worked out the last time, so ...

Reaching over, I barely touch the side of her chin. She looks up at me, and I lean forward a little. Wearing half a smile, my eyes jump to her mouth, to her eyes, and back again. We're already so close, it doesn't take much for the distance between us to disappear. When it does, I try to keep my grin off my face and in my head.

Just like the first time I kissed Lucy, adrenaline runs through my veins. It doesn't take a few minutes of making out or anything else but the feeling of her lips on mine. It's an instant reaction, a high I've never felt before with anyone else. When her fingers wrap around my wrist, to steady my palm against her cheek, I think she feels – or hope she feels – the same way I do.

"I think Photography 101," I mumble mid-kiss, "is my new favorite class."

I can feel her smile against me before she leans back. "I might have to revise the syllabus. Not everyone covers the same material."

"Good," I say and wrap my arm around her waist, "because I like where this is heading."

"Which is where?"

"To more lessons and more practice with me, your favorite student."

Her brow jumps. "My favorite, eh?"

I nod. "I can totally tell what you're thinking."

"Really?" She looks skeptical. "What am I thinking right now?"

"That Aaron's kinda hot, and I'm really cute, and we should make out some more before someone comes looking for us, like my scary cop uncle." I shudder.

Lucy's mouth falls open. "Wow. That's ..."

I expect her to say "completely wrong."

"... remarkably accurate. Except for the scary part."

"Yeah?" I grin and lean forward.

"Yeah," she whispers against my lips.

CHAPTER TWENTY-ONE

Lucy

"Ugh!" Izzy jerks back from the mirror. "How much more time do we have?"

"What happened?"

"I stabbed myself." She turns her whole body around to look at Delaney and me. Mascara is smeared under her one tearing eye. "It would help if I wasn't cursed with the shortest eyelashes on the planet."

"They make vitamins for that." Delaney comes to her rescue. "Some sort of supplement I read about."

"Please fix it," Izzy begs. "I'd rather not look like I got punched in the face when the guys get here."

Delaney pretend curtseys. "As you wish."

I laugh and Izzy smiles as Delaney wipes away the black streak now trailing down her face.

With my best friend's crisis averted, I finish putting on some lip gloss. The girls talked me into using makeup, since we're all going out to celebrate Delaney's eighteenth birthday. It's the first "normal" group thing I've done in a long time, but it feels right. When they first suggested it, I didn't get as much anxiety as I usually do. Wes and Harrison have turned out to be sweet guys, especially to my friends, and I haven't had to deal with any June drama in weeks. I honestly can't believe she's kept her word – but I'm not going to question it. Life is a lot easier when you're not constantly looking over your shoulder.

"Why are we going ice skating again?" Izzy asks Delaney. "It seems like an odd I'm-an-adult-now party choice."

I make a face at her. Although I'm not too sure about my own balance on skates, I say, "Way to be supportive."

"Well, it's not common." She shrugs. "I didn't mean anything bad."

"We're going because I like it," Delaney says, unaffected.

"Do you do it a lot?"

Delaney shakes her head. "When I was little and my parents felt bad after a bender, they'd take me to the store and buy me whatever I wanted. Once, I got ice skates. I only used them a few times, though." Her eyes light up. "Since it hasn't been cold enough to freeze Holton Lake yet, I was excited when I found a rink that had open skate times."

I frown as a thought pops into my mind: a slow-motion movie of me falling flat on my face. "Videos are not allowed," I announce.

"I second that," Izzy agrees.

"What about pictures?" Delaney steps back to admire her mascara correction. "I would like to document my day."

"Well, yeah." I nod. "We can stage those."

Twenty minutes later the guys arrive, and we scramble down the stairs like characters in a cheesy rom com. After saying goodbye to Delaney's aunt and uncle, we open the front door to find three cute boys wearing lopsided smiles.

"Welcome to the Man Van," Harrison says as we all climb into a silver minivan.

"The Man Van?" Izzy asks as Aaron and I head to the rear bench seat.

"Yep." Harrison grins. "It's the name I came up with to de-soccer mom my ride. When your parents get a new car and give you the option of keeping the old one, you go with free."

"Wise choice," Delaney says from the front seat and leans over to kiss Harrison on the cheek. "You know where we're going, right?"

"I think so. Pull the directions up on your phone just in case."

Harrison backs down the driveway, and Wes pulls everyone into a conversation about choosing a restaurant to visit after we skate. As the front of the van weighs the pros and cons of Mexican food versus Thai, Aaron bumps his knee against mine.

"Are you ready for this whole triple date thing?"

"I think so."

He smiles. "You look nice."

I smile back. "And you smell good."

Aaron always smells good. And looks good. And compliments me. He's more gentlemanly than I thought most guys could be these days. The last few weeks have been some of the best of my life, and I realize a big reason why is because of him. Of course my friends have helped; they've always been there. But it seems like Aaron helps me breathe. I don't have to think around him, just *be*.

He squeezes my leg and scoots as close as his seatbelt will let him. "So, I guess I should let you know ... I haven't been on skates in years."

My face scrunches. "You live on a lake."

"And I love all summer lake activities."

"Oh. Well, I think the last time I skated I was ten."

Aaron chuckles. "Then this should be interesting. There is one good thing about Delaney's choice, though."

"What's that?"

"We'll have to hold on to each other the whole time."

I can see his sly look in the dim light of the van, and now it's my turn to laugh. "Any excuse, huh?"

"You know it," he says and kisses the back of my hand.

When we get to the rink, it's a lot more crowded than I expected. We have to wait in line to rent skates, and after we each trade our shoes for a pair, we head over to a seating area to put the death traps on. Yes, I'm getting more concerned about this activity the more I see people racing around the ice.

"Make sure you tie them as tight as you can," instructs a staff member as she wanders through the area. "You'll want as much support as possible."

I do as I'm told, and when I stand, Aaron asks, "You got it?"

"I think so." I may have overdone it; I can barely wiggle my toes.

"You guys," Delaney gushes. "Thank you so much for doing this. You have no idea how much it means to me. This is already the best birthday ever."

Her smile is so big, I think her face might split in two. I've never seen her so happy or excited before, and it makes me grin. Her behavior is more typical of Izzy, and I wonder for a second if they're rubbing off on each other. Regardless, it's nice to see Delaney like this. She's been through a lot, and she deserves to have a good time.

"Then let's get the party started," I say and look back at Aaron.

He gestures for us to walk ahead of him. "After you."

Delaney offers me her arm, and I link mine through hers in an exaggerated, goofy way. It's easier to walk in the skates than I anticipated, and it gives me a little confidence. When we reach the slippery surface, I look for Izzy and Wes and find them already coasting around at a decent speed. How is that possible?

Harrison and Aaron are behind us, and as soon as I step onto the ice, I slide. "Whoa," I say, letting go of Delaney and reaching for the edge of the boards. Harrison ends up right beside me with a somewhat terrified look on his face.

"Please don't tell anyone about what you see tonight," he pleads.

"Ditto," I say. "I already discussed a no video rule with your girlfriend."

"C'mon." Delaney appears next to Harrison. "Take my hand. It's okay."

As the two of them slowly glide away, I feel hands on my waist and hear a voice in my ear. "You want to hang on to the side a couple times around?"

Looking over my shoulder at Aaron, I nod. "That would probably be a good idea."

He gives me a quick kiss.

With one hand running along the boards and the other circling Aaron's waist, we make it around the ice one time. As Izzy and Wes fly by us, she waves at me.

"Show off!" I half yell at her. Looking at Aaron, I say, "Apparently she has a career in the Ice Capades I don't know about."

"And Wes must speed skate in his spare time," he grumbles.

Determined, I put a little distance between Aaron and me. "All it takes is bravery and a little balance, right? I'm not afraid of a few bruises if I fall. Are you?"

"Hell no."

"Then we can do this."

"Hell yeah." He smiles, then pretends to be serious.

By the third or fourth time around, I've let go of the side and we're keeping up with most of the amateur skaters around us. The rink is playing a local radio station while we skate, and the music helps me create a rhythm with my small strides. As I get more confident and move faster, an exhilarating feeling takes over. I can't imagine what it would be like if I actually knew what I was doing.

Soon we're all cruising at a good pace, even Harrison, and I have to admit this is a lot of fun. Aaron and I alternate between holding hands, to him holding onto my waist from behind, to the two of us racing each other and our friends as best we can.

"Harrison wants to see if he can beat me," Aaron says. "You push me and Delaney will push him, and we'll see how far each of us go."

"Okay," I say and try to slide to a stop while attempting to keep my balance.

Once Harrison and Delaney are lined up next to us, the two of us girls push the guys as hard and as fast as we can. Laughing, we let them go and watch their "race," not paying attention to the fact that we're also moving.

"Look out!" Delaney yells just before she collides into me. With nothing to stop us except each other, we both lose our footing and go down. It doesn't hurt when our butts meet the ice, so we lie there laughing until the guys, and Izzy and Wes, make it back to us to help us up.

Soon, we all decide to take a break and head to the concession stand.

"So," I ask Izzy after we sit down, "how come you never told me you could skate?"

"Because I didn't know. Beginner's luck, I guess." She reaches for a chip. Dipping it in some nacho cheese, she adds, "You're not doing too bad yourself."

I frown. "Um, did you miss me fall a few minutes ago?"

"Nope," she says between crunches.

"Do you want some of this?" Aaron rips off a piece of his soft pretzel and holds it out toward me. "It's pretty decent."

"Thanks."

I take it from him and pop it in my mouth. As I do, he slides his plate between us and his body over, so his leg and shoulder are touching mine. As the conversation picks up around the table, a warm feeling spreads through me ... and not just from Aaron's touch. I feel surrounded by good people, too. Who knew this mixed up bunch – two juvenile delinquents, a yearbook geek, and three lacrosse players – could become part of a happy ending to a pretty crappy beginning.

"Oh, look guys. It's the new cast of *Friends*."

My whole body tenses at the over-the-top, sarcastically sweet voice behind me. My heart stops, and everyone else either turns around or looks up.

"Are you kidding me?" Aaron mutters under his breath.

"Let's see." June practically prances to the end of our table and into my line of sight. She looks a little hyper as she braces both hands against the metal top and leans forward, grinning and causing Izzy and Harrison to lean back. Some of her girlfriends stand around her, along with a few guys Aaron knows.

"You," she points at Izzy, "have to be Monica because you're so anal about everything."

Izzy's face contorts. "Excuse me?"

June ignores her. "Which makes you Chandler," she continues, moving her index finger over to Wes. It then lands on Aaron and me. "You two have to be Ross and Rachel. Cute but clueless," she says, then uses her accusing finger to flip her hair. Her eyes land on Delaney, and she adds, "That makes you Phoebe because you're so *artistic*," she twists the word, "and Harrison is good 'ole Joey. Which makes sense, because he was dumb enough to tell us where you'd be tonight."

All eyes land on Harrison, and he puts his hands up in defense. "Jason and Max asked what I was doing this weekend, and I told them. It wasn't an invitation." His eyes narrow and land on the aforementioned duo. He repeats, "It wasn't an invitation."

"Don't care," June says and starts to back away. "We just want to hang out with all the "cool" kids." She uses air quotes when she says cool, then rounds up her entourage and shouts, "To the skate rental!"

As they walk away, I look at Aaron with wide eyes. "Did that seriously just happen?"

He shakes his head like he can't believe it either.

"I'm so sorry," I hear Harrison apologizing to Delaney. "I did not invite them here." His eyes meet mine. "I swear," he says.

"I believe you," I tell him. "She's … she's just …"

"Acting really strange. Don't you think?" Izzy asks. "I mean, she's always weird, but don't you think she was weirder than normal? All happy but mean underneath-like."

"I think that's typical for June." Aaron puts his arm around my shoulders. "So, what do we do now?"

I feel the weight of everyone's stares as if the decision is up to me. It's not. It's Delaney's day, and it should stay that way. These last few weeks without drama have been amazing, and I don't want to lose that feeling. I can be good at ignoring things, at least for another hour or two.

"Well, I say we continue as planned." I raise my hand. "Anyone else?"

Izzy's arm shoots up. "All in favor of pretending the ignorant troll doesn't exist, say aye."

Four more "aye's" sound around the table.

"Good," I say and pour the last of my candy into my palm. "Sour Skittles anyone?"

It doesn't take us long to finish our snacks and get back on the ice. Aaron and I skate hand in hand, but I confess I'm paranoid. I'll be watching my back the rest of the time we're here.

"You're not paranoid; you're justified," he says. "Plus, you're being an awesome friend by sticking this out for Delaney."

"She'd do the same for me," I say without hesitation. *Probably more*, I think.

"I just don't get it." He shakes his head. "June's been quiet for weeks. What triggered her now?"

"I have no idea."

Suddenly, a playful scream rips through the rink. We turn and find June at the opposite end of the ice, lying on her stomach while her friends hold theirs in laughter.

"This is so stupid!" she laugh-yells loud enough for everyone to hear.

Aaron rolls his eyes. "God forbid she isn't the center of attention."

Ignoring the disruption, we continue skating, slower now so we won't catch up to June before she picks herself up. Unfortunately, she decides to hang out by the boards where she fell, and we have no choice but to pass by. Refusing to acknowledge her, we just keep going – which earns us a comment to our backs.

"What? You're too good to say hello?"

Aaron somehow manages to stop on a dime and turns, pulling me around and into his side. I end up flush against him with my head at his shoulder and my free arm around his waist for balance.

"What do you want, June?" he asks with more force than I expect. "Why are you here?"

Her eyes flash. "That's none of your business."

"I think you made it our business when you found us in the lobby."

"I just wanted to say hi." She wiggles her fingers at us in a wave, but I see it more as an attempt to cast a spell.

"You ..." He gives up and sighs. "Whatever. C'mon, Lucy."

Aaron starts to leave and I follow, since we're still connected. We only make it a few feet before hearing, "You can't protect her forever."

Aaron glances behind us. "Watch me."

His words make me scowl. Protect me from what? June's snide remarks and pranks? When we're farther away from her, I say, "I never asked you to watch out for me."

"I know."

"Then why did you say that? You're not required to be my bodyguard."

"But what if I want to guard your body?" His eyebrows jump, and I try to give him a serious look while holding back a smile. Releasing my hand, he wraps his arms around my waist from behind. "We're together, right? Why wouldn't we look out for each other? It kinda comes with the boyfriend/girlfriend territory."

My heart stops for the second time tonight, but this time in a good way. Did he just make us official?

"Okay," he says in my ear. "Is it my imagination, or did you just get all tense?"

We glide to a stop by the corner of the rink, and I turn in his arms to face him. "You said the b word."

He pretends to think. "Body?"

"No."

"Birthday?"

"No."

"Bungee jumping?"

"What? Stop playing dumb."

He grins. "Well, according to some people, I am cute but clueless."

I smirk. "You said boyfriend."

"I also said a lot of other things. Is that bad?"

"Well ... no." I look up at him. "It's just the first time you've said it, so ... do you really want that title?"

Instead of answering me, Aaron leans down and catches my mouth in an entirely inappropriate-for-public-but-mind-blowing kiss that leaves no question. After a few seconds someone whistles at us, making me pull away before I really want to.

"Was that a clear answer?" he asks before resuming his grin.

"Crystal." I smile back. *Holy crap.*

Taking a few steps out of Aaron's arms, I get the bright idea to race him.

"Sure, 'cause we're so good at skating," he agrees sarcastically.

"Damn right we are," I say with fake confidence.

I want a head start, so I say, "Readysetgo" as fast as I can, pushing away from him with my right foot, then my left. After I get a few strides in, I look back to see him behind me, pretending to catch up.

Laughing, I face forward again but not before something hits me hard from the side. The shove forces me to lose my balance, and I think *Shit!* as I trip over my own feet. I can't regain my balance, and all I can see are the boards heading toward my face. I put my arms out to brace myself.

And everything goes black.

CHAPTER TWENTY-TWO

Aaron

What the hell?!

One minute Lucy is skating away from me, and the next June comes flying out of nowhere and plows right into her. They both go down, except June lands on her side and Lucy hits the boards then flops to the ice like a ragdoll.

"Lucy!" I'm by her side in less than a second. I look her over in a panic before gently shaking her shoulder. "Can you hear me?"

She mumbles something but doesn't open her eyes. I don't see any blood, so I take that as a good sign.

"What happened?" Izzy and Wes appear beside me, followed by Delaney and Harrison.

"Did I just see what I think I saw?" Delaney sounds like June's breaths are numbered.

Speaking of, my head snaps up to find her being helped to her feet by Kat and Jessie, Max and Jason. Never did I think she would stoop this low.

"Back away, please. Back away," a staff member from the rink comes shuffling across the ice in tennis shoes. She kneels down next to Lucy and makes sure she's breathing before lifting a radio to her mouth. "We've got an injured skater. Call 911."

Lucy's eyes blink open and dart from face to face. "I'm all right," she croaks and tries to sit up.

Immediately five pairs of hands – six, if you count the rink lady – reach out to stop her to a chorus of "No, no, no."

"You need to lie still until the ambulance gets here and the EMTs check you out," she says.

A voice comes over the walkie talkie. "911 wants to know if the person is responsive."

"Yes," the rink lady responds. She looks at Lucy. "What's your name?"

Lucy tells her, which she repeats over the radio. She then looks at us. "Can you keep her talking while I wait out front for the ambulance? Make sure she doesn't move."

"Yes," I agree for everyone.

Before leaving the ice, she shuffles over to June to make sure she's okay. June answers whatever questions she asks, holding up her hands in what looks like, to me, an innocent "I don't know how this happened" gesture.

Bullshit.

"June is an effing psycho!" Izzy leans down next to Lucy. "Are you really okay?"

Lucy frowns. "She hit me? On purpose?"

"What do you think?"

Even though I want to strangle June, I don't think upsetting Lucy about her is going to do any good. I try to change the subject back to what Izzy asked and focus on Lucy's face. "What hurts?"

"My wrist." Then, she touches above her eyebrow gently and flinches. "And my head. I should have an awesome bruise tomorrow."

I hope she doesn't have a concussion. "Are you dizzy at all?"

"I don't know. I've barely moved."

"Guys." Delaney's voice catches our attention. "Are we ready to tell those assholes we'll meet them in the parking lot or what?" She cracks her knuckles, and a love-struck look takes over Harrison's face.

"No. Don't," Lucy answers.

We all scowl at her. She's too nice.

"No," she notices our expressions, "what I meant was don't do it now. Wait until I feel good enough to join you."

Okay, maybe the niceness is finally wearing off.

"Out of the way, please."

We all back up to let the EMTs through with a rolling stretcher. A man and a woman approach Lucy and stop, then kneel down and start asking her questions. I watch as they start the standard concussion protocol – I know since I've had one – before someone else catches my attention. Trailing in behind them, in uniform, is Lucy's Uncle Tony.

"What are you doing here?" I hear her ask as he stops to stand over one the EMTs.

"I heard your name over the scanner," he says. "We monitor all the 911 calls at the station. What happened?"

As the EMTs and her uncle continue to assess Lucy, I cross my arms and look around. The open skate has come to a complete stop, and a lot of people have left the ice. My eyes find June's, and I give her the dirtiest, nastiest look I can make. Why is she still here? Is she soaking up the aftermath of her assault? Because that's what it was, despite the lies she will try to tell.

"You." Lucy's uncle suddenly appears in front of me. "Let's talk." He looks over at the rest of our group. "You kids might want to turn your skates in for your shoes. They're taking Lucy to the hospital, just to triple check everything."

Wes and Harrison, along with Izzy and Delaney, nod and comply, even though I'm sure they're confused as to how I know a cop.

"So." Uncle Tony pins me with a stare. "What really happened here? My niece told me she fell, but I'm pretty sure she's lying."

I'm torn on what to say. Obviously, Lucy doesn't want him to know, or she would have mentioned June. But what good does it do to protect her? Maybe if someone talks to her other than us, she'll back off for real. My eyes dart to the left and back again. I hope I won't regret this.

"You see that girl over there? Her name is June Summers. She ran into Lucy. If you ask her, she'll tell you it was an accident."

Lucy's uncle casually glances behind us. "But it wasn't'?"

"No. June's been bugging Lucy all year. She's ... she was Cody Cunningham's girlfriend."

"I see." Uncle Tony focuses back on me. "And by bug, what do you mean?"

"She's been pretty loud about who she blames for Cody's accident. She messed with some social media stuff and Lucy's locker. She wore a prison jumpsuit with Lucy's name on the back to a Halloween party, and I'm about a hundred percent sure she wrote "bitch" across Lucy's scholarship picture."

"Anything else?"

"Just a lot of talk, you know? She's forced my friends – Cody's friends – to choose sides. Lucy's had to tip-toe around because she's afraid she'll piss June off."

"Okay." Lucy's uncle nods. "I'm going to have a little chat with Ms. Summers. She should see the light after that. If not, I'm going to ask you to let me know of any more incidents."

"Will do, Mr. ... Uncle Tony, sir." What's this guy's last name? "Oh, and uh ... I don't think Lucy wanted anyone to know what I told you."

"Don't worry. I won't tell on you. Not when she's been the happiest I've seen her in a while."

He kind of smiles at me, and my shoulders relax. As he heads over to June, I decide to skip watching that mess and make my way back to Lucy. She's on the stretcher now, ready to be rolled out.

"We'll meet you at the hospital," I say.

She eyes me suspiciously. "You told him."

"Told him what?"

"That June ran into me."

Amongst other things. "Um, yeah. Because she did. Accident or not, there's a ton of witnesses."

"She's gonna be mad."

"So? Let her. We'll set her straight in a parking lot soon, right?"

Lucy rolls her eyes but smiles. "Yeah. I guess we will."

215

IT's nine in the morning on a Sunday, and I just got back from the grocery store with ingredients for a sundae.

Vanilla ice cream. Hot fudge. Whipped cream. Maraschino cherries. And nuts.

Can't forget the nuts.

After I put everything away, I stare at the clock on the stove willing time to go faster. I couldn't sleep, even after leaving the hospital late. It took a while for Lucy to be seen, longer for her parents to come tell us what was going on, and even longer for her to be discharged. She doesn't have a concussion, but her wrist is fractured. We all stayed in the waiting room talking about what happened until she came out with her temporary cast. I'm supposed to go over to her house after she's had some time to rest, but the wait might be torture. I tried to kill some time by shopping – to bring her something to take her mind off things – but at this time in the morning, there were zero lines at the store. At least we'll be able to check 'hot fudge sundae' off her demand list later today.

Plopping down on the couch, I turn on the TV and flip through the channels until I come to what looks like a boring documentary. Hoping it will put me to sleep for a few hours, I leave it on with the volume low. My parents are already up and doing their thing, but my sister is still asleep.

Setting my phone on the cushion next to my head, in case Lucy decides to call, is the last thing I remember. The next thing I know, the sound of the doorbell makes me bolt upright.

Blinking, I check the time. It's almost noon. I wait for someone else who lives in this house to see who's at the door, but no one does. Did they leave? The bell rings two more times before I pull my ass off the couch to answer it. And as soon as I do, my stomach drops.

It's Lucy's uncle Tony.

"Hello, Aaron."

"Hi." I nervously glance behind him. "Is everything okay?"

He nods. "I hope you don't mind, but I asked Lucy for your address."

"Oh, no, that's –"

"Can I come in? I just have a few questions."

"Sure, of course, yeah." I step back and hold the door open for him to enter. After he's inside, I'm not sure where to go. "Do you want to sit at the table or –"

"Wherever is fine."

I end up leading him into the living room, to the couch where I was sleeping a minute ago. He takes a seat on the edge of the cushion and gestures for me to join him.

"Aaron, I had a long talk with June and her parents last night."

"You did?" I'm surprised. "She's in that much trouble?"

"Tell me ... when you say 'trouble,' what do you mean?"

"I ..." I pause. That's a weird question. "Obviously, she did something bad enough to get her mom and dad involved."

Uncle Tony adjusts his weight on the couch. "Aaron," he uses my name again, "do you know of anyone or anything besides June that might be bothering my niece? Or anyone else at the school?"

"What do you mean?"

"I mean, has anyone else bullied her? Said things? Have you seen other kids being harassed? Are drugs an issue?"

"Drugs?" My expression twists. "I've never seen drugs at Holton."

"But you have seen other kids bullied."

"No." I shake my head. "Lucy's situation ... it's a first for me. Honestly."

"So, you're saying no other kids have been picked on at Holton High?"

"I'm sure they have been, but not that I've seen." What is he getting at?

"What about your friend, Cody? Was he ever pressured?"

Holy shit. The blood drains from my face. "I-I don't know," I stutter. "Why?"

He sighs. "I'm just trying to get an idea of what goes on at the school. My conversation with June was ... enlightening."

Fuck. What did she say?

"Let's get back to Lucy," Uncle Tony continues. "June has been the only one bothering her? No one else?"

"Well," I clear my throat, "her friends went along with it, but only because of June. I doubt they would have done anything if it weren't for her."

He nods. "And what about Allie? What can you tell me about her?"

I can barely speak. "Who?"

"You don't have a friend named Allie?"

My mind races along with my pulse. "N-no. Did June say we did?"

"No, not directly. I overheard the name when she was talking with her parents. It seemed as if she blamed her actions on this girl, but when I asked them about it, they acted as if I'd misheard."

June's parents know about Allie? *She's* behind this? I close my eyes and open them again. Did I really wake up or am I dreaming?

"I'm going to assume you don't know what she was talking about."

Shaking my head, I shrug, trying to look innocent.

"I guess it doesn't matter," Lucy's uncle says, "as long as there isn't anyone else who has it out for my niece."

"Not that I'm aware of," I say, trying to push my thoughts aside. "I mean, her friends might have a bad opinion of Lucy, but if you tell June to stop, I'm sure they'll listen if she has a change of heart. They seem to follow along pretty easily."

"Well," Uncle Tony pauses. "I'm not sure when she'll be able to change any minds."

"Why?"

"Sorry. It's personal." He starts to stand. "I'm sure word will get around soon enough, though. I'd hate to be in high school again."

Uh, okay?

Uncle Tony starts to make his way to the door, so I do, too. "I won't take up any more of your time," he says. "Just, please, if there's anything going on with Lucy you think I need to know about, tell me." He reaches into his pocket and pulls out a card. "I'm asking personally, not as a cop."

"Absolutely," I say as I take it.

Once he's out the door, I race for my phone, my fingers flying over the screen to get ahold of June. *We need to talk.*

I pace waiting for her to respond. I can't believe her parents know. *They know.* And they never said anything?

Like hell we do, nark she sends.

You owe me, I type. *I just had a visit from the police. He asked me about Allie. Any idea how he knows???*

A minute or two passes, probably because she's trying to figure out how to lie. *I don't owe you a damn thing,* she says. *Don't be stupid. He knows because you ratted me out.*

What? *I never said anything about that.*

Then how did he figure out I was high?

Wait. *Huh?*

And now my parents are fed up and they're sending me away to some rehab camp. So thanks for that, asshole.

I'm so confused. *Why would you need rehab?*

She types and stops, types and stops. Finally, *For 'Allie' you idiot. You know, my drug problem??*

I read her text three times. *What drugs?*

Painkillers from when I separated my shoulder in regionals last year. Jesus, I thought Cody told you this.

That is *not* what he told me.

My body plops down on the couch as I squint at my phone. None of this makes any sense. Why would Cody lie? Besides, I saw–

Aaron? He told you, didn't he?

I'm not sure what to say. He did ... but he didn't. *I guess I misunderstood.*

My phone rings immediately. Taking a deep breath, I swipe the screen. "Hello?"

"You. Cannot. Tell. Anyone." June sounds like she's grinding her teeth. "I wouldn't have said anything if I thought you didn't already know."

"Where will your friends think you are?" I ask.

"On vacation. My parents are planning a trip too, so everything looks legit. You can't screw this up."

I rub my aching forehead. "Why all the secrecy?"

"Oh, gee, I don't know," she gets sarcastic. "How about my reputation? My family's reputation? My *scholarship*?"

"Okay, okay. It's just ..."

"Just what?"

"Cody was covering for you and not himself?"

"Of course he was covering for me. He *loved* me. I had to keep everything on track for college, and he protected me. Especially at school. Why? What did he tell you?"

"He said–I thought he was cheating on you."

"C'mon, Aaron. Cody would never cheat on me. Do you even know anyone named Allie?"

I thought I did. My mind swirls with all the things Cody told me, showed me. I remember him telling me June was being difficult; I remember him saying he didn't want to hang out with her anymore. This was why. Damage control was too much.

Suddenly, my head snaps up. "Did Cody try to break up with you?"

Her silence answers my question.

"He did, didn't he? And you threatened him. You said you'd tell his recruiter about the *one* time he used steroids."

"He couldn't leave me. I needed him."

"Jesus." I jump to my feet. "Do you realize he did what he did because of you? He got drunk and crawled under a car because he thought you would ruin his life!"

Her voice is finally quiet. "I know."

I stand there in silent shock as my anger builds. The more I find out, the more my head pounds. I've been so worried about keeping Cody's secrets – and one of them isn't even true. On top of that, June *knew* she caused Lucy's pain from the very beginning, and yet she just kept piling it on and on. For what?

"Look, I've gotta go," June says. "Please keep Allie between you and me."

I don't respond.

"Aaron?"

She hangs up before I say another word.

CHAPTER TWENTY-THREE

Lucy

"You're supposed to be enjoying this with me, you know."

Reaching across the table, I tap Aaron's bowl with my spoon. The clanging sound brings him back to the present.

"Sorry." He blinks. "I was just thinking."

He quickly scoops up a big bite of ice cream and smiles, but I can tell it's forced. He's been distracted ever since he showed up on my doorstep with an armful of sundae supplies. At first I was happy to see he brought dessert; I've barely eaten anything since the rink last night. Now I'm wondering if his surprise has more to do with him than an item on my list of "demands."

After eating another cherry, I ask, "Do you want to talk about it?"

"About what?"

"Whatever's bothering you."

He grimaces and opens his mouth, but before he can say anything, I add, "And don't tell me nothing's wrong. I'm the queen of pretending I'm okay when I'm not. I know the signs."

He starts to roll his eyes, but my shrug and empathetic look stops him. Dropping his spoon, he leans back and runs his hand through his hair. "I don't want … I can't …" He lets out a breath. "Damn June and everything she's done." He looks me square in the eye. "I think I hate her."

I abandon my ice cream, too. "Well, she's not my favorite person, either."

Aaron looks down like he's trying to decipher a puzzle. "I don't think I've ever said that about anyone in my life. And she pushed me to it." His eyes soften as they meet mine, then they jump to the grayish-blue bruise above my right eye. "Are you sure you're feeling okay?"

"I am." It's the truth. My wrist only aches now; it's not throbbing like it was last night.

What June did sucks on a massive scale. I never expected anything like it to happen; comments, threats, stupid games, yes. But her putting hands on me? Never. I really don't know how I'm supposed to go to school with this girl. What if she tries something again? I'm sure my friends, and Aaron's, will keep an eye out for me, but they shouldn't have to. I should be able to go about my day like any other person, but I don't think I can.

"I think seeing us together outside of school made her snap." My face falls. "I don't know if I can finish the year like this." I wave my cast around.

Aaron's expression twists as he slides his chair closer to mine. "You can."

"I mean, I want to be there," I admit, "but only because of you and Izzy and Delaney and the guys." I let out a frustrated sigh. "I'm just so tired of everything."

"No." Aaron shakes his head. "I meant you *can*. June is –" He stops.

"What? June is what?" *Fill in any number of adjectives here,* I think.

"She's leaving."

"What do you mean?"

Aaron doesn't say anything. Instead, he scrubs his face with the palm of his hand and when he's finished, he looks exhausted. "Can I ask you a question?"

"Sure."

"Izzy is your best friend, right? Have you ever lied to her? I'm talking about a huge lie."

I pause, not that I really have to think about it. "No. I've told little white lies, you know, to get out of something she might want to do but nothing crazy. Why?"

Aaron sets his jaw. "Because Cody lied to me."

I close my eyes briefly at the sound of a name I didn't expect. "What did he lie about?"

Aaron looks at me but through me as his eyes glass over. A moment later, he shakes his head and his thoughts away. "I promised him, on my life, I would never tell." He laughs sarcastically. "And it was all to protect fucking June."

Suddenly, he stands and walks a few steps away. He's upset, and I've never seen him like this before. I want to tell him Cody must have had a good reason; after all, he was his best friend. Not that lying is good, but maybe it was his last resort.

"And you know what kills me? I *believed* him." He sounds like he's talking more to himself than to me. He turns around. "I can't figure it out. I've talked to her; he showed me proof."

"Proof of what?" My brow creases.

"He told me he was –" His voice falters.

"He was ...?"

Aaron puts his hands on his hips and looks at his feet. Standing, I walk up to him and wrap my arms around his waist. He's helped me so many times; now it's my turn. "Tell me," I say, trying to catch his eyes.

He rests his forehead against mine. "Cody told me he was sleeping with Ms. Wright."

I freeze. "The teacher?"

He nods against me. "He told me her name was Allie. He showed me text messages and pictures. Except there is no Allie. Only June."

I lean back to look at him. "How do you know?"

"I talked to June this morning."

He's obviously messed up about this, and I want to be supportive, but his source is questionable. "Are you sure *she's* telling you the truth?"

"I'm pretty sure." He blows out a defeated breath. "Your uncle stopped by today. He hinted that June wouldn't be around, then mentioned the name Allie, although he didn't know what it meant and asked me. I lied to him."

"Go on."

"After he left, I messaged June to ask her why she would say that name, thinking we were keeping the same secret. Turns out ..." He scowls. "She's being shipped off to rehab for drugs, thanks to a discussion between her parents and your uncle."

"Wait." My brain scrambles. "June's addicted to drugs?"

"Apparently so." He shrugs. "And, she and Cody gave her problem a name. Allie."

I squint in confusion, trying to think.

"Oh come on!"

"Ha-ha, gotcha!"

My thoughts are interrupted by loud shouts and the sound of an explosion coming from the living room.

"How can you attack your own son?!" My brother's voice is high-pitched on 'attack' and low on 'son.' My dad and my brother have been playing some online video game since I woke up.

"In Destiny Corps Three, you are not my son." My dad sounds like he's trying to be Darth Vader.

Shaking my head, I meet Aaron's eyes. As I open my mouth to start our conversation again, I hear, "Oh gross!"

Turning, I see my brother, Will, walk into the kitchen.

"Are you guys making out in here?" He makes a disgusted face as he opens the fridge. "I'm telling."

I drop my arms from around Aaron's waist and cross them. "We weren't making out."

"Who's making out?" My dad walks in a millisecond after I speak. "No kissing in the kitchen." He grins. "For sanitary reasons, of course."

Oh my god. My cheeks suddenly burn at a hundred degrees.

"Nice to see you again," my dad says to Aaron. "Hope we didn't keep you too late last night."

"No, sir. I would've stayed longer, if Lucy needed me."

"Hospitals are never fun. Thanks for hanging in there with us."

Aaron smiles like we weren't just having a serious conversation – a conversation we need to finish.

"Okay, we," I motion for Aaron to follow me, "need to get some homework done."

Aaron looks lost for a second, then rearranges his features. "Yep, ah yes. Important yearbook business."

"We'll be up in my room," I say and head for the stairs.

"Yeah, so they can make out in private," my brother snickers under his breath.

I glare at him as I walk by. "Be nice. I'm injured, twerp."

He sticks his tongue out at me.

When we make it upstairs, I take a seat on the bed and apologize. "Sorry for the comedians down there. We were in the middle of something serious."

"It's okay." Aaron sits down next to me. "I'm glad your dad isn't as uptight as I thought he'd be. You know, judging from his picture in the office."

He gives me a crooked smile, and I roll my eyes. "He's the polar opposite of uptight." Tucking one leg beneath me, I move closer to Aaron. "I just can't believe ... I never would have guessed June was struggling."

"Me, neither," he says. "Although, it kind of explains some of the things she's done."

I'm quiet.

"Not that it makes it okay," he rushes to add. "Nothing about what's happened makes anything okay."

I agree. Looking down, I pick at my cuticles. I've thought terrible things about June for months. Am I supposed to feel bad now that I know she has a problem? Obviously, Cody cared about her. Otherwise, why would he come up with such an insane lie? Ms. Wright would have gotten in huge trouble if it came out. Like felony trouble. So ... is it truly false?

A thought jumps into my head. Sliding over on the bed, I reach under my nightstand to pull out last year's yearbook.

"What are you doing?" Aaron asks.

Flipping to the faculty pages, I find Ms. Wright's picture, then turn the book around so Aaron can read it. "Ms. Wright's first name is Nicole."

He scrutinizes the page.

"I'm just trying to help, to figure out why Cody made up the story he did."

Aaron lets out a long sigh. "Same here." He closes the book and pushes it away. "I guess my lack of looking at the yearbook supports Izzy's claim that everyone should take it seriously." His voice is bitter. "I would have confronted him a long time ago."

We sit in silence. After a minute or two, Aaron reaches for me and I move closer, draping my legs over his lap. His thumb traces circles on my knee before he says, "I don't want you to think I'm some gullible idiot."

"I don't think that."

"It's just ... I caught Cody in Ms. Wright's classroom; we were supposed to meet up to grab something to eat before our game, and he didn't show. They were in this close, intense conversation, and when they noticed me standing there, they both jumped back, mumbled something, and he walked out. When I asked what was going on, he told me they were hooking up."

I internally shudder at the thought. "And what did you say?"

"I said I didn't believe him, and he went into this long explanation about how she'd been coming on to him in class. He said he decided to see if she was serious, since June was getting on his nerves. According to him, Allie–Ms. Wright, had a thing for younger guys."

My expression gives away my true feelings. Is this conversation really happening?

"He even sent me pictures." Aaron reaches for his phone. "He said she sent them to him."

Aaron scrolls through his cell, then hands it to me. It's a text message thread with Cody. There are several pictures, but as I look through them, I can't tell if they're Ms. Wright or not. Most of them are too dark to tell who's in the photo, and some show the girl with her head turned or just her chin and chest made it in the frame. These pictures could be of anyone, but I can understand how Aaron wouldn't question Cody. In the same situation, I wouldn't doubt Izzy.

"I'm sorry he lied to you," I say as I hand the phone back.

"Yeah, well … the only thing I know for sure is he had some weird conversation with Ms. Wright." He pauses. "She's tried to talk to me a few times since school started, too."

"She has?"

"I blew her off." He smirks. "I wasn't exactly nice."

Knowing what he knows now, he has to be curious. "You should talk to her," I say. "Maybe she can give you some answers."

He snorts. "I'm not sure I want any."

"Don't you think you deserve them?" I ask. "Cody dragged you into this, and it's clearly not okay with you."

"How would I even start that conversation?"

"I don't know, but … I'll go with you."

He gives me an uncertain look.

"Listen, the woman kicked me off the student council because of Cody. I'm part of this because of him, and you said it yourself – if we're together, we should look out for one another. Let me at least try to help."

Aaron's quiet for a few seconds before his eyes meet mine. "Are you sure?"

"Yes."

Maybe it's wrong, but the more I learn, the more cautiously optimistic I feel. Ever since that night at the Field, I've felt like things have been happening to me for no real reason. But now, knowing about June makes me feel less insane; here I was thinking I was the crazy one and now I know she really does have a problem. Maybe if Aaron finds out more about Ms. Wright and Cody, he can find some peace of mind, too.

THE NEXT MORNING, Aaron picked me up early, betting Ms. Wright would get to work at the crack of dawn like all the other teachers do. He wanted to get things over with before the majority of kids showed up at Holton. Now, we're standing outside her cracked classroom door, deciding whether or not to knock.

"Ready?"

Despite looking like he'd rather run through the school naked, Aaron steps forward and raps on the door. "Hello?"

"Just a moment," we hear from the other side.

Seconds later, Ms. Wright appears. Her eyes widen a little when she sees us standing there. "Aaron, Lucy. This is a surprise. What can I do for you?"

Aaron's mouth opens, but words don't immediately come out. I gently nudge his arm with my elbow, letting him know I'm here and he's got this.

"Um ..." Aaron clears his throat. "Earlier in the year, you said I could come talk to you if I needed to. Do you have a few minutes?"

"Absolutely," she says and opens the door wider for us to come inside. Once we do, she shuts it behind her. "Have a seat." She gestures to the student desks in front of hers.

As we do, she pulls a chair over to sit near us. "So, what's on your –" She stops. "Lucy, what happened to your arm?"

Before I can answer, Aaron asks, "Does the name Allie ring a bell?"

Ms. Wright's eyes dart between us before they land on me. "June Summers did this?"

Despite the situation, my heart jumps. She *knows*. If she knows about June, she must know about Cody, too. "Yes," I answer. "We got into a ... thing Saturday night. The police are also involved."

Ms. Wright loses her professional posture and slumps in her chair. "I was really hoping things were getting better."

Aaron shifts in his seat, agitated. "Can you tell us what's going on? What's *been* going on? Because Cody never told me the truth, and I know you two were involved somehow."

Ms. Wright leans forward, clasping her hands between her knees. "You're right."

I think Aaron and I stop breathing.

"Do you remember when I followed you into the girl's bathroom a few weeks back?"

My eyes land on Aaron as he nods yes.

"I caught Cody doing the same thing last spring. I found him holding June's hair as she vomited in a sink; she was violently ill. I asked if they needed help, but Cody said no; it was just a stomach bug. I could tell he was lying." She pauses. "So, I decided to pay closer attention to them for the next few weeks."

"What did you see?" I ask, intrigued.

"June showing up later and later to my first hour class. Absences. Cody turning in her missing assignments and asking for copies of notes. When June was here, her mind wasn't; her work wasn't up to par." Ms. Wright sighs. "I *knew* something wasn't right and thought she might be pregnant. I tried to approach her, but she kept avoiding me. The next time I saw Cody, I asked him about it. I told him if he wasn't truthful, I was obligated to call her parents."

"And?" Aaron presses.

"He told me to go ahead, because they knew. His did, too. My assumption was wrong; June wasn't pregnant. She couldn't get off the painkillers she was given for an injury, and her parents asked Cody to help cover for her until she could. When I did call to confirm, everyone involved backed up what he said."

My eyes grow wide as Aaron's narrow. "Why would he confide in you?"

"I think he was fed up the day I asked – the day you walked in on us, I believe. He was trying to maintain his grades and his sports *and* June's academic and social life – all under the radar. Since the adults involved knew, there was nothing more I could do other than lend an ear when he needed one. He ended up coming to see me quite a bit, since he was forbidden to talk to his friends about it."

"So why the code name?" Aaron asks. "Cody led me to believe Allie was you, and you two were a ... couple."

Ms. Wright's mouth falls open. "What? No. I suggested he and June name her problem to make it easier to discuss, but as far as what you thought –" she vehemently shakes her head – "I'd lose my job." She stands and starts to pace. "I guess that's why you weren't exactly polite when I tried to talk to you."

Aaron looks down. "Yeah."

So that's it, I think. Cody found a friend in Ms. Wright, one who wouldn't spill June's secret, although I know Aaron never would. It still doesn't explain why he created such a fantasy. Was it an escape to get away from reality? Or was it an excuse in case Aaron ever walked in on them again? Maybe he just panicked and said the first thing that came to mind.

Ms. Wright stops pacing. "I wonder if that's why Cody stopped coming to see me in those days before ..." She faces me, her expression filled with sympathy. "Before."

That one word is all she has to say. I look away to avoid her stare.

Ms. Wright crouches down in front of my desk. "Lucy, you have to believe I had the best intentions when I removed you from the student council. Cody was under a lot of pressure, and I didn't want that for you. Maybe I was too close to the situation; I don't know. But I didn't want Holton to lose another student. I didn't want you to become suicidal, too. Lord knows you had enough to deal with."

My hearing suddenly goes fuzzy. "What did you say?"

"I didn't want to lose you, too."

My eyes jump to Aaron, and he looks like he's seen a ghost. Or maybe he is a ghost; I've never seen him so pale. The fuzzy feeling in my ears turns into the slow thud of my pulse.

"Aaron?" My voice is small.

He blinks before he turns on Ms. Wright, angry. "Why would you say that?"

"Because Cody called me to say goodbye." Tears start to form in the corners of her eyes. "He thanked me for trying to help and hung up before I could speak." She stands and clears her throat. "It'll haunt me forever."

Aaron slams his fist down hard on the desk, and I jump. Cody did what he did on purpose? He was drunk enough to think that was his only option?

"Lucy." Aaron's voice shakes. "I didn't want you to find out this way."

Wait, what? He knew, too? My insides start to knot. "What are you saying?"

The pain on his face is indescribable. "I was on the phone with him." He closes his eyes. "I heard –"

I'm out the door. My heart is pounding, and the sound of lockers slamming and kids arriving makes me feel claustrophobic and sick. I need to leave. I need to get out of here.

"Where are you running off to?"

I look up, and a wall of bodies suddenly block me. Their faces blur, but I'm sure they're June's friends. I remain silent and try to get around them, but they won't let me through.

"June isn't here today. Want to know why?" a male voice asks.

I shake my head, looking for a way out.

"Because you got her kicked out of school, bitch."

"Hey. Watch your mouth." Aaron is behind me, then suddenly in front of me. "I talked to June yesterday; she's on vacation."

The guy, whoever he is, laughs. "That's what she told us you'd say."

They're closing in on us, or maybe it just feels that way. My pulse races, and I'm about two seconds from hyperventilating. I need to sit down, but if I do, they'll probably crush me.

"Why don't you go away, Jason," Aaron says. "This has nothing to do with you."

He's right. And it has nothing to do with me. Or us.

"Tell them," my voice cracks. Aaron swings his head around to look at me. "Tell them the truth." June's an addict, and Cody killed himself. That has nothing to do with either of us.

Aaron looks confused, or maybe it's my blurry vision. He shakes his head no.

"Tell them, damn it!" I shout. I'm sick of paying for their actions.

I hear Harrison ask, "What's going on?" the same time I hear a loud crack. Jason's fist hits Aaron's jaw and sends him flying. Arms yank me back, and I almost fall before I see Harrison and Wes jump into the biggest fight I've ever seen. A mob fills the hallway as more kids rush to either watch or join the action, and I keep getting shoved to farther and farther away from Aaron.

"Lucy!"

I turn and see Izzy and Delaney running toward me with wide eyes. "What in the hell is going on?"

All I can do is stare at them. "I don't know."

I don't know anything anymore.

CHAPTER TWENTY-FOUR

Aaron

"Does anyone want to explain to me why half of my lacrosse team is bleeding?"

My right eye stares at the ground while the left is covered with a bag of ice. I catch Coach's shoes in my periphery, as he paces between the only five unoccupied floor tiles in his office. We were all brought here, once Principal Hughes and a few others broke up the fight.

"Well?" he barks.

Bodies shuffle and ice packs crinkle as everyone avoids looking at Coach but me. Our eyes lock and his widen, as if to say 'speak up,' but I don't. As much as I want to tell the truth, I can't. None of the guys will believe me. Not now. They'll think I'm making up shit to cover my own ass.

Breaking our staring contest, I look at the floor again. There are three pencils, a pen, and a huge ball of dust under Coach's desk.

He sighs, annoyed. "If no one is going to talk, I will. Listen up."

More shuffling, more crinkling.

"I'm only going to say this once. If any of you, and I mean *any* of you, get caught up in something like this again, you *will* be kicked off this team. No questions asked. Got it?"

The room fills with mumbled responses. "Yes, sir." "Yes, Coach."

"Now get out of here and get to class."

Everyone begins to leave, so I do, too.

"Not you, Matthews. Sit."

Containing a frustrated sigh, I turn around and fall into one of the two chairs in his office. Do we have to talk about this now? The only thing I want to do is find Lucy; I have no idea what happened to her after Jason threw his first punch. We need to talk; I need to apologize. I need to explain why I kept Cody's secret.

Both Harrison and Wes give me sympathetic smirks as they walk by, even as Harrison sniffs his bloody nose and Wes blots his swollen lip. Once everyone is out of the room and the door shuts hard behind them, Coach leans against his desk and crosses his arms in front of me.

"So, Captain." His voice loses its edge and sounds more disappointed. "You want to fill me in?"

I try not to scowl, but I end up doing it anyway. "No, not really."

He sighs. "Who started it?"

Cody, I think. "Jason."

"Why?"

"He was getting in Lucy's face, so I stepped in."

"To defend her?"

I nod.

Coach scrubs his palm over his face before walking behind his desk. "I'm afraid this is going to keep happening if we don't do something about it."

My brow jumps, causing me to wince when I move my eye. "We?"

"Obviously this is something you can't handle on your own, and I have at least ten futures riding on this season, including yours." He sits down, then clasps his hands and leans forward on his desk. "So, what are we going to do?"

Like I know. I throw out my hands, dropping my bag of ice and catching it against my leg. "I can't change people's minds."

"Can't you?"

"Don't you think I've tried?!"

"Apparently not hard enough."

"Really? You have no idea what we've been going through!" I know I should check my tone, but I don't care anymore. I'm angry, I'm fed up, and the side of my face aches like it's on fire. "Cody's girlfriend hit Lucy this weekend, and now she has a broken wrist," I say, irritated. "Some of your players were there."

Coach frowns, but I keep talking. "June's been shipped off to some drug rehab camp, except she told our *friends* Lucy got her suspended to hide her little secret. And on top of that, this morning right before the fight, Lucy found out that Cody –"

I stop myself. Words are just falling out of my mouth.

"Lucy found out what?" Coach asks.

I let out a heavy breath and slump back in the chair. Screw it. What's the point in hiding it anymore? "Cody killed himself. He ... committed suicide."

Coach closes his eyes and remains silent, so I stare at my knees as the words settle over me. It's an awful, yet freeing, feeling to finally say it out loud.

After what feels like forever, Coach clears his throat. "I'm going to need you to start from the beginning. Talk to me, kid."

WELL, the cavalry has arrived.

My mom, Ms. Wright, Principal Hughes, Coach, and Mr. Evans – a school counselor I've only met once in my life – are all crammed into the principal's office with me. My ice pack has warmed to a baggie of water, and I balance it over one knee while I ignore the adults. The only person I want to talk to is Lucy, and she's not answering any of my messages. Granted, none of them have been delivered, which tells me one of two things: either she shut her phone off, or the battery died.

"I don't understand, Aaron, why you didn't come see me."

My head snaps up at the sound of my name. Is this guy for real? "I don't know you," I say to Mr. Evans. "Why would I tell someone I don't know a secret I swore to keep?"

"But the school makes it very clear that help is available if you're troubled. We have posters."

"Posters?" I scoff and hold up my phone. "I shouldn't have to tell you this, but if it doesn't show up on here, it pretty much doesn't exist."

"Aaron." My mom's tone warns me I'm out of line.

"No." I look at her and shake my head. "This is only the second time I've spoken to this guy. The first was in the eighth grade when I had to plan my high school career. Which," I point at him, "was wrong. You shouldn't have let me register for four years of PE." My eyes swing to Coach, and I catch the side of his mouth twitch as he suppresses a smile.

Principal Hughes starts to speak. "So, what I hear you saying is we need to step it up as far as reaching out to students ..."

Movement outside the office window catches my attention, causing the principal's voice to fade in my mind. Through the open blinds, I see Harrison and Wes walk by, followed by the girls, followed by ... Lucy.

Before I can take another breath, I'm up and out the door. I vaguely hear my mom ask where I'm going, but I don't answer her. There's someone I need to talk to.

"Wait up," I call out as the group reaches the next corner in the hallway. Wes and Harrison glance back at me but don't stop, so I jog to catch up. When I turn the corner, I expect them all to be there waiting, but they're not. Delaney blocks my path with her arms crossed and a pissed off expression on her face.

"What?" I ask.

"You're an okay guy and all, but you need to get your shit straight," she says. "I'm sick of watching our girl get hurt."

"Same," I say.

"So, don't be the one who does it." She tilts her head and sets her jaw. "This is your only warning."

I'm confused.

She steps to the side so I can see Lucy. She's leaning against a wall several feet away staring up at the ceiling. I start to walk toward her and Delaney follows, like she's escorting me. Did something happen that I don't know about?

When we reach her, I stop walking. Delaney pauses too, long enough to give Lucy a tiny smile and a bump against the arm. Then, she heads in the direction of the cafeteria.

"I can't believe it's lunch time already," I sigh. "I've been talking to them for hours." I reach for Lucy's hands, and she gives them to me.

"Talking to who?" she asks.

"Coach. Principal Hughes. My mom." I pause. "I've been trying to get ahold of you."

She nods. "I turned off my phone."

"Why?"

"So I could think." She finally meets my eyes and notices the side of my face. She looks sad as she reaches up to touch it. "Are you all right?"

"Yeah. After the first few punches, I think I got shoved around more than anything."

She looks down again. "Aaron, I –"

"I'm sorry I didn't tell you the truth," I blurt out. "You deserved to know. I really thought I was the only one he talked to that night. Hell, I was on the phone with him right when it happened … he made me swear. What was I supposed to do? I tried to get him to tell me where he was, and he wouldn't. I panicked and started to run. And then when I found him, all I wanted to do was get him *out*."

My voice unexpectedly cracks, and Lucy closes her eyes. She moves her head back and forth in quick little movements, like she's trying to shake my words out of her ears. "Don't … I get it," she says. "I don't need details. I was there."

Damn it. "Sorry," I apologize again. Wrapping my arms around her, I pull her against me.

"Aaron," she says into my chest, "we have to tell them."

"Hmm?"

"We have to tell them." She leans back. "Your team. June's friends. We have to tell them the truth."

"We can't," I say.

"Why not?"

"Because they'll think we're lying. They believe June above all else, remember? There's no way they'll take our word for anything."

"We have to try. If we don't, they're just going to keep coming at us."

"Let them." I shrug. "We know what's real and what's not."

"No." Lucy steps out of my arms. "I'm tired, Aaron. I'm tired of being their punching bag. Literally." She waves her cast in front of me. "Maybe you can take the hits, but I can't."

I understand where she's coming from. "Believe me, I'm sick of it, too. I don't want anyone laying hands on you ever again."

"And I don't want anyone hurting you, either. Or our friends. Wes and Harrison were bleeding. *Bleeding.* Because of us."

"I know, and it sucks. We just need some time. If we do tell everyone, it has to be done in a way no one can question."

Lucy lets out a heavy breath, and her hand shakes when she pushes her hair off her forehead. I hate that she's so upset.

"I feel so guilty," she whispers. "Cody, you," she gestures to my face, "the guys, Izzy and Delaney. They don't need our problems."

I step toward her. "They're our friends. They understand."

She concedes with a nod, but I can see tears appear in her eyes. "I'm being as honest with you as I can. This needs to stop."

"It will," I promise her. "I'll find a way."

"But not right now."

I shake my head. "I don't know what to do right now."

Lucy's face falls and I try to hug her again, but she stops me. "We – you and me – we're the only reason bad things are happening."

My expression twists.

"If you take us out of the picture, it ends." She looks at me as a tear slides down her cheek. "No one else gets hurt."

I don't like where this is going.

She looks away from me, down the hall, and wipes beneath her eye. Then, she wraps her arms around her middle. My stomach feels like lead.

"What are you saying?" She doesn't answer me and stares down at our feet. "Are you ... are you breaking up with me?"

Lucy stays quiet for a moment before she sniffs. "Yeah," she says, then meets my eyes. "Yeah, I think I am."

Wait. This isn't what I want. I don't think it's what she really wants either; we can't let them *win*. My mind races, trying to find the right words to tell her it will be okay, when Delaney's voice jumps in my head: *Don't be the one who hurts her.* She knew something was up. Do the guys know, too?

"I just can't handle it," Lucy whispers.

My shoulders sag. I don't feel the way she does; I don't want to lose her. But I can't force her to be with me. She's scared. What happened this morning shouldn't have happened. Her broken wrist shouldn't have happened, either.

When I reach for her this time, she lets me hold her and she squeezes me back.

The hall starts to fill with kids heading to the next lunch period, so we let each other go and she wipes her cheeks again. I may not have tears, but I feel like someone pulled out my heart, crushed it in their hands, and then put it back inside my chest upside down.

"I'll make this right," I say as she starts to walk away. All she does is give me a miserable attempt at a smile, as if to say, "I want to believe you."

As I turn around to leave, my hands clench into fists. I hate how other people are interfering in our lives; I hate that we have to end so they will act decent. It's then that I make myself a promise. Whether it means Lucy and I end up together or not, I *will* fix this. I don't know how, but I will.

Because she deserves it.

Because we deserve it.

CHAPTER TWENTY-FIVE

Lucy

"You're such a badass."

I don't feel like a badass. In fact, I feel the exact opposite. Which would be ...

"What's the opposite of badass?" I ask, mumbling into the pillow I have squeezed to my chest. Izzy and Delaney are over for a girl's night on a Monday because, you know, that's what you do when the biggest fight in Holton history breaks out over you, the dead kid, his girlfriend, and your now ex-boyfriend. If he even was my boyfriend. We were official for a whole weekend.

A sad, deflated New Year's Eve horn sounds in my mind. *Wooooooo.*

"The opposite of badass would be a lame ass, which you are not," Delaney says, plopping down on her stomach next to me on my bed. "You took control of your mental health. You let Aaron know you can't live with things the way they are anymore. That was brave." She air-kisses my temple. "Now, give me your cast."

Half-heartedly, I extend my right arm like I'm donating blood. Delaney sits up, pulls a bag of Sharpie pens closer, and goes to work creating a masterpiece on the plaster.

"Don't use red, okay?" I'm still having a hard time with that color.

"Noted," she says as she pulls the top off a mint green marker.

"Please explain to me again," Izzy says, sitting up from the floor, "how breaking up with Aaron was a good idea."

It's wasn't, I think and close my eyes. I wish I could take it back. My head knows it was the right thing to do, but my heart is mad. No, it's furious.

"Luce?"

I open my eyes and focus on Izzy's face. "It's for the best."

"Why?"

"Because," I swallow. "If we aren't together, all the craziness stops. Everything can go back to normal."

Izzy sighs and scoots closer. "When are you going to realize that normal isn't a reality anymore?" She gives me her "I'm sympathetic-but-you-need-to-pull-it-together" look.

"I meant the way it was pre-Aaron. When all that happened was whispers and stares."

"Oh, so you're opposed to assault?" Delaney quips.

"I'm opposed to all of it, but yeah," I sigh. "I'm not okay with fists being thrown."

"Or your boyfriend keeping secrets from you." Delaney makes a face and raises an eyebrow.

My stomach sinks. "Yeah, that too."

While Izzy taps her finger on her chin in thought, the idea that Aaron lied to me resurfaces. Okay, he didn't necessarily lie, but he didn't tell me everything, either. Half of me understands why; it truly does. The other half ... not so much. While I always accepted that Cody held some responsibility for what happened, Aaron knew I blamed myself the most. Did he really think telling me the truth would do more harm than good?

"I still can't believe Cody killed himself," Izzy says. "It seemed like he had it all. That choice is so ... final." She shudders and hugs herself.

"We're all battling something," Delaney says as she caps a marker. "Who knows what else was going on with him? I mean, I've got my parents, Lucy has her situation, June's on drugs, you've got ..." Delaney looks up. "What do you have?"

Izzy shrugs. "Nothing, I guess."

"Okay, well, not *everyone* has something." Delaney goes back to drawing. "Things aren't always what they seem."

"Oh my god." My body jerks to a sitting position, ripping my cast out of Delaney's grasp.

"Hey!" she complains.

"What is it?" Izzy asks.

"That's what he meant." My eyes meet Izzy's. "At Central. I asked Aaron why he was being so nice to me. He said it was because he knew how I felt; he said I needed to remember things aren't always what they seem."

Her face lights up. "See? He was trying to let you in on the secret without giving anything away." She kneels up from the floor and leans over the side of my bed. "You should call him and tell him you've had a change of heart."

Delaney snorts and reaches for my cast again. "That wouldn't make anything better."

"Why? She'd have her boyfriend back."

"But that's not the problem." Delaney concentrates as she turns a line she accidentally drew from my movement into an antenna. "She'll always have Aaron." Pausing, she gives me a small smile. "You two being together isn't the issue. He knows that. It's everyone else's reaction."

"Exactly," I say, irritated. "It's like they *know* how to get under my skin and make me feel nuts. I don't understand what they get out of it. Hurting and intimidating people shouldn't be fun."

"No, but it probably brings them closer." Delaney shades in a butterfly wing. "You know, the whole mob mentality of it all."

"Ugh. That's not right," Izzy says.

"It's not, but I guarantee if Lucy and I got ahold of our community service friends, we'd have a mob of our own. Well, a bigger mob anyway."

"And they'd be on our side ..." Izzy's voice drifts off, and I can see her wheels turning.

"Don't even think about it," I say. "I don't have any community service *friends*."

"I do." Delaney grins.

"Stop."

Izzy reaches for my free hand and squeezes my fingers. "It's just not fair. You should be able to do whatever you want with whomever you want and not feel bad about it."

"I know." And that's the truth. I *do* know. I just wish I was strong enough to keep them all out of my head. I wish I could be strong enough for Aaron.

"I guess all we can hope for is that they'll move on," Delaney says, rotating my arm a little, "even though I'm not opposed to another royal rumble."

I roll my eyes, and she continues. "It might take some time since June blamed you for her "vacation," but if they do leave you alone, it's almost as if her puppets are yours. You'll have bent them to your will without them even knowing." She chuckles low in her throat. "You'll be the puppet master."

Her voice gets raspy when she says "puppet master," and I manage a laugh. "That sounds kinda sinister."

"I like it," Izzy says. "It's about time you had some control." Standing, she lets go of my hand. "Still," she sticks out her hip, "I wish there was something more we could do."

"Aaron said telling the truth is off the table," I sigh. "And he's right."

When everything went down, I was willing to bet my most precious commodity, my sanity, that telling June's friends everything we knew would stop the fight. To me, there was no reason why that wouldn't work. Aaron's refusal to agree upset me, but in the last few hours, his words have taken root in my brain. People will only believe June right now, and she's not going to spill her secrets. Her story is hers to share, no matter how shitty she's made things. And regardless of what Cody's decision was, it was still *his* decision. We're not the right people to tell the world.

"So, that only leaves option B," I say after explaining my thoughts to my friends.

"And B stands for breaking up," Izzy dead pans.

"What else could I do?"

Izzy rolls her eyes. "Well, maybe June will set the record straight when she gets back. Isn't admitting you're wrong one of the twelve steps?"

"If you follow them," Delaney mutters, still focused on my arm.

She would know.

Just then, Izzy's phone goes off. Pulling it out of her back pocket, she checks her messages. "It's Wes. He says Aaron's pretty bummed. He and Harrison are making him go out for wings."

Delaney stops drawing. "Food sounds good."

Izzy grins. "Food sounds great."

Oh, fantastic. Here we go. I get to be the party pooper and break up the three sets of Musketeers.

"Guys, I don't think –" I start, stopping Delaney while she gathers the markers into a pile and Izzy from reaching for her jacket. They both look at me expectantly.

"– I should go with you," I finish.

"Duh. Of course you should come with us," Izzy says. "We're all still friends."

She must have missed the first part of my sentence. "No, that's not what –"

I'm interrupted as Delaney pulls me off the bed by my good arm. "You need to eat, too," she says. "We'll make it quick."

"And what if they don't want us there?" I ask with a specific person in mind. "We weren't invited."

"There's no way they wouldn't want to see *us*." Izzy smiles, giddy with the idea of surprising Wes.

Slowly, I reach for my hoodie and pull it over my head, hoping to hide inside it. What kind of friend would I be if I rained on their parade?

Fifteen minutes later, and against my better judgement, we pull into the local wing place. Anxiety has been creeping up on me the whole ride; I shouldn't have come. This is going to be beyond awkward. As Izzy finds a parking space, my heart starts to pound. I can't do this. I need to be the badass Delaney said I was and put my foot down.

"You guys go inside," I say when they open their doors. "I'll wait here."

"What?" Izzy turns around in her seat. "You're not coming in?"

"I can't. It's too soon … it's too weird. I'll just chill in here."

"Are you sure?" Delaney looks concerned. "I thought you were hungry."

I frown at her. Those words never left my mouth. "No, my appetite disappeared at about eight 0'clock this morning," I say. "Go see the guys. I'll be here when you're done."

By the looks on their faces, I can tell they don't want to leave but, on the other hand, they do. "Seriously. I'll be fine," I reassure them. "Eat so we can go back home."

Reluctantly, they step out of the car. When they do, I undo my seatbelt and flop over on my side in the backseat. Closing my eyes, I plan to spend the next probable hour reliving all the stupid decisions I've made – including this one.

Moments later, a knock scares the crap out of me and my body bolts upright. My eyes meet Aaron's as he peers through the window. Obviously, my friends couldn't keep their mouths shut. Why are they so bad at ignoring me?

"Hey," he says after opening the door. "You okay?"

Even though I'm recovering from a small heart attack, I say, "Yeah."

Sliding next to me on the seat, he closes the door behind him and remains silent as his eyes roam the dark cab. Finally, they meet mine. "You couldn't stand to see me, huh?"

Is that what they told him? "No," I rush to say. "I'm the one who doesn't want to be seen."

"Why?"

"Because. I'm terrible at faking my mood." *Plus, I'm pretty sure I'm not your favorite person right now.*

Aaron sighs and slouches down in the seat, so he's staring at the ceiling. "Well, that's one thing we have in common."

Leaning back, I mirror his pose.

"Are you sad we broke up?" he asks.

I might as well be honest. "Yes. I'm not sure it was my best idea."

He turns his head to look at me. "But?"

"But ..." I shrug, defeated. "Something had to be done."

He nods. "I agree."

I pick my head up. "You do?"

"Yeah." He holds out his hand, and I wind my fingers through his. "I don't like your decision, but I understand why things can't keep going this way." He's silent as he runs his thumb over mine. "Just promise me something."

"What?"

"When I come up with a solution, regardless of if it works, you'll think about giving us a second chance."

Even in the dim light of the parking lot, I can see his bruised and half-swollen eye. Why would he even want another chance with me, especially if his "fix" doesn't fix anything?

When I don't speak right away, he adds, "I'm not asking you this out of guilt, if that's what you're thinking. I do feel bad about keeping Cody's secret from you, but not from anyone else. You know I could care less about them. What matters is us, and I already miss you."

As my heart stutters, my eyes close for a second to process his words. I may not understand why he feels the way he does, but that doesn't mean I don't like it. It doesn't mean I don't regret the decision I had to make, and it certainly doesn't mean I don't want him in my life.

"I'll think about it," I say quietly.

"Good." Leaning over, he places a full kiss on my lips, one I don't want to end. When it does, he says, "I'll stop bugging you now," as he reaches for the door handle. "I have some work to do."

I'm still a little dazed by what just happened. I didn't expect to have this conversation tonight, if ever. When he sticks his head back in the car to remind me to lock the doors, all I can do is nod. An odd swirl of emotions is sitting in my chest, and I can't name it.

As I lean over the console and into the front seat to hit the lock button, I watch Aaron shove his hands in his back pockets as he heads toward the restaurant door. He doesn't go inside, though. My eyes follow him as he keeps walking and disappears around the corner.

THE NEXT MORNING, I'm standing at my locker thoroughly convinced I should have found a way to skip today. I'm exhausted. Delaney and Izzy staying over didn't help me sleep. They wanted to know all the Aaron details and overanalyze them to death. Then, when they did doze off, I was left alone to continue thinking about him. I'm going to need some extra time with Dr. Marie on Friday.

Yawning, I reach for my English binder and my copy of *The Scarlett Letter*. We're almost at the end of the semester, which means we'll move on to another novel soon. I forget what the syllabus said; hopefully it's something a little more upbeat and less depressing. I'm over discussing the ostracization of Hester and Pearl. It's too close to my own life.

"Good morning!" Delaney says from behind me in a sing-song voice she never uses.

When I turn around, she's fighting to keep a straight face. "What are you doing?" I ask suspiciously. Izzy looks just as confused.

It's then that I notice she has one arm behind her back. When she brings it around to the front, she hands me six pink roses tied together with a white ribbon.

"Aaron gave these to Harrison to give to me to give to you." A sly smile creeps across her face. "Take 'em."

Just as I wrap my hand around the stems, Izzy says, "Oh, there's a note!" Now she's grinning from ear to ear.

There is a note. They both stare at me like I just received a rare and precious gift. I mean, it's really nice but this isn't how you normally start a break up.

"Read it already." Izzy's usual impatience is showing.

"Give me a minute," I huff as I tuck my book and binder beneath my arm. I'm sure it's a personal message, but okay.

I take my time unfolding the paper just to irritate my friend, even though I'm anxious to read it myself. When I get it straightened out, I read Aaron's words:

L –

I haven't forgotten your list. By the time you receive a dozen roses, I will have done everything I can to make things right. Don't forget your promise.

– A

CHAPTER TWENTY-SIX

Aaron

"Did she do it?"

Harrison lifts his chin and looks over my shoulder. "Yes. Flowers delivered."

"Okay." I let out a breath. "Let's do this."

After I left Lucy last night, a brisk walk helped clear my mind. I needed a plan. But what? I knew the truth should be told, and that I could do; screw all these secrets. The hard part would be making people believe it. Through no fault of my own, I'd lost their trust.

And that's when it hit me.

I needed to win my "friends" back.

"Ready?" I ask Harrison.

He nods. "Do you really think this is going to work?"

"With time," I admit, then silently pray, *Please don't take forever.*

"All right. I'm going in," Harrison says as he starts to back away. "Prepare for an outpouring of support."

"Great." Sarcasm drips from my tongue. Support *is* what I want, but only as a means to an end. As far as I'm concerned, my teammates and June's friends have shown their true colors. Maybe we'll work through that one day, and maybe we won't. Right now, I just need them to accept me back into their group.

"Hey, Harrison." I stop him before he gets too far. "Thanks."

He nods again and salutes, then heads off to start spreading the news of my break up.

Opening my locker, I take my time grabbing what I need for my first class. Since I made it a point to be early today, I have some extra time. Curiosity gets the better of me, and I peek around my locker door in Lucy's direction. She's already gone. I wish I could've seen her reaction when Delaney gave her the roses, but I didn't want to stare in case someone saw. I hope she liked them. She never told me what color she wanted; all I knew was not red.

Never red.

A moment later, I can feel a presence behind me. Several presences, actually. Turning around, I find myself staring at Jason and Max, Harrison and Wes, Luke and Evan from lacrosse, and randomly, Kat. News of my relationship's demise must be like moths to a flame.

Perfect.

As my eyes bounce around the group, I say, "What?" They don't need to know I purposely sent Harrison to fill them in.

"Your boy says you no longer have a girlfriend." Jason crosses his arms. "That true?"

He sounds *so* concerned about my well-being – not.

"Wow. How kind of you to check on me." I sound just as irritated. "I'm surprised you didn't throw hands and ask questions later."

Behind him, Harrison widens his eyes at me in a silent message. *Be nice.* I can't help it; I automatically default to defensive around these guys, especially after yesterday when Jason's knuckles danced with my face. I do, however, need them if I have any chance at getting Lucy back.

Slumping my shoulders, I will my expression to pretend to regret what I said.

"Sorry," comes out of my mouth. "I've had a rough couple of days."

Jason's jaw twitches. "So ... you guys are done?"

"Yeah. We are."

Jason glances from left to right; my guess is he's checking to see if anyone believes me. When no one says anything, he smirks. "It's too bad you wasted so much time on her. How was it volunteering for charity?"

I hear a snicker or two and close my eyes. One, because he's an idiot. And two because he's trying to get a reaction out of me. I force myself to stay calm though, no matter how much I want to strangle him.

"Funny," I choke out and hate myself for it. "Everyone makes mistakes, you know?"

He should know. He's made a ton of them, and so have I; even this conversation feels wrong. But getting to know Lucy was never a bad decision.

Jason finally loses the smartass expression. "Just one more question." He grins. "What's it like to kiss a killer?"

Holy hell, I can't stand this guy. How did I ever consider him a friend? As my blood pressure rises, I notice both Wes and Harrison's jaws drop. They can tell I'm about to snap.

Just as I'm about to step into Jason's personal space, I hear Cody's voice in the back of my mind say *he's testing you*. It makes me pause long enough to pull my shit together.

"You know what they say," I reply through gritted teeth. "Don't knock it 'till you try it."

Jason laughs, breaking the tension. The other guys follow, with the exception of my real friends and Kat. He holds up his hand for a high-five, and it pains me to give him one.

"It's good to have you back, Captain," he says.

The warning bell rings. As we start to make our way to our classes, Jason points at me. "See you at lunch, man."

I guess I've been invited back to the cool kids table.

"Well, that was easy," Harrison says quietly as we let the rest of the guys get ahead of us.

"Really? Because I was about to rip into him." My stomach feels queasy just thinking about what I said. Even though it wasn't much, it was still gross.

"Remember the end goal," Wes says from my left. "It'll be worth it."

"Right. Totally worth it," I repeat. "Gotta keep my eyes on the prize."

Harrison and Wes disappear into their classroom, and as I keep walking toward mine, I hear, "What's the prize?"

I stop in my tracks and turn. Kat is a few steps behind me. Shit. How much did she hear?

She raises an eyebrow, as if asking me the question again.

"Kat ..." I say and drift off as my mind races for something to say.

When I can't find words, she shakes her head and walks away. As I watch her go, I'm left with a sinking feeling.

Great. I've already screwed up, and my plan has barely begun.

IT'S next to impossible for me to sit through first period. I need to talk to Kat. If she tells the guys I have an ulterior motive, I'm done. *It's done.* I have nothing else up my sleeve to make things right.

Sneaking my phone out of my pocket, I send her a message. *Can we talk?*

Sure, she sends.

When? Can you skip anything today?

I'll be in the library for research next hour.

I'll meet you there.

When the bell rings, I don't even stop at my locker or bother going to my next class. I head straight to the library, where I wait between the stacks for Kat's class to show up. When they do, I peek in between the top of the books and a shelf until I spot her. She's looking around too, so I drop – well, slam – my book and notes on the ground to make some sort of out-of-place noise. It earns me a few puzzled looks, but it also earns Kat's attention.

"Smooth," she whispers when she reaches me. "You could've just texted me that you were hiding in fiction A through D."

I roll my eyes, even though that would have been more practical.

My impatience has left little room for logic. "Let's see if we can find a study room," I suggest.

At one end of the library are three small rooms reserved for group projects and club meetings. Thankfully, only one is being used. We step into the one on the end, and I shut the door. Kat sits down at the table, and I sit across from her.

"So ..." I say.

"So ..." she responds, nodding her head like this is uncomfortable.

"Um ..." I have no idea how to start this conversation. "About this morning."

"You mean this morning when you were pretending with Jason?" Her expression turns doubtful. "Or the whole fake break-up thing in general?"

I frown. "There is no fake break-up thing. Lucy ended it yesterday after the fight."

Her eyes grow wide. "Seriously?"

"Yeah. Seriously." I sigh. "Too many people were getting hurt. She thinks everyone will settle down if we're not together."

"Wow." Kat slumps back in her seat. "That makes me so sad."

"It does?"

"It's obvious how much you care about her. You've done so many sweet things in spite of us." She makes a face. "When you find your person, you'd do anything for them. I was really rooting for the two of you."

I'm so confused that I close my eyes to clear my head for a second. "Sorry," I say, refocusing on Kat. "You were rooting for us? Forgive me if I find that hard to believe."

"Well, rooting silently, of course." She looks down. "I'm really sorry, Aaron. We used to be close, and I let things ... get away from me."

"You think?" I try not to be sarcastic, but what she's saying is going to take a minute to sink in. This isn't why I asked to talk to her, but if she's going to be open, I might as well take advantage of it. "Why did you go along with June, then? It's not like you. Or at least I thought it wasn't, but you're always right by her side."

Sitting up, Kat swallows and her demeanor changes. "We all have something to hide, Aaron. Even June. Even me."

Wait. "So, she was blackmailing you?"

"We were ... kinda blackmailing each other."

If she knew I was pretending with Jason earlier, she sure as hell knows how lost I am right now. "What?"

Taking a deep breath, she says, "I assume you know Lucy didn't get June suspended."

"Yeah no, she didn't. And June's not on vacation, either." I know that's classified information, but I'm beyond caring right now.

Kat's eyebrows shoot up. "You know about rehab?"

Holy shit. "*You* know about rehab?"

We stare at each other in silence for a few seconds. If Kat knows June's biggest secret, did she tell her about Cody, too? Is it possible that Kat could be my lucky charm when it comes to telling everyone the truth?

"Okay." I scoot my chair closer to the table, closer to her. "I found out about June's problem from Cody." No need to confuse Kat with all the Allie BS. "He asked me not to say anything, and then she asked me not to say anything. How do you know?"

"I ..." Kat starts, then stops. "It's personal."

"Listen." I don't want to push her, but I could really use her help. "Can we trust each other? Like old times?"

She gives me an apologetic smile. "I think so."

"I only want to set the record straight with my team and your friends. My plan is to earn their trust too, so when I tell them what really happened, they'll lay off Lucy. If it works, I might stand a chance with her again."

"And if it doesn't?"

"At least they'll know. Lucy's been completely shit on, and none of it is her fault. What Cody and June started, I can end. She deserves that at least."

"I agree, but ..." Kat's face scrunches. "What did Cody do? He made some bad decisions, but he didn't *decide* to have an accident. I mean, Lucy didn't either, but that doesn't mean someone isn't responsible."

The look on my face must reveal my darkest feelings because when Kat notices, she blinks and sits back. "What?"

"It wasn't an accident," I say. "Cody ... Cody made a choice."

Her confusion morphs into understanding after a few seconds. "No," she says, her voice a whisper. "Are you sure?"

"I was on the phone with him when it happened." My throat threatens to close, so I clear it. "He asked me not to tell anyone, and I tried to stop him, but ..." I drag my palm over my face to regroup. "I couldn't. I didn't."

Kat blinks away tears. "Does June know?"

"She might assume." I shrug. "When I confronted her, I told her he did what he did because of her. She said she knew, but she might think he just got wasted because of her. She threatened to tell his recruiter about some steroids because he tried to leave her."

"Oh my god." Kat seems genuinely shocked. "I had no idea."

"You didn't notice her acting weird? She never complained about Cody?"

"Well, yeah. We all noticed her mood swings, but she's always had an attitude, you know? It got worse after Cody died; she had more of a temper and she slept a lot, but I just assumed she was coping the only way she knew how. That was, until I found out about the painkillers."

"Did she just come out and tell you?"

"No." Kat looks around and shifts in her seat. "This summer, I was at a mall about a half hour from here. I saw June talking to some guy, and the girl I was with recognized him. She said he used to go to her school, and he was into drugs and stuff. She said he was bad news."

"So, you confronted her."

"I planned to, but she ended up confronting me first."

Huh? I can feel the crease in my forehead.

"When I got home, she was waiting for me in the driveway. She'd seen me at the mall, but she didn't know I'd seen her, too."

"Okay and?" Girls go shopping every day. "Are you not supposed to go there without her or something?"

"She saw me kissing someone."

Okay. "Who?"

Kat hesitates. "My ... girlfriend."

Come again? "Who?"

"My girlfriend."

I'm having a hard time comprehending. "What?"

"Aaron." She reaches across the table and grabs my hand. "I'm not into guys."

I'm so confused. "I ... you ... really?" Wait a minute. "You're gay?"

"Last time I checked."

No way. "Hold on." I lean forward. "Did you know this when I kept asking you out?"

She smirks. "I've pretty much known since birth, so yeah."

I feel so stupid. "Why didn't you say something?!"

"Because I wasn't ready. And besides, would you have been okay with it?"

Why is that even a question? "Um, absolutely." I move my hand under hers and lace our fingers together. "Why are you hiding this part of yourself?"

She shrugs one shoulder. "It feels like I have to."

"Did June make you feel that way?" As if I needed another reason to dislike her.

"No." Kat rolls her eyes. "It's more like a lifetime of stigma." She squeezes my fingers before letting them go. "Anyway, I was so shocked she knew, I told her if she said anything, I'd tell everyone she met up with a dealer. And then ..."

"... and then everything came out," I guess.

She nods. "I went along with her vendetta against Lucy to save myself. I didn't want to give her a reason to out me before I was ready."

Leaning back, I sigh. "I get it. It doesn't mean I like it, but I understand. But just for the record, I'm on your side."

"Thanks." Kat gives me a small smile. "And I'll help with Lucy, if I can."

Can things really be so easy? "Then you'll back me up when I tell the guys? There's no way they can dispute the both of us."

"You want to tell them June's secret?"

"And Cody's."

Kat looks uncertain.

"What?"

"I know she's done some horrible things, but I don't feel right just throwing June's business out there like that. I wouldn't want that to happen to me."

Oh no. Now's not the time to develop a conscience. "What else can I—we—do? It's not like either of them gave Lucy a choice."

"I know." Kat frowns. "Maybe ... we could just ask her? Or warn her? Just something other than blindsiding her."

"How are we going to that?" I try not to sound annoyed.

"June's in an inpatient rehab for thirty days. I know where it is, and I know she gets her phone back for an hour on Fridays. She can have visitors then, too."

My eyebrows shoot up. "Are you saying what I think you're saying?"

Kat reaches for my hand again, but this time to shake it. "Road trip?"

I grasp her fingers in agreement. I really don't want to visit June, but if this is what it takes, I'll do it.

CHAPTER TWENTY-SEVEN

Lucy

It's like he's a magnet. *Stop staring! Stop it. Stop.*

"You okay?"

My eyes jump to Delaney before looking down. "Yep. I'm fine." Fiddling with the plastic bag in my hands, I pull out my sandwich. *It's fine. I'm fine. Everything is fine.*

"Just spill it," Izzy says after biting off a piece of Twizzler. "Seeing him over there bothers you. I know it bugs me."

I shrug one shoulder as I chew. Despite knowing why he's not sitting with us, it's still annoying to see Aaron look so comfortable with his old friends. And the fact that I'm letting it annoy me is bugging me, too. Maybe more than him laughing with Max right now.

"Lucy?"

"What?"

"You're staring again."

Damn it.

"If it helps," Harrison says, "he's never given flowers to anyone else. At least, not that I know of."

"He's trying to do the right thing." Wes looks around Izzy, who is sitting next to me. "Trust us; we'd tell you if he wasn't legit."

I shoot the guys a small, commiserative smile. "I know. And technically, I broke up with him, so ..." I don't know how to explain myself. "I shouldn't care what he does."

"But you do." Izzy starts to give me her know-it-all look but sighs instead. "I don't think yearbook is a good idea for you today."

She's probably right. "What do you suggest I do, oh Editor-in-Chief?"

"Get out of the classroom," she says. "Why don't you pick up a camera for a change? There's got to be something–"

Delaney, who's sitting across from us, looks up over our heads. "NHS. Packing donation boxes for the holidays."

I turn around. There's a poster taped to the cafeteria wall about the community service event this afternoon. *Perfect.* Except ... "I'm sure Alex is already assigned to it."

"Well, I'll unassign her," Izzy says. "Besides, isn't she behind on the Adopt-a-Pet pics? You know, the last volunteer thing NHS did? I haven't seen any."

"I think so," I say, and it's the truth. It will be nice to do something different, something I've started to miss doing. Although I haven't used one of the school cameras since last spring, and now I have a messed-up wrist.

"I'm going to go and start playing with the cameras," I say as I stand and grab what's left of my lunch, "so I can get my settings right." And, if I'm honest, avoid Aaron altogether.

"Okay, see ya," Izzy says as Delaney waves at me with her mouth full of chocolate milk.

About twenty minutes later, I wander into the auxiliary gym. The National Honor Society has lined the floor with a bunch of eight-foot tables. They've set up an assembly line starting with empty cardboard boxes on one end, which are passed along and filled with donations until they end up full by the propped-open emergency door. Then, they're taken outside and loaded into what looks like the bed of a pickup truck.

Spotting the advisor, I walk over to let Mr. Stewart know why I'm there.

"Oh, okay, great," he says as he packs canned vegetables into a box and slides it over. "Take your time."

After I figure out how to get the best hold on the camera with my bulky cast, I manage to turn my brain off as I walk the aisles clicking away. I'm taking way more pictures than necessary, but this is fun. And I definitely want to waste the whole hour.

"Hey."

A familiar voice pulls my eye away from the camera. "Oh, hey, Nick."

"Yearbook?" he asks as he glances toward my hands.

"Yeah." I smile.

"Bummer. I thought maybe you'd joined NHS." He smiles back. "Crazy how close to Christmas it's getting, isn't it?"

I nod. "Even though you guys are doing a good thing here, I'm really looking forward to break."

"I think everyone is looking forward to break. Speaking of," he pauses as he shifts a box, "how long will it take yours to heal?"

"Six weeks."

"Ouch." He shakes his head. "I'm sorry. June has some serious problems."

You don't know the half of it, I think. Then I wonder … "What did you hear? About what happened, I mean."

"Just that she slammed into you and broke your wrist. Now she's suspended and off on some exotic vacation while you're stuck here with the battle scars. Not fair, if you ask me."

Definitely not fair, although she's definitely not on vacation.

"Did I get it right?" he asks.

"Mostly."

He frowns as if asking "What did I miss?" and mentally, I kick myself. What can I add? "It's not a clean break," I say to offer some extra information. "Only a hairline fracture."

My phone pings from my back pocket, saving me. Hanging on to the camera with my good hand, I try to grab my phone with my wounded one. When I can't grasp it, Nick says, "Here. I've got it."

He slides it out of my pocket and hands it to me. "Thanks," I say, even though he could've reached for the camera instead.

I look down to see a message from Izzy: *Delaney and the guys want to hang out after school to do homework and get something to eat. We're headed to Wes' so heads up.*

Ugh. I love my friends, but I don't like being the fifth wheel. I've tried and learned that lesson pretty quickly. Izzy is my ride now that I'm not with Aaron.

"You don't look happy," Nick observes.

"No, it's fine. Izzy just made some plans without me."

"And that matters because?"

"She's my ride home." I use my thumb to open up my phone. If I call now, my mom can probably come get me.

"Well, I can take you, if you want," Nick offers. "I can give you a ride home."

"You can?"

"Sure."

I consider it. Why not? Izzy and the gang can hang out, and I can go home and hibernate. It's a win-win.

"Okay," I say. "Thank you."

He smiles. "No problem."

APPARENTLY, it's a problem.

"I don't understand why you won't come with us." Izzy pouts. "You can't be alone *all the time.*"

Watch me, I want to say. Instead, I sigh. "One afternoon is not all the time."

"Humph," she grumbles. "Call me psychic, but I can see this becoming a regular thing."

I grin and shut my locker door. "I won't call you psychic, but I'll call you psycho."

Izzy sticks her tongue out at me. "Ha-ha."

As I heave my backpack over my shoulder, I turn and see Nick walking toward us. "Have fun," I say to Izzy. "See you in the morning."

"Yeah, yeah," she mutters and waves me off.

"All set?" Nick asks as we meet in the middle of the hallway.

"Yep."

We walk side by side until we get to the parking lot and his car. He opens the door for me, which is completely unnecessary.

"You don't have to do that," I say. "I'm fully capable."

He shrugs. "My mother programmed me well."

I can't argue with that. After I climb in and he shuts the door, it takes all of maybe two seconds for my phone to ping. I pull it out of my backpack as I settle my bag on the floor between my feet.

Are you in Nick Anthony's car?

It's from Aaron. Looking up, I quickly scan the other parked cars. Where is he?

Yes, I type.

Why?

I need a ride home.

As Nick gets settled in his seat, Aaron sends *Where's Izzy?*

I guess this is a problem for him, too. *She's busy. What's the big deal?*

It's not until Nick pulls out of the lot and on to the main road that Aaron responds. *You could've asked me.*

What? *That makes no sense.*

"So, you live off of Runyan Creek, right?" Nick asks.

"Yes," I say, frowning at my phone.

"Is there a problem?"

"What?" I look up at him. "No. Yes. I don't know."

He gives me a confused smirk.

"Things are weird right now," I say, then correct myself. "I mean, a different weird than before. Things were never not weird."

He nods. "That's understandable. Look at your arm. And then

whatever happened between you and Aaron." He pauses as he stops at a light. "Did you guys really break up?"

"Yeah," I sigh. "It was too much for me right now."

"Wait." Nick looks concerned. "*You* broke up with *him?*"

"Yes." I shoot him a curious side-eye. "Why?"

He steps on the gas. "It's just ... he's ..."

"Out of my league?" I suggest.

"No, no," Nick backtracks. "I just don't know many girls who would do that. Especially with him. He's got one of those reputations, you know? Perfect at everything."

He is pretty perfect, I think sadly. "Well, perfect or not, it doesn't change the fact that people want to make things hard for us."

"Do you want to talk about it?" Nick asks.

He must not have been at Harrison's Halloween party. "No, I won't bore you. Didn't you hear? I have a therapist for that." It surprises me how easily I can admit seeing Dr. Marie now.

"Hmm," he pretends to think and smiles. "Yeah, I think I did hear that."

After I direct him through a few more turns, we pull up into my driveway. "Thanks," I say again when he stops the car. "I really appreciate it."

"You're welcome. And I hope things get less weird," he says as I open the door. "If you need any help with the lessening of the weirdness, just let me know."

As those words leave his mouth, Aaron sends me another text. *You know he likes you, right?*

Huh? No, he doesn't. Does he?

"Okay, well, bye," I say, feeling stupid now. I don't want to stick around to find out if Aaron is right. Not today, even though Nick's a nice guy.

Once I make it inside and up to my room, I text Aaron back. *You're wrong. And how would you know anyway?*

It takes him a moment to respond. *I saw the way he was looking at you at Fall Fest. He's a goner.*

Give me a break. Flopping back on my bed, I send *I don't have time for this mess.*

Neither do I, he responds.

———

LATER THAT NIGHT, while my family sleeps, I'm lying in bed staring at my dark ceiling. Aaron didn't text me again after his last message, and I'm awake wondering what he meant. Does he seriously have potential Nick jealousy, or did he really mean he doesn't have time for this mess–the mess being me. Did I piss him off getting a ride from Nick? It shouldn't matter. Yes, I know he's "working" on things, but we're not together. It bothers me to see him with his old friends, including the girls, but I'd never say anything to him about it.

My head rolls on the pillow, and my eyes land on the shadowy outline of the roses he gave me. Since they're only a few days old, in the daylight, they're still bright and beautiful. Now, they look like some sort of dark, contorted creature. Why do I have a nagging feeling that as they fade, my hope of any type of normalcy does too?

Unexpectantly, my phone lights up on the nightstand. Grabbing it, I read a message from my brother: *I snuck out.*

I was awake before, but now I'm wide awake. He's only thirteen! *Where are you?*

Owen's.

Why?

To hang out all night.

Owen lives within walking distance, but it's still about a mile away. Will walked all the way there alone after midnight?

Dude, that's not safe.

I need you to come get me. I'm sick.

Oh, really. *Sick like how?*

Sick like I just puked.

What? I'm not walking twenty minutes to Owen's in the cold. No wonder he's sick; it is the beginning of December. He's probably coming down with the flu.

Well, I guess you just got caught. Wake up Owen's parents and ask them to drive you.

They're not home.

Are you kidding me? *Then I'll wake up Dad.*

No!! He'll ground me.

Yes, but what's the alternative? I can't drive, and Will can't walk home alone, in the dark, puking his guts out.

My mind races. If this had happened a week ago, I'd call Aaron. I could still call him, but that would take more time. I could call Izzy or Delaney, or Harrison or Wes, and I know they would help. I really don't want to involve them, though. Relying on others can suck sometimes. I really wish I could rely on myself.

It's that thought that makes me sit up. Why can't I rely on myself? What's stopping me from at least trying?

My phone lights up again. *Lucy? Don't get Dad.*

Tossing my covers back, I use the flashlight on my phone to find a pair of socks and my coat. Pulling everything on and then shoving my feet into my slides, I text my brother back. *Hang on. I'm coming.*

I hope.

After creeping down the stairs and quietly finding my car keys on the hook by the door, I slip outside and speed shuffle over to my car. It's so cold that it's started to snow, and a thin layer of flakes covers the windshield. I'm definitely not walking now. If I can't drive, then Will's busted.

Sliding behind the wheel, my heart starts to race. I haven't done this in so long. As I start the car and turn on the wipers, my vision gets blurry. *Okay. It's okay*, I tell myself, scrunching my eyes shut and then blinking to clear them. It's only a mile. It's only a mile.

It's only a mile.

As I fasten my seatbelt, I take a deep breath in through my nose and push it out through my mouth, like Dr. Marie taught me. I do it a few more times, completely filling my lungs, before I put the car in reverse and slowly back down the driveway.

When I turn out onto the road, I continue my deep breathing. My entire right leg is shaking as I push on the gas, and my palms are sweaty. Thank god it's so late and no one else is out. My eyes dart back and forth, looking for anything that might jump out in front of me. A deer, a dog, a cat, or god forbid, a person. Jesus, why did I just think that? *Don't think about that.*

I'm only going a whole six miles per hour, and when Owen's house comes into view, I could almost cry with relief. When I pull into the driveway and stop, my hands are shaking so bad it takes me a bunch of tries to text Will "I'm here" instead of gibberish. Moments later, he comes out the front door, holding a plastic grocery bag in one hand and clutching his stomach with the other.

"You drove," he says with surprise, even though his face is as white as a ghost.

"Yeah, and don't breathe on me," I say. I don't want whatever he has. "How did you expect me to get here?"

He answers by dry heaving into the bag, and I decide to up my speed to ten miles per hour on the way home.

When we get there, all the lights in the house are on, and there's a figure standing in the doorway. Will's still going to get grounded, but I couldn't be happier. Despite my trembling, I want to scream from the rooftops. I did it. I did it. *I did it!*

"Do you want to tell me what in the hell is going on here?" my dad asks when we walk up to the house. "We heard the car start."

Once inside, I gesture toward Will, so he can explain. When he opens his mouth, all that comes out is "blaaahhhhrgghhh" as he pukes into the bag.

"Oh my goodness!" my mom comes rushing from the kitchen.

As she tends to my brother, I walk up to my dad and throw my arms around him. He squeezes me back stiffly, since he didn't expect my hug.

"I drove," I whisper into his shoulder, smiling. "I drove."

CHAPTER TWENTY-EIGHT

Aaron

"Y ou ready?"

"Ready."

It's Friday, and Kat and I are skipping school to visit June. She can only see people during a one-hour window, so we need to head out if we're going to make it there on time.

"She knows we're coming?" I ask as I settle into the passenger seat of Kat's old Blazer.

"If she reads her text messages when she gets her phone back, she'll know *I'm* coming." Kat adjusts the heat in the cab. "Are you cold? This thing takes forever to warm up."

"I'm good." I'm also fidgety. Today could be the day this all ends. Once I get June to agree to share the truth, it's just a matter of time before people accept it and move on. Only a matter of time before I can prove to Lucy things are good, and she won't need other people to take her home anymore. Like Nick.

Damn, that irritated me. Even after Harrison told me the reason why she decided to ride with him, I still didn't like it. And not because I don't trust Lucy. But Nick? He's not stupid. He saw an opportunity.

He *sees* the opportunity. What if Lucy decides I'm not worth the headache? I feel like I'm on a deadline.

"So, where is this place again?" I ask Kat.

"It's near Kalamazoo, in Augusta. It should take us about two hours to get there. The Mt. Olive Counseling and Rehabilitation Center."

"Sounds fancy."

"I think it is. June's parents never do anything small."

She's got that right. "Well, if the length they went to cover up her problem is any indication, then no, they don't do anything small."

Kat smiles. "True, although I meant they always want the best of the best. I guess I would too, if it were my kid."

"Yeah, but you would have dealt with this sooner," I say. "I mean, if June's parents had taken this seriously from the start, recruited some professionals, maybe Cody would still be here."

"Maybe," Kat concedes. "But then again, we don't know every detail about how things went down. I don't think there's an instruction manual for this. Just like when your kid tells you they're gay."

I scowl. "Your parents aren't ..." I pause to find the right words. "They're supportive, aren't they?"

"They are, and they really like my girlfriend, Dana." Kat looks over at me. "But, if you ask my one aunt and uncle, or my grandparents on my dad's side, that part of me doesn't exist. And if you ask some of my cousins or my brother's girlfriend, *I* just don't exist. Period."

My jaw drops. "Why does your brother put up with that? You're his baby sister."

Kat shrugs. "Let's just say I really, really hope he doesn't end up marrying her." She shudders.

About an hour into our drive, we make a quick pit stop to get snacks at a gas station and then get back on the road. The closer we get, the more I eat – I'm slamming cheddar cheese Combos like there's no tomorrow. I didn't realize this would stress me out so much.

When we pull into the rehab center, it's only a few minutes after noon, when the visitation hour begins. After Kat turns off the ignition, she lets out a deep breath. "We don't have a game plan, do we?"

"No, not really." I rub the back of my neck nervously. "Let's just hope she's feeling well and in a good mood. Maybe she'll just be happy to see people." Although probably not me. We should have thought this through a little better.

"Well, here goes nothin'," Kat says as she pushes her door open.

"Wait," I stop her. "If June doesn't want to see me, I'm okay with it. I'll leave. But promise me you'll ask her about Lucy. Promise me you'll try to get her to do the right thing."

Kat looks at me like I've lost my mind. "Of course," she says. "Would I come all the way out here otherwise?"

"Okay." I nod. "I just wanted to make sure we're on the same page."

"We are."

After a short walk across the parking lot, we enter through the front doors and walk into a lobby similar to a doctor's office but way nicer. I let Kat do the talking as she tells the attendant we're here to see June Summers, and we're her friends from school. She takes our names and asks us to have a seat while she goes to let June know we're here.

"What if she refuses to see either one of us?" I ask as I sink into an oversized plush chair.

"She won't," Kat says. "If I know anything about June, it's that she's curious. Or I guess you could say nosey. If she sends us away without finding out why we're here, the curiosity will eat her alive."

Minutes pass. When the attendant returns, she says June will see the both of us.

"See?" Kat sends me a knowing look when we stand.

The woman leads us farther into the building until we come to a large room that, to me, looks like a lounge. Round tables are spread throughout, and one wall is lined with windows and potted plants while couches and coffee tables line the remaining three. Over half the space is occupied with people, and there, sitting by herself on the far end at one of the tables, is June.

"Well, this is a strange combination," she comments as we sit down across from her. "You didn't tell me you were bringing company." She looks at Kat.

"Well, we weren't sure if you wanted company," Kat says slowly.

"You have until one o'clock," the attendant reminds us before walking away.

The three of us fall silent. I don't know where to begin. In these seconds, I take a moment to look at June. She looks healthy but tired. She's dressed down in sweats and a hoodie with her hair in a ponytail. She's not wearing any makeup, which I don't think I've ever seen, so maybe that's why her eyes look a little purplish underneath.

"How are you?" Kat asks. "Is it nice here?"

"Oh, it's the best."

I see she hasn't lost any of her sarcasm.

"It's just like a spa, except every minute of your day is planned, and you don't get a say in any of it. There aren't any massages or mani-pedis, but there is a lot of talking and mediational yoga. Oh, and the most awesome part? Feeling like complete ass as I detox."

Shit, I think. She's not in a good mood.

"I'm so sorry," Kat says and reaches for June's hand. "Did they say when you might start to feel better?"

June keeps her arms crossed and shrugs. "Eventually," is all she says. Then, her eyes fall on me. "What brings you here, Aaron? Are you concerned about me, too? Or are you still trying to get in Kat's pants?" Her eyes light up as she leans forward. "Do you want to know a secret? That will never, ever happen."

"Wow," I say and shake my head. "Will you never stop? Look around. You're here to get well. You should take advantage of it."

June rolls her eyes. "Yeah, I know. It's just a little hard to be positive when it feels like a freight train is running you over. I can't even stay asleep long enough to escape it."

That does sound like hell. "It'll get better," I say, "and you'll be stronger for it."

"Did you really come all the way out here to encourage me? You haven't been my biggest cheerleader, Aaron. Like, ever." She then turns to Kat. "Why is he here?"

"Because we had a talk," she says. "There was a huge fight. The guys confronted Lucy for getting you suspended, and Aaron stepped in."

"Of course he did." June looks unimpressed by my chivalry.

"Your friends think you've been kicked out," I say. "They're blaming Lucy for something she didn't do. She wanted me to tell them the truth, but I knew they wouldn't believe me. We need to set things straight. Kat and I, we want to tell our friends the whole truth. About you. Cody. Everything."

She doesn't hesitate. "No."

"Excuse me?"

"I said no."

Kat tries to explain. "June, listen –"

"No, you listen." She lowers her voice to a hiss. "This is *my* life. You don't get to run your mouths about it. Say whatever you want about Cody, but leave me out of it."

I can feel my blood pressure start to rise.

"You mean like you did?" Kat leans forward. "Lucy has a life, too, and you decided to run your mouth about her. How is that fair?"

June's eyes narrow. "You used to be on my side."

"Only because you were holding Dana over my head."

June shuts up for a minute as her eyes dart between me and Kat.

"Yeah, he knows," Kat says.

I think I see a brief flash of defeat in June's eyes. This might be my chance to talk some sense into her. "After the fight, because it was at school, Coach, Mrs. Wright, the principal ... they all know the truth about Cody," I say. "And because they know about him, they know about you, too."

"So, what?" June throws up her hands. "You're going to blackmail me while I'm sitting in rehab? Really?"

"No," I say. "I'm just telling you some people already know, so why not tell your friends the truth? Then, they'll leave Lucy alone. She deserves that."

"And what do you get out of it? Lemme think." June sarcastically puts her finger to her chin in thought. "Oh! Right. You get to be with your precious girlfriend with no strings attached, hanging out with the guys, and leading the team to victory." She laughs. "The only reason you're here is to make things easier for you."

"You're not wrong," I say. I won't lie.

"June," Kat tries again, "think of this as moving forward. Don't be selfish."

June's mouth falls open. "*I'm* the one being selfish? What a joke." She suddenly stands. "You two are the ones who want to trash my reputation, and I say hell no. How is not wanting to lose everything being selfish? I've already lost Cody, and I still have to go back to that school." She turns to leave but stops. "My life. My secrets. Don't you dare say a thing."

"June –" Kat tries to reach for her arm, but she shakes her off and walks away.

Kat sighs and looks at me. "Well. That didn't go so great."

My stomach sinks to my feet. No. No, it didn't.

I SULK the entire ride home. I should win a trophy for the worst road tripper ever.

By the time we pull up to my house, Kat and I have exchanged few words. When we left Mt. Olive, I volunteered to drive, so she wouldn't have to. She spent most of the time staring out the window after I didn't have much to offer in the conversation department.

"So," she says after I put the car in park, "have you figured everything out yet?"

"Absolutely not," I say and let my head fall back against the seat. "I'm sorry I wasn't better company."

"It's okay. Today didn't work out."

"That's an understatement." I sigh. "You really tried, though. Thank you."

"That's what friends are for." She reaches over and gives my arm a small jab. "So, what's plan B?"

"Other than ignoring June and doing what I want, I'm out of ideas," I say.

Kat gives me a wary look. I know she doesn't want me to do that, and without her behind me, I'm back to square one. I have no credibility, which sucks. I have nothing else to try.

Nothing. Zero. Nada.

I blow out a frustrated breath. "Any suggestions?"

"Since you asked ..." Kat takes her seatbelt off and turns her body toward mine. "You want to fix things, right? Make it all go away?"

"Yes."

"Have you ever stopped to think that's not possible? You can't change the past."

I can't stop my eye roll. "Yes, I'm aware of that."

"Okay. So, here's an example. What happens if you have a really bad game? As in, you get totally smoked. You're mad about it, pissed off; you're tired because you tried. You dwell on it for a while, but over time, you start to forget. It stings less, because other things occupy your mind."

"No. It stings less because we can figure out what went wrong and fix it so it doesn't happen again."

"Ugh. Bad example." Kat shifts her weight. "All right; I'll use Cody. We're grieving him now, because he just left us. But you know how this works. Over time, grief lessens. There will always be sadness, but there will be happiness, too."

I can feel the doubtful expression on my face. "And you're telling me this because ...?"

"All I'm saying is the fix for this is probably time."

That's not what I want to hear.

"The holiday break is coming up, and I don't care how old you are, everyone gets excited about Christmas. We won't be in school for a few weeks, and people will be busy with skiing and snowboarding and vacations. When we come back, they'll have better things to talk about."

"Until June reappears."

My words take the wind out of Kat's sails. "Aaron ..." she groans. "We can't tell the truth about June. I accused her of being selfish, and I stand by what I said. But we'd be the same if we tell."

"I know." I rub my forehead. "I know. Stop being logical."

It's quiet in the cab again. Defeat starts to settle over me. I promised Lucy I would make things right, and I can't. At least not any time soon; not until some magic idea springs into my brain. I hate that I was hopeful earlier.

"We can learn how to send subliminal messages to our friends over break," Kat suggests. "Or do you know anyone who does hypnosis?"

I give her a small smile. I'm grateful she's still willing to help. Unfortunately, I think she was right before. All we have is time.

And I don't think it's on my side.

CHAPTER TWENTY-NINE

Lucy

"Oh yes, it's ladies' night, and the feelin's right, oh yes, it's ladies' night ..."

"Dad." I shoot him an annoyed stare. "Stop."

"Oh, what ... a ... night." His voice gets lower as he opens the refrigerator door.

"Dad!"

"What?" He smiles. "I can't sing?"

"You've got that right," my mom mutters, which makes Delaney and Izzy laugh. "Where are you three headed?" she asks.

"Just the movies," Izzy answers. "We're going to see *Love vs. Love.*" She bats her eyelashes at a feverish pace. "It's supposed to be romantic."

"A romantic *comedy,*" I clarify. I'm definitely not in the mood for two hours of mushy swoon.

"God forbid we see a drama."

I sigh so hard I think I tweak a rib. We're a week into break, and this is the first time I've been able to pry my friends away from their boyfriends for a night. It's not that I don't love Harrison and Wes, but it's been exhausting trying to fit in with the four of them.

"Don't listen to her." Delaney drapes her arm over my shoulders. "She's just upset that her present from Wes was a gift card to Applebee's."

I frown at Izzy. "But you love Applebee's."

"I know." She crosses her arms. "I just thought he'd give me something a little more sentimental."

"You know what Lucy's dad gave me for our first wedding anniversary?" my mom asks.

"Hey, now." My dad pauses mid-sandwich making. "We don't talk about that."

"A vacuum."

Our mouths collectively drop as my mom nods with a smirk. "Yep. A freaking Hoover."

"Dad!" I say in shock.

"It was twenty years ago!" my dad defends himself. "And our old one broke."

"Humph," my mom grunts and then looks at us. "Girls, let me give you some advice. When it comes to gifts, always be clear about what you *want* vs. what you *need*."

Point taken.

Not long after the enlightening, yet odd, conversation with my parents, Izzy, Delaney, and I are on our way to the movies. What's new about this is I'm the one driving. Ever since I had to rescue Will, I've been pushing myself to drive farther distances little by little. This evening's trip will be my longest.

"So," Delaney leans forward from the back seat, "it just dawned on me what your mom said. Maybe you should be more direct with Aaron, and tell him what you want."

"She wasn't referring to relationships," I say.

"Still, it's been awhile since you two talked."

I'm painfully aware of that. "He said I'd know when he's done all he can. I'm not going to bug him about it." *Because I might not like what he tells me,* I think.

"I would think you're entitled to a status update." Izzy sounds irritated.

In all honesty, I would love that. Sure, I've gotten a little information here and there from Harrison and Wes, but all they tell me is he hasn't given up ... and I shouldn't give up on him.

"Can we not worry about Aaron tonight?" I ask. "There's so many other things to talk about. Like the fact I'm going the speed limit on the expressway."

Both Delaney and Izzy lean to look at the dash, then let out a whoop and start clapping. "Good job!" "Congratulations!" they say in unison. It does feel good to do a normal everyday thing without hyperventilating.

Actually, a lot of things have felt good over the last few weeks. Driving for one, but school has been so much easier without June there. It's like her mere presence created tension. Something Aaron is doing must be working, because no one has said anything to me or so much as looked my way since we broke up. The only awkward part of the day is yearbook, when I strategically try to avoid him other than a quick hello. Without all the nonsense around me, I can feel some of my confidence coming back.

"Now that you've accomplished another goal," Izzy says, "I think you should call Aaron. Just tell him you hope he's having a good break."

"Or that you want to meet up. For coffee," Delaney adds.

"You know I don't drink coffee," I scoff, and my brain suddenly flashes back to homecoming, when Aaron and I were on the run from the party police. When we stopped at the diner because I thought he wanted coffee, and we ended up with hot chocolate instead. Which I still owe him for.

Silently, I sigh. Memories like that, when they randomly pop into my head, make me miss him. I miss him regardless, but I'm not going to tell my friends. They'd just push me harder, when I'd rather do things in my own way.

When we get to the movies, the lobby is packed. The lines from the ticket and concession registers wind all the way to the entrance doors.

"This place is popular tonight," Delaney muses.

"Do you guys want to share a large popcorn?" Izzy asks, reading the concession signs over our heads. "Since there's free refills?"

"Sure," Delaney and I agree.

While we wait, we figure out what we want and hand our cash over to Izzy, since she'll use her debit card to make things faster. Izzy and I always sit in the very topmost row of the theater, against the wall under the projector, and we want to get those seats.

"I'm going to add some extra butter to this," I say when I'm handed the bucket of popcorn. Since I still have my cast, I can't juggle all the boxes of candy and drinks. "I'll meet you guys over there."

Delaney and Izzy nod, and I weave my way through the lines and around the corner to the seasoning station. I make sure not to drown the kernels, even though I'm tempted. Buttered theater popcorn is the best.

When I finish and turn around, the back of a guy several feet in front of me catches my eye. I could swear it's Aaron, so I do a double-take. He's not wearing his varsity jacket, but a leather coat instead. I can't see his face, but his walk is familiar. So is the grey beanie on his head. He disappears into the crowd just as Izzy and Delaney find me.

"Ready?"

"Yep," I say, tearing my eyes away from the spot where I last saw him.

Luckily, we're able to get our top row seats in the movie theater for *Love vs. Love*. Actually, our theater is only about half full, which means something else big must have just come out. If Aaron were here, what would he see?

And with who?

Stop it, I chastise myself. He does have friends, too. Not that he's here with Harrison and Wes; we'd for sure know about that. And why does it matter? It shouldn't matter. Unless ...

"Are you two setting me up?"

Izzy and Delaney stop mid-chew. "What?"

"Are the guys here?" It wouldn't surprise me if they came up with some plan for us to run into them later.

"Um, no," Izzy says with a look of confusion. "Wes is visiting his grandma for the weekend. I thought I told you."

"And Harrison is stuck doing "family time" since he's been with me a lot over break," Delaney adds. "Why?"

"You just ... you brought up Aaron a lot in the car. I wouldn't put it past you two to arrange some sort of accidental meeting."

"Who us? Never." Delaney puts her hand to her chest and pretends to be shocked. Then, she grins. "No, we didn't plan anything. It's a good idea, though."

Izzy nods in agreement. "Shame on us for not thinking of it."

The lights dim as the first preview starts to play. I settle in my seat, preparing to be entertained. I can't remember the last time I dedicated any time to a movie. Oh, wait. That would be when I went to Aaron's, and we watched *Scream*. My pulse skips at the memory.

Good grief. I pick up my Coke and down half of it. I'm not sure what's going on with me, but I really need to do a better job of blocking that boy from my brain.

Thankfully, minutes in, the movie does it. It turns out to be really funny and sweet, and something I think we all needed. I lose track of time until it's over. As we're walking to the lobby and laughing about the main character's hilarious waxing mistake, Delaney suddenly grabs my arm and shoves me behind her.

"What the-?!"

"Shhhh!" she says. Izzy keeps walking, so she grabs the hood on her coat to stop her. She stumbles backward before she turns and says, "Hey!"

"Look." Delaney's eyes are wide as she nods over to our left.

Suddenly, I regret eating all the popcorn that I did. Standing there, just far enough away for us to stare without being noticed, is Aaron and Kat. It was him.

"Maybe they're here with a group?" Izzy whispers.

"They could've just run into each other," Delaney says.

We watch as Kat hands Aaron the drink she's holding. He takes a long pull from the straw, then hands it back to her. She takes a drink too, before reaching into her pocket to check her phone. She shows him whatever is on the screen and he smiles, taking it from her and typing something.

Yeah, no. They're here together.

My heart starts to pound.

The evidence is clear as they start to walk toward the lobby doors, and he drapes his arm around her shoulders. Delaney has to reach for Izzy again and hold her back as she starts to march in their direction.

"We're just going to let them get away with this?" Izzy asks, incredulous.

"No," Delaney says with controlled calm. I can tell she's seething. "We're going to ask Lucy what she'd like us to do."

Both girls cross their arms and stare at me, waiting for an answer. Part of me wants to confront him, and the other part wants to run away. I'm so tired of running away.

"You know what?" I start walking. "I think maybe I deserve that status update."

We head out to the parking lot faster than we normally would walk. My eyes scan the darkness looking for Aaron's truck. I'm not sure if we're going to be able to find it. Even if we do, what am I going to say? I'm not sure what's going to come out of my mouth.

"Over there!" Izzy points.

When I look, I see both Aaron and Kat getting inside the truck. I start to run in their direction because, hey, why not embarrass myself to the fullest extent? I know when Aaron spots me because his eyes about pop out of his head. He gets out of the cab and shuts the door just as I stop a few feet in front of him.

"Lucy," he starts.

I have to catch my breath. "I ... saw ..." I swallow. My eyes dart to Kat and back again. "What?" So much for coherent sentences.

"There's nothing going on." He holds his hands up. "I swear. We're friends."

"Since when?" My breathing returns to normal.

"Since she's been trying to help me with June. Really," he walks toward me, "I'm just trying to figure things out."

I glance between the two of them again and Kat looks speechless, kind of like a fish with her mouth hanging open. "And you need her help at the movies?" I ask.

Aaron's expression falls. "We just wanted to get out and do something. It's not personal."

This weird swell of jealousy builds in my chest. "So, this is okay, but I can't get a ride home from Nick?"

He starts to speak, but I cut him off before he can. "Because the last time we talked, you seemed pretty mad about that."

"That's only because he likes you."

"And she doesn't like you?" My brow shoots up.

"She ... uh ..." Aaron looks back at Kat and then at me again. "No, she doesn't."

That was convincing. I start to back away. "You know ..." My voice goes quiet. "All you have to do is be honest."

"I am being honest." He looks pained as he steps toward me.

"If things have changed, I don't need you to be my hero," I say. "You can move on. It's okay." It's really, really not okay, but what else am I going to say? I broke up with him because it was too hard for me. He doesn't owe me anything.

"Nothing's changed," he says adamantly. "Please trust me."

I want to.

"Come on, Lucy. Let's go," Delaney says.

Her tone tells me she's heard enough, and I think I have, too. I saw what I saw. I guess it could've been friendly, but pigs can fly.

As we walk back to my car, Aaron doesn't try to stop me. When we get there, Izzy asks, "Do you want me to drive?"

I shake my head. "No, I'm good."

"Are you sure?"

I shoot her a sad smile. "Yeah." I can do this. I don't know why I can, I just do.

As soon as we're out on the road, Izzy exclaims, "What in the actual hell?" She pulls out her phone and starts texting. "If Wes knew about this ..."

"Oh, I've already sent a few messages to Harry," Delaney says from the back seat. "If they've been holding out on you, Lucy, I swear ..."

I bite my tongue and focus on the road.

By the time we reach my house, both of my friends have spent the entire time bickering back and forth. Not with each other, but with their boyfriends over text messages. Both guys claim to know nothing about Aaron and Kat while apologizing to me through Izzy and Delaney.

"Do you want us to stay over?" Izzy asks when get out of the car.

I really don't. It's not that I don't love these guys, but I really feel like crying and I'd rather do it alone if I have a choice.

"You don't have to," I say. "Besides ..." I reach for my phone. Yeah, there are some messages from a certain someone. "I think I'd like to talk to him alone."

"Okay. But call us if you need us," Delaney says before hugging me.

After the girls leave, I head upstairs to my room, take off my coat, and flop down on my bed. This night went so sideways; it's frustrating. Reluctantly, I unlock my phone to read Aaron's messages.

I'm sorry. Please believe me when I say nothing is going on.

Lucy?

Can you text me back?

I know you're mad. Can you call me? I want to explain. There are things you don't know.

You've got that right. So many things.

I try to respond to Aaron, but I keep typing messages and deleting them. Finally, I settle on the most straightforward thing I can think to say. *I need some time.*

A stray tear escapes my eye, and I wipe it away. A clean break would have been best; I could've ended all this tonight. I should've told him it's over and to stop trying, but something wouldn't let me. I physically couldn't type those words.

Since I don't want to debate what I sent, I decide to block his number. My finger shakes when I do it, but I know how easy it would be to give in to another conversation. Then, gathering my strength, I pull myself off the bed and walk over to my dresser. Another tear falls as I pick up the now dry and dead roses - the hope I had for some kind of normal - and throw them in the trash. It's time to move on.

I just wish I knew what that meant.

CHAPTER THIRTY

Aaron

Time.

I can't tell you how much I hate that word. Not to mention the concept itself. It's either moving too fast or too damn slow; there's too much of it or not enough. There's never a perfect length.

As I drag my sorry ass into school on the first day back from break, all I can think about is time. Lucy said she needed some, but apparently the rest of our holiday vacation wasn't enough. She wouldn't respond to any form of communication, so I finally broke down and asked Izzy and Delaney what I could do. They confessed she blocked my number, which felt like a sucker punch. It was proof of what I already knew – she was done with me. I shouldn't have gone with Kat to the movies. I shouldn't have said anything about Nick.

And I shouldn't have believed I could fix this.

Lucy will never get her full dozen roses.

When I make it to my locker, I try to focus on opening it but instead my eyes wander down the hall to where Lucy should be. I catch a glimpse of her, and my heart stops. She's looking at me, too. It takes everything in me not to sprint down to her and ask her to leave, so we can talk and work things out. Would she go with me if I asked?

"There's only one way to find out," Cody's voice challenges me in my head.

"Hey, stranger," Kat says from behind me.

Mentally, I flinch. The last person Lucy needs to see me with is Kat. I turn around, to try and block her from Lucy's view.

"Hey," I say. "Sorry I didn't text you back last night. I was –"

"In a mood?" she guesses and then raises her eyebrows.

"What? No."

"What, yes," she says. "Don't tell me you weren't overthinking today. First day back, first day around Lucy ..." she drifts off. "Anyway," she straightens her posture, "remember when I said I would help if I could? Back when we talked in the library?"

"Yes, and you did. You did everything you could with June."

"Well, after that epic failure," she looks over her shoulder. "Harrison! Wes! C'mere."

My friends have just arrived, and they wander over. Wes asks, "What's up?" while Harrison shoots me a look I interpret as "Dude. You're not starting off too great here."

"Would the three of you please escort me to Lucy's locker?" she asks as she takes a few backward steps.

Whoa. "Wait, why?" I ask.

"There's one thing I can clear up," she says, "and I'd like a little support while I do it."

Harrison and Wes look confused, but agree. I'm pretty sure I know what she's thinking, and as we walk, I whisper, "You don't have to do this. Not for me."

"It's more for me, actually," she says. "When the time is right, you know."

Izzy is the first to notice our group approaching. She pokes Lucy in the arm to get her attention, and when she sees us, she tenses. Delaney turns around when she realizes they're not listening to her anymore.

"Hi," Kat says when we reach the girls. "I just wanted to introduce myself. I'm Katherine. Kat for short."

"Umm ... we know?" Izzy says with an uncertain look on her face.

"Well," she takes a breath, "Lucy. I want you to hear the truth about Aaron and me. From me."

Lucy blinks a few times before she lets out a skeptical, "Okay."

"We're friends. We've known each other a long time. Since, like, the second grade."

Actually, I think it was the third grade, but I don't correct her.

"Anyway, I just want you to know," she looks around our group, "I want all of you to know, I'm gay."

If it wasn't for the noise of the other students oblivious to us, you could hear a pin drop. Wes and Harrison look like they've been hit with a brick, and the girls look a little stunned, too.

"Soooo," Kat says after a few awkward seconds, "there is no Aaron and me. At least, not personally. I mean, intimately. I mean, romantically."

"I think they get it," I stop Kat with half a smile.

"Oh my god," Delaney comes to. "Is this the first time you've told anyone?"

"On my own terms? Besides my parents and Aaron, yeah."

Delaney rushes forward and wraps Kat in a bear hug. "Good for you," she says as she squeezes her. I try not to laugh. Kat doesn't know what to do with her arms and gives Delaney a weird shoulder pat.

"Wow," Harrison regains consciousness. "I never knew. Um, congratulations, I guess?"

Kat laughs sarcastically. "It's not a prize."

Harrison shrugs. "What else do you say?"

"You say thank you for trusting me." Lucy takes a few steps. "For trusting us."

"I just wanted to clear the air," Kat says. "I can't put up with Mr. Mopey anymore." She jabs me in the side with her elbow. "And I definitely don't want to be in the same league as June." Kat meets my eyes. "Aaron will fill you in. I'm sorry for the things I've done."

Lucy nods and then looks at me.

"Okay!" Izzy claps her hands together. "Why don't we all give Lucy and Aaron some spa –"

The warning bell rings, and everyone groans. As they turn and start to make their way to class, Lucy backs up to shut her locker door.

"Can we talk after school?' I ask as she slams it, secretly hopeful.

When she turns around, my heart pounds. "How about we skip yearbook and talk then?"

FOR THE PAST THREE HOURS, I've been thinking about nothing other than what I want to say to Lucy. I think I may have missed an entire chapter review, but I don't care.

Just as we're ready to pack it up and leave third hour, an announcement comes over the PA: "Welcome back, Huskies," Mr. Hughes' voice crackles through the speaker. "We have a special assembly planned for the next part of your day. Please head to your fourth hour class for attendance, then proceed to the gym. Thank you."

What?? *Ugh.* Why can't things ever work out for us? Next hour is yearbook, and they're taking attendance, which means it'll be next to impossible for Lucy and me to skip.

Damn it.

Regardless, I sprint to class because it feels like I've been waiting an eternity. When I make it there and see Lucy, she gives me a "What can you do?" shrug. I mouth "After?" and she nods yes. We can probably sneak away undetected as everyone leaves the gym.

Once we're there, I really want to sit next to her, the girls, and my real friends, but instead sit with my lacrosse team and Kat. It's only the first day back, and I'm already fed up with this keeping-up-appearances-post-break-up thing. I look over my shoulder into the bleachers to see where Lucy is and find her about ten rows up. Irritatingly, I also spot Nick sitting directly behind her.

"Do you have any idea what this is about?" Kat distracts me as she looks around the gym.

I shake my head. There's a podium set up under one of the basket-ball hoops, but that's always there for an assembly. I don't see the band or Spirit Committee, so I really have no clue.

"Good afternoon, students," Mr. Hughes says after he walks up to the mic. A large group of people follow him in and stand against the wall. Teachers, including Ms. Wright, coaches, including my coach, other staff, and ...

Oh my god. My stomach sinks.

"The staff here at Holton hope you all had a relaxing break," Mr. Hughes continues. "We hope you've come back ready to tackle the rest of the school year. With that said, it is a *new* year." He glances over his shoulder. "We have a special guest here to talk to you today about a new program we're implementing going forward." Mr. Hughes turns and gestures behind him. "Holton High, I'd like you to give your full attention to Mr. John Cunningham."

As Cody's dad walks forward to shake the principal's hand, my chest constricts. Why is he here? My teammates also look confused; I doubt any of them have seen Cody's dad since the funeral.

"Hello," Mr. Cunningham says as he sets some papers against the podium. "Thank you for having me today. As Mr. Hughes said, my name is John Cunningham, but some of you may know me better as Cody's father."

All whispered conversations and feet shuffling come to a halt at the sound of Cody's name. Mr. Cunningham has the gym's full atten-tion; all you can hear is the hum of the school's ventilation system. I glance up at Lucy and see both Izzy and Delaney have an arm around her.

"My son," he continues and looks down at his speech. "My son ..." he drifts off and goes silent. Taking a breath, Cody's dad looks up and unexpectedly finds me in the crowd. I'm sitting in the first row of bleachers to his right, so I'm not hidden, but it still catches me off guard. He then looks around at the familiar faces of the lacrosse team, sets his hand on his speech, and crumples the paper into a ball.

"I'm just going to do this," he says into the mic before clearing his throat. "My son, Cody, was a smart kid. A lot of you knew him. He was outgoing, friendly, and pretty damn athletic. He had a bright future. He had a good heart, but he could be a smart ass, too."

Subdued laughter trickles throughout the gym.

"Many of those things describe all of you," he continues with a small smile. "You, too, are smart. You have close friends, maybe you're athletic, or artistic, or a musician. And you're loved." He pauses. "Like Cody was loved."

The crowd falls silent waiting for Mr. Cunningham to continue.

"Yet, despite all those wonderful things, my son struggled." He glances over at me and our team again. "He was anxious. He worried. He was scared. And he put a lot of pressure on himself. In fact, he put so much pressure on himself, to be the perfect kid, the perfect student, the perfect player, the perfect boyfriend, that he made a very real, very final choice."

Whoa. A cold sweat breaks out on the back of my neck. I can feel eyes on me, and when I look up, Lucy's wide-eyed stare meets mine. It's only when Cody's dad starts talking again that I look away.

"Today, I'm here to tell you my son, Cody, committed suicide."

It feels like all the air has been sucked out of the room. Kat's hand finds mine and clenches it while I try to focus. I can hear people whisper as they process the information; I can feel them stirring around me. Everyone knows now. How long has his dad known? He must hate me for not coming to him myself. Did Coach tell him because I told Coach?

"A lot of you might feel the way Cody did," Mr. Cunningham's voice draws our attention back to him. "And that's why I'm here. To share my son's story in the hope that it will prevent another tragedy. Some of you look shocked, and that's okay. Cody was struggling. And if you're struggling too, you're not alone. Your principal, teachers, and I, we want to help."

Mr. Cunningham turns and says something to Mr. Hughes, who joins him at the podium. "Thank you, John." He pats Cody's dad on the arm. "Holton High, today we're announcing a new outreach program. It will be available to you at any hour, any day of the week, and you may use it in-person or anonymously."

One of the teachers hands him a paper, which he holds up. "These flyers will be handed out as you leave the gym, but first, please take out your phones."

Everyone with a phone looks confused but complies.

"We want you to add a new number," Mr. Hughes says. "The name of our program is Twenty-Three. Please enter it into your phones. It was Cody's –"

"Jersey number," I say quietly at the same time as Mr. Hughes.

"Then add the following contact information," he continues.

As he rambles off the phone number and email address, I type it in robotically along with the people around me. As Mr. Hughes goes on to explain about the help line, I vaguely register the words licensed, counselors, and referrals as I stare into space. A vision of Cody appears a few feet from his dad. He looks at me and shrugs, saying, "What'cha gonna do? I have no control over my old man." Something he used to say when his dad would holler the loudest from the stands.

Smiling at the memory, I shake my head.

"Well, that secret is out of the bag," Kat whispers from beside me.

Yeah, I think. And I thought I'd feel better about it.

We're dismissed soon after, and I immediately stand. Of course, everyone else does too, and I look for Lucy in the sea of students. I want to find her, but I also want to talk to Cody's dad. He deserves an explanation as to why I went to Coach instead of him.

"Aaron."

I feel a hand on my shoulder and turn around, winding up face to face with Jason.

"Did you know?" he asks.

My expression must give away the truth, because his eyes widen and he leans back.

"Damn," he mutters.

Satisfied with his reaction, I start to head toward the gym exit with Kat. "Do you see Lucy?" I ask as I look over everyone's heads.

"There." She points to the side, toward the podium where everything was announced. "She's talking to Mr. Cunningham."

Huh? "I'll catch up with you later," I say and push my way through the Holton High student body. Once I'm close, my presence catches their attention.

"Aaron," Cody's dad takes a few steps toward me. "I was hoping to talk to you."

Words escape me as I look between him and Lucy.

"Mr. Cunningham wanted to tell me he knew who I was," Lucy says, her voice uncertain. "A few months ago, back at the restaurant."

"You knew?" I ask, confused.

Cody's dad nods. "When your child dies, you know every detail. Or, at least I needed to know every detail."

Before I can figure out what to say next, he places his hand on my arm and reaches out to Lucy with the other. I can tell she's reluctant to take it, but she steps closer and does.

"You two have been through so much," he says. "I've wanted to talk to you for some time, but things ..." He pauses. "Let's just say they are what they are. Lucy," he grasps her hand tighter, "I want you to know we don't blame you. Cody's mother and I ... it's not your fault."

Lucy looks dazed.

"Our son made a choice. An impaired choice, but a choice nonetheless. You didn't ask to be a part of that."

Lucy's eyes tear up as he turns to me. "And Aaron, you've also been living with this secret."

My voice sounds weird around the lump in my throat. "He asked me not to tell anyone." I realize now how ridiculous that sounds. "How did you know?"

Mr. Cunningham squeezes my arm. "Nicole – Ms. Wright, she reached out. She'd talked to Cody right before ... and there were some things he was going through –"

"We know about June," I say, glancing at Lucy.

"I see." He sighs. "Then you probably know about our financial worries, too. We told Cody we'd make it work if he didn't get a full scholarship, but he was determined to make that happen so he wouldn't burden us."

Mr. Cunningham's voice fades as my mind travels back in time, to when Cody said Allie – June – threatened to tell his recruiter about his steroid use. I had no idea his family was having money trouble; he never once mentioned it. Now I know why the possibility of her running her mouth intensified everything.

"... that's why we wanted to start this program. If it only helps one kid," Mr. Cunningham's voice takes center stage again, "I'd like Cody's memory to be about more than his death."

Both Lucy and I nod as Cody's dad releases us and takes a step back. "I'm not going to take up any more of your day," he says as he looks around the nearly empty gym. "But, Aaron, I'd like to talk again soon, if you're feeling up to it. Cody's mom and I, we ... have questions."

"Absolutely," I say, now that I know there's nothing left to hide. As Mr. Cunningham says goodbye and starts to walk away, my last thought strikes me as odd. There was never anything to hide this whole time.

"So," Lucy blows out a breath, "today's been fun, huh?"

"So much fun." I shoot her a commiserative smile. "I guess we should expect nothing less by now."

She smirks.

As we start to walk out of the gym side by side, she says, "I never expected that to happen. Did you?"

"Never. But I'm glad the truth is out. At least, I think I am."

"What do you mean?"

What do I mean? I don't even know.

Out in the hallway, I walk around the corner to one of the benches in the gym lobby and sit down. Lucy sits next to me. Her cast catches my eye; the plaster decorated but all worn and tattered, especially around her fingers. Reaching under her wrist, I cradle it in my hand and she lets me.

"How much longer?" I ask.

"Another week. I'm starting to lose patience. I guess you never realize how long six weeks really is."

When she says it like that, I think the opposite. Has it really been almost a month and a half since that happened?

Stupid time.

"What is it?" she asks. "Are you okay? I mean, a lot went down since this morning."

"I'm fine." I nod. "What about you? You understand what happened with Kat, right? I didn't ask her to come out to you today; she just kinda grabbed me and the guys and did it."

"Can I be honest?"

"Please."

"If she hadn't said anything, I don't know if I would have completely believed what you told me about her. When we weren't talking, my brain was everywhere."

My eyebrows jump. "I thought Harrison and Wes told you –"

"They did," she interrupts, "but I'm still a little insecure when it comes to you. It's not like the two of us make sense."

"Whoa," I stop her. "Who said that?"

"No one. But c'mon," she gives me a sarcastic stare, "we've been through more stuff than any couple I know."

She's right. I reach for her cast-free hand, and she lets me take it.

"Dr. Marie and I are working on it," she adds. "She thinks it might be a good idea for you to talk to her, too. If you want. If we decide to be an us. Still." She pauses. "I'm having trouble with words."

She looks down, and my adrenaline spikes at what she said. I try to contain my smile. "Your words are fine."

Lucy meets my eyes.

"I'll take you up on that. I'd really like for there to still be an us."

Smiling, she sets her casted hand on top of our joined two. "Okay. Good."

"If it makes you feel any better, the whole time we weren't talking I was convinced you had dumped me for Nick," I confess. "Even though –"

"Even though our friends said otherwise," she finishes and half laughs. "We're a mess."

"But I like our mess." I squeeze her hand. "I've missed it."

Lucy moves closer to me, and we sit in silence for a few moments. I think we're just happy to still be together. I know I am. Eventually I say, "I'm sorry I couldn't deal with June. Kat and I tried; we really did."

Lucy shakes her head. "Don't worry about it. Part of why I wanted to skip with you is to tell you that I'm learning. There's so much we can't control. There's really no 'normal,' and things will never go back to the way they were when Co – *he* was here. They just won't."

She still can't say his name. "So, we'll just deal with June? If we have to, I mean."

"Yeah." She looks up at me. "That's what we'll do."

Behind her, Cody appears, grinning. He gives me a double thumbs up before shoving his hands in his pockets, slowly turning, and walking away. As he fades, I wonder if this is the last time my mind will conjure him. I don't want it to be.

"What are you looking at?" Lucy glances over her shoulder.

When she faces me again, her lips are so close to mine, I only have to move an inch to place a kiss on them. Someday, I'll tell her about my Cody visions. Just not today.

"Want to get out of here?" she asks.

"Sure. Where are we going?"

"I have no idea," she says and stands, "but I'm driving."

"What?" I say in disbelief.

"There are things we can control, and things we can't." She reaches for my hand. "Let's start with you and me."

I stand with her. "And driving?"

She grins. "And driving."

ACKNOWLEDGMENTS

I hope you enjoyed Lucy and Aaron's story. There are a few people I'd like to thank for pushing me to complete it. The idea for *Seven Ten Third* first popped into my head in 2014, but I wasn't able to start writing it until 2016 (see *Sparrow* and *Cardinal*). Then, as life tends to do, things got busy, and I was only able to work on it in bits and pieces.

First, super thanks to the OG beta support team: Tara, Shannon, Joelle, Erica, and Breena. Thank you for agreeing to read my words, putting up with my slow pace, and giving me feedback. I can't tell you how much it helps! You've told me this is an important story to tell, and I agree. I hope I did the subject matter justice and more people feel the same.

Of course I can't leave out my mom, mother-in-law, and Aunt Gloria. You kept asking me about the "next book," despite receiving a grumpy answer about it possibly never getting done. Thank you for reminding me you want to read my writing, even when I wasn't sure I could make it happen. Love you!

And finally, thank you to Marissa, my writing cheerleader from Florida. In all honesty, if it wasn't for you falling in love with Emma, James, and Dane, and then falling in love with Aaron, I wouldn't have tried so hard to complete this story by your birthday. I know I failed in that regard, BUT I did get you some more chapters in that time! Having someone the same age as my characters enjoy this story was the motivation I needed to finish. So, truly, thank you. I look forward to reading more of your own writing in the future – you have a gift.

ABOUT THE AUTHOR

Sara Mack grew up with her nose in books and most notably got caught reading *Flowers in the Attic* behind her Trapper Keeper in the 8th grade. Twenty years ago, she married the guy she met at the gas station and now has two kids, two pups, and two fish. She has an unnatural affinity for iced tea, dark chocolate, and true crime docs. Writes paranormal, contemporary, and YA. Reads everything.

Connect with Sara:

On Facebook:
https://www.facebook.com/sara.mackauthor

On Twitter and Instagram:
@smackwrites

Website and Email:
http://smackwrites.wix.com/saramackauthor
smackwrites@gmail.com

OTHER BOOKS BY SARA MACK

Sparrow

Cardinal

The Guardian Trilogy

Guardian

Allegiant

Reborn

Available on Amazon, Smashwords, Barnes & Noble, Kobo, iBooks